Hurnungaz

the Dark Breath of Earth

Praise for 'Lore of the Sælvatici'

This is a fascinating collection of short stories, narrative poems and pagan inspired folklore type stories of the darker ages. The tales are dark and visceral. There is nothing 'cuddly' about them. This is grim dark foe folk-law that has more in common with real folk-law than many modern interpretations of folk-law you might chose to read.

There is a grim fascinating beauty to this collection, which is in essence background material for a larger body of work. that larger body of work is a re imagined version of the Robin Hood mythology. If this is anything to go by that too will be grimmer and darker than you would generally expect. There isn't much in the way of Lincoln Green and merry thigh slapping going on here. The narrative poem structure of much of this work only adds to the sense of agelessness and timelessness of the stories. They read as if meant to be performed.

Performed on a dark summers' night, under the stars, around a campfire that crackles and spits as if it will rage out of control at any moment.

Performed by men and women with antlers tied to their heads, least you hope they are tied on, not grown.

This is visceral, dark, grim and engrossing stuff. It feels real, it feels like the folklore of an England long vanished and forgotten, when Sherwood was a boundless forbidding Forest full of spirits both benevolent and malicious, often both at the same time. Hunter and hunted. Stag and wolf....

Mark Hayes, author of 'Passing Place: Location Relative'

Praise for 'Hurnungaz'

Some books are easy to review. This is the other sort because it is brilliant and at the same time it definitely won't be to everyone's taste.

We all know Sherwood as a place of camp, swashbuckling adventure. Sherewode, on the other hand, is a mysterious, dangerous forest where old Gods walk, and many of the monsters are human. Called by mad stag goddess Caerne, The Hooded are rising to fight the forces invading the forest.

This is definitely a folk horror novel. It draws heavily on folklore, and it's both violent and unsettling. There's a lot of death, and the constant threat of sexual violence, but there's nothing unbearably graphic. However, the story is not folk-horror shaped. In many ways, it is the people who are the source of the horror – as is normal in the genre. But there are no innocent outsiders here, no Pagan traditions impinging on a modern world. Everyone is complicit in some way, and the dark, violent horrors of the forest are of everyone's making.

The cast is massive and there are a lot of different perspectives. If that's a dealbreaker for you, don't venture in. You have to spend a while trusting the book as it hops around between the huge cast and trusting yourself that you will be able to keep track of them all. To further complicate matters, while these characters echo familiar folk from the Robin Hood stories, they are not as you know them. This is deliberately unsettling and disorientating at times. There's an intrinsic uncanniness to it.

The writing style is often like an early epic – like The Tain, or Beowulf, or something of that ilk. The language and phrasing is poetic, and often stark. The deeper we are in the forest, the more mythic the writing tends to be, and that also means that we don't spend a lot of time exploring people's feelings and motivations, that we just get the raw encounter with action.

Each one of the many characters believes in what they are doing. Their motives vary – revenge and greed are dominant forces, but care, protection, religion, and all the messy things religions inspire people to do are in the mix. While the old gods are present and unsettling, it is without a doubt the things characters do in the name of Christianity that are most disturbing. This is a vey mediaeval take on Christianity – full of burning people for the good of their souls, and seeing the forest as the enemy.

The main reason I know this is folk horror, is because of the way it will make you want to move in, if you're that sort of person. If you're drawn to the murder village, or looking for Cabal, if you'd welcome the bloodied stag girl with too many sharp teeth, if in your darker moments you would take out people who destroy forests for personal profit, then Sherewode will speak to you. If you identify with outcasts, with folk at the margins then you'll feel at home here. That's what folk horror does best.

This book is part of a series. You don't need to have read any related material to jump in, and I will be reviewing the others – I have two more to read at present.

Nimue Brown, druidlife.wordpress.com

Hurnungaz

The Dark Breath of Earth

Steven C. Davis

Wulfenstæg

First published in Great Britain in 2024 by Tenebrous Texts

Translated from the old Ænglish, re-interpreted and
presented by Wulfenstæg
Edited by Laura Jane Round and Dan Martin

Typeset by Tenebrous Texts

Hail Freya

Hail Gwynn ap Nudd

Hail Manawydan ap Llŷr

There were bodies, everywhere. Flies, buzzing. An unreal sound. Blood was thickly splattered; friends' faces contorted in death. Severed limbs. Shattered weapons. Body parts.

Singed bodies. Roasting pork. Crackling.

Sick. Bile rising. The stench of death, of piss, of shit, fear and terror. Smoke from something burning, drifting lazily into the damaged sky.

They couldn't *all* be dead.

Bodies in huts. Bodies on the practice grounds. In quiet corners, in ones, twos or threes.

Bodies, dead, riven, decapitated, everywhere.

Blood, and more blood.

Abject terror. The creature, the thing that had done that –

A whirlwind of *terror*steel flashing and biting, rending, hacking and slashing. Piercing eyeballs and ripping gizzards. Hacking off hands and slashing throats.

Inhuman.

Radiant with the hero-light, twisted and malevolent.

Lightning made manifest. A horror show, the darkest stuff of the bloodiest legends brought to life.

From the dark, something horrific strayed.

**

Even in Londinium they had heard the news.

The Cathedral of the Christ of the East – their jewel – had been attacked. Destroyed, some whispers said.

That, rather than the Sheriff's missive or the intense, irate, letter from the Black Bishop, had moved the King's mind into action.

They had attacked with fire and wild creatures, the reports said. Demonic, Hel-borne creatures. Hundreds of outlaws.

Gisborough had scoffed at that.

Even on the muddied, flattened track, the sound of the soldiers with him was impressive. In double file, snaking out behind him, scaring all the denizens of the dark forest, the thunder of hooves and the rattle and creak of chain and leather.

Gisborough grinned. It was good to be freed of the madness of the Black Bishop. Good to be back in the saddle leading a force of soldiery. It might be more gamekeeper than he'd have liked, but it was no checking tally-counts or being obsequious to a mad monk.

First stop was the supposed-destroyed site of the cathedral to see what the real result was, to talk to survivors, to see if they could be tracked.

Then D'Hallowcross.

Then the Hooded.

**

Brother Blacwin drew his robe tighter. Night was coming on and he was still a mile from his rude shelter at the edge of the village.

Something screeched. An owl, he thought.

Something laugh-screamed. A fox.

What those outlaws had done at the Cathedral site was terrible. Those poor people, Blacwin thought, so lost and confused that they would attack a holy place, that they would attack people who cared for them, who only wanted to make their lives better.

Ignorance was no excuse. They had to be punished, of course, but he hoped pity would be shown them. The stories must have been exaggerated in the telling. Almost all buildings burnt down. Dozens of soldiers slain.

He shook his head.

Something scream-screeched.

Shadows lengthened.

Blacwin looked around. The way was known to him through the trackless wilderness that was Sherewode, but tonight it seemed – strange.

Shadows shifted though no wind blew.

There were odd sounds, and he knew most of the sounds creatures of the forest made.

He sighed, pressing his beads tighter in his hand. There were a few wolves' heads in the forest, misplaced, lost, abandoned people, but they had no cause to attack him, a penniless brother of the Christ of the East.

The poverty of the brothers of the Christ of the East was well known. They lived on the generosity of the villages they served. They were not rich men; riches were a distraction.

He flinched as the shadows moved.

As the shadows closed in around him.

**

Ymbere slipped silently through the shadows, two rabbits on his belt. The traps had worked; they always did.

He grinned. One for himself; one to sell in the morning. It was too late to light a fire; the other villagers would be suspicious. Raw or leave it, the eternal decision.

He saw the trackway and slowed, checking either way, coming to a halt and listening.

The Forest breathed.

He could hear the foxes, the owls, larger creatures, further away. The faintest breath of wind disturbing the branches.

Nothing to worry about.

He lingered, even so.

The Hooded had been gone for weeks or months. Rumours were uncertain. Verderers had started returning to the forest.

Ymbere grimaced. Whoever they had been, they had done a good job of driving the Normans out of the forest in fear for their lives. That they should return –

He scowled and moved rapidly across the trackway in seconds, moving almost before he'd made the decision.

He returned to the gloom on the far side and paused again.

No one had heard him, no one had seen him.

He headed off.

**

Discordance. Angenijs was staring down a sunken lane, shrouded by overhanging trees through which no light reached – and yet patches of light sparkled and twitched.

The far end was solid darkness that moved. That reached towards her and, wary, drew back. That undulated like the waves hitting the sea shore and being driven back.

She blinked.

Rubbed her eyes.

Looked again.

The sunken lane had dropped lower. Water pooled along it, seeping out of the banks. The darkness at the far end was diminishing. She could smell smoke. Distant fire.

She turned and looked back. Her brother looked up at her, wide-eyed, trusting. Instinctively, she held her hand out.

He got up and ran to her.

She took him by the hand and ran for the sunken path.

Ran for the wyrd.

**

The first rays of the rising sun caught the dying body hanging in the rusted metal cage.

Piss, shit and blood leaked from it.

Their wool was stained. Their face was lined with cuts from a sharp knife. Their eyes glittered brightly, angrily, clear blue.

A crow balanced on the rusty cage.

Spikes had been driven through the man, pinning them into the cage, condemning them to a slow, painful, death.

Muscles trained to wielding weapons were helpless: wrists and ankles were chained tight to the cage.

The crow cawed.

Its meal would be ready soon.

**

Savaric froze. The shadows moved in the clearing. A creature, not human. Hooked, bloodied claws. Grey skin. Mottled brown furred legs, ending in broken hooves. A trailing beard, filthy with blood and mucus.

Savaric wrinkled his nose. It stunk of shit and blood. Something noxious.

'I, smell you,' it rasped, turning its head this way and that. Small, saggy ears flapped.

It stamped a hoof and a fallen tree branch snapped cleanly.

It peered intently at the undergrowth.

Can it see me?

'I, am free,' it burbled. 'Cernunnos is gone. The walls tumble. My people will soon be free.'

Savaric grimaced.

The creature turned, close to facing where he hid.

'I, know you are there.'

He realised it was having trouble breathing.

'I, will find you.'

It moved towards his hiding place.

**

She crooned softly, enjoying the smell of blood and piss and shit. The chamber was deep underground; deep in her dominion.

Winchester crooned, stroking one of the broken bodies.

The man gulped in terror.

Winchester grinned.

'Why are you still alive?'

'Because, because,' he fumbled.

She laughed. 'You betrayed the Christ of the East,' she screeched, dragging her nails down his thin leg. 'You did not stop those wretches! Those Hel-bound creatures!'

She tore his other leg.

The brother of the Christ of the East whimpered, blood trailing down. Three weeks he'd hung there. There had been five, at the beginning.

Five people – brothers and soldiers – that the Abbess had taken from the Cathedral site. Two had died almost immediately under her questioning. Three had survived – two brothers and a soldier.

Winchester scowled. There was pleasure, in hurting them. Not hurting them, no, she was doing this for The Christ of the East. She was loyal. She was obedient. She had to know everything that had happened – how it had happened – why it had happened – so she could find these – Hooded.

'They were the ones who took my pet from me.'

The brother whimpered in his chains, looking at her.

'The Christ of the East speaks to me!' she bellowed, seizing a warm iron and striking him on the leg with it.

He screamed, a fresh wave of pain and fear dribbling out of him.

'Tell me of the Hooded!'

**

Gisborough stared. The land was cracked and broken, torn open. Smoke drifted from some of the fissures. The air smelled of death. His horse snickered, uneasy. He heard other horses' discomfort.

Remnants of buildings still stood. Smoke or mist still seemed to linger around them. The sun blazed down but the day was hotter still: the air was heavy and nauseous.

'This is the site?' asked the commander of the King's Own, Berenger.

He nodded to the red-haired soldier. The man might look like a warrior or mercenary for hire – and he was a very good fighter – but he was also a good diplomat, used to the courts of the King and the King's machinations.

'It is. From Hel might not have been wrong.'

'It is,' Berenger spoke surprisingly softly, 'like some battlefield in the Holy Land, where Hel-fire has been used. What should rip the ground open like that but Hel-fire.' He shook his head. 'It's one thing to see it in the Holy Land, but here,' he patted his trembling horse's neck. 'What are your orders?'

Gisborough inclined his head towards the heart of the site, where remains of half a dozen buildings still smouldered. 'The Cathedral is beyond those. That they still stand in some form, that is where –'

Smoke or mist had gathered between them and the shattered buildings but he could see it roiling.

'Dismount,' Gisborough hissed, 'the horses cannot cope, cannot go onto the site. Have some men stay with them in case –'

The mist curled away and he saw a man walking towards him, dressed in a long brown robe, over which they wore leather armour. A face he recognised, a thick beard: clean shaven cheeks. Dark eyes. An unmistakeable air of authority.

'Is that one of them?' Berenger asked.

Gisborough shook his head, brows furrowed, vaulting down from his horse.

On the man's back he could see he carried an immense axe.

'See to the men. The horses,' he ordered, moving forwards.

'William!' the approaching man grinned. 'Ware the shadows, friend William. You are not forgotten.'

Gisborough stared.

The man chuckled, thrusting his arm out in greeting as he neared.

William took his arm. 'I never thought to see you again.'

'We do what we must.' The man nodded. 'It is good to see you again. I never expected to be back, and yet here I am.'

'Does your brother know you are here? Your brothers?'

He shook his head. 'They will know soon enough. You will take message. The Black Bishop will expect them soon; will expect all his benefactors to make visit and reparation.'

'Reparation?' William stared.

The man nodded. 'Had more troops been provided. Had this Hooded band been hunted down.'

William nodded. 'That is my mission. From the King.'

'I see the King's Own are with you.'

Gisborough grinned. 'It was the destruction of the site that tipped the King's mind to sending soldiers north to investigate.'

'My lord,' Berenger appeared at his side. 'Men and horses sorted.'

Gisborough nodded to his brother in arms. 'This is Berenger of Willenhala, commander of the King's Own.'

Berenger looked at the axe-carrying man. 'And you are?'

He chuckled. 'I am seneschal to the most noble Brother Gascon, called by some the Black Bishop. He is the voice of the Christ of the East –'

Gisborough could feel the power, the command, in the man's voice. He kept his face studiously blank.

'Grand Architect of the Christ of the East's plans. This is not just a cathedral, Berenger of Willenhala. This is the heart of what will be the first city of the Christ of the East.'

Berenger stared.

'From here, the infectious root of paganism will be stamped out. We will fight fire with fire if we must. It has taken hold deeply. These Hooded are just one such example. Burn the woods, chain the peasants, slay their heroes. We have much work to do between us all.'

Gisborough nodded. The man wasn't mad at all.

'And I,' he continued, 'I am Hallowcross. Geoffrey of Hallowcross.'

**

'What do we have here then, priest?'

Brother Blacwin shook his head. 'I am a brother of the Christ of the East. I have no money, no possessions. I am here to save people's souls.'

There were five of them, he thought. Looming, menacing, shadows. A sliver of moonlight here and there glinted off eyes and knives.

'Nothing to pay the toll, then?'

'Toll?' he quaked.

The wolf's head snickered. 'There's always a toll. Your head, perhaps, priest.'

'I am no priest,' he reiterated.

'And suddenly not so scared, either,' another voice added.

The speaker glanced at the one who'd spoken.

'You're right. He's not so scared. So let's say –'

There was a whistling sound. The speaker staggered backwards, choking, an arrow piercing his throat.

**

Ymbere headed away from the trackway quickly and silently. The thought of rabbit, even raw – to tear it apart with his teeth. The fur would be useless, the meat raw and bloody. But still meat.

Wait for sun up. Build a fire.

The temptation to have both. His stomach rumbled. It had been a while since he'd had anything to eat – and the smell would carry, would draw other villagers in.

Selling one was right, but still – he gagged, stopping, staring down.

Two crossbow bolts seemed to have grown from his belly.

He blinked owlishly. That couldn't be right.

**

The sky was so bright. The yellow star burned, causing Angenijs to shield her eyes. She drew her brother, Diederic, to her; half carried, half dragged, him under the shelter of a tree.

The air was clear, neither smoke nor smog nor mist. She could smell many strange and foreign things. But the tree was solid, recognisable. The flowers in the field around it were familiar but unrecognisable. Beyond the field there was a steep rise to one side; a thick forest covering of trees on two sides; on the remaining side the field dissipated into a marsh.

She could feel her skin tingling. She clutched her brother tighter. The world was different. Bright.

The Undrentide path that had drawn her here – had drawn her brother here, though she had brought him with her without thinking – was gone. There was no sign of it; a sinking path between trees, overhung with branched shadows and water seeping through –

She shook her head.

'Well, we are alive.'

She stared at the disturbed silence. The voice was hers and not. Strange and alien, unknown, though she knew what she had said.

We are alive she whispered to herself. Ripples rebounded. The world – she shuddered. The world was alive and *different*.

'If this is my wyrd –'

**

Bwyd lit the cairn and stepped back. He'd managed to free the man, but he'd died in his arms. He didn't know him but he recognised the tattoos that adorned his body.

'Caerne,' he whispered. 'Dissever me never. Hold my brother close. Carry his spirit free to the hills of his home. Let his axe rise and fall beside you. Let him soar. Let him hunt the Normans in his ancestral home.'

The fire crackled and raged, catching hold. Grey clouds lined the sky, hard and close, austere. He wrapped his robe closer. A black robe, that of a brother of the Christ of the East.

Bwyd grinned.

Whoever had killed one of the Sælvatici would pay. Llewellyn would see to it. The man had been tortured in a way his people never would. Someone had been determined to make him hurt and offer the final insult: not to care enough to kill him, but leave him to die in agony.

Bwyd stamped his stave against the ground.

'Fly well, my brother. You will be avenged.'

In the distance, a few days' hence, he knew, Llewellyn and his keep. His home. And an answer to the reason why he had been asked to return.

'Caerne, protect me. If you live. Give me wings. Give me speed. Caerne, from the dark, guide me home.'

**

'So, this, is the world of Cernunnos.'

Savaric hunched in tighter, hoping against hope that he had not been seen. The creature, Hel-beast, whatever it was, moved closer.

'Little being,' it drooled. 'I, can see you.'

A clawed hand caught his head; wrapped fingers in his hair and pulled him up.

He screamed. The creature was strong; stunk of brimstone and shit.

'Little creature,' it slobbered, licking its lips. 'The walls break. The sheep will rise up. The cattle in their fields –'

She – it – grasped his arm. Twisted.

Savaric screamed, not wanting to look. His arm, his wrist, his hand, felt *wrong*.

'The walls tumble,' it crooned.

There was a snap. Savaric felt sick.

'Cernunnos is gone,' it burbled. 'My people will rise.'

A hand grasped his throat. Squeezed. The hand on his head *twisted* –

**

'So what can you tell me?'

'It was them,' the man gibbered, 'the Hooded. There was the dark haired archer. The warrior, the King's Man.'

'And how are you still alive?' the Abbess crooned.

'I was knocked unconscious,' the soldier said. 'I saw the attack. We charged – Hurnungaz. He loosed,' he shook his head. 'I saw him notch a single arrow. He loosed,' he gasped, choking and swallowing.

'Carry on.'

'Water,' he whimpered.

Abbess Winchester chuckled. 'Water would have put out the fires. They burned the Cathedral. Fortunately,' she sniggered, 'fortunately much of it was stone. The Black Bishop is already rebuilding it bigger, stronger, taller,' she breathed, feeling a touch of something – female. Inappropriate.

'To watch one of them,' she almost drooled. 'The bastard archer –'

'Hurnungaz.'

'To watch the bastard archer twist at the end of a rope. To watch him burn –' that, *that*, was a pleasing thought.

An inappropriate thought, given her female form. I am Hel clothed in flesh. Inappropriate flesh.

To tear his belly open. To watch his innards pour out. To cascade. To glisten. To –

Her eyes rolled back in her head.

'He burns,' she crooned. 'He glistens, blood bleeding out. His power leaves him. Knife blade glistening trails across his chest. His power absorbed. Oh! By the Christ of the East –' she gasped. 'To watch him swing in the breeze. To watch the drip, drip, drip. To watch the life die in his eyes. Destroy him and,' she shuddered again. 'His death and I will ascend. I will ascend!'

**

Thrydwulf crouched by the stream. It was surprisingly deep; fish thundered in its depths, sparkling and yet out of reach –

He plunged his arm in, gritting his teeth. The water was icy. He could see the fish, and they were still beyond him.

He moved closer, stretching out beside the stream, clutching hold of the ground with one hand, plunging his other hand deeper.

Something kissed it. He twisted his hand but the fish was gone. He spread his fingers, forcing himself to remain immobile.

A few fish. The King would not miss them. No one would know. It would stop the rumbling of his belly.

Indescribable. He blinked, feeling cold. *Really* cold.

Turned his head and struggled to sit up.

His hand stayed where it was. Two verderers, in Nottingham's colours, stood over him, grinning. One carried an axe, from which blood dripped.

Thrydwulf blinked again.

His hand!

The other verderer raised a loaded crossbow, pointing at him.

Loosed.

**

Hurnungaz waited.

Aeons passed.

Stars were born, crossed the heavens of the Christ of the East, and died out.

Whole lineages of stag-crow crossbreeds rose and fell.

Kingdoms rose and fell to rise again, before falling into decay and disrepute.

He withered from flesh to bone to dust to earth and rose once more, stag-blooded, created by violence.

The sky was green.

The sky was yellow.

The sky was the colour of madness.

Stars burned and died and blazed forth once more –

The stars were her eyes.

Her eyes.

From the dark –

Her eyes glowed green

Her eyes glowed yellow.

She was there and her eyes were the colour of madness. Her eyes were the colour of life. Her eyes blazed and suns burst from the verdant and ebbed and flowed back to the green.

'I am Stag.'

She stamped her hooves on the rock and the rock shattered: valleys formed.

'Why am I here?'

She snorted. 'The rocks do not question their existence. The mountains do not ask why. The stag does not ask why, just that it must.'

'Am I –' Hurnungaz hesitated. 'I killed – the stag. There was – metamorphosis. The corpse of the stag –'

Her teeth were locked on his throat.

'I failed!' she screamed, her voice full of his blood.

Hurnungaz shuddered awake, sitting up.

'Ratatoskr!'

Wulfrun stirred. 'Freya? Iseulde!'

Hurnungaz looked around. It was still dark. Dark and still. The forest was silent. Quiet. It hadn't been the same since – since – since they'd attacked the cathedral.

Since Caerne had loosed all kinds of creatures and Hel beings on the site.

That had drained him. Wulfrun had all but carried him away from the site. He hadn't seen Caerne leave. Didn't know if –

'Is she dead? Drained?'

Raven whimpered in sleep. The young man was learning fast. How to stay hidden. How to build fires. How to hunt, how to fish. How to kill.

So few of us left. Bwyd, disappeared after the battle. Hereseige gone before. Muna, Mar, Tam, all gone. Sciuridae.

He frowned. 'Ratatoskr. My dream.' He frowned. 'What does it mean?'

Godwin grunted. 'Something Norse.'

Hurnungaz looked up at the man and nodded. 'Yes. I'll ask Wulfrun when he wakes.'

Godwin made a face.

'Why aren't you sleeping?'

Godwin grimaced. 'Everything's,' he shrugged. 'I don't know. I thought, after the battle,' he grimaced.

Hurnungaz nodded. 'That it would make a difference. That everything would be – better.'

Godwin nodded. 'They know. They know we are a threat now. If we haven't got them all,' he shook his head. 'It might be better to scatter. Lie low. Reform,' he trailed off.

Hurnungaz sat up straighter, shaking his head. 'No. If we scatter, we're easy prey for them. The brother in charge of the site, he wasn't there. No Gisborough, no one really leading their soldiers. We got lucky. Damaged them. We have to regroup and continue what we were doing.'

'Without Caerne?' Godwin asked.

Hurnungaz shook his head. 'I think – I think if she was dead. Or gone. I think I would know. I would feel it. She may be – resting. Recovering. We cannot just lie here. We need to move on. Regroup. Gather more. Continue the fight back.'

Godwin nodded slowly. 'It will be better when Sir Roger and Hereseige return.'

Hurnungaz looked away.

Quellavera. I hope you're safe and on your way home.

**

Candles guttered in the deep cave. They were far underground. The opening chambers of the cave were low to the ground, mostly filled with an icy, fast flowing river. They had scrambled along the bank of the river, sometimes wading in it, for what had seemed like hour upon hour, until, at last, they had come to a parting of the ways.

The river had returned, deeper, underground, disappearing into the rocks in an unfollowable manner. The cave had slanted to the right, dropping down slightly before broadening out in height and breadth and heading gently upwards.

Hugi had been able to see in the pitch blackness. She could discern shapes, angles, but not clearly. Hugi, for all his crow-like nature, could see perfectly.

There was a natural bier-like rock formation in the middle, half hollowed out. She had built a fire in that: Hugi had flinched away from it but needed the warmth. He sat around the corner from it now, knees drawn up, head tucked down, leaning against the rock, accepting the warmth but out of reach of the flames.

Mar lay on top of the bier.

Mar the assassin.

Mar the boy.

Mar the girl.

Their clothes were drying out in front of the fire. Muna had found them, had tracked them down. Their arms, their thighs, their chest, had been cut by their own knives.

They had done that, and lain down to die.

She had collected their knives, their weapons and their clothes; had gathered them up. Had called for her brother long into the night and the following morning until he had appeared.

Mar the unknown.

The fire warmed the rock and Mar lay on the rock and the rock warmed them. But they did not wake.

There was still life in their lungs, in their heart. Still a slow heartbeat. But no consciousness, no waking.

Candles on stone niches flickered. They were so deep underground no light would be seen. A breath of wind reached them occasionally, from tiny cracks, tiny fissures, that stretched all the way to the world above.

But here, below, they were all safe.

Muna began washing Mar's body again. The wounds they had inflicted had bled, but not enough to drain their body. Not enough to send them to death's domain.

Something else had happened. Mar's body bore signs of having carried another, of having been a mother. Why someone should choose to hide that part of themselves so thoroughly –

She smiled, remembering the lust and anger Mar had felt towards her. Wondered at it. Was Mar drawn to her? Did Mar hate because she was female and Mar felt she could not be?

And what of the child born to her?

Muna shook her head. The cave was their safety, all of their safety, for the moment.

**

*Terror*steel and joy. Malevolence.

He could feel it spreading. Grinned, shuddering, feeling the pleasure ripple through him. His verderers were in action. No mercy. No kindness. No forgiveness.

He smiled. Ripples. Terror would take hold of the forest. Bend the peasants to his will. Bend the Saxons to his will. In time, the Normans.

There was nothing to match him. Nothing to challenge him. Nothing that could withstand his fury.

Scáthach. He had disposed of her easily enough. She was a fool, relying on her reputation, not taking precautions, not being cautious enough. He had come upon her people without challenge. Yes, she had been a good warrior –

He chuckled. Not good enough.

She had not seen him. Not *recognised* him.

When the hero-light transformed him, he had ripped her apart as if she was an insect. Oh, it had been a *glorious* slaughter.

Scáthach trained few men, preferring her own sex in everything. Had trained them in swordsmanship and hand to hand, in all manners of fighting styles.

He had found and slain – slaughtered – them all. Found them on the training fields. In the barracks. Cunny to cunny and nose to cunny. In the quiet corners with swift fingers and silent lips. In their own beds and others, naked or in full armour.

He had taken eyes. Taken toes. Hacked and slain, reiving them as if they were hay bales to be torn apart.

Some were nursing young or bearing young. Being mothers. All had died in a crimson wash.

All had died. *Terror*steel and malevolence.

That had been a good day.

**

St. John looked up as the outer door opened. Gisborough, followed by a red-haired warrior. He frowned, waving his men at arms to stand down.

'Gisborough!' he hailed.

The man raised a gloved hand in greeting, sweeping down the hall towards him.

'My lord,' he grinned, 'can I introduce commander Berenger, of the King's Own.'

'Commander,' D'Hallowcross inclined his head. 'I take it the King has taken up my suggestion?'

Gisborough nodded, flourishing a scroll and handing it to him.

'Warden of Sherwood?' he raised an eyebrow.

The knight nodded. 'The King felt – as titles go – that was appropriate for what He has tasked me to do.'

'It was my title,' he snapped.

Gisborough withdrew another scroll and passed it over. 'The King's orders.' He glanced at the soldier with him. 'It may be a test.'

The Sheriff stared at him for a moment before scanning the scroll. He shrugged and threw the scroll back onto the table.

'Excuse us Berenger. Are you staying, Gisborough? I can find room for your men.'

Gisborough nodded.

D'Hallowcross summoned his seneschal. 'Escort Berenger. Ensure his men are settled; the outer barracks can be emptied for them. See that the stables are available and there's ostlers ready. Then find them food.'

The man nodded and withdrew, Berenger accompanying him.

'Well, Gisborough? What news?' He grinned, taking a swig of his wine; signalled for a servant to fetch a goblet for his guest. 'How is the Black Bishop's site?'

Gisborough accepted the goblet, taking a deep swig.

'The forest feels – empty.'

St. John grinned. 'My verderers are out in force; I have a new man in charge of them. He is ruthless. Training them to be ruthless. The site?'

Gisborough half-smiled. 'I met the Bishop's new seneschal.'

'Oh?'

'Your brother, my lord. Geoffrey of Hallowcross.'

The Sheriff stared. Snorted. 'Never thought he'd leave the Holy Land. He was war-mad. Liked the – freedom – to be – indiscrete. Towards prisoners.'

'Oh?'

'I don't know if the Christ of the East talks to him, or his own demons talk to him. He is,' he shrugged. 'He and Brother Gascon are well suited.'

Gisborough nodded. 'I didn't realise – until I saw him at the site. I met him, years ago. He saved me from,' he shook his head.

The Sheriff took another mouthful of the wine. 'You think the King stirs the pot?'

'Money and prestige that was yours, my lord, he has given to me. Unless there was anything in the missive from Him I am not aware of.'

D'Hallowcross scowled. 'No. That's the second source of income I've lost. Was the Black Bishop at least injured?'

'I don't think so.' Gisborough finished his wine and held his goblet out for more. 'As far as I know him, I trust Berenger. A solid King's Man, but surprisingly competent, not just a swordsman.'

St. John nodded.

'The site is – I do not know what the Bishop will do. The ground is ravaged and torn open. Smoke still leaks from some of the fissures. I think the cathedral is mostly unscathed, but the barracks, the stables, guest quarters, much has been burned down.'

The Sheriff couldn't hide his grin.

'The demands from the Bishop have not yet started, but they will. Your brother tells me he is still most furious that the money from Lincoln was stolen.'

'These Hooded.'

Gisborough nodded. 'The King was holding that against you. My lord. By passing the mantle of Warden of Sherwood onto me,' he paused.

D'Hallowcross raised an eyebrow.

'He has no wish to stir from Londinium. The forest is – was – outlaw-infested. There appears to be a cessation of outlaw activity since the attack.'

The Sheriff nodded. 'My new captain of the verderers is ruthless. My soldiers raid the villages randomly now, tracking down any wolfs head, any outlaws.'

Gisborough nodded. 'There will have to be a planning meeting. I have one hundred of the King's Own to hunt them down with.'

D'Hallowcross grinned. 'Tales of them,' he shook his head. 'Some say they wait near the cathedral site. There are stories of them being seen in York, in Austerfield, in the Marcher-lands.'

Gisborough snorted. 'That's the last thing we want. Marcher lords and the Hooded in union.'

He nodded. 'Most of Sherwood is trackless. There are a few recorded incidents, I have details. But nowhere obvious that could be a base.' He frowned. 'Do you need to keep your men in one unit? Blocks of twenty, criss-crossing the forest, could be quite useful. Flush them out from wherever they're hiding.'

'There are tales from some of the survivors. The leader, Hurnungaz, has some unusual skill with a bow.'

The Sheriff finished off his wine and held his hand out for more.

A servant scurried over to refill his goblet.

'Would a group of fifty or a hundred negate this skill? I am not interested in,' he paused.

'My lord?' Gisborough asked.

'I want them hounded. On the move. Keep as many villages under watch as possible. Hunt them up and down the country if we have to.'

'That would take a lot of men.'

D'Hallowcross nodded. 'It would. Do what you can. I am intending to reinforce my control over the Saxons, the peasants, those who owe us their fealty.'

'What are your plans. My lord.'

St. John sniggered. 'It has been too long since there has been a tourney. An opportunity to impress upon them natural Norman superiority.'

Gisborough smiled. 'What do you intend?'

The Sheriff sniggered. 'Something – to attract the fools. Why,' he grinned. 'A silver arrow! Something shiny with no value. And,' he raised his goblet to Gisborough. 'It will be a good opportunity to gather a few lords together.'

'The Bishop?'

He shrugged. 'Indirectly. It is to everyone's benefits if the outlaws are swept from the forest. With tougher verderers, villages being watched, more patrols mounted and on foot.'

Gisborough nodded. 'Give them no hiding place. Turn the very people they claim to represent against them.'

He nodded. 'And a bounty for any signs of Pagan activity. This forest god. If we destroy their shrines, their sacred places, even their believers.'

'More souls for the Christ of the East.'

The Sheriff nodded sombrely. 'The Black Bishop is,' he shook his head. 'A madness consumes him. I will not stand in his way.'

'There was a man; an architect. He heard voices as well. An attack by the Hooded killed him. There is the Abbess as well.'

'Winchester.' The Sheriff grimaced. 'She is madness personified. Second only to the Black Bishop.'

Gisborough nodded, putting his goblet down. 'Thank you for the drink, my lord. I should check Berenger and his men are settled.'

D'Hallowcross nodded. 'Of course, of course.' He grinned. 'You'll join me for a meal tonight? You and Berenger?'

Gisborough nodded. 'Of course, my lord.'

**

Brother Blacwin sketched the sign of a cross in the air. Three of the outlaws lay dead and the rest had fled.

He looked up at sounds in the undergrowth. Oh no, not more –

A figure emerged from the undergrowth, clothed in ragged, patched clothing, a bow slung over his shoulder. Another stood behind them, almost invisible in the lengthening shadows.

'I am Brother Blacwin.'

The man nodded. 'I'm Tam.' He jerked his head at the person stood behind him. 'That's Alain in the shadows. We mean you no harm.'

'You were the one who – killed those men?'

Tam nodded. 'I am. Luckily for you.'

He inclined his head. 'Thank you. I do not know what they had planned, but,' he shrugged. 'I can give you a prayer. I have no money, not even a single coin to thank you.'

The man shook his head. 'I – we – are not looking for coinage. We keep the forest safe for those innocents.'

'Bless you,' Brother Blacwin sketched the cross in their direction. 'Do you work for the Sheriff? Brother Gascon?'

'The Hooded,' the one called Tam said.

He frowned. 'Why, they're wolves' heads. The worst of them, I've heard. Pagans and rapists. Idolaters.'

Tam chuckled. 'That we are not. Well,' he shrugged. 'I have no court with your Christ of the East. But I scarce have court with Caerne either.'

Blacwin shook his head. 'That cannot be. You – you attacked the Cathedral site?'

Tam nodded. 'It is a blight on the forest. Trees chopped. The land blessed by,' he scowled, shaking his head.

'Do I detect an accent?'

'Highlands,' Tam scowled.

'What brought you south?'

The man's scowl deepened. 'I – we – can escort you to your village, if you wish. We have nothing against you.'

Blacwin found he was shaking his head. 'You are – truly – of the Hooded?'

Tam nodded. 'We are. I was one of the first Hurnungaz recruited.'

The brother stared. 'You carry out unholy rites and sacrifices to your dark deity?'

Tam frowned even more. 'No. Caerne's,' he shook his head. 'She's powerful, yes. Really powerful,' he stressed, 'unlike your Christ of the East. Your priests –'

'Brothers.'

'Eh?'

'Brothers. We're not priests. We seek to save the villagers' souls. They so easily fall into bad habits. We ask for nothing; give everything we can to save them.'

Tam snorted.

'I,' Blacwin hesitated. 'I am called to save the souls of the village that gives me lodging. But, I believe, there may be a greater calling here.'

The man raised an eyebrow.

'Would you allow me to accompany you?'

Tam scowled. 'I'm not betraying the Hooded, nor Hurnungaz, for you.'

'I am no threat,' Blacwin protested. 'I am Anglo-Saxon. These are my people I am trying to save. I owe nothing to the Normans.'

Tam snorted. 'You think us wolves' heads, outside the law.'

'You've killed people!'

Tam nodded. 'Ay.'

Blacwin stared. 'How black must your soul be?' he whispered.

Tam shook his head. 'Not as black as the soul of the man who murdered my son. Who raped and murdered my daughter.'

He stared. 'What? What did the justices say when you went to them?'

Tam shook his head, scowling. 'The man was a nobleman. I saw what he'd done. I killed his man at arms. I killed him.' He sighed. 'But my daughter was still dead. My son still dead. My line wiped out, there was nothing for me in the Highlands.'

Brother Blacwin sketched a cross in his direction. 'I am sorry for you. That should not have happened.'

Tam snorted. Looked away.

'Hurnungaz,' he said softly. 'He has a power, comes from Caerne. I thought him a devil-worshipper at first. I had a band,' he snorted. 'I always knew who to rob. Who to let pass through unmolested. And then he came.'

'What did he do?'

'He slew my men. Loosed a single arrow and three men of mine died. Loosed another and three more died. They broke and ran.' He shook his head. 'He spared me. Spared me,' he said, with a touch of bitterness, glancing at the brother. 'I sometimes think it would be better to be gone, to be with my Aoife once more.'

'You still live,' Blacwin said softly. 'There is still hope.'

'Hope for what?' Tam turned half away. 'My wife died a while ago. Both children murdered. I came south, got –'

'There is me,' said a voice behind Tam.

The young man moved into the open. 'You saved me from the burning building. If you hadn't been there, I would have died.'

He had pale blond hair; looked thin and nervous. His accent was of Londinium and he looked out of sorts.

'Hello,' Brother Blacwin smiled. 'You're scared here, aren't you?'

**

Decision made, Angenijs headed for the trees, her brother's hand in hers.

'You'll see. We can't stay hiding all the time. We need food. Drink. Someone will find us.'

The trees loomed. Dark and twisted, oaks and unrecognisable trees whose frames twisted and creaked in the slight breeze.

Branches trembled.

Leaves skittered in the breeze.

'I know it's not our world,' she answered her brother's silent look. 'I don't know *how* we're here. But we are. So we must find help. We must be strong.'

A path ran into the woodlands. The girl took it, her brother clutching her hand tightly. It was dark under the shade of the branches, dark and cool.

She paused, looking back. The single tree in the field almost gleamed in the sunlight. Bright, bright, sunlight that had hurt her and her brother's eyes.

She turned and headed deeper into the forest.

**

Bwyd smiled, leaning on his stave. The castle at Clun was before him, less than an hour's walk. His feet were sore. He was tired. He could do with a long soak and a lot to drink. A whole roast chicken to eat. More food than was probably available. Fresh clothing.

He shook his head and resumed walking.

He spotted them too late: three figures on small, shaggy, hill ponies, moving to intercept. There was nowhere to hide; no shelter to run to. He stopped walking, holding his stave crossways.

'Caerne, guard me.'

The three warriors approached, keeping out of reach and staying well apart from each other. One carried a stave; another a crossbow; the third an axe.

'State your business with Llewellyn of Clun.'

Bwyd smiled. The Welsh accent was music to his ears.

'By the dark breath of earth,' he grinned, 'is this how you greet a brother?'

One of them stared, half lowering their weapon. The other two studied him closely.

'Name yourself.'

'By the dark breath of earth,' he repeated, 'I expected the recognition phrase.'

The soldier carrying the crossbow lowered it, scowling softly. 'Dissever me never.'

He nodded. 'My name is Bwyd. I am Sælvatici. I serve Caerne. I work with Hurnungaz of the Hooded. I was summoned by my lord of Clun, Llewellyn. I have seen the body of one of my kind – one of our kind – in the corpse cage. What has happened here?'

The axe-carrying soldier shook his head. 'Much has changed since you were called away, Bwyd of the Hooded. My Lord Clun will tell you directly. You two,' he glanced at the other two, 'head back, ensure a bath and food, ale. I will tell Bwyd what I can.'

**

'There is the matter of the tithes, your grace.'

Abbot Simon scowled at Lucianna.

'Did I say you could speak, mistress?'

She lowered her gaze, shaking her head.

'Lower your top,' he instructed.

She obeyed wordlessly.

'That,' he smiled, studying her, 'those are how you retain your position. Do not presume to speak. Do not presume intelligence.'

She shook her head again.

'Although I do have a use for your mouth. Come here, girl.'

She scurried over.

The Abbot drew his robe up. When she was in position, he threw it back over her.

'Your – tongue – is useful to me, child. Your appearance is enjoyable, but speaking detracts from your beauty. Do not do so again unless you are responding to a question of mine.'

She seemed to nod, her mouth otherwise engaged.

He grinned, picking up one of the sheaf of parchments. 'Now then –' he grimaced. 'Slower, girl. Enjoy it. Your mother certainly did.'

He skim-read the parchment. Thought, idly, about having her tongue plucked out, but that would probably ruin her. A convent, he thought, smiling, leering, as she got her positioning perfect. Somewhere she cannot spill her secrets. Somewhere she cannot obtain any satisfaction.

That, his smile broadened. That would be a good end for her. Find someone to replace her.

A wicked thought came to him and he grinned. *That* would be appropriate.

**

'I was just scrumpin' apples, sir.'

The verderer grinned, drawing a knife.

'Sir, please,' Cyneburg begged. 'I can offer you – summat.'

She ran her hands over her chest. Flicked her skirt up – she had undertrews on, but lifting the skirt was enough to entice local boys.

She'd had plenty of experience with *them*. Verderers were just local boys who'd been given power by the Sheriff.

She ran her hands over her chest again, slower, emphasising her shape.

He grinned. 'What's your name, girl?'

'Cyneburg, sir. You can have – whatever I have. To atone for – what I did.'

She tucked her skirt into its waistband.

'Whatever you want, sir.'

He thrust his knife at her chest mutely.

Cyneburg drew the tunic up and discarded it. She was cold: she'd not had a verderer before, but she'd had several of the local boys. Knew what they liked. What they wanted.

She tugged her trews down.

'How do you want me, sir?'

'Turn around,' he growled, grinning.

Cyneburg hurried. She had done it before. Sometimes it hadn't been great. Other times it had been quite enjoyable. She doubted the verderer would take long about it.

And at least then she'd be able to say she'd had a man.

She heard him bite into an apple.

His hand caressed, squeezed, her cheeks. Moved to her thighs: between her legs.

'How many have you had, little Cyneburg?'

'Not many, sir. Just boys. Not a man like you.'

He withdrew his hand: she made a disappointed noise.

She heard the apple be discarded.

He pulled her to him: she could feel his interest pressed against her lower back.

'Theft is still theft and thieves deserve –'

She felt the knife touch her throat. There was pain, a coldness, the cry died in her throat –

**

'What do we do?' Raven asked.

Hurnungaz paused. 'I don't think Caerne is dead. But with Hereseige gone, Bwyd disappeared, Tam and Sciuridae gone, possibly caught or killed during the battle, Mar and Muna as well,' he trailed off.

'Hereseige will return,' Wulfrun said. 'We need to still be here when he's back.'

'How long does a journey to York take?'

Godwin pulled a face. 'As long as it takes. If he and Sir Roger are having to accompany Quellavera to a ship,' he shrugged helplessly.

Hurnungaz nodded. 'We cannot wait for him to return. It could be months. But with five of us only –'

'Does Caerne's gift still work?' Wulfrun asked.

'Gift?' queried Raven.

'I loose one arrow, there are three in flight.' Hurnungaz shook his head. 'Often in practice no. When I need it, if I call to her, yes.'

'Call to her then,' suggested Merik. 'My brothers sent Fauld and I to you. You – you *are* the Forest, Hurnungaz. You will raise Sherewode.'

'We could wait with Merik's bear-kin?' suggested Godwin.

Hurnungaz shook his head. 'That would be weakness. We need to rebuild. We need to show we are still here. The knights, the lords, the Norman bastards, are sending soldiers back into the forest. Verderers. We may have spent a fair bit in attacking the cathedral, but that's not the war won. The battles continue.'

'But with less men,' said Wulfrun.

Hurnungaz nodded. 'Would you prefer to return to Gringeleia and Lady Perric?'

He scowled. 'James, her son, is a good lad. Lady Perric's nice but she's no Freya.'

'But you could?' Hurnungaz raised an eyebrow.

Wulfrun's scowl deepened. 'I will not see Freya and Iseulde until I am in the

Halls with them. I will not meet Freya, having been with another woman. She is my wife!' he thundered.

Hurnungaz looked away.

'And I serve Ullr,' he added. 'Someone has to pay. One day, I will find de Saintcrow and de Syloc. Both will pay. But I will not go alone,' he moved to his feet, angry. 'I am of the Hooded!'

Hurnungaz lifted his head suddenly. 'Wait. There is – something.'

**

Hugi had rebuilt the fire and it blazed inside the cave, hotter than ever before. Muna leant against the side of it, dripping in sweat, Mar in her arms.

The assassin still – slumbered. They had slept for days, if it was sleep. Sweat glistened on their back. On their arms.

'What if they never wake?'

Hugi looked up and shook his head. The care was evident in his deep set eyes.

'Wōden,' she murmured. 'Hear my call. This one is useful. Important to Hurnungaz and the Hooded. Saving them would help us.'

The fire continued burning. The low candles around the cavern kept burning as they had previously.

Nothing changed.

'Wōden. I am your raven. Your hand. Your messenger, your scout. I ask for your assistance. Life is a struggle. Wōden and Ullr and now Caerne. She is powerful indeed. She acts in a way you cannot. She could rule Sherewode; could drive you out.'

She looked at her brother.

He frowned.

'Wōden –'

Mar coughed and spluttered, moving unexpectedly.

'Mar!'

They opened their eyes and screamed.

**

Gisborough grinned at his bed companions. Evgania, the daughter of Warwick. A dark-haired and dark-eyed beauty, full in the bust and hips.

Jenny of Loxley, a serving maid, white-blonde haired, thin in the hips and chest, a Hel-cat who enjoyed scratching and biting.

The things Jenny had done to Evgania while she'd lain across him, while he'd been inside Warwick's daughter. The serving maid had drawn blood with her teeth and claws.

Evgania had enjoyed it. She enjoyed it even more when he'd disciplined her. And even more again, when he'd put Jenny atop her and disciplined her with his gloved hand.

Evgania lay face down, worn out, still slumbering, her back torn up and her buttocks bruised. Jenny lay on her back, wide awake and grinning, one hand between her legs, stroking herself.

He pushed her hand aside, striking her there.

She quivered and moaned, her blue eyes intense.

'My lord,' she whispered, 'you have a need to spend yourself in me.'

He rolled her onto her belly, drawing her back onto him. 'You weren't unenjoyable,' he grinned, sliding into her. 'Whose property are you?'

'D'Hallowcross,' she answered, moving against him of her own volition. 'If you hold still, my lord,' she said after a moment, 'I can do it all for you. You will enjoy it all the more.'

William let her, hands loosely on her hips. She was, probably, one of St. John's discards, but she was accomplished at what she was doing.

He grinned. The sort of thing he would never have got as seneschal to Brother Gascon. At least the mad brother hadn't been around. And seeing Geoffrey again! That was unexpected and delightful, though he'd sensed Geoffrey had more to say, when Berenger wasn't around.

'My lord,' her voice caught, 'I know they're small, but if you would care to stretch around and grab my tits, I will finish you off.'

William was surprised to find himself complying. He took her in hand, pushing down on her.

'My turn to tell you to lie still. I will finish myself off in you.'

He held her tightly, thrusting into her.

She moaned and gasped obediently.

With one final thrust he relinquished her, pushing himself up from her.

She giggled. 'That was most enjoyable, my lord Gisborough.' She rolled over onto her back, sweaty and clammy and sticky. 'I am glad my commodity brought such relief.'

He nodded and began dressing. 'I have a meeting with D'Hallowcross. See that the bed is made and the room properly fit before you leave.'

'Yes, my lord.' She giggled. 'Can I play with the daughter of Warwick before I finish?'

He looked over at the slumbering girl. 'Do what you want with Warwick's daughter as long as she's alive and has no cause to write to her father.'

He headed out for the main hall. D'Hallowcross had wanted to talk of nothing but wars and campaigns and the Holy Land last night, and Berenger, particularly, had been an eager participant in the conversation.

A fire blazed in the main hall. D'Hallowcross raised his mug in greeting and signalled. A servant scurried across, carrying plates of foodstuffs for him.

'Sleep well, William?'

William grinned. 'When I slept, I slept well, St. John. Thank you for the bed warmers.'

St. John chuckled, taking a swig of his ale. 'They are a good pair. Evgania likes being broken and Jenny likes breaking her.'

Gisborough chuckled.

'What are your plans, Gisborough?'

Gisborough took a swig of his ale. 'I think a regular patrol, maybe twenty of the King's Own, to guard the Cathedral site.'

The Sheriff nodded.

'The King's Own,' he paused.

The Sheriff continued to eat his breakfast, unhurried.

'They are – an iron glove. To have them watching villages would be a waste of time. My lord.'

D'Hallowcross nodded. 'Indeed.'

'There were towns, villages, you mentioned. Perhaps a show of force in them. Rattle them. See what falls loose.'

D'Hallowcross grinned. 'I will get you a scroll with a list of them. I have men out there, both in the forest and the towns, villages, cities, keeping a watchful eye out for them.'

Gisborough nodded.

'I know the main routes, my lord. It strikes me there are many places we would miss. Some, with eighty armoured, mounted, warriors, would be all too easy to miss.'

D'Hallowcross nodded. 'Concentrate on the larger places, the main roads.' He paused. 'Tell me. Did you enjoy Jenny?'

Gisborough paused, fork halfway to his mouth. 'Yes. For a serving maid, she seemed – well trained.'

The Sheriff chuckled. 'It amused me to make her a serving maid. She was given to me by Elizabeth of Loxley.'

Gisborough frowned. 'And she is?'

St. John finished his mug and held it out for a refill. 'She is a hag. She was married to one Robin of Clun, nephew of her previous husband.'

Gisborough grimaced. 'A Marcher lord?'

The Sheriff shrugged. 'I don't know. But it's him who's become this Hurnungaz.' He chuckled. 'A Norseman I know says it's – bastard. Illegitimate son.'

Gisborough narrowed his gaze. 'What can she tell us of her brother?'

The Sheriff shook his head. 'Very little. I had hoped to make her a spy in York's camp, but she saw through it.'

Gisborough continued eating his breakfast.

'I am minded to offer her to you. If you want her.'

Gisborough raised an eyebrow. 'You want a spy in my camp?' He chuckled. 'As bedwarmers go, she is good, yes. But I've the King's Own to lead. No time for –'

The Sheriff snorted. 'That's exactly why you need someone who's just for you. And no,' he shook his head. 'I have no interest in your plans, other than where they overlap with mine in clearing Sherwood of outlaws. We could be of assistance to each other.'

Gisborough pushed his plate away. 'The King takes your title and the monies associated with it and gives it to me. You are – pardon me my lord – almost overly friendly. You offer me a girl you freely admit is a spy.'

The Sheriff pushed his breakfast away, taking a swig of his ale. 'I believe one of my men has been turned. He is, I am reasonably certain, one of these Hooded.'

'And your thoughts towards him?'

'He no longer serves me. I want him dead. I want them all dead.'

Gisborough narrowed his gaze. 'There is more. My lord. Something personal.'

The Sheriff met his gaze calmly. 'Jenny is surprisingly competent. She knows many of the villages. Her brother is – was – a minor Anglo-Saxon nobleman. She has value beyond a bedwarmer.'

'And you've not used her as such?'

The Sheriff looked away. 'She was given to me as property. I used her as property.' He looked back at Gisborough. 'If it will allay your suspicions, I will take coin for her. Buy her off me. She has no love for her brother.'

'I would want to talk to her first.'

The Sheriff nodded. 'Of course. You know where she is.'

**

'I'm Alain,' the shy young man said. 'I'm a scribe.'

'Bless you, child. What has brought you into the wilds of Sherewode?'

He glanced at Tam. Brother Blacwin saw the man nod.

'I worked for Brother Gascon. There was a fire,' he shook his head. 'I wasn't well.'

'I got him out of there,' Tam added.

Brother Blacwin nodded.

'The Black Bishop's mad,' Tam growled.

Blacwin started to object, then changed his mind. 'I have never met the man. I cannot say. I know he will have what is best for those in his care at heart in all he does.'

Tam scowled. 'He cuts trees down. He blesses the land. He hangs peasants for looking at him wrongly and steals money from the poor.'

The brother raised an eyebrow. 'How do you know he steals money from the poor?'

Tam stared, scowling. 'Money is sent to him. Tithe money from the people of Sherwood. He pays soldiers, stone masons, he burns the trees and destroys everything he finds.'

Brother Blacwin shook his head. 'I am very grateful for your assistance, friend Tam. And you, young master Alain. I suspect I would not be alive now, but for you, but I cannot agree with what you say. And I have a village to attend to, so I must,' he trailed off.

'Go on then,' Tam scowled. 'We'll see none murdered by mistake, but you're wrong supporting the mad bastard bishop.'

He almost smiled. 'And your mad bastard archer? I have heard the tales. He can draw animals from trees. He need loose only one arrow and three good men die.'

Tam snorted. 'Ay. He's got a power. But good men?' He shook his head.

'Friend Tam –'

The man scowled. 'I'm not your friend. You're a supporter of a mad monk who wants to kill and destroy everything –' he turned away.

'Stay,' said Alain.

'Stay?' Tam whipped around.

Alain nodded. 'Please? I've been having – terrible nightmares. And then the fire.' The young man looked at the older. 'Please, Tam. I'm grateful for your saving me, but he's a brother of the Christ of the East.'

'Suppose,' said Blacwin softly, 'you brought me to your demon archer and let him decide?'

'You think him a demon?' Tam asked, a twinkle in his eyes.

Blacwin smiled. 'No, I do not. Demons are – not what,' He shook his head. 'If you will let me – learn more – will you let me with you?'

Tam stared.

'Please,' said Alain.

Tam glanced at the younger man: nodded grudgingly.

**

The trees creaked. Groaned. Shadows dappled them and branches moved, sending a scurry of leaves and acorns drifting down upon them.

'There's something up there,' Diederic whimpered.

'There is not,' she reassured, holding his hand tighter.

The path was nothing but a rutted mud track, barely wide enough for the two of them side by side. As they ventured in, the daylight and field gradually disappearing behind them, the track began narrowing.

'We should have stayed in the field,' her brother protested weakly.

'The sun was too bright,' she reminded him. 'There was only the tree for shade. We have no food. We need water. We need,' she shrugged.

'Will they find us?' he asked.

'They will,' she nodded. 'They will track us through – wherever we are.' She looked around, trying not to shudder. 'This is a strange place, but we will find help. They will find us, in time.'

**

'What happened?' Hurnungaz asked.

'I don't know!' Caerne screamed.

They were in a deeply buried grove. The trees were twisted and blackened. There had been grass once, but the land was dead now, cracked mud and melted rock.

Blood leaked from Caerne's ears. Oozed from her nipples. Trickled down her thighs. Her fur was mostly gone, only traces remaining, the skin beneath raw, burnt. She was bald, her horns gleaming white, cracked with black fragments. The merest stump of her tail remained. Even her hooves were cracked, weeping pus.

Sciuridae lay at her feet.

Without moving, Hurnungaz knew he was dead.

'What happened – with Sciuridae?'

Caerne sighed. Her face was gaunt, eyes pure yellow. 'I killed him. Took everything he had.' She sighed. 'It didn't help.'

'The attack?'

'The Wulfenstæg drained me,' she giggled, her hand snatching to her crotch and away again. 'I came so hard the world ended. All that power, pouring through me.'

She dropped to her knees, face pressed to Sciuridae. 'He was my brother,' she howled, throwing her head back, fingers clawing at her chest and belly, drawing blood.

'My brother! And I killed him.'

She clutched at her throat.

Hurnungaz dropped to his knees, pulling her hands away.

She stared at him blindly.

'I killed him,' she whispered. 'Fed on him like he would recharge me. Tried to take my energy back from him but it's hers. It's hers!' she screamed, staring at him.

'Whose?' he asked gently.

'Crow-bitch!' she screamed. 'Her god murdered my father!'

Hurnungaz nodded gently.

'You fucked Quellavera,' she said softly, staring at him nastily, licking her teeth. 'Poured all my power into her quim. Her belly bulges with it,' she giggled. 'There's a beast in her belly.'

Hurnungaz stared. 'I – did,' he replied softly. 'She's pregnant?'

She dragged him into her embrace. Pulled him down so that they lay awkwardly, half-hugging, over Sciuridae.

'It was just – sex,' he said, after a while.

'It should have been a triumvirate,' she whimpered softly.

'A threesome?'

'No.' She grimaced. 'I gave some of my power to you. I gave some to Sciuridae.' She sighed. 'Your power is all but spent and I have too little to give you any. I drained Sciuridae to take back what I had given him and he had already given his to the crow-bitch.'

'Muna.'

'Crow-bitch.'

Hurnungaz sighed. 'Had he not, what would draining him have done?'

She raised her head. Tears were leaking from her eyes. 'It would not have killed him. It would have drained him, left him tired. It,' she shuddered, looking away. 'It tore him in half. I tore him in half.'

'What can I do to rebuild you? To rebuild me? The Hooded – there's four others, still. We're all – weary? Worn out.'

'Patterns have been broken.' Caerne heaved. 'New patterns have to be made.'

'What do you mean?'

'Take them out hunting. Teach those who abuse the forest people to fear the Hooded. Normans, slavers, verderers, anyone who hurts my people.'

'Will that – help you?'

She nodded weakly.

'You said about a triumvirate?'

Caerne lifted her head. 'I have almost no power. You have none. There is no one.'

'Wulfrun?'

She tilted her head back. 'Ullr.'

'Hereseige?'

She shook her head. 'He does not truly believe.'

'He's alive?'

She nodded.

'What about – Mar?'

She tilted her head sideways, baring her teeth and growling. 'Crow-bitch.'

'He's with Muna?'

Caerne studied him for a moment.

'The assassin,' she answered slowly. 'There is a thread to the Old one as was. I appeared to them in Erin. There are,' she grimaced. 'Whispers of Wōden around them. No.'

'Tam?'

She shook her head.

'Bwyd?'

She opened her mouth but stopped.

'He is alive,' she almost mewled.

'Where?'

'Wales.'

'Could it be done?'

'Not over distance.'

'Can something be done – a new triumvirate formed – if Bwyd and I were here?'

Caerne raised her head. There were sparks of green in her yellow eyes. 'It may be. Rebuild the Hooded. My people need you. Forge new patterns.'

Hurnungaz nodded. 'It will be slow going.'

She nodded, huddling even closer to Sciuridae.

'He is dead,' Hurnungaz said softly. 'There is nothing to be gained.'

Caerne raised her head. Her eyes blazed yellow. 'He is my brother!'

Hurnungaz nodded. 'And the first to join me. Your power drew him to me.'

She scowled at him, burrowing underneath Sciuridae's body. 'He keeps me safe. I need to rest, Hurnungaz of the Hooded. I am drained.' She sighed. 'You have a task, Robin,' she added, mockingly.

**

'By the dark breath of earth!' roared Llewellyn. 'Brother Bwyd!'

'My lord!' Bwyd raised his hand in greeting. 'Dissever me never, my lord.'

The hall was smaller than he remembered it. Long pennants rippled in the breeze from the high windows. Fires burned in each wall, causing shadows to dance.

But there were only four tables, forming a rough square in the middle of the hall, and less than half a dozen men sat at each. There was the smell of overcooked meat; stale rushes.

Llewellyn stamped up to him. He had flaming red hair; a big beard, and ice-blue eyes.

'Brother!' He flung his arm out in greeting.

Bwyd took his arm. 'My lord.'

He was pulled into a bear-hug. 'My lord? You my lord me now, eh, Bwyd?'

He was recognised; there were cheers from the tables and stamping of mugs, or axes against shields.

'You look – wearied, my lord.'

Llewellyn sighed, and stood less tall than he had done a moment before.

'There is much you do not know, and much that is sad, and some that is perilous. But it is good to see you!' he rallied again. 'Has it been a long trip from the heart of Sherewode?'

Bwyd nodded. 'And odd, leaving my comrades, my brothers in arms behind, saying nothing, telling them nothing. But you are still, are always, my lord, Llewellyn.'

Llewellyn clapped him on the arm. 'Good man. A flagon!' he roared. 'Wine for Brother Bwyd, returned to us.'

Serving maids appeared, one rushing up with a goblet, another a sack. Others appeared, refilling the warriors' mugs.

'There are,' he spoke softly, 'fewer here than I expected to see, my lord.'

Llewellyn nodded, taking a mouthful of wine. 'Fret not! They are not dead, but scattered for safety's sake.' He grimaced. 'It is a heavy thing to talk of now. Let us drink, reminisce, we will talk seriously in the morning and rebuild. Plan,' he slurred slightly. 'Plan,' he repeated, looking meaningfully at Bwyd. 'There is much to plan.'

He pulled away. 'Stoke the fires!' he roared. 'Let the wine flow. Bring more food!'

The warriors cheered, bashing goblet on tabletop or axe upon shield.

'The Sælvatici!' Llewellyn roared. 'The Sælvatici rise once more!'

The roar in response shook the rafters.

**

The tree was adorned with old skulls and threads of many colours, some so old the tree had grown around them. It was in a clearing remote from any village, buried deep in almost unbreachable thorn-infested undergrowth.

The verderer grinned, pushing the thief before him.

The man stumbled and fell.

'So,' the verderer grabbed the man's tunic, half kneeling on his back. 'What we have is an altar to their heathen god. You prayed here, didn't you? Sacrificed virgin girls here, eh?'

The thief shook his head, whimpering. Both hands of his were bandaged; he was missing two fingers from his left hand, the little finger from his right.

'But that's alright, you see,' the man sniggered. 'You see, we're making another sacrifice. You,' he kicked the former archer. 'Too many useless people.'

He dragged the thief towards the tree. Flung him against it, grinning when he heard a crack.

He drew a knife, slitting the man's throat.

'Mythical forest god,' he sniggered, 'come see your dead servant. We will wipe your backwards, scummish, belief from this land.' He shook his head. 'The Christ of the East wills it.'

**

From the dark, he could smell *them*. One of Scáthach's own. A survivor. A bitch. Scáthach's daughter or lover, he couldn't tell, couldn't care.

One of them survived!

He breathed heavily, feeling the weight in his lungs, feeling the fire. His hand cramped, tendons twitching.

They – survived!

His shoulders flexed. His back trembled. They were here – in Sherwood. He ground his teeth together.

His jaw trembled. His head pounded. His ribs cracked.

The power poured through him.

The Marcher lands had only been a start.

Here, he cackled maniacally. Here, the forest would run red.

He ripped a tree out of the ground and flung it out of his way. Screamed in rage, enjoying the silence of the forest afterwards.

Picked up a boulder and tossed it into a tree, grinning as the tree was torn out by its roots.

He screamed wordlessly. Plunged his fists into the trunk of an old oak, feeling the power and rage flow through him.

'I will find her!'

The oak exploded.

**

The cart moved slowly, creaking, the ponies tired, the day closing in. The farmer sat at the front, whip in hand, bundled up against the weather. The cart was low; filled with sealed bags of corn. Spilled corn filled the floor of the cart and trickled out behind it.

'Nothing there,' said Wulfrun, scowling. 'Farmer.'

Hurnungaz glanced at him; at Godwin and Merik. 'Stop him.'

They shared a look and moved out from the trees.

'Whoah!' the farmer jerked his reins. 'Where did you come from?'

'What's in the cart?' asked Godwin.

The man clutched the dagger at his belt. 'Nothing but corn. I've no coin. It's from three villages, their crop.'

'Really?' said Raven, moving into the open.

The farmer scowled at him. 'Who are you, boy? You look like you should be working the fields still.'

Raven looked at Godwin. 'Villages send their corn for sale, yes. Nottingham or elsewhere. But not just entrusted to one man. They take turns, several men. In case of outlaws.'

Merik chuckled, drawing his knife. 'What have we here, then? Who are you really?'

'There were – no men to spare,' the man protested. 'There are been no outlaws since that – attack. Broke them, the villagers reckon.'

Hurnungaz moved into the open, arrow nocked on the string. 'You're not one of the Forest.'

Wulfrun drew an axe. 'The corn's not corn, is it?'

'Hey, you can't do that,' the man protested.

Raven was suddenly there, stood on the edge of the cart, a knife to the man's throat.

'You're no villager,' he hissed.

'Don't kill him for it,' Wulfrun said, splitting one of the bags of corn.

Corn poured out.

'See?'

Raven pushed his knife deeper.

Hurnungaz smiled as the sound of coins clinking together began.

'Merik, Godwin, unhook the ponies from the cart. Give the Sheriff's man one; let him ride to Nottingham.'

'He'll murder me,' the man protested. 'Tis his money.'

'The Sheriff's money?' Wulfrun kicked bag after bag of corn. All jingled. 'He sent you corn to take back into Nottingham?'

The man whimpered. 'The villagers – the villages gave it to me.'

'Oh,' said Godwin, moving in, 'a taxman.'

**

'The Sheriff tells me you're a spy.'

Jenny whipped her head up, her eyes ablaze. 'I am no spy,' she hissed.

Gisborough raised an eyebrow. 'I hope Warwick's daughter remains – intact.'

She grinned, a fire in her pale eyes. 'Mostly.'

He chuckled. 'My power doesn't impress you.'

'Why should it?' She sat up, pulling the sheet over the sleeping woman's body. 'I was Jenny of Loxley. Now I am Jenny of Nottingham.'

Gisborough grinned. 'Sister to the outlaw Hurnungaz.'

She spat. 'His bride was a crone. He was only interested in hunting and fishing, in spearing maidens on his rod.' She snorted. 'He abandoned me. Why should I feel any loyalty to him?'

'Indeed.' He drew up one of the chairs, putting his feet on the bed. 'Tell me of York.'

Jenny snorted. 'Dresses as a man. Likes being ploughed. The King wants her with child; I doubt she wants it.'

'Why?' he frowned.

'Because she's not stupid.'

His frown deepened. 'She's – the King's cousin.'

Jenny nodded. 'As soon as she's pregnant, it's all about her offspring. D'Hallowcross' offspring. The future of Nottingham and York.' She scowled. 'Unless it's a girl.'

'If it's a boy?'

She shrugged. 'It will inherit York. Nephew to the King.' She chuckled. 'A pawn.'

Gisborough narrowed his gaze. 'And what are your own – intentions?'

She stared at him, radiating fury. 'I would like to see my brother swinging from a noose. I would like to see him torn apart by wild ponies. I would like to see him in pain, bleeding, dying.'

Gisborough chuckled. 'I have one hundred of the King's Own. The King has commissioned me to hunt him down. Track him wherever he goes.'

She shook her head. 'You'll never find him.'

He raised an eyebrow.

'My brother *knows* Sherewode. Sherwood,' she corrected herself.

'Could you?'

She shook her head. 'He's not my brother anymore. Some woodland deity has captured him.'

Gisborough nodded. 'The Old gods still have powers here.' He grimaced. 'Allowing for that, could you track him? Suggest what he might do, where he might go?'

She shrugged. 'I don't know. What is it to me?'

'You would be no camp follower.'

She raised an eyebrow.

'The Sheriff has offered you to me, for coin. Robin, this Hurnungaz, is my intent. I need him captured. You can help me.'

'And I'm no camp follower?'

He shook his head. 'No. There may well be hard riding. Hard nights. Not much for – a lady's sensibilities.'

Jenny snorted. 'I'm no lady. I'm an Anglo-Saxon noblewoman, or I was. I can draw a bow, I can use a stave, I can think at least as well as a man.'

'So where would Robin be? He successfully assaulted the site of the Black Bishop's cathedral. Why has there been no news recently? I do not know if the site is still useable by Brother Gascon.' He shook his head. 'It makes no sense. In his position, I would be crowing about it. I would be ensuring everyone knew I had destroyed the cathedral.'

Jenny shook her head. 'He's not interested in that. He's moved on.' She sighed. 'He's stalking another prey – more gold, like the wagons from Lincoln?'

'How do you know about them?'

She chuckled. 'Everything comes through Nottingham. I hear everything.'

Gisborough scowled. 'Your impression of York? Of D'Hallowcross?'

She smirked. 'York is dangerous. She thinks she's powerful.'

'And?'

Jenny sniggered. 'And she is. D'Hallowcross,' she made a face.

'What?'

She shook her head. 'He *could* be. Something has upset him; one of his plans has been interfered with.' She scowled. 'He lingers, like a spider waiting for a fly. If he went after something instead –'

Gisborough raised an eyebrow.

'He has troops, he has spies, he has ruthlessness. He holds back. Something,' she shook her head again. 'He is a hard nut. I cannot break him. He doesn't trust me.'

'And me?'

She chuckled. 'An arrow being drawn back. You served in the Holy Land.' Her grin dropped away. 'I see the shadows about you.'

Gisborough blanched.

'You were the Black Bishop's seneschal. You've got yourself something you're far more suited to.' Her grin returned. 'You'll do well, Gisborough. Whatever happens with my former brother. You command respect. You have authority. You have might.' She grinned. 'Crush Hurnungaz, and you will have much more.'

**

Her son, impaled on a sword. Scáthach, beheaded, defiled. Her sisters, her fellow warriors, murdered, slaughtered all –

Bodies on fire, bodies locked in love skewered on spears, bodies ripped and torn apart.

Blood. Her mouth was full of blood. Buried alive unconscious under a cairn of bodies. Heads, hands, feet, hacked off randomly. Sources of pleasure hacked at and defiled.

Flies, buzzing. Piss and shit. She was alive. Buried alive. Fear. Terror.

Had anyone survived?

Was her son alive?

Was he still there, waiting for her, knowing she still lived?

Mar opened her eyes.

She was engulfed, hands tearing at her, teeth biting –

Mar flung herself backwards and out of the trap, unarmed and unarmoured, screaming –

Hit the ground hard, winded.

The air was cold; cool. Somewhere dark. A dying fire, surrounded by stone. Candles in the walls –

She backpedalled furiously.

A figure stood over her, skeletal thin, bone white. A huge penis, black-veined, pulsing. A crow-headed figure, screeching, bending down towards her –

**

Alain followed Tam almost blindly. He had been – in a delirium. Lost. That creature – the creature that had sat on his chest – or had it?

Londinium. Scribery. The creature –

But this was Sherwode. *Sherwood.* There were no straight lines. Tam, these Hooded, they would have no need of a scribe.

But Brother Blacwin – he shook his head.

It was all confused, a jumble of thoughts, spinning.

It was these Hooded, possibly even Tam, who had loosed arrows at Sir Gisborough and him. Who had caused him to shelter in the abandoned chapel with the knight –

He shuddered.

But it was Tam who'd rescued him. But for Tam he would have died in his sleep, or awoken too late, the cathedral site under attack from the Hooded and creatures straight out of Hel running loose.

Tam had tried to tell him that it was merely boars, with some stags and wolves; even a bear or two.

It was straight out of a tale.

**

'I like the look of you.'

Bwyd raised his head. Llewellyn snored, face down on the table. The fires were dying down. Scattered groups of two or three warriors still talked and drank but none near him.

'I am Aneirin.'

He looked up at the woman who stood beside him. A thick, green, robe. Her face was in shadow from a hood, but he could see the twinkle of her eyes.

'Young Bwyd.'

She opened the robe enough to reveal she was naked beneath it. An emerald pendant on her chest.

'If you are not fully incapacitated by alcohol, I have a small chamber. Some company this night would be pleasing.'

**

Mar stared in terror.

'Hugi,' said an exasperated voice, 'sit down! You're scaring the assassin.'

Mar blinked. Stared.

Muna knelt before her, tufted black feathers at her crotch, under her arms. Wings seemed to sprout from her back, wings that were visible and invisible, wings that she could see through.

'You were a boy,' Muna said softly. 'You lusted after me.'

Mar scowled.

'Does Raven – know?'

She nodded. 'Raven knows I'm not a boy. I was injured. A blade cut my chest, was bleeding freely.'

She looked down. There were relatively fresh cuts on her inner thighs, her belly, her chest, her arms.

'Why, if you were trying to kill yourself,' Muna began.

Mar snarled. 'If I'd wanted to kill myself I'd have driven a blade into my heart.' She scowled. 'I wished for death. I longed for it. I wanted to feel death's final embrace,' she sighed.

'You're alive.'

Mar scowled.

'Do I need to keep your weapons from you?'

Mar raised an eyebrow. 'I'll kill you if you try and stop me.'

Hugi rasped in anger. The firelight made him look even more – Hel-like.

'Put that cock away Hugi or I'll cut it off you and feed it to your sister!'

Hugi glowered.

'You lusted after me, Mar. Why?'

'I wanted to hurt you,' she scowled. 'If I'd been a boy I would have. Every which way imaginable.'

'But you're a woman.'

'This,' she gestured to herself. 'This mewling quim. Once. Just once does a man have it, and I get pregnant. Have a son.' She shuddered, pain coming in waves.

'Mar!'

She drew back, shaking her head. 'I hate you, Muna.' She spoke through gritted teeth, shaking. 'I was a warrior of Scáthach. No man was my equal. Now I'm,' she shrugged, scowling.

'You're a woman, Mar. A mother.'

Mar launched herself at Muna. Knocked the woman over and slammed her head into the ground. Grabbed a handful of hair and pulled her head up. A knife was in her hand.

'Muna,' she hissed, gazing up at Hugi. 'Would you like me to cut your tits off for your brother to eat?'

Hugi glowered but didn't move.

'Would you?' Mar pressed the blade against Muna's neck. 'Because that's what he did.'

She shuddered.

Flung the knife away.

She was lifted effortlessly. Hugi leaned in, screeching wordlessly –

**

'And what would you want?'

Jenny grinned. She was voracious, taking and wanting more from him than any bedwarmer ever had before.

'Well, I'm no lady.' She chuckled, sprawled in his bed, naked. 'But then you can see that, you like that.'

William nodded. 'Marriage would never happen.'

She shook her head. 'That's not what I want. I want to ride with you. I want to hunt my brother with you, my lord. I want to keep you warm at nights. I only ask –'

'Oh?'

'Spare me no luxuries. Do not treat me as a weak and feeble woman. I can use a bow, I can ride a horse.' She grinned. 'I can use a stave and I know knife work.'

'And you would betray me when your brother is found?'

She snorted. 'If you would let me be the one, I would loose an arrow into his belly. Let him see I am the one who ends him.'

'An extra mounted knight?' He frowned. 'You would need arms, armour, weapons.' He shook his head. 'D'Hallowcross wants me to buy you from him. I've no mind to spend money on armour for you as well.'

Jenny grinned. 'Supposing I got you money. You could make me your squire. Leather armour, trews, jerkin.' She shrugged. 'I can steal most of that from D'Hallowcross. I would be an attentive squire. And on cold nights,' she spread her legs, hands on her thighs. 'I could provide warmth and company.'

He frowned. 'How would you get money? You are a good bedwarmer, but I doubt you could earn enough coin –'

She sat up, scowling at him, throwing a pillow angrily. 'My lord!'

He batted it away.

'You would throw pillows at me until coin fell out of them?'

She sat up, drawing her legs in under her. 'Warwick's daughter. Her father dotes on her and she's a slut. If she were to be kidnapped, he would pay good coin for her.'

Gisborough raised an eyebrow. 'And how would you do this? How would you get a message to her father?'

'She has a silk scarf her father gave her as a present. If he were to receive it, with the rightly worded message –'

'You would need to get through to him.'

She nodded. 'I can write. And I am a serving maid. I pose no threat.'

'And kidnapping the girl?'

She grinned. 'Evgania likes me. She likes being hurt. I could arrange for her to take a turn about Nottingham. She would ask me to accompany her.'

William shook his head. 'It is a distracting fantasy, but D'Hallowcross would not allow the pair of you out without escort. While he tries to sell you to me, he likely may keep you under close watch.'

'If he thought you remained in here with me –'

Gisborough shook his head, a little reluctantly. 'Alas, I have a command from the King. Hurnungaz is not the only one I seek, but all the Hooded.'

Jenny nodded. 'Then I have a suggestion, my lord.'

Gisborough nodded. 'Tell me. Then I must be off.'

**

Sir Richard sighed gently. It has been so long. A mild breeze blew. The sunlight was dappled, strained through the overhanging branches. The armour no longer chafed, nor was he even really aware of it. After fighting in the Holy Land for so long –

He blinked. Too many years staring at unending sand plains. Too many years with a too bright sun. Too many years away from his homeland. Away from his people. His home.

There was something on the path ahead. Something – small. The forest creaked and stretched around him. He could hear bird song. The snuffling of small creatures in the undergrowth.

Sir Richard proceeded slowly, cautiously. Two figures, children, perhaps, gradually became clearer.

He had heard the tales of the outlaws of Sherwood: outlaws of Sherewode, ancient forest land. The Hooded, from what he had discerned from the tale tellers and minstrels, were the most powerful of them.

The most feared of all the outlaw bands.

As he got closer to the children, he saw their skins were pale and oddly-hued, possibly stained from the dappled sunlight.

He raised his hand in greeting.

'I am Sir Richard of Verysdale. Are you lost?'

They were a boy and girl; the girl older, who clutched her younger brother's hand tightly.

'I mean you no harm,' he smiled. 'Where are you from?'

The boy looked terrified. He drew his horse to a stop some distance from them, glancing around. If they were bait, dismounting was the stupidest thing he could do.

But the look on the children's faces –

He swung down from the horse, leading it to one side of the track, looping its reins around a low branch.

He lowered his cowl and smiled. Removed his gloves, running fingers through his thinning hair.

'I am Sir Richard of Verysdale. Do you recognise my voice? Are you, perhaps, Welsh?'

The girl smiled, a little shyly. The boy had moved so he stood more behind his sister.

Their skins were strangely hued. The colour was not from the shadows of the trees, but in their skins. Pale green skinned they were, subtle but noticeable.

'Have you come far?'

He knelt down and held his hand out. The girl, slowly, approached, a shy smile on her face.

**

Bwyd woke late in the morning. The woman still lay beside him, leaning on her elbow, looking at him. Her chamber was small, rushes on the floor. They'd used her robe as a bed; there was a small pile of blankets and furs in the corner, unused.

'Good – morning.'

She smiled. 'Good morning, Bwyd.' Her voice lilted in a way he found very attractive.

She reached a hand out, cupping, caressing, him. 'Is the young Sælvatici of Sherwode ready for more?'

She had long, red-brown, hair that fell past her shoulders, receding. Dark hazel eyes. There were wrinkles at her lips, her eyes. A wild, tangled, thatch. Sagging breasts that swung freely.

'Aneirin.' He frowned. 'I know that name.'

'Of course you do,' she chuckled. 'I taught you sword and stave when you were young. Of an evening I taught lessons at the fireplace. Myths and legends of our people. Heroes of old.'

Bwyd widened his eyes, staring. 'Aneirin!' He gulped. 'Warrior woman and word smith.'

She nodded, sitting up.

Bwyd stared up at her. Sitting up, her face seemed more lined, her body heavier. Stouter.

'I have passed the age where I can bear children, though I have nursed many in my time.' She patted his knee. 'It was a most pleasing night, but I see my time with you –'

'No!'

Aneirin chuckled. 'You want one more story, perhaps, for old times' sake.'

Bwyd shook his head, sitting up, taking her in his arms and drawing her close.

'You taught me much, Aneirin.' He kissed her, sliding his arms around her back.

'Much,' she smiled, kissing him back. 'Perhaps this old war horse has one more lesson in her.'

She bore him down, straddling him.

**

'Put her down, Hugi!'

She was lowered back to the ground. Hugi scowled; turned and walked away from her into the darkness.

A moment later she heard a splash.

'An underground lake?'

'A deep stream. It's what led us in here. This cavern is quite deep. There is no way in or out except through the river.'

'I was brought here.' Mar scowled. 'From Erin. I was being trained to be a warrior. I was – I am – very good. My son was growing fast. The son I'd never wanted.'

'I am Wōden's right hand,' Muna said softly. 'Hugi is his left hand. I am – memory.'

'Memory?' Mar raised her head.

Muna nodded. 'I can take you back to any memory you wish to. Or I could, possibly, take those memories from you.'

Mar shook her head. 'A bastard butchered all of my kind. Slaughtered them. Hacked bodies. Defiled living ones. Stabbed my son on a spear like he was meat, to be skewered and cooked on a fire.'

Muna looked away, looking queasy.

'He would hunt me, if he knew I lived. I hunt him.' She sighed. 'I was sent here, but he is not here. I will have to find the Old one.' She grimaced. 'Caerne came to me. If she were around, if she still existed –'

'She still lives. I think.'

Mar narrowed her gaze. 'You think?'

Muna nodded. 'This land has long been fought over by three gods. Cernunnos, Wōden and Ullr. Wōden and Ullr conspired; tricked and slew Cernunnos, thinking to take this land for themselves.'

Mar raised an eyebrow. 'And?'

Muna almost smiled. 'Caerne rose out of the ashes of Cernunnos. She scares me. Wōden and Ullr tend to need to work through others. She can,' she shook her head. 'She is power. Personified. She is mad.'

'I need to see her. She will know how to find the Old one.'

Muna shook her head. 'I cannot help you. I summoned her once,' she shuddered.

'And if I ordered you to do it?'

'You could kill me. I am quite weak here. But if you want to summon her, I will not support you. If you wanted to kill me, you would likely succeed.'

Mar stared at her. 'Were I a boy, I would rape you. You know my secrets. I would rape you. Break your arms. Break your legs. Snap your scrawny neck.' She smiled, baring her teeth. 'Pluck every feather from your carcass and burn them.'

Muna shook her head sadly. 'You are alive. Your clothes are beside the cairn, as are your weapons. I cannot help you further.'

**

They emerged in a field in which a single tree grew. Mist lingered. Rain drizzled softly. The air smelt – different.

Radewych raised a hand, calling a halt. Her people spread out carefully, cautiously, weapons and shields raised in readiness.

The wyrd path which had led them to this place was long gone. The children they followed were not in sight.

The field, to one side, seemed to dissipate into a river and a marsh. To the other, an unknown forest. The forest was the most likely.

Radewych took a deep breath.

The air was fresh. Things were growing. Moist and decay. Living trees. Decaying plants. Creatures of the undergrowth.

Inhabitants.

She nodded, heading for the forest.

**

'You saw our brother in the cage?'

Bwyd nodded grimly. 'I did, Llewellyn. How did it come about?'

Llewellyn sighed, pouring ale into a mug and passing it over; pouring a drink for himself. Apart from them the hall was almost empty. Two servants were working on relighting the nearest fire; a third was carrying in a laden platter with plates of food on for them.

'You know – we have lost kin?'

Bwyd nodded sadly. 'I do, my lord. Aneirin told me. I am sorry. I will say words for them.'

Llewellyn smiled; nodded. 'Thank you.' He sighed. 'I am glad she found you. She was great comfort to me –' he looked away.

The servant slid the tray of food between them and withdrew.

Bwyd took a hunk of meat and a hard bread roll.

'As if that was not bad, terrible, enough,' Llewellyn shook himself. 'A man came to us, just after. Called himself Paol.'

He snorted. 'I thought him an ally. He was Celt. A fiercesome warrior.'

'It was his work?'

Llewellyn nodded grimly. 'He played the part of an ally. He knew – a little – about the Sælvatici, though none of our phrases.' He sighed, scowling.

'What happened?'

'He asked for a contest, to test his skills. I agreed. We train daily, our own new blood or the young of Marcher lords. I said yes.'

'Oh,' Bwyd said softly.

Llewellyn nodded slowly. 'Three of my men were dead before I realised.' He looked directly at Bwyd. 'He is *fast*.' He shook his head. 'I carry war in my fist, but he.'

Bwyd drained his mug. Refilled it.

'I reined him in. An accident; an oversight.' He shook his head. 'Speed. Power. A hero-light flickered about him.'

Bwyd stared. 'None have had the ability for so very long –'

Llewellyn nodded. 'He persuaded a man of mine – a good man, a family man, to join him in a private fight. He swore he'd only use one blade.'

Bwyd grimaced. It *should* be only heroes who carried the hero-light. A gift from the Goddess, from the land, from the People. If one should carry it who was unworthy –

'He disarmed him. Put him in the cage. Tortured him.'

Bwyd felt sick.

'I – had insight. I knew he wanted to slaughter us, to destroy the Sælvatici. I sent most of my men away to different parts of Wales.'

'And they were safe? What of those remaining?'

'We –' Llewellyn sighed. 'We buried ourselves deep in the tower. He burned the stables. Tortured, killed, some servants who'd not fled fast enough. In time he moved on, though angry.'

'He wanted the Sælvatici dead? Does he work for the Normans?'

Llewellyn shrugged. 'I suspect not. A man like that, following orders is not in his nature. He is chaos. Power. Rage.' He shook his head. 'I think, at the end, he thought of or scented something – someone – else to hunt. I do not know who.'

Bwyd nodded. 'That is not good news, my lord.'

Llewellyn looked up, grim. 'I worry. I have – saved – the Sælvatici, but at what cost? My friends. My brothers. My leadership as well?'

'What would you have me do? Why did you call for me?'

Llewellyn smiled. 'Aneirin is capable in many ways. She is up for what I want of her.'

'And that is? My lord?'

Llewellyn grinned. 'You are young, Bwyd. One day, perhaps, you may command the Sælvatici.'

Bwyd stared. 'My lord! That is not something I would choose.'

Llewellyn chuckled. 'Sometimes, those that command, are chosen against their will. If you are, then accept it.'

'But if it is a position –'

Llewellyn finished his mug and poured another. 'Yes. You are my choice, but that may have no influence.'

'I am – honoured. But that would mean –'

Llewelyn nodded. 'Yes. The one you call Hurnungaz – Robin of Clun. He has his priorities. You have yours.'

'And mine is – the Sælvatici?'

'If it comes to it, yes.' Llewellyn chuckled. 'But I have something for you first.'

Bwyd took another mouthful of the ale.

'Tides are turning. This man. Your attack on the unholy cathedral. News is sporadic.'

Bwyd nodded. 'We lost a few men during the attack. I did not see the brother behind it all, he was skulking out of sight, I suspect.'

Llewellyn closed his eyes for a moment. 'You will return to Hurnungaz. You will take Aneirin with you.'

'Aneirin?' Bwyd grinned.

Llewellyn smiled. 'And ten of the bowmen. They will join your Hooded.' His smile broke into an angry grin. 'We need to *fight*, Bwyd. You and Hurnungaz, the men you have, you have done what we could not. Fight the Normans. Fight the Norse. Fight the oppressors!'

**

Gisborough reined his horse in, pointing to the village below them.

'There. We go in hard and fast. Shake them up. Seize the headman. Anyone else who looks capable. Take them and withdraw.'

Berenger nodded. 'And then?'

Gisborough buried his scowl. 'We return here. Question them.'

'Why not in the village?'

'I want the village – unsettled. Threatened. We can come in, take their head-people, threaten anyone we want, kill anyone –'

'I am not sure,' Berenger havered. 'Unless –'

Gisborough shook his head. 'They do not know that. Remaining in their village to question them, there is too much they could take strength from. We seize them, remove them, torture them.'

'Have you a mind for torture?'

He shrugged. 'I will do what is necessary. Killing; maiming. It tends to loosen tongues.'

Berenger nodded. 'As you say, my lord.'

**

Muna drew the dress back on, trying not to shiver. The underground river was icy cold. Mar – Mar terrified her.

Hugi was long gone, she could sense that. Mar was – rage, personified. Not something she wanted to deal with.

She sighed.

In the shadows at the back of the cavern where she waited, a pale hand, carrying a bundle of clothing, emerged from the water.

She waited, not knowing whether to flee like her brother or wait and face – whatever Mar did. Whatever they said.

She sighed. She had tracked Mar down after the battle. Knew Mar could track her far easier and quicker than she'd found the assassin.

They emerged slowly from the water, eyes glittering.

Blades were strapped to their thighs, outer and inner. To their forearms. To their belly, their back, even between their breasts.

They flung their clothes onto the rocks; scrambled up.

'If you keep looking at me like that, I will plunge a blade deep into somewhere very painful.'

'You hate me. Want to kill me.'

Mar snorted. 'I don't give a fuck for you, crow-girl. I will happily pluck your feathers. I would happily shave you with my knife-blade, but only if I thought it would hurt you in some way.'

'It won't hurt me. I am Wōden's raven.'

Mar was suddenly there, a knife at her throat. 'I don't like you, little crow. Look at me too often and I will take your eyes.'

'I could be your lover, Mar. I will keep your secret. You do not need to fear me.'

Mar scowled. Her hand moved to Muna's breast.

'What a soft heart you have,' she scowled. 'I will not take your eyes until I have made you watch me slaughter your brother.'

Muna flinched. 'Please no,' she begged.

Mar laughed. 'Soft. The offspring of Wōden's soft cock.' She grinned, baring her teeth in an imitation of Caerne. 'Stag Daughter will rend him apart and feast on his entrails.'

Muna managed to pull free: staggered back a little.

'A storm is coming,' Mar grinned, her eyes bright and feverish. 'Run, little crow girl. I will dissect your brother later.'

**

Hurnungaz loped through the forest easily, moving as swiftly as for the joy of it as much as anything.

Wulfrun was gone, taking the taxpayer's stolen coin to the nearest villages. Bwyd was alive. Hereseige was alive. Tam was alive. Mar and Muna were alive.

Sciuridae.

Sciuridae. He sighed.

And Caerne. Alive but damaged. Broken. Weak. Tired.

Raven and Merik and Godwin ran with him. Raven was growing in confidence, had proved his worth already.

New patterns, Caerne had said. Bwyd would be part of that. But Bwyd had gone, left, without a word –

But Bwyd was Sælvatici. Bwyd would return.

There was a broad trackway ahead. Two men, in long white robes, emblazoned with red crosses, walked down it.

Hurnungaz grinned as the men started turning towards them –

'Semicircle!'

They fanned out around the two. Both were heavily armoured and armed; one had drawn a huge sword, wielding it two handed.

'We are Templars!' the knight roared. 'Face us and die.'

Hurnungaz drew his bow and nocked in one movement, arrow aimed at the speaker's face.

'I loose, and an arrow takes each eye and a third your mouth. We are the Hooded. This is Sherwode!'

'There are only four of you,' the other Templar grinned. He was dark haired; taller than the other.

'I loose,' Hurnungaz matched his grin, 'there's only one of you.'

'Do you know Sir Roger de Lisle?' Godwin asked.

The sword-wielding Templar stared at Godwin, eyes narrowing.

The Forest breathed around them. Leaves swirled, scattered by unfelt breezes. Insects chittered. Trees creaked.

'He has not been seen in the preceptory for a while,' the dark haired Templar said.

Godwin nodded. 'He took me in. Saved me from an outlaw gang.'

The sword-wielding Templar studied their faces carefully. 'You,' he gestured at Hurnungaz, 'you are the devil worshipper?'

Hurnungaz chuckled, tracking the speaker's movements, knowing, *knowing*, that to loose would kill the Templar.

'I was created by Caerne. I was brought forth from who I was. I am Hurnungaz.'

'There are still only four of you,' the other Templar smiled. 'Against two of the most highly trained knights in the world. Hurnungaz,' he half inclined his head. 'Whom the tales tell carries power in his bow. The rest of you,' he shook his head. 'A tribal warrior, an Anglo-Saxon, a boy. None of the tales tell of you.'

'There are more of us,' Hurnungaz responded, grinning.

'Perhaps. However skilled with swords or clubs you might be, I see no chain. No toughened leather. My brother strikes at the boy, the Anglo-Saxon, they go down. They stay down.'

Hurnungaz smiled grimly. 'He doesn't get the chance. I loose, he dies.'

The sword-wielder snorted.

'Sir Roger went to York,' Godwin spoke softly. 'He was accompanying – a maiden on a quest. She sought to return to her people in the Holy Land.'

A howl rose around them. Figures were everywhere, some half naked, painted and streaked; all clutched clubs, axes, primitive weapons.

He loosed. Three fell, arrows in their throats.

The sword-wielding Templar turned; he was almost overwhelmed but his blade was sharp and heavy: blood and limbs flew.

Godwin and Merik loosed arrows, but the wave of attackers was tidal, converging on them from all around.

The taller Templar hacked and slew dispassionately, bodies piling up around him.

Merik, Godwin and Raven had formed up together, the two men protecting the younger warrior.

Drawing sword and blade he flung himself into the battle.

**

Lightning rumbled. Thunder flashed.

Muna flung her head back.

Flee.

Muna turned and ran. The clouds boiled, erupting, hail stinging and lashing.

She fled through the storm, unheeding, uncaring, not knowing why, not knowing from whom or what she fled.

The ground turned to mud. Her feet turned but somehow she kept running. Trees creaked and tilted, hailstones ricocheting off them, near blinding her.

Muna fled, knowing *something* was following her.

**

Bwyd found Aneirin in the kitchens, helping to prepare food.

'Llewellyn says – you're coming with me?'

The kitchens smelled of ale and meat. Carcasses hung off to one side, salted. There were tubs of roots and vegetables. Servants bustled about, sharing knowing looks and grins.

Aneirin grinned, concentrating on the task in front of her – skinning a hare.

'I am. I command the archers Llewellyn is giving to you. I lead them; the Sælvatici ride to join the Hooded, Bwyd.'

He nodded. 'Llewellyn said – after his wife died, after his faithful hound died –'

'I was a comfort to him. It's only sex, Bwyd. He'd lost so much that was his. Took his rage, his grief, into my arms and I helped him.'

Bwyd shook his head. 'It wasn't that I wanted to talk about.'

Aneirin raised an eyebrow. 'Normally its sex men want to talk about.'

He blushed. 'Not sex, no.'

She seemed to sober. 'Come with me then.' She grinned at the others. 'No juicy details for you.'

A few grinned in response.

She led him out to the open yard; a small corner of it, sheltered on three sides by the natural and manmade defences. Clouds scudded overhead, black and purple, threatening but not delivering the expected rainstorm.

'I didn't know you worked in the kitchens.'

She snorted. 'Warrior woman and word smith. What I am supposed to do when there are no battles, when it is not time for tales to be told?'

Bwyd hesitated. 'I don't know.'

'I might sit at Llewellyn's high table, but that doesn't mean I don't know how to skin animals. How to make broth. How to train the young.' She grinned. 'You see the glamour and not the mundane. Both are who I am.'

Bwyd nodded slowly, side-tracked and distracted.

'What do you want to know about?'

'This – man. The hero-light.'

Aneirin grimaced. 'Paol.' She shook her head. 'An evil, wicked man. Llewellyn rallies the Sælvatici well, but with the death of his kin and the terror Paol brought, his position may not last.'

Bwyd nodded. 'He said I would be his choice, if –'

Aneirin nodded. 'His choice may count for nothing. His instruction is to support the Hooded. The Sælvatici, the Marchers, the Welsh, will one day march in force to support Hurnungaz and his Hooded. We are merely – the first wave.'

Bwyd nodded. 'Good. And this Paol?'

Aneirin shuddered. 'I have swallowed the seed of the demon.'

Her voice was stark, the bones visible in her hands.

'I was a distraction. He will come for me in time. I am,' she shuddered.

Bwyd reached for her but she pulled back, a furious expression on her face.

'He will come for me, Bwyd. You could not stop him. Llewellyn did all he could – scatter his forces so that Paol could not slaughter them, and barricade himself in the tower.'

She shook her head.

'Frankly,' she continued after a moment, 'I'm surprised I'm still alive. I'm surprised he didn't find a way into the tower; didn't burn it down around them.'

'Around everyone you know.'

She scowled. 'I know far more people that you might think, Bwyd.' She sighed. 'Hurnungaz has power. Several of the Hooded have connections to other gods, other sources, I have heard. We will, likely, need all of them.'

**

They stood in a circle, side by side. The longsword wielding Templar, Grimgyth, who fought passionately and wildly, clearing a swathe in front and to either side of him.

To his right, Godwin, with club and knife, finishing off any Grimgyth missed.

He fought methodically, unceasingly, untiring, sword and blade taking life after life.

To his right, Raven. Half shielded by him, the boy darted forwards and back, knives flashing, finding stomachs, thighs, necks. Stabbing and retreating. Stabbing and retreating.

To his right, the other Templar, Dægmund, who fought coldly, methodically, the opposite of his companion Grimgyth.

To his right, Merik. Merik fought with axe and knife, bear-cloak swinging, protecting him from club and knife and grasping fingers.

And to his right, Grimgyth.

The circle was unbroken.

The circle was flickering steel and death and blood flew and the bodies piled high and still they came on in a wave –

He realised the attackers were silent, no wars cries, no shouts, no cries, even as they fell before the scything circle of steel.

One moved among the onrushing flow of attackers who was different.

Economical of movement.

Methodical.

Lethal.

They barely seemed to move and yet bodies piled up around them as they moved – almost leisurely – towards the defensive circle.

They were clad all in black, where the attackers wore rags, scraps of clothing or nothing. They wielded knives as if they were an extension of their arms and throats were slit and hearts were pierced and bellies were sliced open.

The oncoming wave stumbled.

Dægmund glanced at him. 'One of yours?'

'Mar!' Hurnungaz bellowed.

The one in black lifted an attacker and threw them onto another. As three went down, the assassin changed direction and cut and killed and slew without pause.

Bodies tumbled before them.

They threw back their head. 'Scáthach!' tore the air, surprisingly light, surprisingly jubilantly.

Hurnungaz grinned. 'The Hooded! The Hooded!'

The circle expanded, bright flashing steel rings slaughtering all around them.

What was left of the attackers broke and scattered.

**

'Lucianna, why is there a missive here for you?'

'Your – your Grace?' she stammered.

He looked up. They were in his private chamber; she was standing with her back to the window; sunlight was streaming in around her.

She was wearing one of his thicker, hooded, brown robes, lined with bear fur, held in place by a chain and clasp. She was wearing nothing beneath it.

He studied her dispassionately, missive forgotten. She was broad and bony in the hips. Strong muscled thighs. A flat belly. Broad shoulders; long arms. Fine fingers. Her face was shadowed from the hood, but she looked down.

'Unclasp the robe,' he rasped. 'Let it fall.'

She obeyed him.

He turned his attention back to the missive.

"My dear sister in the Christ of the East, I hope this finds you well.

"I am desirous of some spiritual enlightenment. I am sorry that, as enjoyable as Nottingham and the pleasures of D'Hallowcross' court is, it does not offer much opportunity for spiritual growth.

"To this end; and please forgive me if this is too bold. My lord D'Hallowcross suggested I write directly to you, you being his brother's mistress.

"Of course, it is not that he thinks you share your night-bed with him. That would be a most unholy thing and he is certain it is not so; as am I.

"But he meant that you serve His Grace De Hallowcross in every matter. The Abbot has said before, it is reported to me, that your activities bring much pleasure to him.

"Please, as sister to sister, and as one faithful to the Christ of the East and so obedient to my lord, His Grace De Hallowcross, allow me to visit for a time to seek counsel and graceful companionship.

"Evgania, of Warwick.

"Residing at Nottingham Castle.

"With all my sisterly love in the Christ of the East."

He looked up. 'Do you know this Evgania?'

'No, your Grace,' she replied, still looking down.

'Why does she seek your company by name?'

'I do not know, your Grace.'

Her body was bathed in sunlight. She really was rather beautiful.

'Is this a subtle threat from St. John? What does he know or hope to gain from this?'

'I do not know, your Grace.'

'I do not think your mother was as beautiful as you, girl.'

She lifted her head in surprise. 'Your Grace?'

'She was – even bigger – than you in the hips. Bigger in the breast. She was a wanton. She had known the company of many men.'

'Your Grace?' Lucianna repeated, horrified.

He dismissed her unspoken concerns with a wave. 'She brought you, as a babe, to me. She wanted a religious, strict, upbringing. She had no money to pay though.'

'And you had – my mother?' she whispered.

'Of course I did,' he snorted. 'She had no money to pay. Otherwise you would have been given to a village. You would have grown to work the fields, your beauty coarsened, married to a pig of a man to bear a brood for him.'

He shook his head. 'Your mother was a rare beauty. I saw what you might grow into, and you are.' He grinned. 'For three years she served me faithfully, on her knees, on her back or on her belly.'

'What – what happened to her?'

He looked up from re-reading the missive. 'I grew bored of her. I had her whipped from the door, cast out into the forest at night, naked and bleeding.' He shrugged. 'And you grow into her likeness more with every day.'

She stared, silent tears sliding down her cheeks.

'Your Grace?' she whispered.

'Shush. Let me read this missive. My brother is up to something.'

**

Gisborough washed his hands in the bowl of water Berenger had had one of his men fetch.

'Nothing of any use!'

Berenger sympathised. 'It takes time, my lord. Perhaps coin, for a different village? See which method yields results.'

Gisborough scowled.

'It could be,' he thought out loud, 'that they truly knew nothing.' He shook his head. 'Whatever else, they were Saxons. Death was a blessing for them.'

'Bur leaves us no closer to finding the Hooded. My lord.'

He scowled at Berenger. 'The Sheriff has his verderers searching for them as well. We move on to the next village on the list.'

Berenger made a face. 'They will learn, in time, we are coming for them.'

Gisborough nodded. 'That is the other way to pursue them.'

'My lord?'

'Choose a village. Commandeer it. Ensure enough get out to spread the word. Fortify it. Close it to all. Wait for them to come to us.'

'Would they know?'

Gisborough scowled. 'None have claimed reward. None have known where they are based. Either they truly don't, or fear of pain or death is not enough.'

'Everyone fears death,' said Berenger.

Gisborough looked up. Shadows. The shadows are its hunting grounds.

He shook his head. 'We could trace every tale, every whisper, to every and any village that mentioned it. I am not sure we would find them.'

Berenger nodded. 'What we need is a tracker. Someone who knows him. Who knows how he might think, where he might hide.'

Gisborough grinned. 'I have an idea.'

**

Wenlock looked around, aware he was looking around before he had even realised he was awake.

The ground he stood on was cracked and broken, bloodied and burned, dead, but it was not the cathedral site.

Wisps of smoke emanated from the ground, though it was cold underfoot.

There was a massive shape, one of the Hooded, he realised.

Sciuridae.

Sciuridae was dead, his spirit long since gone.

But there was the merest spark – underneath.

The corpse was heavy. It took everything he had to push it up a little, to see pale, gaunt limbs. Patches of burnt fur. Weeping wounds that still wept blood.

He crawled down and burrowed in, setting his back against the corpse. The creature hadn't crawled beneath it to die, they had crawled beneath it to hide, to escape, to neglect their duties.

Wenlock scowled at them.

He put his back against the corpse and it was softer. Squishier.

With a supreme effort he managed to push the corpse back, to have it half roll away.

The stench of death was indescribable.

Caerne lay sprawled on her back.

Her legs were cracked, hardened like tree roots. A myriad of cracks, from the soles of her hooves to her crotch.

Wenlock blinked, realising there was not a patch of fur nor hair left on her body.

Her – opening – was swollen, blistered and cracked. The cracks in her legs either led to or emanated from it.

Her face had sunk in on itself, looking horrific. Her tongue lay half out of her mouth, thick and swollen. Her arms were similarly cracked to her legs: the cracks seemed to be climbing up her throat and across her shoulders and down.

Only in her chest, particularly over her heart, was there any sign of life. There were drying trickles of blood on her breasts. Fresh blood still oozed from her nipples, but it oozed sluggishly.

'Old one,' he whispered, belatedly remembering he was the Old one.

Wenlock wrapped his arms around her, drawing her out from underneath the body. She was light, fragile, bony. An almost husk of a being.

'This is a bad place for you, Caerne. This is death. You are dying.'

The mad godling didn't respond. There was no light in her eyes, though they were open.

Wenlock drew her in tighter, and then they were back in his burrow.

**

'We have no way of knowing where they are!'

Radewych glanced at her compatriot.

They subsided.

'This is a rich and fertile land. They could be anywhere; lost in the woods or taken in by a lord or a village.'

'We are not giving up on them!' another protested.

She stared at the speaker coolly.

They subsided.

'The way back is gone, even if we were to leave them. Which we are not. Angenijs and Diederic are our priority. Our responsibility. We find them and restore them to the kingdom – or die trying.'

She studied the other four. They nodded.

'I have no knowledge of how we came here. A path between lands. I think this is the land of the Engels – the Saxons.'

A couple grimaced.

Radewych shrugged. 'We will worry about returning – with the children – when we have them. That is –'

'Rade!' one of her patrol shouted.

She turned. Figures were sprawling out of the trees all around them, twenty or so, masked, hooded, armed and armoured.

'To arms!'

**

'Mar,' Hurnungaz grinned. 'Good to see you.'

The assassin looked up and scowled. 'He's here,' he hissed. 'Here!'

Hurnungaz frowned. 'Who?'

Mar grimaced. 'The one I seek. He's here.'

'Who were those?' asked Godwin.

'Peasants,' muttered Grimgyth.

'No,' Hurnungaz shook his head. 'Not peasants. Not a single word. No war cries. No cries in pain. And far too co-ordinated.'

'Hel-summoned?' asked Dægmund, raising an eyebrow.

Mar started cleaning their blades.

'Old things gather in this place,' Hurnungaz said, glancing at Mar. The battle had changed them. If anything, they were darker. 'Caerne,' he hesitated, remembering the broken stag-daughter. 'Maybe something was loosed in our attack upon the cathedral.'

Dægmund frowned. 'That is not something to boast of.'

Hurnungaz shrugged. 'We defend the Forest. Her people. Brother Gascon threatens that. We oppose that.'

'And we know Sir Roger,' added Godwin. 'He worked with us.'

Dægmund nodded slowly. 'You are worthy fighters, Hurnungaz. We will continue on to our preceptory. Should we meet again,' he paused.

Grimgyth grinned. 'Then there might be a reckoning.'

Hurnungaz inclined his head to them. 'Thank you, both. You are free to travel Sherewode, we will not stop you or your kind.'

Dægmund raised an eyebrow. 'We are holy knights of the Christ of the East. Do you truly think you could stop us?'

Hurnungaz chuckled. 'We are the Forest. We are Caerne. You are honourable warriors. Honourable allies or enemies.'

Dægmund smiled. 'A reckoning may come, Hurnungaz of Sherwood, but it is not one we would seek. Look to your people. We will look to our beliefs.'

Grimgyth nodded his head. 'It was a pleasure to fight beside you. One day, perhaps,' he grinned.

'Indeed,' Hurnungaz inclined his head.

The two Templars departed.

'What of Muna?'

Mar looked up, scowling. 'She fled from me.'

Hurnungaz raised an eyebrow.

**

'York wants me to attend a – celebration?'

The messenger nodded. 'Yes, my lord. She feels,' he paused.

'Well?'

'She feels she may have been too – harsh on you. My lord.'

'Too – harsh?'

The messenger nodded; a warrior by the looks of it, probably one of his wife's soldiers.

'York wishes to receive Nottingham into her,' there was a pause, 'city. She wishes to extend the curtesy to you that you extended to her.'

'Oh?'

'She is planning a feast in your honour, my lord. She has a new cook. She wants to show you what,' he coughed. 'What Yorkshire can bring to Nottinghamshire. My lord.'

The Sheriff sighed, taking a sip of his wine. 'When is this planned for?'

'Whenever you can make it, my lord.'

'Our marriage?'

The messenger coloured slightly. 'I was informed of it, my lord. It is not common knowledge.'

'Why do you think she wants me in York?'

The man raised an eyebrow. 'York is a hard and just commander, my lord. But she is still a woman, with a woman's needs.'

He raised an eyebrow. 'You would talk of my wife's needs? Of your commander's needs?'

'She bad me tell you,' he hesitated again.

'What?' St. John scowled.

'She looks forwards to receiving you – personally. My lord. For as long as you would like to – entertain her.'

He chuckled. 'So she grows horny and her loins are empty.'

The man didn't answer, eyes downcast.

'I have plenty of bedwarmers of my own. Why should I put myself through the journey for a woman and a meal?'

The messenger raised his head a little. 'I believe the King has sent her a missive, my lord. He expects to hear news of her pregnancy, and is unhappy that no word has been received.'

St. John chuckled. 'I will think about it.' He dismissed the messenger. 'Ale,' he called, stretching his arm out.

A servant ran up: refilled his flagon.

He took a mouthful. 'Fuck York by the King's order, until she is pregnant.' He grinned. 'Seneschal!'

**

Bwyd felt his loins stir as Aneirin strode into the courtyard. She wore a huge stag's crown of horns, from which hung feathers, skulls of smaller creatures, glistening, still-wet entrails and more.

Her hair was long and loose, unbound. She was painted for war: blood markings upon her face and arms, breasts and belly. She wore a leather skirt, tightly knotted and wrapped around with belts. Hand axes and knives hung from the belts, a heavy weight of them.

She stared at him. Grinned, flashing her teeth. They were blood-red.

'We march to war, men of the Sælvatici. Women of the Sælvatici. Bwyd. We march to war!'

The archers roared with her. The guards on the walls roared with her.

The ten archers were male and female, some fully clothed and armoured in wool and leather, some in wool and chain, some just in wool and some in nought but their skins.

The men on the walls began stamping their feet, slamming pikes and axes against the stone.

The courtyard rang with steel and stone.

'You march to war!' bellowed Llewellyn.

The fortress resounded with Sælvatici war cries.

'To war!'

'To war!'

'To war!'

The walls shook.

The walls shook.

The walls shook.

'Sister Aneirin! Brother Bwyd!'

The walls shook. The Sælvatici roared.

'You march for Sherewode. Sherewode and the son of the Sælvatici, Robin of Clun!'

The walls shook. The air shimmered.

'You march to Hurnungaz and the Hooded!'

The walls shook. The air shimmered.

'You march and the spirit of the Sælvatici marches with you! The spirit of the Marchers is with you. The spirit of the Welsh is with you!'

The roar was resounding.

**

"My dear sister in the Christ of the East," the Abbot dictated.

He took a mouthful of the rich, red, wine.

'Have we more of this?'

Lucianna raised and bobbed her head. 'Yes, your Grace.'

"My dear sister in the Christ of the East. It pleased my heart to receive your missive, though we have never met."

He studied Lucianna for a moment. Sent in disgrace to a nunnery, I think. Pregnant and outcast, her tongue removed so none can know her shame or whence it originated.

He grinned. Once I have no more use for her tongue, or her, that is.

"It displeases me to learn that Nottingham does not offer much opportunity for spiritual growth. I am given to understand that Nottingham holds many secret and private chambers. Private places of prayer, where many a maid has spent time on her knees."

He grinned at the last line.

"I am a pure and virtuous maid. Servicing the Abbot is my only joy and one that gives me the greatest pleasure."

He grinned. 'Slut that you are.'

Lucianna coloured slightly, eyes still downcast.

"I have meagre possessions and the Abbey does not hold sufficient guest chambers to your status, but if you would not consider it unbecoming, I could share my simple bed and lodgings with you whilst you seek counsel and graceful companionship."

"Lucianna.

"Residing at Gresham Abbey.

"With all my sisterly love in the Christ of the East."

'There.' He grinned. 'That will do. See that it is sent to D'Hallowcross.'

'Yes, your Grace.'

'Tell me, Lucianna.'

She looked up.

'Tell me your thoughts on a woman sharing secrets with another woman.'

'I – I do not understand, your Grace.'

'I know of this Evgania. She is Warwick's daughter and one of my brother's bed warmers.'

'Oh.'

'Oh indeed. When she arrives, I want you to seduce her.'

'My lord! That is wrong.'

'What is wrong? That I use you in such a manner, or the thought of two women,' he shuddered.

'Two women together, your Grace,' she grimaced. 'It is wrong.' She smiled at him, a little shyly. 'I am your property, my Grace. Your Grace,' she blushed, flustered. 'You may command me to do what you will.'

'But you find the thought of laying in love, with a woman, disgusting.'

She nodded. 'Yes, your Grace.'

He grinned. 'But you will do it anyway. And when I have learned all of her secrets, and all of my brother's secrets that she holds, then I will punish you for it.'

'Yes, your Grace,' she mumbled, eyes downcast again.

'I sometimes think I am too lenient upon you, Lucianna.'

'Yes, your Grace.'

He scowled, exasperated. 'I had your mother flogged into the forest when she failed to entertain me. Do not bore me too early, Lucianna. I would miss your body.'

'What would you have of me, your Grace? The ink is drying, the messenger cannot be sent yet.'

He grinned, beckoning with his finger. 'Come here.'

**

She clung to him, shrivelled, barren, empty. Her hair was gone, her head bore only horns, small, almost soft.

Her fur was lost in its entirety, not a single hair upon her body. Her tail was almost of nothing. Her breasts were shrivelled and shrunk, her nipples no longer oozing black substance.

He had packed her tightly in the earth. Had packed her tightly with earth. Her lips, her legs, were no longer cracked and broken; though her hooves were still cracked, they no longer bled pus.

Wenlock cradled the former godling in his arms. Hurnungaz was creating new patterns, returning the Hooded to the Forest. The creature she had created was still out there: still had some of her power.

He could feel Bwyd returning to the Forest, a powerful man, power in his fist.

All three would be needed to bring Caerne back.

He sensed something and looked up.

Power –

A patrol of five warriors, unlike any he'd seen before. Clad in leathers of grey, black and green, each heavily adorned with weapons.

Their leader, a woman, drew a pair of longswords.

To her right, one carrying a stave, but each end of the stave bore a knife blade and crossguard.

To their right, another woman, carrying possibly even more weapons that the leader. In each hand she carried a hand axe.

To the left of the leader, a warrior wielding a morning star and a spiked flail.

To his left, a woman carrying a pike, its shaft adorned with knife points.

Facing them a ragbag assemblage of outlaws, in tattered and torn clothing, wielding clubs, knives, a rusty sword or two.

An assemblage of twenty or more, desperate, hungry, at the end of all hope, to face five such armoured warriors.

The woman spoke. She spoke a language Wenlock knew not, and he could understand many. The five fanned out into a semicircle.

The outlaws charged –

Their leader dispatched two easily.

Her warriors fought coolly, methodically.

No rage or passion.

Professionally.

In seconds the five were cleaning their weapons. The wolves' heads had been slain efficiently.

Wenlock shivered.

Caerne stirred.

**

Gisborough held his hand up: the patrol eased to a halt behind him.

There were bodies everywhere.

Pagans, outlaws, peasants, he didn't care.

They were dead. About twenty of them, poorly armed, poorly clothed.

'Berenger!' he grinned.

The man moved up beside him.

'Someone's cleaning up Sherwood.'

He nodded absently. 'Whoever did it – all the bodies are the same. None of whoever they attacked.'

'A larger band – these Hooded?'

Gisborough frowned, dismounting and moving around the corpses.

'Set men to check for tracks.' He shook his head.

'No one's been slain by arrow or bolt,' Berenger said.

He nodded. 'Yes. Not the Hooded.'

One of his men yelled: Berenger hurried over to confer.

'Tracks, my lord!'

Gisborough looked up.

'Five. On foot. Not that long ago.'

'Mount up!' Gisborough called. 'Whoever they are, we have them!'

**

The water bubbled and burst, spilling over the edge. The rill wound its way through his grounds, but this grove, where the land dropped, where the water sang as it cascaded over the edge –

Richard smiled at the playing children. Angel – he wasn't sure that was her name, but it was close and he knew not their tongue; she knew only a little of theirs, though he was teaching her to speak his language.

The boy child – Deederich – spoke little, and only his own language. But it was obvious he loved his older sister and trusted her.

The sun sparkled, dappled through the leaves.

Children's laughter –

His fingers clenched for a moment. He had not expected to hear children's laughter again. Not since –

He had left the Holy Land, sick of war, sick of death, sick of bloodshed. There was no one waiting for him in Verysdale.

His wife was dead, his son killed in a tourney. There was no one he –

And then the children – not Welsh, despite what he had first thought.

Born to wealth, pampered, but still children. And why shouldn't children be pampered. He had spared his son a little; had he spared him less –

Would Henry have been a better knight? Would he have survived the tourney?

Richard sighed, smiling, watching the children play.

There was money – a little, but perhaps enough. Someone to look after them. A tutor, to help with learning the tongue. Entertainments for them.

Whoever they were, wherever they had come from, they were children in a strange land.

He felt his heart swell, most unexpectedly. He crossed himself. By the Christ of the East, he muttered, they shall know nothing but joy and peace in my little sanctuary. I will shelter and protect them, I will make enquiries, but they will be safe here.

**

Hugi stopped. Turned and stared.

A creature watched him. Horned it was, like a stag, but the body of a wolf. Deep set eyes of Hel-fire.

It breathed aggressively, baring its teeth. Mist curled from it; mist rose from where it had been.

He held himself still as it moved towards him.

It growled.

Hel-spawn. I am Wōden's own, his left hand. I am *thought*.

It moved to circle him, keeping its eyes on him.

Hugi grinned, moving his arms, imitating flight.

The creature hissed, slowing, eyeing him warily.

Wōden. Guard me.

**

'Halt! Halt and surrender!'

They were crossing a broad plain. To the left it fell away, too steep to descend. To the right, a tributary of the Trent roared and pounded in full roar, treacherous and deep, fast and furious.

The five warriors were halfway across the plains, heading for the distant treeline.

Gisborough grinned.

Berenger glanced back, making hand gestures.

The King's Own began spilling out to either side of them, forming up into four ranks deep, ten to each side.

Enough to run the five warriors down.

Gisborough studied them.

They bore no colours, no standards, no tabards. Mercenaries or outlaws.

Mercenaries, considering the number of weapons each seemed to carry. But an odd outfit. Long weapons, but only two of them. Not enough to stop a cavalry charge. Mace, axe and sword. Highly skilled he wagered, but unknown.

Gisborough grinned. He had eighty of the King's Own, the most highly skilled warriors, at his beck and call.

'Thoughts, Berenger,' he asked.

'I don't like the two spearmen. They slew that outlaw band; they're ruthless.'

'We've plenty enough –'

Berenger made a face. 'I'm loathe to lose good men, and that I fear we will in this conflict. They're not the Hooded. Talking may achieve news of them.'

Gisborough frowned. He wanted to clap heels to the horse. Wanted to thunder across the plains.

An echo of the Holy Land. Charging the heathen savages. The sun baking down. The enemy dressed in robes, no defence against blade or bolt.

Those that could fight, were savage indeed. But most were no threat, just there to be slaughtered.

He shook his head. If I charge, there's no guarantee any will follow.

'None carry bows, that I can see.'

He nodded to Berenger. 'We move, slowly. Let them see our might. Our number. We will get close, then you and I move to – talk.'

**

Aneirin was leading the way, crossing a wide clearing, the archers scattered out behind him, moving through the undergrowth.

She flung her hand out behind her, fingers stiff: Bwyd stopped and the archers stopped, slipping silently into shadows.

Three figures moved into the clearing, leering at Aneirin.

'What have we here then?'

'I reckon that's a freshly slaughtered stag she's wearing. There's a penalty for that.'

'Mmm,' agreed the third, grinning. 'Reckon its worth a tumble or three before we take its hands.'

'Aged meat,' said the first. 'It'll be tough. Look at its tits. Passed its prime.'

The three verderers flanked Aneirin, surrounding but out of her reach, their attention focused on her.

'It's mad,' said the second. 'Mad, or a Marcher.'

'A Marcher?' the first one scoffed. 'It's got the tits of a wetnurse. Probably half the Marcher lands has had it.'

'So?' said the third. 'It's in Sherwood now. Those tits are ours.'

'Why don't you come try them?' Aneirin asked. 'There's still some life to them.'

'Don't –' the first warned.

The third verderer lowered his crossbow and approached her.

Bwyd saw Aneirin pull her shoulders back. The third verderer was entranced, as good as dead. The other two were suspicious, watching closely, crossbows still held with intent.

The verderer grabbed her.

Aneirin pulled him to her. Bwyd saw her right arm plunge back and forwards.

The verderer gasped, staggered, losing his grip –

Aneirin picked the verderer up and flung him at the nearer of the other two verderers.

The remaining man fell: Bwyd hadn't even heard the bow strings, but half a dozen arrows peppered his body. The rest were in the man Aneirin had slain.

The third tried to rise, pushing the body off.

'He's mine,' Aneirin hissed, crossing to him and kneeling down, drawing a dagger.

**

Mar flung up their hand for silence. They could feel – something.

Raven watched them. Knew their secret. They would kill Raven if –

They would kill Raven – as their own child had been killed.

They bit their lip.

Hurnungaz. Hurnungaz always suspected something.

Something wasn't right. Something was approaching. Something – not quite human. Something greater than human.

Muna. They hated and – as much as it loathed them to admit it – feared Muna.

A woman. Openly. In Sherewode. In a white dress.

She wanted to rend Muna's wings –

Why am I she when I hate her?

I want to hurt her. I want to pluck her wings. Pluck her feathers. Cut her brother's cock off and feed it to her. Watch her face as I tell her what it is.

Something – human. But accompanied by – power. Something – something of Caerne.

That didn't please her.

If I was a boy, I would rape Muna. Terrorise her. Torture her.

Why?

I could not hurt Raven. He needs protection. She glowered. I would hold him to my heart and keep him safe if I could.

Mar glared. He makes me soft.

Muna – she makes me hate.

She makes me stronger.

Mar grinned, thinking about holding Muna down and hurting her.

A wolf! *A boar!*

The wild boar came barrelling out of the woodlands, thundering towards her –

They could sense Merik and Godwin reaching for weapons –

'Hold!'

The boar launched itself, knocking Mar onto her back, driving the wind out of her.

Its grizzled, ugly, toothy, snout was in her face.

A thick tongue licked her face. It slathered and dribbled on her, peeing a little in its excitement, snorting and wuffling. It settled down, crushing her ribs, breathing heavily.

'Wulfrun!' called Hurnungaz, standing above them.

Wulfrun laughed. 'Pissed yourself, Mar, or is that your little friend?'

The others laughed.

Wulfrun crouched besides her, his wolf next to him.

'I would offer you my arm to draw you up, but your boar looks happy with his bed.'

Mar glowered at Wulfrun. 'Help me up, brother.'

Wulfrun's wolf sniffed at the boar.

The boar growled back.

Wulfrun stroked his wolf. 'You know Mar. This is his boar. He's as fierce a fighter as you are. You are both of the Hooded.'

The boar shifted round.

Mar tried not to wince, feeling a pain in her chest.

'Come on,' Wulfrun held his hand out to the boar. 'We were hunting.'

The boar waddled off her. Mar gulped for breath.

Raven smiled. Merik and Godwin tried not to smirk.

Wulfrun stood up smoothly, offering his arm. 'Come on, brother. We've Normans to hunt.'

Mar grabbed his arm. Jumped to their feet. 'And Irish. There's an Irishman here now. We hunt him as well.'

'Ullr!' bellowed Wulfrun. 'Freya and Iseulde!'

'Scáthach!' cried Mar.

'The Hooded!'

'Caerne!'

**

'What is your wish for me, my lord?' Angelica asked.

St. John looked up as the door opened.

'A missive, my lord,' his man called, waving a parchment.

St. John grimaced. 'Who from?'

The man shook his head. 'It is marked with the sign of the cross. And the Black Bishop's own seal.'

He grimaced. 'The Black Bishop's request. Gisborough said it would be coming.' He looked up at his man. 'Unfortunately, you arrived too late to find me. Leave it on the table. Arrange a carriage and guards – send word to York that I am intending to visit her. I will set off within the hour.'

'Yes, my lord,' his man placed the parchment on the table and hurried off.

He looked again at the Moorish slave girl. She was stood next to him, naked, in front of the fire. Her skin was a surprisingly deep brown, black at the tips of her breasts and her cunny. Her long hair fell to her hips, unbound, blacker than night, purple in some lights.

'I am off to York, to plough my wife at the command of the King.' He grinned. 'I could use a travelling companion. Have you travelled much before, Angelica?'

'Only when I was brought to this country, my lord.'

He snorted. 'From others, that might have earned them a whipping.'

'My lord, do I not please you?'

He grimaced. 'I've lost a man of mine and money that should have been mine. Another has been given a title and source of money.' He scowled. 'And, I fear, I may have to give another away.' He clicked his fingers. 'Come here.'

She came and stood next to him, so close the black-purple hair at her hips brushed his fingertips.

He straightened his fingers: she moved closer.

'That is better,' he grinned, stroking the hidden valleys and ridges.

'My lord,' she gasped.

'I am taking you to York. You will beg sanctuary of her.'

'She will suspect I am a spy,' she gasped, 'my lord.'

'Indeed, she will.' He pushed his fingers a little deeper, enjoying the way her breath caught, the way her thighs trembled.

'I will have to hurt you before we get to York. Make it believable that I will hurt you, kill you, if you return with me.'

'My lord,' she whimpered, biting her lip.

'Indeed,' he said, grabbing her arse and pulling her closer, pushing his fingers in deeper still. 'I will regret losing you, but you will be a useful spy in her camp. I will find a way for you to pass messages on, if you are successful.'

'If I am not, my lord,' she trembled, sweat pouring off her as she sought to control her passions.

'I will see to it that York knows you are a spy. She deals with them personally. Slew the last one she found herself.'

Angelica whimpered, her body climaxing.

The Sheriff withdrew his fingers. 'Clean yourself up. Get dressed. We leave in the hour.'

**

'We have come to take the children back!' spat one of them, a woman, staring angrily at him.

They were impressively armoured and weaponed, but they were only five of them. A mercenary band – but interested in children?

Gisborough raised an eyebrow. 'What children?'

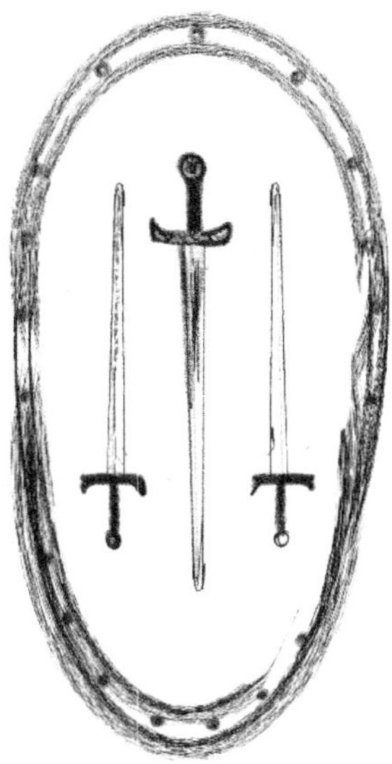

She stared at him with loathing.

'As you can see,' he gestured back towards the King's Own. 'I far outnumber you. Perhaps you will tell me who you are. Whom you serve. Who allows such disrespect from their captain of guards.'

She said something in her own tongue. He caught the meaning of a word or two.

'Flemish?'

'Anglo-boy?' she sneered in return.

He could see Berenger struggle to hide his smirk.

'I am Sir William of Gisborough. Commissioned by the King, given one hundred of the King's Own, to seek the Hooded. I am Warden of Sherwood. Commander of these men and responsible for these forests. You are trespassing, and you will answer my questions or I will slay you all.'

'The hooded – boys?' she frowned. 'I know no hooded boys.'

He glared at her. 'Hooded. Hood – ed. They are an outlaw band.'

She looked blankly at him.

'It's plain this is not your country. You're here without a letter from the King. Without permission. Everything you have is forfeit. Where is your boat?'

'My,' she frowned. 'Horse that rides on waves?'

One of her men said something. The other three laughed.

Gisborough clapped his hand to the hilt of his sword.

'I think you cannot help us,' she said calmly. 'You are all about boys and horses and these are toys, but they do not help us. Go, or we will dispose of you like we did the others.'

Berenger moved his hand.

The King's Own moved as one, horses responding easily even as the men drew swords in readiness.

Gisborough chuckled. 'By the time they reach you, you will already be dead. There are too many of us for you to succeed. Surrender, now.'

The King's Own broke into a gallop.

The warriors, the mercenaries, grinned, preparing their weapons.

'I am on the King's business!' he bellowed, half rising in the saddle.

'You are,' she frowned, 'an itinerant peddler?'

He roared, drawing his sword.

The ground was rumbling. The King's Own would split and move around them: would ride the five down with minimal loss of life.

The five moved back, as he'd known they would.

The ground was rumbling. The two with longer weapons were at the front, but all five were constantly shifting, watching, moving, shifting into a preferred defensive position.

Better defensive position. Gisborough tried not to grin. They might take down a couple of the soldiers; four, even, if they could force the horses to scatter. But that still left thirty-odd coming at them from one direction, fourty from the other.

They were as good as dead.

Gisborough grinned. 'The King's Own!' he bellowed, standing in the stirrups.

**

The creature launched itself and Hugi caught it, holding its snapping jaws away from his face. Twisted and threw it –

It landed and whipped back onto its feet, racing in, growling.

Hugi caught it again and lifted it, throwing it upwards into the trees.

It crashed upwards, howling and snapping, and then it was falling faster than it'd risen –

He moved back hurriedly.

The creature landed on all four hooves. Its legs wobbled. It hissed deep in its throat, stalking him slowly, keeping low to the ground.

Hugi grinned; moved in.

**

Three arrows flew over their heads and struck the leading warrior. He pitched backwards off his horse, which bolted, dragging the man with it, straight into the path of one of the cavalry charges.

That cavalry line broke perfectly, shearing away to avoid the commander. Neither were an immediate threat.

Her patrol moved perfectly to face the other cavalry charge.

Radewych grinned. Arrows were falling amongst that charge now, the line at the furthest end was crumpling as horses fell and men fell.

She could see, further back, a stand of archers loosing at the cavalry. Three figures were running towards the cavalry, weapons drawn, and – there appeared – to be a wolf and a boar thundering with them across the plains. War cries and screams echoed: she grinned.

'Split!' she ordered, drawing her swords, 'take them!'

Her company broke ranks.

Two of the archers were now running to assist the others, leaving a single, dark haired, figure loosing into the cavalry charge.

She saw him loose a single arrow, but three were in the air. Three! Impossibly three –

Bodies fell, horse and human.

Arrows flew at an inhuman rate, buckling the left flank of the cavalry charge.

Whoever the man was, Radewych thought – was he one of these Hooded –

The five newcomers now moved as one, spreading out, almost upon the broken edge of the charge.

The cavalry charge broke upon them.

**

Caerne opened her eyes. Flecks of the palest green swam in the deep yellow. An unblinking yellow.

'Food,' she bleated.

She was little but warm bones, long hands, sharp teeth. Wenlock nodded.

'Live? Dead? Cooked?'

'Living,' she hissed. 'Always living.'

Wenlock concentrated, and then they were on the edge of a field. Grey clouds loomed but sheep cropped the grass.

Caerne lay on the grass, a broken bundle of limbs. There was almost no life to her. Wenlock withdrew.

Time passed.

A lamb moved slowly closer, cropping the grass.

It moved closer.

It licked at her skull, at her horns.

It nibbled its way down her flank.

Caerne rolled, surprising it, causing it to bleat, but she held it close and its cries subsided.

It nibbled at her neck.

It nibbled at her empty breasts.

She wrapped her arms around it, holding it tight to herself, and looked up at him.

'I cannot kill it,' she bleated helplessly.

Wenlock moved out of the shadows and drew his stone knife.

Caerne stared up at him, terrified and helpless.

Wenlock slit the lamb's throat, pulling its head backwards. Its blood gushed, spraying out across Caerne.

Caerne screamed, locking her jaw onto the lamb's torn throat, sucking and guzzling and biting.

He rubbed his bloody hands on the fleece.

She rolled again, spreading the carcass, ripping its belly open.

'Caerne,' he began.

She thrust her head into its belly, chewing and swallowing, drinking the hot blood.

At last, she raised her head. Blood dripped from her. Rubbed her hands over her face. Rubbed her hands over her head. Rubbed her hands over her breasts.

'That was so good.'

She licked her lips. Clamped a bloody hand between her legs and crooned.

'More, Wenlock, more.' She rocked from side to side gently. 'So much more, Wenlock. Sheep, goats, cattle.'

She licked her lips again, swallowing.

'Their life – sustains you?'

Caerne nodded. 'Blood. Life. Bwyd is returning. Hurnungaz is pattern building.'

She rubbed her hand slower between her legs. 'I will need more soon,' she crooned. 'A stag. A wolf. A bear.'

She closed her eyes. Her face was horrific – sunken, blanched, drenched in fresh blood, dripping.

**

Hurnungaz ran, but he was too far away. The charge of the King's Own had been broken and the soldiers were retreating, taking Gisborough with them.

Bodies lay piled around, both horses and men. Insects buzzed and the air stunk with something other than blood, death and shit.

'They got Gisborough away,' Wulfrun grimaced.

He nodded, breathing heavily for a moment.

Four of the warriors who'd stood against Gisborough and his men remained. Their leader looked up, a tall woman, hooded in a long leather cloak and heavily armoured.

'You are these – Hooded?' she called out.

He nodded, grinning, moving towards her.

'I am Hurnungaz.'

'Radewych.'

'You are outlaws.'

He shrugged. 'Who just saved your lives.'

She looked at her fallen comrade.

'Not all of us. But thank you.'

He nodded. 'This is unsafe. The land is too open. If Gisborough is not badly injured, they will regroup and return.'

She nodded. 'We seek children. We do not know this land.'

'You seek children?' Hurnungaz asked, hand on the hilt of his sword.

Raven had moved up beside him on one side, Wulfrun on the others.

'Not just any children,' she grinned. 'We kill those who steal children.'

'Explain yourself then,' Wulfrun grunted.

Radewych gazed at Wulfrun coolly. 'The two children we seek were stolen from our patron. They were under his protection. We do not know how they arrived here, but we followed them through –'

She half turned her head and spoke quickly with one of her warriors.

'Through a tunnel of water and earth? There was a path, and light, and pulsing darkness,' she shook her head. 'I can barely understand it in my mother tongue, let along in the tongue of the Anglos.'

'And the children?' Raven asked.

Hurnungaz noticed his hand was on his knife.

'We are here to keep them safe. To return them to their patron,' she hesitated, 'if they so wish. Or to see them safe here, if that is their wish.'

'I think there's movement in the trees, far side,' Godwin said, hurrying up. 'We should –'

Hurnungaz nodded. 'Head for where we were. Radewych? You are free to join us. I would like to know more.'

She nodded, glancing at her comrades and talking rapidly.

One of the others hoisted their deceased warrior onto his shoulder.

'We move,' Radewych said, nodding to him.

**

Alain sat up, looking around. The night was full dark. Hel-creatures screamed and strutted all around them, but Tam and Brother Blacwin slumbered on, untroubled.

They'd been walking for days.

Their legs hurt.

There was no sign of these Hooded, and he wasn't sure how he felt about them. Brother Blacwin – a brother of the Christ of the East, a touch of familiarity amidst the strange, unearthly, eerie, never-ending forest, seemed to think they were not the Hel-summoned creatures some of the tales told them to be.

Destroying the citadel of the Christ of the East!

Burning everything to the ground!

Destroying –

But Tam had saved him. Tam was one of the Hooded. The Hooded – Hel-creatures – wouldn't save someone who was part of something they were trying to destroy, surely?

That. He shuddered. That creature.

Was I mad? Am I dreaming, now? Was it real, did it sit on my chest?

He grimaced. Whatever it was – fantasy, delusion, nightmare – it had –

It had what? Londinium was straight lines. Cleanliness. Order.

The forest was –

Alain shuddered.

Was it these Hooded who had loosed arrows at him and Gisborough and forced them to spend the night together in the former chapel?

He shook his head.

It would all be clear once he met the Hooded.

**

'What do you want to ask?'

Bwyd looked up in surprise.

Aneirin was squatting by the low fire, cooking the three hares they'd caught. Three of the archers were on guard; the others were resting, sleeping if they could.

She had laid her magnificent crown of horns to one side. For comfort and movement she had removed the leather skirt: wore nothing but a belt, from which hung a profusion of axes, blades and other objects.

By Bwyd's reckoning they'd pass south of the cathedral site. Then it would be a case of tracking Hurnungaz and the others, if such a thing were possible.

'If it's sleeping with me again, I'm not in the habit of taking the same man twice.'

Bwyd looked up, surprised, but shook his head.

'No, I wanted to ask more about the man, Paol, that came to Clun.'

She snorted. 'I would rather talk of fucking and long nights of intimacy. Holding a friend close as our pleasure intermingles.' She smiled grimly. 'It was a most satisfying night and morning with you, Bwyd. You could use more experience,' she broke off, glowering.

'But you'll not be the one?'

'You want to know about Paol?' She grimaced. 'Tall and red-haired, like Llewellyn.'

'He slew three Sælvatici without any effort. Defeated and tortured a fourth.'

'I know!' Aneirin snapped. 'I was there.'

Bwyd looked away.

'Hurnungaz has a power that comes from Caerne. There is something about Mar,' he paused. 'Something of – the Old ways. Muna has power; from Wōden. If – when – we face him, all we know about him will be useful.'

Aneirin turned away. Concentrated on the cooking.

'Before – the combats. Llewellyn was upset. His hound.' She sighed. 'He agreed a feast. Tried to make light of the event, but his heart wasn't in it.'

She sighed again.

'What happened?'

'Llewellyn came to my room,' she said, after a while.

The fire crackled and spat.

Bwyd knew better than to prompt Aneirin.

'Despite what I had told him, he wanted me.' She sighed. 'As mother to his son, as lover, as wife. I turned him down.'

She looked away.

'He had not long left, than Paol came to me.' She grimaced.

Bwyd wanted to know about the grimace.

'I was lonely. I was desperate. I was sad.' She shook her head. 'I wasn't seeing.'

'What?' Bwyd couldn't contain himself.

She scowled at him. 'We fucked. He has – inhuman appetites.'

He looked away.

'I thought we were done,' she continued, softer, though still bitter. 'He made me kneel before him. The hero-light came upon him. He burned my lips, my tongue. He filled my throat, my lungs. His seed burned in me and I was helpless.'

Aneirin scowled. 'I lay on my bed, his seed coursing through me, and I had no strength to move, no strength to speak. I half expected him to kill me then and there.'

She shook her head. 'At the feast the challenge was set and three Sælvatici died.'

'I'm – sorry.'

She shook her head again. 'Before he left me, he said he would come for me before the end.' She sighed.

'There is no –' Bwyd spoke softly, 'no guarantee of safety with the Hooded. But there might be strength.'

She gave him a bittersweet smile. 'I shall face Paol again. He is powerful enough on his own, without the gods' intervention.'

**

Wenlock grimaced. They were in a clearing. Caerne was crouching on her haunches patiently, elbows on her knees, arms outstretched.

They had been waiting a long time already.

Weak, afternoon sunlight slanted through the trees. He could sense woodland creatures all around, all too small to threaten, most too small to be seen.

Caerne was waiting for something specific.

She was still hairless, her tail nothing but a stump. Her legs, her hooves, appeared healed. She was beyond thin: gaunt, her ribs visible, her veins and muscles all but visible.

Her eyes were more yellow than green still, her teeth sharper and seeming more numerous, her jaw stronger.

More of a predator, less of a stag, Wenlock thought.

He turned, feeling the motion before it happened: a pair of hares sprang into the clearing, unheeding of him or Caerne.

They sprang across the clearing –

And Caerne snatched them up, sinking fingers deep into one's body, ripping the throat out of the other.

Blood sprayed.

Caerne rent and tore, shredding their bodies, swallowing their entrails, their blood, their bones.

She ate noisily, lustily, smearing their blood over her face, her body.

'Why,' Wenlock asked softly, 'why do you need to eat creatures? What does it give you?'

Caerne raised her gaze. Sparks of green flickered in the yellow.

'Belief does not sustain me, and who would believe in me? The daughter of Cernunnos, given life by a stag's death, filled with the power of the Forest, taking the shadows left by Cernunnos.'

She licked her lips. Licked and swallowed.

'I was created, I came into being, because of death. I am Death, the Stag's daughter.' She began licking her fingers. 'I gave my power to two, and both gave it away.'

'They didn't know –'

'Sciuridae knew,' she screamed, 'Sciuridae knew! He was brother-kin, my creation caused his. My creation,' she burst into tears.

Wenlock stared.

She shuddered. 'The Wulfenstæg,' she whimpered. 'It was too powerful. It drained me. It tore my power from me.'

She looked at him warningly. 'It is still out there. The Wulfenstæg. If it finds me it will kill, it will drain, it will end,' she shuddered again.

She howled.

'You have me,' Wenlock said softly.

'You, little one,' Caerne matched his tone. 'You have power, but it is not mine. The Old one brought Mar to this land. They are the crow-bitch's now.'

'Muna?'

'Muna,' she crooned. 'But Muna's not Muna anymore. Muna's powerful.'

'What happened?'

She looked at him. Licked her lips again.

'Muna's not Muna,' she whispered, crying softly, staring at what was left of the hare carcasses.

**

'Lucianna! Lucianna! Where the devil are you?'

His mistress came running.

'I'm sorry, your Grace, I was –'

'A missive from Warwick!'

'Your Grace! News of Evgania?'

He held his mug out. She hurried to fill it.

'Ha!' He snorted. 'Warwick calls his own daughter a strumpet. There has been,' he chuckled. 'He is casting her out. Sending her to a nunnery.'

'A nunnery? You may not find what your brother was after –'

He scowled at his mistress. 'Warwick requests I send you to counsel her: she has been through some distress, apparently.' He grunted. 'Then you are to take her to Winchester.'

'The Abbess de Winchester.' Lucianna grimaced.

'The Black Bishop's mad voice speaks to her as well. If this chit is being sent there, she will not be seen again.'

'What do you want of me, your Grace?'

He grunted, picking up another missive. 'Go to Warwick. I will send two brothers with you. You will accompany her to Winchester.'

He grinned, taking a swig of the red wine. 'And when I say you will accompany her, you will seduce her. It is an abhorrent act, a thought, but you will do it.'

She stared at him. 'Your Grace, how can two women,' she trailed off.

'Seduce her. Find a way to seduce her. It is all – abhorrent.' He shuddered. 'I want to know what my brother was playing at, what is going on.'

Lucianna dipped her head. 'It will damn my soul, your Grace. But if you command it.'

'I do,' he growled. 'Your soul is of no interest to me, only your body.'

She bowed her head. 'Your Grace,' she whispered.

He pulled the missive opened and cursed. 'Hel's-balls. The Black Bishop wants more of my brothers. And coin,' he shook his head. 'Will no one rid me of this mad bastard brother?'

**

Hugi bounded back to his feet.

The creature stalked him, eyes of green, eyes of fire, eyes – seemingly at times, of cloud or smoke.

It was real enough and also – not.

It stunk like a Hel-beast.

It smelled of the stag-girl.

He grimaced. A stag but a wolf, feral, Hel-summoned, Hel-drawn –

It sprang and he caught it, ignoring the slavering jaws, and flung it, hearing it crack against a tree.

He stumbled.

Blood streamed down his side.

The creature got to its feet once more, shaking its head, baring its teeth and growling.

**

'Tell me of these children.'

They had found shelter for the evening: a thick stand of trees, tightly interwoven, nigh impenetrable, and certainly not by those on horseback.

Hurnungaz had led them across three streams, including reversing direction and walking upstream through one, lest Gisborough thought to have dogs with him.

Night had fallen. Mar had caught two hares and cooked them – away from their resting place – so that everyone had a mouthful of warm meat, at least.

'We are,' Radewych said, 'warriors of the north.' She frowned. 'Not north but,' she shook her head. 'We serve our liege lord. He took the children in as his wards. They have food, instruction, in time the boy will become his heir and the girl will be married off. She is,' Radewych smiled. Paused.

'She is called Angenijs, her younger brother is Diederic.'

Hurnungaz nodded. 'How came they to be wards?'

She made a face. 'We are not a kingdom. Our liege lord is a good man, but there are border wars. Skirmishes.' She sighed. 'Their parents died. He has no children of his own; took them in as his kin.'

He nodded again. 'Sherewode is a vast territory, covering most of the land. They could be hiding anywhere.'

'Hiding, or captured.' She frowned. 'They may be dead, but we will not stop looking until we have found them, one way or another.'

'And what of your – deceased comrade?'

'Our tradition. We will take his body to a river. We will tie him in it and weigh his body down. The,' she paused, searching for the words, 'the horses of the river, they will eat his body and return it that way. It is but an empty cage; Kugene is long left.'

Hurnungaz nodded. 'None of the streams we crossed are deep enough; his body would be discovered quickly. There is a tributary of the Trent to the north, three, four, miles perhaps.'

She nodded. 'If you will give us a guide, we will rest and take our brother's body to the sea.'

Hurnungaz nodded. 'Of course.'

**

'Will you tell me a story?'

Richard smiled, and moved to crouch beside the bed that Angel was in. It had been his son's room; had stood empty for so long –

He nodded. 'Of course I will. What would you like the story to be about?'

Angel was learning their language quickly. Deederich wasn't. He spoke only occasionally, and only to his sister, and in their own language. His skin still seemed quite green, whereas the strange pigment was beginning to fade from his sister's skin, and he had no idea what caused it.

'Do you know,' she frowned, struggling for the words. 'I don't know the words.' She looked up at him. 'Will Deed be alright?'

Sir Richard sighed gently. 'I hope so. You are learning the language; he is not. Did he speak much before?'

She shook her head. 'No. He did speak, but not much. His thoughts were,' she scrunched up her face again. 'With the horses of the air? He would talk about things that weren't there.'

He nodded. 'I have sought and found two people to help me educate the pair of you. To help you both to learn our language.'

Angel nodded slowly. 'Do you know how to – go home?' she asked, a little shyly. 'You are very kind, but I miss,' she clamped her lips together, moisture in her eyes.

He stroked her hair gently. 'I do not, I am afraid. But we will look. I will have messages sent. Someone in the court of Londinium may know,' he grimaced.

The thought of contacting the court was not a welcome one. He had excluded himself, after Henry. Having no one, he had gone to the Holy Land. He sighed. There was a tiredness in his bones. The warmth and the sun and the glittering sand might be good for his health, but he missed the trees, the rolling hills, the plunging valleys: he missed Sherwood, even with the rain and the damp and the mist.

It will cost but it will be worth the cost. If I can find their kin, their way back to wherever they came from.

He shook his head. Perhaps they are what drew me back, unknowing. He stroked Angel's head again.

'Sleep child, sleep. I will keep you and your brother safe.'

He smiled. And I thought I had no one here for me.

**

'We come from the dark. We are the dark. We are myth, we are god, we are legend.'

She was free. Had driven off –

'I am Muna. I am the eyes of Wōden. I am Hooded.'

Jackin had wanted to rape her. Jackin was dead. Mar had wanted to –

Mar was female. Hard. Dead inside.

Mar. She almost purred.

'Wōden watches. Ullr stalks the forest. Caerne rises, a wild power, a mad stag-daughter, a Hel-creature.'

'We are Muna. We are the eyes of Wōden and the memory of the Forest.'

She bared her teeth and laughed, running her hands over her new form.

'Breasts. Loins. Wings.' She frowned. 'Hurnungaz holds Caerne's power. Seduce him. Fuck the power out of him. You – *we* – can take it from him.'

'Wōden commands I keep a watch. Caerne is an unknown.'

'They buried me alive,' she hissed. 'I want vengeance.'

'I am Wōden's servant.'

'Caerne will be weakened if you take Hurnungaz' power from him. Ride him. Offer his soul to Wōden. With Hurnungaz' power we can take Caerne.'

Muna laughed.

'You know nothing. Caerne would rend us limb from limb.'

Muna paused, thinking, remembering, searching.

'Caerne is weak,' she growled. 'She summoned something beyond her control.' She laughed. 'She is with the Old one. She can barely kill a lamb.' She grinned. 'I can sense her.' She bared her teeth again. 'She will barely feel it when you drain Hurnungaz. Take him,' she insisted. 'Then we can take the mad godling. I can taste her power.'

**

Wystan crept to the edge of the swamp, staring in terror and fascination.

Night was falling, though the sky was still light. From the swampy ground, more like a low-lying fetid lake, interrupted here and there by patches of gorse grass, mist rose.

A naked woman stood in the midst of the lake, head bowed.

There was nothing to see and yet –

Long, clean limbs. One leg was in front of the other; arms outstretched, hands hanging loose.

Wystan stared.

The woman's hands were unnaturally long, twice the length of his own.

Birds squawked and whistled and creatures made sounds from all around, but nothing paid attention to the woman in the water.

Was he mistaken? Was it some kind of dead, barren tree, the solitary living thing rising from the surface of the swampy lake.

And then there was a strange cry. A swan, stark, almost blindingly white, flapping its way across the lake. A single, solitary swan.

The sky changed, darkness onrushing.

The swan flew in front of the dead tree-woman –

She *moved*, her hands catching the swan, ripping its wings from it, pulling it to her, ripping into it with her teeth.

Blood sprayed. Feathers sprayed.

He could hear the crunching of bones. Feathers were swallowed and spat out.

Night came on and the creature raised its head.

Wystan couldn't be sure: it seemed to be staring straight at him, though it was too dark to see its eyes.

And then it began moving, heading towards him.

Wystan turned and fled.

**

Kugene was the shortest of the five of them, Hurnungaz noticed. His skin had the faintest of green touches to it.

Radewych and her people said no words over him, simply attached a rope to his body and knotted it to a tree root that straddled the river bank. Then they weighed his body with stones.

Radewych spoke quickly to her people in their language; after a discussion she grinned, turning back to him.

'This forest is unknown to us. We would – assist your help? We want our kin safely restored or their deaths known, so they can be avenged and we can return to our liege lord.'

'You know how to get back to him?' Wulfrun asked.

'A horse of the sea,' Radewych answered, studying the Norseman closely. 'Your words tell me nothing of where we are. I need to see a map of the waterways, the seas, the oceans. From that we can navigate our way back.'

'You could – be free here?'

She shook her head. 'Free of our obligations? It is who we are.' She sighed. 'We have been five for so long. Kugene was the next to join the pentamerous after myself.'

'Five?' Wulfrun frowned.

Radewych nodded. 'A five pointed star. The four compass points and being true to yourself.' She looked back at him. 'I would like to find those warriors again. They had no idea who we sought, but they broke our pentamerous.'

Hurnungaz nodded. 'That was Gisborough. It looks like he's got some help.'

Wulfrun snorted. 'They were the King's Own,' he shook his head. 'They were truly formidable once.' He chuckled. 'The King's guard. Except some of it is second sons and those refused by the clergy. They've more money and training thrown at them than natural temperament.'

'You were – a King's Own?' Godwin asked.

Wulfrun nodded. 'When it meant something.' He glowered. 'I still have debts to pay.'

Hurnungaz grinned. 'We don't know where to start looking for Angenijs and Diederic.' He nodded to Radewych. 'But we can backtrack to the battlefield and hunt Gisborough and his men.'

Radewych nodded. 'Yes.'

**

'Whose are they?' Aneirin hissed.

'Beorma,' Bwyd answered. 'A small town. The Normans favour it.'

A column of soldiers was coming down the trackway: about twenty. They wore leather armour and carried axes and knives: no bows that he could see.

'Stay out of sight. I'll test their loyalties.'

Before Aneirin could respond, he strode out from behind the tree.

'Brothers!' he called out, raising his hand.

The column slowed, hands on weapons. Their captain continued a few more steps before stopping.

'Brother? What call has a Welshman in the Kingdom of Mercia?'

'The kingdom of Mercia?' Bwyd raised an eyebrow. 'Did Mother Hode not die in vain? Does Mercia stand against the Normans?'

There was a tightening of arms, hands on hilts.

'Hode was a traitor, long dead, just like Athelstan.'

'You know your history.'

'And you're a long distance from the Marcher lands, Welshman. Why are you here?'

Bwyd grinned. 'I am one of the Sælvatici. Forest guardians.'

The captain chuckled. 'Forest folklore. Your forest god is dead. The Christ of the East is blessing the forest. Superstitious nonsense is being swept away.'

'So you stand for the Normans and the Christ of the East, Beorma-man?'

The captain gave him an odd look. 'Beorma,' he grinned. 'Beorma stands for Beorma.'

'The Normans favour your town. The Normans slay Anglo-Saxons, the old Ænglish, with impunity.'

The captain snorted. 'And you, brother? A Welsh Pagan, wandering free in Sherewode. Can your capering in the woods and staining yourself in woad turn the tide? The land is drowned and we struggle to survive on our own.'

Bwyd grinned. 'Have you not heard? Sherewode does not stand alone. Sherewode belongs to the Hooded.'

The captain scoffed. 'The forests cover the land, Pagan. No outlaw band, no wolf's head outfit can run it.'

Bwyd chuckled. 'Have you been to the site of the cathedral of the Christ of the East? The ground is riven. Buildings still burn. The Forest does not stand alone. The Forest fights back.'

The captain narrowed his gaze. 'And do you, perhaps, have companions in the woods? Are we currently surrounded by a ring of steel, waiting to slay us all?'

'Where do you stand on the Normans?'

The captain chuckled, smiling at him. 'I have already told you Beorma stands for Beorma. What the Normans do,' he shrugged. 'They are not Beorma.'

'But you take their coin.'

'If a superior force offered you coin and did not look too closely, what would you do, brother?'

'I would want to know their intentions before taking any coin.'

The captain snorted, shaking his head. 'Beorma standing against the Normans? We would be flattened.'

Bwyd smiled. 'Beorma standing with the Hooded? We will support you. Help keep you free.'

The captain gave him another look. Shook his head. 'This is not a conversation for now.' He grinned, turning his head to the side.

The soldiers drew axes: the column began walking.

'Beorma stands for Beorma,' the captain repeated. 'Another time, perhaps. Ask for Rúne.'

Bwyd stepped back. He could feel the watchfulness of the Sælvatici, arrows on the string. He shook his head, stepping back off the trackway to let the Beorma-men pass.

**

Angelica gave a startled scream.

D'Hallowcross looked up. 'What?'

She pointed.

They were on a main thoroughfare on the approach to York itself, though still a few miles out. The road was lined with gallows. Some had long-rotted carcasses still swinging in the breeze. Some were far more recent.

'They're a warning.' He grinned. York was effective, if nothing else, given all her other faults.

'What did they do?' the girl whispered.

He shrugged. 'Does it matter? Thieves, outlaws, peasants, Pagans.' He shook his head. 'It's about crowd control. Let the serfs know what happens if they step out of line.'

'That's –'

'Now then,' he smiled sourly. 'It's time you became terrified to return to Nottingham with me.'

She went to speak again but he shook his head.

'You forget your place, girl. You are nothing to me. Disposable.' He forced himself to smile, standing up, drawing on his leather gloves.

**

'Did you understand any of what she said?' Hurnungaz asked Wulfrun softly.

The Norse nodded, stroking the wolf's head. 'A little. They're not Norse. Of Viking stock, but not quite.' He shook his head. 'There's any number of smaller territories that aren't kingdoms, that are countries. Some of them have very well trained armies, specifically because there is so few of them.'

He nodded. 'Do you – would you – trust them?'

Wulfrun grinned. 'They will be honourable to their code. They are fearsome warriors.' He sniggered. 'It's time we hunted Gisborough. Get rid of one lord and send a message.'

Hurnungaz nodded. 'Let's find them.'

**

The creature charged.

It surged across the clearing and Hugi knew in that moment – not that he'd been wholly unaware before – that the creature he faced was Hel-borne.

It howled and the clearing shook. Trees snapped. Trunks imploded. A storm of leaves and branches lashed at him – and through the flurrying leaves, the creature lunged for his face.

Hugi caught it around the neck but the weight and speed toppled him.

It snapped and bit, drooling, its breath stinking of blood and death.

He tightened his grip but it was simply too thick in the neck, too heavy, too powerful to strangle.

'Wōden!'

He hefted and the creature rolled, snapping again at him, locking its jaw onto his arm.

Hugi screamed.

**

The stag was silhouetted on the brow of the hill. Its fur was damp, sparkling in the sunlight as it cropped.

Wenlock watched as Caerne walked up the hillside towards it.

The stag raised its head, looking at her for a moment, before returning to cropping the grass.

Caerne stroked its flanks. Ran long fingers lightly over its horns. Stroked the line of its jaw.

Wenlock tensed, expecting Caerne to slit the creature's throat.

She vaulted instead, sitting on its back. It shifted, adjusting, returning to eating the grass. Caerne caressed its back, its flanks.

Kicked her heels into its flanks. It jerked its head upwards and set off, galloping. Caerne flung her arms around its throat and clung on.

**

Jenny waited until the sounds calmed down; at least one of them was snoring already. The brothers were comatose, having drunk the wine she'd prepared for them. They'd been out of it before anything had begun.

She slipped silently into the tent, her eyes adjusted to the darkness. Lucianna, the Abbot's mistress, slumbered on her back. Evgania of Warwick lay with her head on Lucianna's chest, dribbling.

There was a small chest against one tent wall; the dowry Warwick was paying to foist his daughter off to the convent. A roll of clothing next to it that had been Lucianna's: Jenny grinned.

Lucianna had been stupidly ignorant about the possibilities of sex between women. Evgania had seduced her with ease, causing the Abbot's mistress to squeal delightedly in a manner which suggested the Abbot had never brought her pleasure.

She opened the chest silently, double checking the two women. Her plan had been to ransom Evgania back to her father, but his renouncing of her had stopped that. Still, with a dowry to ensure her acceptance –

She drew the two bags out of the chest and checked their contents: weighed them thoughtfully. There would be plenty enough.

Jenny tucked them into her bodice. She knew roughly where Gisborough was. Would find him, once she had made herself into a suitable squire for him.

She grinned in imagination. He was a lusty, powerful man, capable of helping her achieve what she wanted. The potential of her brother's death was a powerful motivator. The potential of William as her bed-mate was almost as powerful.

She slipped out of the tent and headed for the horses.

**

'They headed that way,' Wulfrun pointed.

The ground was torn up, the route the column took obvious. There were scraps of clothing, blood, armour, fragments of shattered weapons.

'As night falls they rest,' Radewych spoke coldly. 'We will fall upon them.'

'Can you tell how many are injured?' asked Hurnungaz.

Wulfrun shook his head. 'There's no dead horses here. They've carried all the bodies back with them. Gisborough was injured; they might not have gone far.'

'We should hasten after them,' insisted Radewych.

Hurnungaz shook his head. 'Slow and steady. They are too strong. But we can dog their footsteps, lessen their numbers.'

'Slaughter them,' ordered Radewych.

'Track them. Lessen their numbers. Teach them to fear the forest.'

'Uh, Hurnungaz?'

Wulfrun glanced at Raven. The young lad was looking towards the distant stand of trees. He reached for his axes. Three figures had left the trees and were heading towards them.

One looked like a youngster, short and slight. Another was wearing the robe of a brother of the Christ of the East. The third looked more like a warrior.

Hurnungaz laid an arrow on the string of his bow.

Radewych and her people spread out, two to either side of them, weapons drawn, though the people made steady progress, not running, and seemed – Wulfrun doubted they were harmless.

'Bait for a trap?' he wondered.

Hurnungaz nodded.

Mar drew their blades, their eyes gleaming, teeth bared.

'Wait!' cried Godwin.

Wulfrun stared. The most warrior-like of the three looked familiar. He wondered if the youngster was, in fact, a girl. The third, the brother, still looked like a brother of the Christ of the East.

'Hurnungaz!' shouted the one in the middle.

'You know them?' Radewych asked.

Wulfrun grinned. 'That's Tam in the middle. What he's doing with a treacherous brother, and not tied up, I don't know.'

'And the third?' she asked.

Hurnungaz grinned. 'Looks like another guest.'

The three neared.

Wulfrun grinned, returning his axes to his belt.

'Brother,' called Hurnungaz, 'this is no place for you. Begone.'

The brother smiled, and sketched a cross in their direction.

Hurnungaz hissed.

Wulfrun gripped the hilts of his axes.

Raven drew a dagger, fury in his eyes.

'Come closer,' Mar mocked softly, 'I will happily slit your throat.'

Tam frowned at the assassin.

'Forming a new band, Tam?' Hurnungaz asked softly.

Tam shook his head hurriedly. 'No. No, not at all.' He gestured to the young lad with him. 'I rescued Alain from one of the buildings on the cathedral site; he was almost burned alive.'

Alain had soft blond hair. A grubby smock, shirt and trousers. Their hands looked soft.

'Not a peasant,' commented Raven.

Alain looked surprised but nodded. 'I was a scribe for Brother Gascon. Tam saved me after the,' he hesitated.

'After we attacked the cathedral site and Caerne summoned Hel?'

Alain stared. 'Caerne?'

Wulfrun grinned. 'Horned. Female. Mad.'

Alain nodded, looking stunned. 'I saw her. It. It came to me in my dreams.'

Hurnungaz grinned. 'She does that.'

'What's with the brother, Tam?' Raven glowered.

Radewych sighed, pointedly.

'We saved him from being attacked by outlaws.'

'We're outlaws,' Raven stared angrily at the brother.

'Does my presence upset you, child?' asked the brother, looking at Raven.

The boy tightened his grip on his knife.

'Why are you here?' Hurnungaz asked bluntly.

'You would be Hurnungaz the demon?' the brother asked. 'We are told you are an abomination, yet you appear no different from your men.'

'Loose an arrow at him, Hurnungaz,' suggested Godwin.

Hurnungaz glanced at his man and shook his head. 'Why are you here, brother?'

'I am a brother of the Christ of the East,' the man declared. 'I have been told that you are a worshipper of Hel. I cannot believe my superiors would lie, but you do not strike me as a Hel-creature.'

Hurnungaz chuckled. 'If I lay an arrow on the string and loose, three take flight. Three die, or three arrows sink deep into the flesh of my target. A gift from Caerne.'

'Ah, yes,' the brother smiled. 'The Hel-beast incarnate?'

Wulfrun snorted with laughter.

Both Hurnungaz and the brother glared at him.

'I,' said Alain, a little shyly, his voice light, 'I believe in the Christ of the East.'

Raven bared his teeth, glaring at the young man.

'We should be tracking down this Gisborough and his men,' interjected Radewych. 'Not standing here talking.'

Hurnungaz glanced at the warrior woman. 'I thought Tam lost. There was a big battle; our Stag-god unleashed all kinds of things to destroy a cathedral and its unholy priests. Tam disappeared after the battle; I thought him dead.'

Tam glanced around. 'Where's Sciuridae?'

**

Hugi *ran*.

He hit the tree, the wolf-creature still hanging onto his arm. The shock ran through him: there was a crack, and the tree shifted, groaning.

He drew back, the creature rolling back onto its hooves, staring at him, drooling, glaring.

The tree splintered, cracking, branches falling, leaves tumbling.

The Hel-wolf howled, turned and ran.

Hugi moved back as the tree collapsed, shaking the ground, tearing its roots out of the ground.

He shook his head, staring at the deep wound in his arm.

**

Muna waited.

The camp quietened slowly. She didn't know who the four strange warriors were, but two of them had left with Wulfrun and Godwin. Two remained in camp. There was no scent of danger about them.

Hurnungaz: she could taste his presence. She licked her lips. Take him, and Caerne would be so much weaker.

Tam. Two more strangers, one a brother of the false god. Raven, Merik – and Mar on sentry duty.

Muna smiled maliciously.

The *girl*boy was moving quietly, looping around the site, almost undetectable. If she'd had to rely on just her eyesight, she'd have missed Mar, they were that good.

Muna grinned.

As they passed beneath her, she dropped onto them, driving them to the ground in perfect silence.

**

Wulfrun scowled, glancing at Radewych.

They'd tracked the King's Own to a small village, south from where the battle had taken place. King's Own now stood guard around it, both mounted and stationary patrols.

A fire blazed in the centre of the village. If the village was large enough to have a blacksmith that might have a fire burning through the night, but not in the open, and in most villages when night fell, there was no light.

Figures milled around the fire, both villagers and King's Own.

'Can you – slip past them? Pretend to be one of them?'

Wulfrun shook his head. 'Not a patrol like this. They've trained together, they'll have worked together for a long time. They'll know I'm not one of them.'

Radewych scowled.

'What do we do?' asked Godwin softly.

'We stay and watch. If they move on in the morning, we track them. If they stay here, one of us carries a message to Hurnungaz.'

**

Mar heard – *something* – then was sprawling on the ground. They reached for their knives – and hands clutched her head.

Mar screamed. *Blood filled her mouth. Fists battered her flanks, scratched and tore at her back, tore the hair from her head –*

Mar screamed. Tried to scream. Feathers choked her mouth, filled her throat. She screamed, trying to break free –

Claws ripped at her cheeks, her neck, her shoulders. Claws shredded her clothes; ripped at her back.

Her son was in front of her, impaled on a spear. Her heart lurched –

She could barely see, there was blood in her eyes, her own blood, pain exploding throughout her body –

And then something exploded against her head.

**

'Berenger!' Gisborough bellowed.

He looked around, angry. He was lying on a low pallet, piled with furs that stunk of animal; there was a door-shaped hole, covered with a rough cloth, and the room stunk of peasants.

His commander hurried in.

'My lord! You're awake.'

'What happened? Where are we?'

'Safe, my lord. We're in Thryingstone. It's the day after we attacked those – foreigners.'

He scowled, sitting up. 'Where's my sword? Why here?'

'We were ambushed, my lord. I gave the sign to flank them, to crush them between our wings, and –'

'And?'

'The Hooded attacked, my lord. Three arrows struck you, knocked you off your horse. The horse bolted; warriors were falling. We got you to safety.'

'You *left* the scene of a battle?'

'To save you, my lord Gisborough, yes. That Hurnungaz has some Hel-sorcery. His arrows broke one of the wings.'

Gisborough rolled his eyes in exasperation. 'He was on the field of battle, and you fled before him?'

Berenger scowled. 'Thirteen men are dead, my lord. In a few seconds. Some from those warriors who'd been in the boats. Most from Hurnungaz.'

'Thirteen?'

His commander nodded. 'His arrows just,' he shrugged. 'Unless we come upon them in surprise, charging them head on may not be the way to do it.'

He frowned. 'Nottingham mentioned something. A tourney; a challenge, to grind the peasants down and remind them who's in command. A prize to tempt these Hooded, and others like them.'

Berenger nodded.

Gisborough scowled. 'Send a messenger to Nottingham. Send for Jenny of Nottingham.'

'A girl?' Berenger frowned. 'It's not really the time –'

Gisborough glowered at his commander.

After a moment, the man withdrew.

**

Gloriana stood in front of the roaring log fire, a bearskin cloak pinned at her neck: nothing else. The firelight gleamed between her legs, illuminating the thick, straw-gold fur that crowned her hips.

She drew the bearskin back, baring her impressive bosom.

'I hope you are not too spent on the Holy Land whore to fill my belly. The King demands to know when I am due.'

St. John scowled.

'She is African. Her skin is much blacker.'

Gloriana snorted. 'She has a cunny and breasts. I know you have ploughed her.'

He shrugged. 'She is a woman under my command; a common whore, nothing more.'

'Common?' his wife raised an eyebrow. 'I had her stripped and bathed. There is nothing common about her.'

He scowled, shrugging.

'She bears many bruises as well, in places no child should.'

He snorted. 'She is my property. I will take her home with me when I am done; finish off what I started.'

'Why did you bring her on the journey?'

'Her cunny is snug. Her arse is tight. She is good with her tongue.'

His wife looked revolted. 'I do not want to know the details of what you do with your whores!'

He grinned. 'Her flesh hides bruises well. Yours will not. You might command York, but I am your husband.'

She raised an eyebrow again. 'I stand naked before you, and you thinking of hitting me rather than fucking me?'

St. John snorted. 'You are unladylike. Lose the bearskin. Get onto the bed on all fours and I will fill your belly.'

Gloriana laughed. 'I am a wild animal, husband. More fun is to be had in the chase and then the catch.'

He frowned. 'Lose the bearskin and on the floor then! Spread your legs and I'll fill you.'

She snorted. 'So crude, so pathetic, *Nott*ingham. The King commands I be pregnant. If you're not up to the job –'

'You would dare, whore –'

He strode in, fist drawn back. She moved in to him, suddenly, knocking him to the floor, straddling him.

'I am the Sheriff!'

'And I am your wife!' she hissed. 'Fuck me, husband.'

He threw her onto her back, scowling, and straddled her, trying to ignore the way she wriggled and writhed, smirking up at him.

'Only one man has had you before, and he barely capable of getting it up?' He raised an eyebrow. 'You wriggle like a common whore. How many men have you known? Which men have used you?'

'I am no common whore –'

He backhanded her and she was stunned. He got off her, rolling her onto her belly.

'Stay down,' he hissed, disrobing. 'I will get you pregnant, but you need to remember your place.' He grinned, fighting the urge to caress her back. 'On the floor, beneath me.'

**

Sir Richard smiled. 'How are they doing?'

Angel and Deederich were playing on the edge of the stream that bordered his lands. A nurse was close by, in case anything untoward should happen.

'Your daughter, Angel, is good with sums. She knows the names of the King and his principal courtiers; she knows the names of most of the major and minor lords around her, be they Anglo-Saxon or Norman.'

He nodded. 'Good. And Deederich?'

There were children playing in his house, in his grounds, again. It had been so long ago, since his son –

The tutor coughed apologetically.

'Yes?'

'You asked about Deederich, my lord?'

'Yes.'

He could almost hear the man's sigh.

'His knowledge of language is poor. He seems to have no interest in it. The cook tells me he eats less than his sister as well.'

Richard nodded. 'Angel has a lusty attitude towards food. She likes meat, sometimes rawer than I think wise. She eats vegetables, fruits, she drinks a little wine or ale. Her brother,' he sighed.

The tutor nodded. 'I would say Angel is a healthy, normal child. Whatever it was that gave her skin an unhealthy hue, it has all but faded. She,' he smiled. 'She likes to learn. She is happy here, I would say. Wherever she was,' he shook his head.

Sir Richard nodded. 'I do wonder about where they came from. Underfed. Obviously a boat or something brought them to this island, but why? To sell them as slaves? They are children, they have no special skills. Was it poor diet that gave them green-hued skin.'

'Deederich still has that, though he eats less, and barely touches fruit and vegetables.'

Sir Richard nodded. 'You know money is no object. I am happy with Angel. Do I need to ask you to send for a physician for Deederich? I give him sunshine, play with his sister, fresh food, things to drink, and he barely eats, he doesn't learn our language.'

'I can fetch a physician, my lord. You know it will not be,' he paused.

Richard nodded, sighing. 'They are – important. They had no one. This is not their home, but I will do what I can to support them.' He smiled at the tutor. 'Fetch the medic and anyone who you think can help. I do not want Angel to lose her brother.'

**

'What news, Godwin?'

The man shook his head. 'They're in the village of Thryingstone. They're dug in. Mounted patrols, warriors on guard. Gisborough's there.'

'Could we attack?'

He shook his head again. 'Wulfrun thinks the men would know he's not one of them straightaway. The village is small; the King's Own are everywhere. There's,' he shrugged. 'I don't know. Fifty, sixty of them in the village. More standing watch.' He scowled.

'What?'

'They sent a couple of riders out; messengers. We got one, but the other got through.'

Hurnungaz nodded.

'You said,' interjected Tam. 'Sciuridae?'

Hurnungaz glanced at the Alba man and shook his head. 'He was with Caerne. He didn't make it; she is still weak.'

'What – happened?' asked Raven. 'I saw things. The ground was heaving.'

Hurnungaz nodded. 'Caerne – summoned something.'

'A Hel-beast?' suggested Brother Blacwin.

Hurnungaz looked at him until the brother looked away, raising his hands in apology.

'The creature tore the ground up. Drained Caerne of her power.' And if you hadn't – Quellavera – he grimaced. 'Caerne – Sciuridae, he,' he hesitated, looking at the brother again.

'I am not a fiend from Hel. Nor is Caerne. But when I loosed an arrow, slew a stag, Caerne was – came into being. I had been Robin; I became Hurnungaz. And Sciuridae,' he smiled softly. 'Sciuridae came into being.'

'And now he's gone?' asked Raven.

Hurnungaz nodded. Radewych's three companions sat in silence, wrapped in their cloaks, listening and watching but not contributing. How much they understood he wasn't sure; presumed they could all understand everything that was going on.

Tam sighed. 'Sciuridae dead. Hereseige – gone. Bwyd – gone.'

'Bwyd's alive,' Hurnungaz interrupted. 'Caerne could sense him. He's on his way back to us.'

'Why did he just leave?' Raven asked.

Hurnungaz glanced at the young man. 'I don't know. Bwyd has obligations. That may be what called him, though I wish he'd said something.'

Raven frowned, looking around. 'Where's Mar? Where's Muna?'

**

'What? Have you? Done?' screeched Hugi.

His sister stood before him, arms crossed over her chest. The Hooded, Mar, sprawled at the ground in front of her. Muna had been carrying her over her shoulder; had simply dropped her to the ground.

'You need a release. It thinks its male. You can show her she's not.'

Hugi stared. Mar was naked, their body scratched and ripped, bloody and torn.

He looked up and stared at his sister. 'Hooded,' he screeched.

She snorted, shaking her head. 'Had she been a boy, she would have raped me, several times over. So I thought you might like to defend me.'

Hugi stared at her, shaking his head slowly.

'We *are* Wōden's,' she hissed. 'His creation. His children. His hands. His ravens.' She shook her head. 'That one is of Caerne and the Old one. We are taking back Wōden's power. Caerne, this Hurnungaz, stole his territory. Sacrifice her to Wōden.'

He shook his head.

'Who? Are you?'

She kicked the girl spitefully. 'We are Muna. We are Wōden's. What are you?'

He bent and lifted the unconscious Hooded.

'Feast on her,' his sister ordered. 'If you are squeamish I will rip her belly open so you can feed on her entrails.'

He shook his head firmly, cradling the Hooded close.

'Mine,' he rumbled.

Muna scowled. 'Take her power. Break her. Weaken Hurnungaz. Weaken Caerne.'

He shook his head stubbornly.

She narrowed her gaze. 'I,' she said, moving towards him. 'Will. Bury you both. Alive.'

**

Abbess Winchester looked up as the two women were escorted into her presence by one of her own and two Benedictine brothers.

One was a peasant girl; the other minor nobility by the looks of it. Both fallen on hard times. She scowled at the brothers.

'Gresham brothers? Of Abbot Simon?'

The brothers nodded, keeping their gazes lowered.

'Be off with you. I have no need of you.' She frowned. 'Wait outside. I will interrogate these girls then you may need to accompany them –'

'My lady,' interrupted the minor noble.

Her man grimaced.

'I am Your Grace or the Abbess Winchester! You do not speak! You answer my questions, chattel.'

The two brothers withdrew. The girl stared at her stubbornly.

'Seneschal, have you a willow-crop to hand? It seems someone needs to be disciplined.'

He nodded, touching the implement where it hung from his belt.

The peasant girl looked up, but didn't speak.

'I know you.' She frowned. 'Are you the Abbot's mistress?'

The peasant girl blushed. 'I run his household, your Grace. My name is Lucianna.'

She frowned. 'Why are you here? Who is this one?'

'This is Evgania of Warwick, your Grace. Her father sends her to you for instruction and discipline.'

The girl stared at Lucianna.

She held her hand out. 'Where is the money? Warwick can pay for her education.'

The peasant girl shook her head. 'We were – there was a maid. Jenny of Nottingham. She stole the money. Your Grace.'

Winchester thinned her lips. The girl can be a servant. Humble her. Make her work on her knees. Make her crawl on her belly.

'Yes, my lord,' she whispered.

She looked up. 'Abbot's mistress. Return to your master with his brothers. The girl will stay here.'

Evgania smiled brightly.

The Abbot's mistress frowned. 'She brings no dowry, your Grace. What will her position be?'

The simple girl, the minor noblewoman, stared at her, at the peasant girl.

'She can crawl on her belly. She can clean the firepits. The privvies. Enough work can be found for her.'

'Your Grace!' the girl said, aghast.

She smiled. 'You, Lucianna. Return to your master. If he wishes to contact the Sheriff, have a replacement dowry sent, or Warwick, I care not which one. Otherwise she remains a common serving girl.'

'Your Grace!' the girl protested again.

She nodded to her man. 'Take her bodice and clothing down. Twenty lashes to her bare back. Then set her to clean the floor of the kitchens.'

The man nodded, drawing the willow-crop.

**

Wenlock stared, horrified and fascinated.

The stag was on its back, its head half-twisted around, legs splayed. Caerne ripped its throat open. Ripped and tore, tugged, opening its belly up.

Entrails and guts, blood and bones.

Caerne ripped its skin apart, thrusting her arms deep into the bloody warmth. She cracked the ribcage and tore the heart out, biting it, crooning to herself as the blood trickled down her face.

Finished, she wiped her hands across her skull, her face, across her body. Fur was beginning to regrow, at her crotch and belly, on her thighs, her arms.

She thrust fingers into herself, riding the stag's corpse noisily, thrusting against the bloodied ruination of their stomach, her free hand clutching and playing at her breast.

Wenlock looked away. He could feel the power in what she was doing, but it was grim, grisly.

Caerne climaxed, slipping and falling into the bloody corpse, panting and shuddering, a beast in heat.

Her tail blossomed, bone-white fur. Fur grew from her shoulder blades; from her rump.

She pushed herself up onto all fours. Blood and pleasure dripped from her. She shrugged, shaking herself. Blood flew – and then something plunged onto her.

**

'Isn't it better,' St. John chuckled, 'when you accept the natural order of things, wife?'

She scowled at him. Her shoulders, arms, breasts and belly were bruised. He had deliberately not struck her in the face.

'I could hurt you more, but you will be the mother of my child. My line.'

She glared up at him.

He put his hands on her belly: she winced.

'Once you are pregnant, as you will be before I leave, then you will keep yourself to your chambers. You will dress as a woman and be womanly in all things.'

'Nottingham –' she growled.

'I am going to take Angelica back with me. Her quim is as good as yours. She can take my lusts better than you can.'

'I am not some whore –'

He punched her in the belly and she gasped, struggling for breath.

'I can slap her around all I want. Your little dominion will come to my child. Once you have born me an heir, you will visit me regularly. I require,' he spread his hands over her belly, 'many offspring. You are young; your womb is fertile.' He grinned. 'Shall I send for the Brother of the Christ of the East to bless you?'

He caressed her breasts. 'He has a low opinion of women. He or his representatives will ensure you act like the woman god made you.'

She scowled.

'The King wants me with child –' she began.

'I think three brethren should attend you at all times. To ensure your purity and holiness.'

'I am your wife,' she growled, 'the King orders I am with child. But I do not want you fucking that little whore.'

St. John grinned. 'I will fuck who I like. Since you will not obey the King's orders and do your wifely duty, in surrendering York to me, then I must sate my desires elsewhere. It is not natural for a man to be – unaccompanied.'

She shook her head. 'This is my kingdom, given to me by the King!' She stared at him. 'But you are my husband,' her voice softened. 'I will keep the child to keep her safe from your – tastes. I do not want to know what you get up to. I will bear your children but this kingdom remains mine.'

'You may have her.' He chuckled. 'When I return to Nottingham, I will have brothers sent to you.' He grinned. 'I need plan a tourney; rid the world of these Hooded.'

'A tourney?'

He nodded, pushing himself into her. She grimaced but didn't fight him.

'Teach the peasants, the Anglo-Saxons,' he grunted.

She took his hands: put them back on her breasts.

'I can think of better uses for your tongue.'

He clutched tighter, thrusting into her. 'A silver arrow,' he grimaced, pushing himself up. 'I'll catch all the Hooded. Hang them. Send their heads to Londinium.'

He thrust harder and harder. Gloriana lay, obediently unresponsive, beneath him.

**

Hurnungaz turned, holding his hands out for silence.

The woods – were alive. For a moment he could smell the spray of a river tumbling over rocks. A towering citadel, remote, in the border village of Clun.

Hurnungaz grinned.

'By the dark breath of earth!' he bellowed.

'Dissever!' roared voices, many more voices than he'd expected.

They were still at their camp: searches had not revealed Mar or Muna, although there was evidence of a scuffle.

He was staring through a sparsely populated stand of trees. There was undergrowth but it did not grow thickly; the trees were not close; sunlight slanted down between them in faint streams.

The Forest moved.

Figures were suddenly there, about a dozen, mostly dark-haired, armed and armoured in leather, stout and tough, led by a familiar figure in a loose robe and a woman wearing a headdress of magnificent horns.

'Hurnungaz!' called Bwyd.

Hurnungaz raised his arm. 'Bwyd! You return to us. What took you from us without a word?'

He approached, grinning. 'May I introduce Aneirin, sword tutor and story smith of the Sælvatici.'

Hurnungaz nodded. The woman, taller than Bwyd, smiled.

'You are Hurnungaz of the Hooded?'

He nodded. 'My forces are a little scattered at the moment, but I have Tam, Raven, Godwin, Merik, Alain, Brother Blacwin,' he paused at the three warriors of Radewych: they had not volunteered names.

Bwyd stared. 'Where is Wulfrun? The others?'

Hurnungaz shook his head. 'Wulfrun is keeping an eye on Gisborough: we injured him.'

Bwyd grinned.

'Who do you bring us, Bwyd? Their presence is welcome.'

Bwyd grinned at him. There were ten figures in a loose semicircle. All were warriors and carried short bows. Most were male, but there were female warriors amongst them.

'This is Madoc. Gwilim. Tegwared.' As he mentioned each name, the man or woman inclined their head.

'Gwion. Ifor. Howell.'

Universally they looked tough. Warriors of the Sælvatici! There were none he recognised; all looked younger than him.

'Llywarch. Tangwystl. Genilles and Myfanwy.'

He nodded to them in turn. 'Welcome to Sherewode and the Hooded. Who do you look to for commands?'

Aneirin caught his look. 'We look to you and Caerne of the Hooded. Llewellyn, Lord of the Sælvatici, sent us to bolster your numbers. More of our kind are coming.' She grinned. 'The tide is turning, Hurnungaz. Terror stalks our lands and the forest. While Llewellyn secures our lands, we must unite to drive the Normans out of our forest home.'

**

Gisborough looked up. The village was, on one side, in a partial bowl in the hillside. A dirt track led to the village, now widened by the passage of the King's Own, but down it now came a single rider.

A fire blazed in the middle of the village. His men hacked trees down to feed the fire and to strengthen the village.

Thryingstone will be where we catch them. Pits are being dug, spiked, for them to fall into. Houses reinforced. In time, waves of the King's Own I will send away from here. Cannot make it too obvious this is a trap for the Hooded. Let them come down here in time. They will not get out alive.

**

Mar opened her eyes cautiously. They were wrapped in a rough blanket, lying in a small nook on a steep hillside. Trees overhung the nook and it was thick with undergrowth, but they could still see –

The crow-headed creature looked up at them.

'Hugi.'

He nodded. 'Safe.'

Mar looked around again.

'Muna – wrong.'

She looked back at him. 'Wrong?'

'Wrong. Hates you. Powerful.'

'Where are my clothes? My weapons?'

He shook his head. 'She brought you. Wanted me to –' he looked away.

Mar stared, horrified. The full sight of Hugi – she grimaced.

'She gave me to you?' she whispered.

He nodded. 'She not my sister. Something wrong. Wanted me to,' he gestured towards her. Towards himself.

Mar stared. Swallowed. 'Why,' she hesitated. 'Why didn't you?'

He looked at her with black, unreadable, eyes. 'Not monster.'

**

'Do you know why I have summoned you, John?'

Her cook shook his head. 'No, mistress. I hope I has not caused issues.'

Gloriana smiled. She was in her outer chamber, a fire roaring. The Sheriff was two days gone, thankfully. Fearghal waited outside the door, just in case she was wrong in her suspicions. John's voice – she grinned.

'Your accent is not from here, is it?'

'Stanage Edge, mistress. I used to be,' he shrugged. Grimaced. 'I've done several things. Been a stone mason. A shepherd. A,' he broke off.

'And where did you learn to cook?'

He smiled. 'Times were hard. Roots. Vegetables. What could be found. Scavaged. Sto –' he broke off again.

'My last cook tried to poison me. He worked for a very bad man.'

The cook, a tall man, didn't reply.

'I find your meals – simple but wholesome. Peasant fare, but for all that, tasty and filling.'

'Am not a man of Londinium, mistress. I cook what I know.'

She smiled. 'I think you are much more than that. John. Of the Hooded?'

He looked up and met her gaze. For an instant there was a connection – and then he bowed his head.

'I doesn't know what you implies, mistress. I am but a simple man, humbled to work for you, Lady Gloriana of York.'

Gloriana smiled. 'You know of who I speak. You *are* of whom I speak.'

He sighed. Looked up at her again.

There was a struggle in his eyes. Passion. Rage. Fear.

'My captain of the guards is outside this room. He is not in here. John,' she smiled. 'We may be able to –' she hesitated. 'Be useful to each other.'

He was wary. Cautious. Since her previous cook had attempted to poison her, she'd been a lot warier about letting anyone get close. Fearghal and others had argued for a known cook, bought for better money, from another lord. But that way lay betrayal. Just as she knew the Sheriff's girl, Angelica, was a traitor, for all the Sheriff had abused her.

But John was – direct. Simple but not simple; a man of the people. He had lacked in confidence when he first came to her, but had grown quickly.

'I am not a soft lord, John, to hunt peasants with a hundred men at my back. I stand with those I command, be they Anglo-Saxon, Norman or other.'

'If I am – who thou sayest I am, then –'

She chuckled. Stood up from her table and fetched two goblets and a wine skin.

John stayed frozen, watching her carefully.

'Are you here as a spy, or was it simply an opportunity?'

She poured two drinks and put one in front of him. Took a mouthful herself and swallowed it.

'I,' he shook his head.

'If I wanted to arrest you as a *potential* member of this outlaw gang, the Hooded, you would already be in my gaol.'

Gloriana took another mouthful, settling back down into her chair.

John, a little reluctantly, took a sip of wine.

'You have given me no cause to doubt you, John. I *may* be wrong, but I think I am right.'

'You said we could be – useful.'

'A stubborn man,' she smiled. Sighed. 'My husband,' she grimaced. 'You know him as the Sheriff of Nottingham. His former man, the man Gisborough, now leads one hundred of the King's Own, hunting these – Hooded.'

John stared, edgy and cautious.

'The King demands I am with child. He had me marry Nottingham. This is my kingdom,' she gestured around, 'but between the King, my husband, and the brothers of the Christ of the East he will send,' she grimaced.

'How can I serve, mistress?' John asked softly.

**

Sir Richard sighed. Deederich lay in his cot, too weak to move.

'What news?' he asked the medic.

The man grimaced. Shook his head. 'It is not good, my lord. There are things that can be tried – leeching and bleeding, but your son is unresponsive to most things.'

'He is not,' Richard began. Shook his head. 'He is.'

'Possibly a Hel-creature has his soul,' the medic continued. 'With a donation, I am sure Brother Gascon would visit. If he could not drive the creature out of your son, none could.'

Sir Richard grimaced. Brother Gascon was a zealot, crazy from the heat of the Holy Land and a dangerous man.

He sighed. But if it would help.

'See to the bleeding and leeching. Send for the Brother. If he can assist.'

The medic nodded. 'I will arrange everything, my lord. As long as you have the money for it.'

He nodded. 'I do. I leave you to your work. Save my son!'

He strode out of the fusty room and out, into his garden.

Angel was sitting with her back to a tree, near to the stream. He crossed to her, trying not to frown.

'You will stain your dress, Angel.'

She looked up, and he could see she had been crying.

He sank to his knees next to her. 'I am sorry, child. Stain your dress all you want. Your brother –'

'He will not – he will not,' she began.

He stroked her hair gently. 'I will spend every coin I have to bring him health. The medic tries leeches currently.'

She grimaced. 'A quackery. It will do nothing.'

He shrugged. 'I must try. Daughter mine.'

She looked up at him, a smile touching her eyes. 'Yes, adopted-father.'

He sighed. 'If I could return you to your people; if they are here, if I could find them. I have men searching,' he sighed again.

She nodded, putting her hand on his. 'They will be led by a woman called Radewych. She is fearsome and lovely. If anyone can find us, she will.'

He nodded.

'There is more, isn't there?'

He nodded again. 'The medic thinks a demon has your brother's soul. He recommends a,' he grimaced. 'A man who has a terrible reputation. I fear,' he shook his head.

She climbed into his lap. 'You will do what is best for Diederich. Thank you for caring, Sir Richard.'

**

Wenlock stared, wide-eyed, as the Wulfenstæg bowled Caerne over. She hissed, hands raised to scratch at the Wulfenstæg, but it headbutted her, knocking her down easily, licking at her face.

Wenlock stared. It was licking the blood from her face.

It stood over Caerne and she stretched her arms up, stroking it, trying not to giggle as its thick, wet, tongue lapped at her face.

'Wulfenstæg, Wulfenstæg,' she crooned.

It shuffled down, licking at her throat.

Wenlock blinked.

'It recognises me,' Caerne giggled. 'It recognises me!'

The wolf-creature licked her chest.

Caerne crooned.

**

'She what?'

Abbot Simon stared at Lucianna.

'The Abbess said, you could write to your brother, or Warwick, for the sum required. Otherwise she would remain,' she grimaced.

'And how was this money stolen?'

'Evgania had a maid. Jenny of Nottingham. I think she used to be the sister to that outlaw.'

The Abbot grimaced. 'So one on my brother's whores steals money from Warwick's daughter, and the mad bitch of Winchester thinks I will write to save the girl?' He snorted. 'On her knees, scrubbing, sounds like the place for her.'

'Your Grace,' Lucianna protested.

He snorted. 'And what is the state of your soul, Lucianna? Did you find the reason for her writing to you?'

She blushed.

'It was her maid who prompted it.'

Abbot Simon shook his head. 'So Nottingham's whore arranged the visit, stole Warwick's money and fled, and you delivered the stupid girl to Winchester?'

She nodded, tears trickling down her cheeks.

'Don't tell me you've fallen for the bitch!' he roared.

She shook her head.

Like mother like daughter, he thought.

**

'Wulfrun.'

Hurnungaz gripped the Norseman's arm. 'Any change?'

Wulfrun shook his head, glancing back at those with him. 'One messenger escaped. The King's Own have the village well fortified. Radewych wants to question Gisborough.' He frowned. 'Welsh?'

Hurnungaz grinned. 'Sælvatici.'

Wulfrun grinned. 'We could attack. Reckon there's still more than us. But if they've the same skill you have.'

Hurnungaz shook his head. 'They don't have Caerne's gift, no. But they even the odds.'

Wulfrun snorted. 'I reckon Gisborough is staying there. Turning the village into a trap. If we charge in,' he shook his head.

Hurnungaz nodded. 'I agree.' He grinned. 'There's nothing to say we can't take a few of them out. The distance from here to the huts – fire arrows?'

Wulfrun grinned.

'What's happening?' Radewych demanded.

Hurnungaz shook his head. 'I agree with Wulfrun. The village is a trap. We passed several groups of riders: the King's

Own are circling, waiting for us to make a move. If we go in, we might not get out again.'

Radewych grimaced. 'There's no indication that the children are in there. But I want him. This Gisborough.'

Hurnungaz grinned. 'We'll take out a patrol or two. Then return tonight. Fire some of the huts, see what happens.'

**

'Why – dress as boy?'

Mar looked at Hugi. They had headed south, heading in the general direction of the cathedral. At least from there, she could look for Hurnungaz and the others. Hugi had been considerate.

He was an ugly thing, not unlike herself. White, true-white, skin. A bald crow's head with a huge beak which made speaking difficult. A huge, out of proportion, cock.

'I had a son.' She grimaced. 'He was murdered. I had lovers, women.' She smiled, faintly. 'I never wanted to be a woman. I never wanted a child.'

She looked away. They were resting in a thick coppice, letting the day slide past, travelling by night mostly.

'There was,' she shook her head. 'I don't want to talk about it.'

Hugi made a concerned noise.

'Why – hate women?'

'I don't,' she scowled. Blinked. Shook her head. 'I don't know.'

Hugi offered his arms. 'Sleep?'

She missed – not sleeping in the earth. Whatever Muna had become, she needed to get to Hurnungaz and the others, that they could – she scuttled over to Hugi.

He wrapped his arms around her like a bone cage. He was heavily muscled and big in every way. She laid her head on his arm, knowing if he locked it around her throat, she'd be dead and unable to stop him.

She trusted Wulfrun. Trusted Hurnungaz, mostly. Trusted Hugi. Trusted Raven.

She snuggled in tighter and let sleep wash over her.

**

Brother Blacwin watched as Hurnungaz strode into the middle of the trackway. They could all hear the column approaching: some of the King's Own.

Hurnungaz was – a conundrum. On the one hand, he was obviously not quite of peasant stock but was Anglo-Saxon. On the other – he sighed softly. He was an outlaw and he should do all he could to have him captured.

But –

He heard the hoofbeats increase and the calls of the King's Own.

Hurnungaz drew back and loosed. Three arrows sprang from his string – he stared in disbelief.

Devil worship. A Hel-gift.

There was the twanging of bow strings all around him. He peeked out again. Most of the soldiers were down, a jumbled pile of bodies, from which horses struggled to rise or pull free from entangled corpses.

A Hel-gift.

**

'Are you awake, John?'

His hand moved to that secret spot that the Sheriff had no idea about.

She gasped in pleasure and surprise. 'You know –'

'My Rose always liked to be touched there.' He opened his eyes and smiled at her.

Gloriana smiled, making herself comfortable. 'Don't stop.'

For several minutes she lay in silence, as John's touch brought her a pleasure she had only ever been able to bring by herself.

She murmured softly, putting her hand over his. 'That was,' she smiled. 'Let your fingers rest.'

He grinned. 'Thou likest 'it?'

She nodded. 'This cannot last. The Sheriff can never know. Once I am –'

He nodded. 'I am a cook. A peasant. A simple man. To be in a lady's bed –'

'Do you know other – secrets?' she asked, berating herself even as much as she wanted to know.

I am losing my head! My cook, a peasant, an Anglo-Saxon, definitely one of the Hooded! And here he lies, his hand between my legs –

If the Sheriff finds out. If the King found out!

'What?' he asked. 'You went – far away.'

'Can you use your tongue as you use your finger?'

He grinned. 'Aye. Arleigh used to like I did that to her.'

'Who was Arleigh?'

He shook his head. 'No one. A seneschal's daughter, too young to tup but not too young for – other things.'

'Other things. You used your tongue upon her?'

He nodded. 'As I would like to upon you.'

She snorted. 'What do you think of me?'

His hand – disappointingly, moved to her breast. 'Any woman that knows her own mind. That knows what she likes.'

'I am not some servant maid or lowly officer's daughter.'

He nodded. 'I know'est. I will please you as you direct, presuming not to take advantage.'

'I don't want,' she paused.

'I don't want my child to be the Sheriff's. He must think it is. Once I bear it, my life may be over. He sends brothers to watch me, to limit me.'

He moved his hand, thumb caressing her nipple. 'I know how to please a woman, if that is what you want.'

She bit her lip as her body responded to his touch. 'If I am discovered –'

'One night, mistress,' he smiled. 'If you want me gone in the morning I will be gone.'

'Is one night – enough?'

'My Rose conceived after just the once.' He grimaced. 'I had to flee, I couldn't afford –'

She put her finger to his lips. 'I really think your tongue should be busy elsewhere, John.'

**

'Why do you hate me?'

Raven scowled at him, shaking his head.

Hurnungaz glared at him.

Brother Blacwin subsided. The young man had a secret; an unfathomable hatred of – something he was connected to.

He sighed softly. Suppose it is not me. Suppose a brother has failed in his calling, has hurt the young man? He shook his head. Such an act cannot be condoned. Reparation must be made – if that is what ires Raven.

They were nearer the village that William of Gisborough and the King's Own waited in. He hadn't contributed to the discussion, but he agreed it was likely a trap.

Hurnungaz and his people had slaughtered ten of the King's Own without any apparent regret. The horses had been stripped of all accoutrements and turned loose. The men had all been slain by arrow: whatever his feelings about these Hooded, they were accurate.

Alain is a believer. He is new to the Hooded. Is his belief what gives Hurnungaz pause from slaying or leaving me behind?

I do not want to be a martyr. But these Hooded –

He saw the arrows take flight, bright spots of fire in the night. They were some distance from the village, shielded by trees, but it was still in sight.

Or it had been in sight, whilst the sun was up.

The arrows flew, too numerous to count and then, distantly, he heard the sounds as they embedded themselves into –

'Father,' he whispered, 'guide the Hooded's targetry. Let none of the King's Own be killed this way. To burn alive,' he shook his head.

A knife pricked his stomach. He froze, turning his head slightly.

Raven glared at him, a finger on his lips.

He nodded.

The Hooded loosed and loosed again. He could hear shouts from the village now, and something was definitely alight: the fire was burning brighter and brighter.

'Withdraw,' the order came down.

He drew back. Shapes were flickering between them and the fire, soldiers, horsemen, he couldn't tell.

Raven grabbed his arm and tugged.

'Come on!'

He turned and ran.

**

St. John smiled, pulling over a parchment. 'Seneschal!'

His man came running. 'Yes, my lord?'

'Prepare messengers. And send for as many scribes as we have.'

'Yes my lord,' the man bowed and withdrew, hurrying off.

'Now then,' he grinned.

'A silver arrow.' He scratched a note. 'Let the Jews pay for it. Embellished. A thing of beauty. Or gold, perhaps?'

He shrugged. 'A tourney. Messengers to all the nearest lords and some from further away.' He grinned. 'An influx of soldiers into the heartland of Sherwood. Representatives from the larger villages, let them try and prove the worth of the Anglo-Saxon stock.'

He grinned.

'And when these Hooded are caught –'

The thought of it not being the Hooded, swinging from nooses, but his wife, appealed to him. When I have a child, she can have an accident. Her attitudes are wrong. Her behaviours – he grimaced.

A messenger has already gone to Brother Gascon. He grimaced. If the bribe was not significant enough for three of his most devout brothers to attend her, to limit her, to fence her in.

He grinned. A representative from York, as well. The honour of the country. Of its people.

He shook his head.

The country, the people, have no honour. The Black Bishop is wrong to dismiss their old gods – he shook his head. Their old gods were not enough to destroy the cathedral site, merely damage it.

This. This, he thought, this will rip the heart out of the country. Prove, conclusively, that the Normans are best. We have taken them over. Our lands. Our laws. Our powers. Our hierarchy. They are all but powerless.

He grinned.

And when I have that man of mine back in my hands, him and all the money he helped steal –

**

Gisborough looked up as a shadow lingered in the doorway.

'Yes?' he growled.

'My lord,' answered one of Berenger's men, 'there's a man here. Says he's a squire from Nottingham.'

'Send him in.'

He took a swig of the wine. A figure moved through the doorway. For a moment bright sunlight blazed –

'My lord.'

The squire removed their helmet, revealing curly white hair.

'Jenny,' he grinned. 'How came you by the clothing?'

She grinned. 'I stole it from Evgania. The Abbot's mistress was taking her to Winchester. If she's any sense, she won't.'

He nodded. 'The Hooded attacked last night.'

Her smile turned into a frown. 'What did my bastard brother do?'

He scowled. 'He and his men slew a patrol previously. They've just vanished. They used fire arrows last night; two huts burnt, but no one injured.'

She snorted. 'He daren't get any closer. Your men chased?'

He nodded. 'They were gone. We found where they'd waited.' He frowned.

'What?'

'My scouts reckon there was about twenty of them.'

'So? You have – a hundred?'

He shook his head, pouring a goblet of wine for Jenny.

'Twenty three dead, and not even a single outlaw to show for it.'

She stared, continuing to loosen and remove her armour and clothing.

'You're intending to?'

'To strip for you, my lord. I understand you must be careful. That is why I thought you might like to carry out a personal inspection.'

He grinned. 'What suggestions have you? If he flees too quickly, and the village is too defended for him to launch an all-out assault?'

'Find some peasants.' She scowled, pulling the shift free of her underskirt. 'Women, the old, children. Hang them.

Surround the village with their bodies. Challenge him to single combat. He has pride: he will not resist that.'

Gisborough smiled, getting up, pulling the underskirt down and lifting her, putting her onto the table.

'I am not to be disturbed for several hours,' he called out.

'My lord,' the guards responded.

'Now then,' he grinned

**

Muna smiled. She could sense the creature, the little godling that was –

The tiny godling. Not Caerne, but something else. Something much smaller, much more insignificant.

I am Muna –

'We are Muna,' the voice in her head insisted. 'They buried me alive. I live again through you.'

'I am Muna. I am Wōden's hand –'

'Your brother will have torn the woman apart by now. You should have let me open her belly.'

'No,' she hissed. 'Mar is not –'

'You would like to fuck Mar?'

'No! I want Hurnungaz.'

'We want Hurnungaz. We will drain him of his power when we sit in his lap. We will drain Caerne. I *will* find her. I *will* rip her open and drain her power. To eat a god's bones and blood –'

She turned as she heard the creature step out from the undergrowth.

It had grey skin, furred legs and hooves. A thick, rasping tongue, floppy ears and a goat-like beard. The stink of rotting meat, of diseased meat, of something –

'What are you?' she rasped.

It shuffled unsteadily towards her. 'I am not Caerne,' she cackled. 'I am here for the cattle. The pigs, the goats. Sheep. Those who have no one.'

She lifted bloody claws.

Muna smirked. 'We are Muna!' she bellowed.

The creature blanched, unsteady on its hooves.

She strode closer – it tried to shuffle sideways.

Muna caught it. Ripped its arm sideways, dislocating it.

The creature screamed piteously.

She tore the other arm. Twisted the legs and pulled them, but was unable to physically rip them off the creature.

It lay on the ground, sobbing and heaving, its limbs twisted and broken.

'Imagine it is Caerne,' the voice in her head spoke to her.

Muna plunged her fingers deep into its eye sockets. As it screamed hideously, she grabbed the thickly twisting, slobbering, tongue, and tore it out.

**

'What now?' Radewych asked, 'There are far too many warriors in that village.'

'We should not scatter too far,' said Aneirin. 'Our strength is the bow. If we split up –'

Hurnungaz nodded. 'We cannot charge into the village. The huts are filled with soldiers. There are more in the woods beyond.' He looked around. 'I would say we were lucky. They were fast to respond,' he glanced at Wulfrun. 'Had they been faster –'

The Norseman nodded. 'They might be second or third sons, but they've had money thrown at them for years. The best training. The best armour. They've been trained to fight side by side, to rely on one another. Standing and fighting them is not an option.'

'A war of attrition?' offered Tangwystl.

Hurnungaz shook his head at the Welsh warrior woman. 'We just escaped. Had Raven not grabbed Brother Blacwin.'

The brother inclined his head towards Raven. Raven scowled but didn't acknowledge him.

'Why do we stay here?' Bwyd asked. 'We have a force of Sælvatici. Gisborough pens us here, hoping we'll attack, and while we do that, others ride through Sherewode unchecked.'

Hurnungaz nodded slowly. 'I am reluctant to leave Gisborough to his own devices. I do not know if any villagers are left alive. And a force of King's Own that strong –'

'He pens us,' Tam said softly.

'Ay?' asked Madoc. 'We are not the ones trapped in the village.'

Tam shook his head. 'No. But,' he shrugged.

Hurnungaz nodded. Reluctantly, he thought, Radewych nodded.

'We are too numerous to travel quickly or subtly.'

'Where is Mar?' asked Raven suddenly.

Wulfrun shook his head. 'I don't know.'

'You would leave a watch on the village?' asked Aneirin.

'I think maybe four groups.' Hurnungaz looked at Radewych. 'How would your people feel about separating, one into each group?'

Radewych looked at her people. 'We were pentamerous. We were five, working as one. Kugene is dead. We are no longer pentamerous.' She sighed. 'My people – do not easily give their names. But.' She looked at them in turn.

'Englara,' said one of the women with Radewych.

'Jerith,' said the man.

'Yasha,' said the other woman.

'If we are splitting into groups,' said Alain, 'may I be in the same group as Brother Blacwin?'

'Bwyd. Aneirin. Are you happy with the idea of separating your people into four groups?'

'What is our priority?' Aneirin asked.

'The children. And any opportunity to defy the Normans, to slay soldiers or verderers, anything to give our people hope.'

Aneirin pressed her lips together. Nodded slowly.

Hurnungaz nodded. 'One group will target the cathedral site. I will not ask you Alain or Brother Blacwin to be in that group.'

'Do we take a compass point each? One in each direction?' Merik asked.

Hurnungaz shook his head. 'I'll lead a group to the cathedral. If the Black Bishop is there, I've the best chance. Wulfrun, you'll lead one towards Nottingham.'

Wulfrun nodded. 'It might be worth paying a visit to the Abbot of Gresham Abbey.'

'The Sheriff's brother?' said Tam.

Hurnungaz nodded. 'Yes. Bwyd, you can lead that.'

'What are your intentions towards the bishop?' he asked.

Hurnungaz shrugged. 'The Abbot could be our guest for a while. See what he knows about the Christ of the East and the cathedral. Let's see if Nottingham will pay for him to be returned.'

'Tam.'

Tam looked up in surprise. 'What?'

'I want you to lead the other group. Find the Trent. Follow it south.'

He blinked in surprise. 'What am I looking for?'

'Mar. Muna. The children Radewych searches for. Opportunities to,' he looked around at the others. 'Gisborough is supposed to be hunting us. If we are elsewhere, robbing and stealing, word will get out. He will be forced out to face us.'

He looked round the assemblage.

'Wulfrun, take Radewych with you, and Alain. Keep an eye on Nottingham. See if you can't cause the Sheriff to bestir from his fortress city, have him drag Gisborough out of the village he's in.'

'Which of the archers?' asked Aneirin.

'Who do you recommend?'

Aneirin looked around. 'Gwion, Ifor and Howell.'

They moved to stand next to Wulfrun.

'Aneirin, if you go with Tam. Yasha as well, and Brother Blacwin.'

'Genilles and Myfanwy as well?' she suggested.

Hurnungaz nodded. 'Follow the Trent. Stay off the paths and see what you find.'

Tam nodded, the others joining him, though he looked unsure.

'Bwyd, take Merik and Godwin. I don't know if the Abbot stirs from his premises much, but he might be a useful prisoner to trade for Gisborough leaving Sherewode.'

'Llywarch and Tangwystl,' Aneirin added.

'Leaving –'

'Gwilim, Madoc and Tegwared with – you?'

Hurnungaz smiled. 'And Raven and Englara. We go to the cathedral site to see what the state of it is. To see if the *illustrious* Brother Gascon is around.'

'That's – it?' Raven asked.

Hurnungaz shook his head. 'Gisborough, one way or another, needs to be dealt with, but not by rushing into a trap. We will return,' he looked around, 'the fight continues, but for now we need to deal with Sir William. If we show him to be failing to patrol Sherewode, he will be called back. He will be humiliated. Disgraced.'

'Good,' muttered Tam.

'And if it – doesn't work?' asked Bwyd.

Hurnungaz smiled. 'I am not minded to throw all of us away in a single attack. We will stir the Forest into action. Gisborough will be humiliated.'

'There is,' Aneirin said hesitantly.

'No safety in numbers. This forest is ours, but if we all stay together,' he looked around, taking his time, 'we risk drawing them on to us. Smaller groups are easier to cross Sherewode. We can be in multiple places at once. If they don't know where we are, they can't hit us.'

Wulfrun nodded. 'Time to rattle some cages.'

Tam nodded slowly.

Radewych looked at her people: held each of their gazes' silently for a moment before turning away.

**

Mar frowned, seeing something pale twisting and turning in the trees ahead of them. Night had fallen and it was dark: cold. She had nothing but the rough blanket to wear and a stout branch to defend herself.

They moved cautiously, Hugi following behind, surprisingly softly for one of his size.

She grimaced as she got nearer and details became clearer.

An old woman hung from a branch, naked, dead, her face contorted, her body bruised and shrivelling, already cold. Her head was at an angle that suggested her neck had been snapped.

Why would anyone kill an old woman and strip her, leave her hanging here –

Freshly dead as well, Mar could tell, holding up her hand to make Hugi pause.

As she moved closer, she caught a glimpse of another. A child this time, naked, hung, tears frozen on their cheeks.

She froze.

Low voices. She signalled to Hugi to hide. Crouched low, pressing herself against a tree, wrapping the blanket tight, hoping the night and the tree would shelter her.

'That's the last of them.'

'Grim business.'

She peeked. Two men, dressed in a dark livery, a short distance away. She hid again.

'Something moved there.'

'A rabbit, a hare, a Hel-beast. I've no wish to be out longer than necessary.'

'We should search.'

'Huh. Kissing up to Gisborough?'

The man spat. 'Hardly. Sitting idle in a village while they pick us off? The man's a coward.'

'That's William of Gisborough you're talking about!'

'I know. Hides in a village. Has us hang children and old women.'

They moved on, their voices still audible for a while.

**

Wenlock watched.

Caerne sat astride the Wulfenstæg, head thrown back. Her fur gleamed in the noon-day sun. She ran her hands over her head, stroking her horns, stroking her hair. She traced the contours of her face, her nose, her cheeks, her lips.

Slid her hands down her throat.

Her fur had regrown, thicker than before he thought. It stopped at her neck, but covered the rest of her. Her legs were not much thicker than those of the creature she sat on; her tail was crisp and bright, fluffy, like a dandelion seed about to burst.

'Bwyd has returned to Sherewode. He is with Hurnungaz,' she murmured, crooning to herself. 'He brings the Sælvatici with him.'

She slid her hands down, tearing the fur until her breasts were bared.

She sat there, soaking up the sun, her fingers caressing her fur.

'I am returning,' she crooned softly.

The Wulfenstæg purred in unison with her.

**

'Who is here to see me?' Abbot Simon demanded.

'His name is Sir Richard of Verysdale.'

The Abbot frowned. 'That name is known to me.' He shrugged. 'What does he want?'

'I believe he is after a loan, your Grace,' Lucianna replied.

The Abbot snorted. 'When I am done with him, send a scribe in. I will write to my brother.'

She swallowed awkwardly. 'About – Evgania, your Grace?'

He looked at her in surprise. 'Why on earth should I write to my brother about that trollop? I suspect Winchester has broken her by now.'

'She is Warwick's daughter. Your Grace.'

'And a woman that you have fucked.' He frowned. 'Maybe I should have Brother Gascon exorcise you.' He looked her up and down. 'Still, it might be more enjoyable driving the devil out of you personally.'

'I am your servant and property, your Grace. You can treat me however you wish.'

'However I wish?' he chuckled. 'Send Sir Richard in. Then fetch a scribe and await my pleasure.'

She bowed and withdrew. An old knight, stiff-limbed, walked in.

'Your Grace. I am Sir Richard of Verysdale.'

The Abbot extended his hand.

Sir Richard lent over the desk. Took his hand and kissed the ring.

'Oh yes. I remember. There was some scandal, was there not, Sir Richard, concerning your son?'

'Henry?' the knight stared at him, hurt in his eyes.

'I was given to understand you had no intention of returning to this country. To die in the Holy Land, I believe.' He grinned. 'And now you are here. How can I help you, Sir Richard?'

He indicated the seat opposite him. Took a mouthful of his wine.

The old man sat stiffly. 'That had been my intention.' He sighed. 'But I missed the brook. The trees. A soft English breeze.'

The Abbot made a face.

'And just as well I returned,' the man continued, not seeming to have noticed his reaction. 'I have been left – two children to care for.'

'How nice.'

'Mmm,' the knight agreed.

Simon stared. The man's fingers were gnarled. Thin and twisted, long callused from holding a sword, though he doubted the man was capable of it anymore.

'Two children,' he repeated, shaking his head. 'One, Angel, my daughter, is a delight. So sharp. So caring. She will make someone a beautiful and dutiful wife one day.'

'That is good.'

'But my son, Deederich,' he sighed again, deeper.

'Your son – what?'

The knight looked up. 'Erik, I suppose. He is not well. There had been physicians, medics. I have paid for tutors. The best food. Sunlight. Fresh air.' He shook his head. 'Nothing seems to get through to him.'

'Perhaps he is possessed,' the Abbot suggested flippantly.

'Yes!' exulted the knight, becoming animated. 'So the medic suggested. That is why I have come to you.'

'Oh?'

'I wish for Brother Gascon to visit him. If he cannot drive whatever possesses – Eric – out – no one can.'

The Abbot raised an eyebrow. 'Then why come to me?'

The old man sighed. 'Because the man will ask a high price. I mean,' he coughed, and it didn't sound healthy, 'donation to the Christ of the East's coffers. I have not the money for what he will ask.'

'And what surety will you provide? How will the money loaned be returned?'

'I can stand Verysdale Hall and grounds against the loan. As for the repayment, I have friends. I am writing to them. They will cover a portion of the repayment each.'

The Abbot grimaced. With luck, he will die and the hall will become mine. It is a small holding, but pleasantly appointed.

After several moment's thought he nodded. 'It is agreed. I shall send for a scribe and draw up an agreement.'

**

Beate looked up at the two men, keeping her expression hopeful and fearful.

'What are we going to do with you then?' the bearded one growled.

The other one, the blond-haired one, took her hand: lifted it.

'Four fingers. She's a thief.'

She shook her head desperately. Her other hand was caught.

'See? Missing a finger on both hands.'

'Can you talk, girl? Have you use of your tongue?'

Beate shook her head desperately: opened her mouth.

The blond-haired man grimaced.

'Are you a thief, girl?' the bearded man asked.

Beate shook her head. Touched herself: held up one finger.

'A girl of negotiable virtue?'

She nodded, catching both of their gazes before hanging her head in shame.

'There's no shame, lass.'

The bearded man touched her arm hesitantly.

'We're merchants. I can spare a coin for a sating. There'll be a bit of food later, not much mind. You can travel on from us in the morning.'

The blond-haired man looked her up and down. 'For your food you can use your mouth on me. I've never had a girl with no tongue before.'

The bearded man rolled his eyes but pressed a coin into her hand.

'No time like now, lass.'

**

Saul looked up as he sensed movement. He had stopped on the edge of a river, a tributary of the Trent. It was mid-afternoon and the river was higher than expected, higher than he was comfortable taking his covered cart through.

Those inside his cart – were quiet. As darkness, as night, encroached, they would awaken and stir, but for now they rested.

He was not so foolish to think they slept.

A woman, a noble lady, rode into view, accompanied by two men at arms. She had short-cut blonde hair; a pale face and hands. She rode side-saddle, hands in her lap. One of her men held the reins of her horse; the other walked closer to her, hand on the horse's back.

She stopped, on seeing him. 'I am Lady Fringilla. What is the issue, tradesman?'

Saul bobbed his head. 'The river is too deep, Lady Fringilla. My way on is across, but it is not safe.'

'Is your cargo heavy or light?'

He shook his head. 'It's not heavy enough to hold the cart down if I drive it through.'

She patted the neck of her horse. 'Have you a rope? One of my men could swim across, tie it to a tree on the far side.'

He stared. 'That is most kind of you, lady.' He licked his lips. 'I am not sure any of my product would be of interest to you.'

He accepted the rope handed to him and passed it to one of the lady's men.

'And what is your product?'

'I sell a range of things –'

'I saw the hand that passed you the rope,' Lady Fringilla interrupted. 'My holding may be small, but my intelligence is not. Do not think me stupid.'

Saul grinned, bobbing his head. 'Yes, Lady Fringilla. My product is women. To serve men. To satisfy men.' He resisted the urge to look smug.

Her man was halfway across the river, having tied the rope to a branch. Even a makeshift guide to support, and the assistance of her men –

'We want her,' a voice hissed, low, from within the cart.

'Are your women so mis-trained that they cannot satisfy a woman?'

He coughed. 'They are not ladies' maids, my lady. Their duty is not to wait and serve. Their duty is – to fornicate.'

She chuckled.

Saul stared in surprise.

'My holding is not far from here. I have only a few servants. I could put you and your people up for the night in exchange for –'

She left it hanging.

Her man reached the other side of the river and tied off the rope. It was secure on both sides.

'In exchange for?' he asked softly.

'In exchange for you letting me look at your ladies once we reach my domain. I choose one and she spend the night with me. In exchange, shelter for the rest of you and a warm meal; a warm, safe, place to sleep.'

**

The blond-haired man lowered his trews and underthings.

'Come on, girl. Wrap your mouth around that.'

Beate stared. You're supposed to entertain me with that pathetic, cold and limp, worm? At least your friend had a bit of vigour and was warm. You worm looks like it'd turn water to marsh.

She put her lips around it, trying not to grimace.

At least both will be fast asleep soon. A warm meal and being sated.

His hand clutched the back of her head.

'It's an odd feeling, no tongue. Still, there'll be no complaining from her.'

'Make it quick. The meat's done. Night's drawing in.'

The blond-haired man moved: she could feel him getting stiffer.

'What's her cunny like? If she's as good with those lips as she is with these, then?'

'If you've a coin, you can find out for yourself. If we sell enough in Nottingham there'll be plenty spare.'

Beate could feel him thickening, his moment coming.

'What, keep her with us, you mean? Cunny, tits and a mouth but no voice. That'll be nice.'

'She's staying with me tonight. I can spare another coin; keep me warm through the night.'

He came, panting and moaning like it was a huge thing.

Beate withdrew, forcing herself to kiss the shrivelled worm.

**

A patrol of a dozen soldiers was riding down the trackway, leading away from the cathedral site. Hurnungaz glanced over at Raven, crouching on a high branch, knife clenched in his fist.

'Ready?' he mouthed.

The dark-haired youngster nodded.

He placed an arrow on the string. Glanced at the three Welsh archers with him and grinned. There were answering grins; arrows nocked.

He looked at Englara. She stood patiently, wrapped in black leather and dark green clothing, almost invisible in the shadows. The weapon she bore was a spear, longer than her but spiked along its length to catch, snag and tear clothing, skin or armour. She saw him looking and nodded.

Hurnungaz grinned.

Loosed.

Three soldiers fell from their horses and there was neighing and screaming and weapons being drawn and bow strings were plucking and arrows whistling and he drew, nocked and loosed another.

Englara moved into the open, her spear knocking two of the remaining riders off their horses. Raven launched himself onto the back of another, knife hand striking at the man's neck.

Hurnungaz dropped onto the trackway, nocking another arrow.

Three were down, dead, not rising. Three still were mounted, one reeling, under attack from Raven. Half a dozen were injured or trying to rise.

He loosed and three of those fell, never to rise. The Welsh archers fired as one and one of the remaining riders fell.

Raven pushed the soldier he'd been grappling with to the ground, blood on his hands, grinning viciously.

'You fight for the Black Bishop?' Hurnungaz called.

The remaining soldier cursed and wheeled his horse around, striking heels to it. Raven flung his dagger but it bounced off the man's armour.

Englara took two of the injured out, stabbing them with her spear.

Hurnungaz drew a third arrow.

'You'll never strike him,' said Gwilim, one of the Welsh.

'A coin says he does,' answered Tegwared.

'You're on,' grinned Madoc. 'He's on horseback, hunched low, the branches are low and overhanging.'

Hurnungaz grinned. 'By the dark breath of earth.'

Sherewode fell silent.

Still.

He loosed –

At a distance, three arrows buried themselves in the soldier's back, throwing him off his horse: it was pulled to the side and galloped into the trees, neighing.

There was a solid crash, a fractured neigh, and silence.

The Welsh cheered.

**

'Who have you lost?'

Wulfrun glanced at Radewych in surprise. They were moving through the deep undergrowth, Alain a few steps behind them, the three Welshmen further back.

'I see it in your eyes.'

He nodded, scowling. Freya – she was there, in front of him, for a moment. Her sparkling eyes. Her rough, coarse, knowing, laughter. Her hands, reaching for him –

'My wife. Freya. I served the King but she was always the better warrior. My shield-maiden. My heart.' He grimaced.

Radewych nodded. 'I miss Kugene. The five of us were close.' She sighed. 'The pentamerous shared everything, and now this Gisborough has broken us.'

Wulfrun nodded. 'My daughter Iseulde. They are in the Halls. I will be reunited with them, in time.'

Radewych nodded. 'And those that slew them?'

He glanced at her again. 'I will find them, in time.'

'You don't search for them?'

'De Saintcrow and de Syloc. I know where one, at least is. But,' he sighed.

'I do not know where the children are. Where Angenijs and Diederic are.' She sighed. 'But you know where someone who has wronged you is. Why do you not seek vengeance?'

Wulfrun stared. Shook his head. 'They – they are in the Halls. They would not,' he broke off.

'What was done to you – think it would not be done to any other?'

'I am Norse,' he growled angrily.

'And are forbidden revenge?'

'Alain?'

The young man moved up to join them. Wulfrun beckoned to the Welsh.

'Hurnungaz said to head for Nottingham. But a longer journey would lead to Scarsdale. In the vicinity is one Magnus de Syloc. My former overlord, he slew my wife and daughter.'

'Kill him,' one of the Welsh hissed.

'We would still be hunting for the children en route. And those of the Hooded who have disappeared,' Radewych said.

'The Christ of the East says it is a sin to kill,' Alain said, softly. 'But I have lost – kin. I know what the hurt is like. In my grief and rage, if I had had the luxury, if I had been capable,' he trailed off.

'Hunt them,' Gwion added, grinning.

'Kill them,' said Ifor.

Howell nodded. The dark-haired, silver-bearded, Welshman rarely spoke.

Wulfrun grinned. 'We head north.'

**

'You're sleeping with me tonight, lass.'

The bearded man was stretched out on the ground near the dying fire. The blond-haired man had moved out of the natural clearing to sleep.

Beate stared, wanting – but reluctant, also – to shake her head.

A coin appeared.

'I'm not trying to cheat you. Come lie beside me.'

She lay down next to him.

'No, lass. Face away.'

That, she didn't like.

He moved in tight and close to her, drawing his cloak over her. He put his hand inside her trews: forced it between her thighs, cupping her.

'I'm a heavy sleeper. If you're a thief, you won't get far, and it'll help my friend not think about having his way with you.'

He squeezed crudely, tightly, bringing tears to her eyes.

'After all, who are you going to scream out to? '

She could feel his breath in her hair.

'We'll fuck in the morning and then we'll see.'

**

'What news?'

Paol grinned at him. 'This is an old and dangerous place, Sheriff. I like it.' His eyes gleamed with fire. 'There is one of these Hooded I want. And one I have been tracking for a while.'

'The date is set for the tourney. Missives have gone to the cities, to the towns. Archers from all over the land will come. The prize of a silver arrow –'

'You think it will draw these wolves' heads into the open?' drawled the Irishman.

St. John nodded. 'It is to remind the peasants, the Pagans, the Anglo-Saxons, that the Normans are their overlords. Catching the Hooded –' he nodded. 'How can they not be tempted? Their man Hurnungaz has some Hel-like power with a bow.'

'Tell me more.'

The Sheriff refilled his goblet. The tall Irishman didn't drink. The man was no knight, but he had something – a wildness – that the likes of Sir Gisborough, for all his knightly training, could never match.

But where William could be controlled, this man – this man was an entirely different matter.

'There is a creature. The peasants speak of it. A forest god. Some say it is a stag. Some a girl.'

The man curled his lip.

'Oh, do not think less of her for that. She led the attack upon the cathedral site. Witnesses say she tore bodies apart and drank their blood.'

Paol scoffed. 'What nonsense! Why, they say that about me.'

'Hmm.' He stared thoughtfully at his man. He was kilted, wiry to the point of his bones almost being visible and there was madness in his eyes.

'I would like to match you against her. Against this Hurnungaz – formerly Robin of Loxley.'

'And his sister?'

The Sheriff blinked. 'You know he has a sister?'

Paol chuckled, and there was an edge to it. 'This forest keeps no secrets from me, Sheriff. Terrified, the rocks tell me. The trees flinch back. The rivers give up their secrets.'

'And you've not caught the Hooded.'

The man snorted, eyes narrowing. 'I've been leading your verderers. As you commanded. My lord,' he added sarcastically.

'I think your services would be better used hunting them.'

The Irishman nodded. 'I will reive them. This Hurnungaz, I will bring you his head. But there's two of them – two women – that I want. The rest I will simply kill.'

'That easily?' St. John mocked.

Paol stared at him, fire flashing in his eyes. 'Scáthach taught me well. So well she was no match for me in the end,' he grinned, baring his teeth. 'That was a joyous day. I will paint the forest with the blood of the Hooded.'

**

"Dearest brother.

"I hope this missive finds you well. It seems your whore, Warwick's daughter, is now a guest of the Abbess Winchester, and without any dowry to soften her stay.

"From what my mistress informs me, who accompanied Evgania to the nunnery, one Jenny of Nottingham, formerly of Loxley, stole her money, having first knocked out my brethren.

"Accordingly, I hold you responsible for what has happened to my brethren, and to Warwick's daughter. Unless you give me reason not to, I shall be writing to Warwick with news of his daughter. I know he has cast her out as a strumpet, but I doubt even a lord such as Warwick would want her in Winchester's care without easement.

"Your brother, the Abbot of Gresham.

Representative of The Christ of the East."

The Abbot sat back and re-read the missive. 'He will pay me for what this this Jenny did to my brothers. Knocked out, indeed. Who does she think she is?' he screamed.

'What of me, your Grace?'

He glanced up at his mistress. The sunlight streaming in caught her straw-gold hair and made it shine, for all it was cut unnaturally short. The robe she wore was belted at the waist; swelled pleasingly at her bust and hips.

He grinned. 'I think it is time I got you with child.'

**

'We could attack it.'

Bwyd glanced at the bear-warrior, Merik. 'We could, but to what end? The Abbot has no guards beyond a few old men-at-arms. Crossing Sherewode he hires guards.'

'He's rich though,' added Godwin.

Bwyd nodded. 'And the Sheriff's brother. What would be the advantage in murdering him?'

'It wouldn't be murder,' Llywarch argued, 'he's following a false god. It would be liberation.'

Bwyd grinned, shaking his head. 'Unprovoked. Attacking a representative of the Christ of the East? If it was that Brother Gascon, the mad Black Bishop, then yes. But Abbot de Hallowcross?'

He looked back across the grounds of Gresham Abbey. Shook his head. 'No. We wait and watch. If nothing happens in a day or two, we circle around and see what we can find.'

'And while we're waiting?' asked Tangwystl, grinning.

**

They paused for the night in a sheltered dell, just up from a tributary of the Trent. Yasha was on guard. Brother Blacwin was already asleep. Genilles and Myfanwy were wrapped in each other's cloaks, snug and deeply asleep.

'Bwyd said – you lost your wife a while ago?' Aneirin asked.

Tam looked up and nodded. 'Ay. Aoife died many a year ago. My children only a few years past.'

'And you've no one for company?'

He raised an eyebrow. 'I thought – Bwyd and you,' he trailed off.

She shook her head, thin lipped. 'No.'

Tam nodded, looking away. Trying not to look –

The robe she was wearing had slipped open: she was naked beneath it. Firelight played across her skin.

'This is a – terrifying time, Tam. We are outlaws. Normans hunt us. Something – terrifying – stalks the land, something that has already visited the Sælvatici. Visited me.' She grimaced. 'I would not be averse to company, even if it were only a warm body to hold me.'

'I lost,' he halted. Trembled. 'I lost the woman I loved a while ago. I had only my children, Aine and Callum. And then they were taken from me, murdered,' he drifted off again.

She rose and crossed to him. Put her hand on his knee. 'You may not be looking for sympathy, but wouldn't it be nice, for a few moments, to be lost in something – someone – else?'

'Aoife,' he said softly.

'I am not taking her place. Would she want you lonely? Would she object to a little portion of happiness?'

He looked up and met her gaze. 'I love her.' He licked his lips. Shuddered. 'It would be nice. It has been so long –'

She moved, straddling him, sitting on his lap, her robe falling away. 'You will have to keep me warm this night, Tam.'

**

'So you suggest?'

'Send missives to the nearby villages. Send them further afield. Until this Hurnungaz faces you in single combat, you call him a coward, skulking in the shadows. He is a boy, nothing more. Let him prove himself; if he defeats you,' Jenny grinned.

'He won't,' William glared at his squire.

'I know.' She smiled. 'But you have to give him hope. Give him a reason to face you. If he defeats you – you will take the King's Own away from here. If he does nothing, you will kill one person a day from a nearby village, proving his cowardice. And if you defeat him,' she chuckled.

'What?'

'Then promise the rest of his people will be free. It's a lie, of course. But separate him from them. A test of courage. Of swordsmanship. Not archery.'

William grinned, nodding. 'Kill their leader and they may scatter. But there's a King's Man – a *former* King's Man – among them, this Wulfrun of Scarsdale. He may be strong enough to lead them.'

'Find out what sent him to outlawry. There will be something you can use against him. He may have fought in the Holy Land; someone will know him, will have something against him.'

Gisborough nodded, grinning. 'Who else is amongst their number? Who or what else will draw him out?'

Jenny grinned. 'There is talk of a woman amongst his people. Muna, I think. No doubt he's fucking her. Capture her, and she'll draw him in for her rescue.'

He grinned. 'I like the way your mind works.'

'And my body.'

He nodded. 'But for the moment, your mind. I need to do something, I need to take action, before the King hears nothing has happened.' He frowned. 'Scouts, as well, to search for the boat of those damned foreigners. See if we can find anything about them; lay a trap for them if they try and leave this country.'

**

Ycenthwaite trudged. The night was black, without a moon. Slivers of cloud shrouded the overhanging trees, but he knew the path. He trudged on.

The air was thick and still. Cloying, fetid. As if it came from Hel –

Ycenthwaite turned, staring. The Old forest stared back at him, silently. He waited. The darkness variegated in blackness and purple-black, and green-black, and cloud-light reflected on glistening dampness. Moistness.

Sweat ran down his spine.

He stared. There *was* something there, he knew it. If he ran, if he looked away, it would pounce upon him, and then there would be no more Ycenthwaite.

No more Ycenthwaite. He sighed.

The Old forest was malevolent and malicious. Sheriff's-men, King's Men, brigands, murderers, Norse, Normans, Pagans, Saxons, the forest was full of them. The Celts, the Old Ænglish, were the worst of them. Offerings stuffed into dead trees to appease their Forest gods.

But they were all just human.

The darkness smiled.

Ycenthwaite shook his head. He was a fool, a moon-struck meanderist. There was nothing *in* the Old forest. It was just old. And dead. And that bishop, that man of the cloth of the Christ of the East, he was building a cathedral in its heart, burning it to ash and salting the ash and blessing it. Soon, nothing would remain.

He shook his head again and turned away.

The Girl god with yellow eyes stared at him, tilting her head this way and that. Her horns gleamed feral white. She bared her teeth, tasting the air, tasting his flavour. She had too many wicked, sharp, small, teeth. Teeth designed for tearing and rending.

Ycenthwaite stared, transfixed.

A wolf padded behind her. A wolf that wasn't quite right –

She was a Stag girl, a creature driven mad by her own existence. She was wolf-mother, stag-bitch, raven-crone, boar-harlot. She stared. Smiled.

'Ycenthwaite,' she crooned.

Ycenthwaite stared.

'Hunting game, Ycenthwaite?' she chuckled.

The wolf neared. Horns rose from its head, a stag's horns. There was no threat from it: no, the threat came from – *from* – he quailed.

The child of Cernunnos.

The mad godling.

Stag-daughter.

'Caerne,' he quailed, dropping his catch.

She snatched the hares before they hit the ground, biting deep into one, blood spraying. She rent the other, throwing portions to the wolf-creature.

He wondered could he shuffle away. His wife would scold him. Would berate him. Would remind him she liked him best when he wasn't there, she liked him best when he brought something to eat, not when he returned empty-handed. But at least he might return.

Caerne began licking her hands.

Ycenthwaite stared. Her hands – its hands – were lean and overlong. White skinned, human skin, though stag-fur mostly covered her.

'What – what are you?'

She laughed. 'You know what I am, mortal. You have granted me a favour. Fresh meat. Fresh hare for my hound. My Wulfenstæg. Do you like him?'

Ycenthwaite glanced around. Moonlight gleamed off black eyes that watched him. Saliva glistened on salivating jaws. A wet tongue that caught the last remnants of hare. It circled the clearing slowly, forcing him to turn, to keep his gaze upon the wolf-stag and the mad godling.

I must be mad.

'We are all mad,' Caerne giggled, pausing to lick the blood from her teeth, 'fear and lies. Terror and grief.'

He nodded. 'What must I do? Am I – a meal to you?'

Caerne peeled with laughter. The wolf took up the hysterical laughing sound, a feral fox in the fading light.

Ycenthwaite stared. I am moon-mad. Cursed. Delirious. I will wake up, and I will be dead, and it will be a relief.

'Ycenthwaite.'

He stared. The wolf padded back into the velvet-darkness of the warm forest.

'Ca – Caerne.'

She turned and followed the wolf, pausing on the edge of full darkness.

'Verderers hunt this night. One I have drowned, one I have hung, one I have taken to wear their head as a crown. Be ware, lest they hunt you.'

**

Muna studied them silently. She could sense the one who served the emptiness, the false god, the hollow shroud. They were no threat –

It was them! The voice in her head raged.

People like them.

They were the ones who buried me alive! They whipped the villagers into hatred, into fear. They were my undoing. I thought them harmless, a sop, meaningless. They betrayed our people. Turned them against me!

Muna winced at the voice shrieking in her head. The woman, the spirit, the witch, wise-woman, whoever she had been, the Christ of the East had obviously caused her death.

He is no threat. I do not sense Hurnungaz or Caerne, either.

The spirit raged. I want him!

She frowned. Unfamiliar scents. Wool and leather; a foreign scent. That was the one on guard. The stink of coupling.

Kill them all, the voice whispered.

No! I am Wōden's! Their deaths do not benefit Wōden.

They will sate me. You do not like being reminded of what peasants can do. What do you think Hurnungaz will do to you, if we do not defeat him. Drain him of his power. If you do not slay them, one of them may become aware of us. And I want that vessel of the empty god.

No.

**

'Do you – hate my sister?'

Mar looked up at Hugi and shook her head. 'No.'

'You – love her?'

She grimaced. 'No.' She sighed. 'She walks around Sherewode in just a white dress!' She scowled, shaking her head. 'Like staying in the shadows and being out of sight doesn't apply to her.'

Hugi raised an eyebrow.

'And I can see her tits!'

His eyebrow rose higher.

'I mean,' she shook her head. 'If I was a boy I'd be turned on. But I'm not. I'm annoyed,' she looked away.

'My sister – annoys you.'

She sighed, exasperated. 'I like,' she grimaced. 'I would like to be a boy. To hold her down. To take her. But I'm not a boy.'

'Girl.'

'Was it the tits, cunny or stretch marks that gave me away?'

Hugi smiled cautiously.

Mar rested back against him. She wasn't interested in him – or anyone – and he wasn't interested in – whatever she was. Even if there had been any interest, it was obvious they were physically incompatible.

'I don't want to be a girl.' She sighed softly.

He put an arm gently around her waist, the other around her chest, and it was nice being held.

'Is girl,' he rumbled softly.

She shook her head. 'I just want to be – violence. To,' she choked up. Looked away, surprised at herself.

'Grief. Rage. Helplessness. Sorrow. Terror.'

'You are Mar the assassin.' He raised his thigh, bouncing her as if she was a babe. 'You need black. Weapons.'

She smiled, and shifted sideways. 'Will you help me dig – a bed – tonight? I want to lie in the earth. But I want to lie on top of you. You keep me warm. You keep me safe.'

Hugi nodded. He drew her in closer and she nestled into him.

**

'It is time you were gone, John. I have risked too much for too long. If the Sheriff found out – if the King found out –'

'So I'm disposable –'

'I said –'

'Relax, lass.' He caressed Gloriana's belly, recently filled. 'Hereseige was never going to be in Yorkshire for long.'

She smiled, putting her hand over his. 'I have a gift for you before you go, however.'

John smiled. 'Doesn't have to, lass. These last few weeks,' he grinned. 'But truthfully, I've cooked all I know so many times over.'

Gloriana nodded. 'There is a reason for my gift. And not just – as thanks.'

John nodded, wondering if he could move his hand to caress her breast one last time.

'Her name is Angelica.'

He raised an eyebrow. 'Eh?'

'The Sheriff ensured I took her into safety. I think she's intended to be a spy on me.'

He frowned. 'Then why –'

'Because I don't want her here. Because she's young and female. Because I'm sure you could seduce her.'

He frowned. 'If she's no outlaw, a life in Sherewode's not for her.'

'She was a whore for the Sheriff. He struck her, abused her, all to make me take her in for her safety.' She sighed. 'The Sheriff intends to have some of the Black Bishop's brothers keeping me safe. Between them and her,' she shook her head.

'I don't know the lass. She should have an option –'

Gloriana snorted. 'Don't be naïve, John. She's peasant stock. A Moor, to boot. Her only value is her quim, her breasts, her mouth.'

'As opposed to your value,' he moved his hand to her breast.

She slapped his hand away.

'I'll have her sent to your chamber tonight. You'll take her – and I mean,' she glared at him, 'what you'll not get the chance to do with me again, John.' Her expression softened.

'A noble woman, married to the Sheriff of Nottingham, niece to the King. And a hunted man? A Saxon man.' She shook her head. 'My gift is the girl. Be gentle with her. Seduce her, take her away with you when you steal away in the night. Do not get caught!' she warned. 'Or all may be revealed.'

'And there's no chance,' he asked, trailing his fingers over her belly.

She slapped his hand away again. 'None from me. If you're still lustful, hie to your chamber. I will have her sent early. Sate yourself on her.'

**

Hurnungaz stared as the man moved into the centre of the bridge across the Trent.

'I know you,' the man smiled. 'I sense the Hel-spawn around you. Hurnungaz of the Hooded.'

Hurnungaz grinned. The bow was in his hand, arrows in their pouch at his hip –

'A fair contest, Hurnungaz. Swords. Yours against mine. Unless you're afeared?'

He chuckled. 'I could kill you here before you even draw sword.'

The man shrugged. There was a military bearing to him. Close cropped hair, a direct gaze.

'That you could try. But I'm fast.' He grinned. 'I would like to see how my skills fare against yours.'

'And you are?'

The man grinned. 'Your challenger. You can call me Geoffrey, since that's my name.'

'And what do I get if I defeat you?'

Geoffrey grinned. 'The sense of accomplishment, knowing you've bested a warrior who's seen long years in the King's service, both in the Holy Land and elsewhere.'

'And if I lose?'

'Hurnungaz,' protested Raven.

Geoffrey shook his head. 'This is a straight fight between you and I, Hurnungaz. Geoffrey versus – Robin, wasn't it?' He grinned. 'Your men go free at the end whatever happens. I merely wish to test my skill against yours.'

'Stick him,' Gwilim hissed.

Geoffrey chuckled. 'So you've got yourself some Welsh bowmen. Very wise. But this is not a competition of arrows on shields. This is swords. Unless,' he grinned. 'You might be a Pagan, Robin, but I think you honourable. I will not goad you with challenges of cowardice, since I know you are not.'

Hurnungaz nodded. 'For a warrior, you like to talk.'

Geoffrey drew his sword slowly. 'I've no wish for slaughter. To third blood?'

**

'I recognise those colours,' Wulfrun pointed at the dozen warriors skirting the edge of the woods they were in.

Alain was close behind him, uncertain and clumsy. The three archers, Gwion, Ifor and Howell were next in line, bows already drawn; Radewych at the end.

'De Syloc,' he grimaced.

'We can take a dozen,' Radewych answered.

Wulfrun glanced at those with him. 'The odds are –'

'I can fight,' Alain protested, 'I've had to before.'

He frowned. 'I thought you were more at home in Londinium.'

'I was,' he answered, almost petulantly. 'But I'm a scribe. I had to fight to get the training, to survive, to get a,' he trailed off.

'It's not the same as knife play, lad,' Wulfrun replied gently.

'But they hurt you!' Alain burst out, angrily.

One of the soldiers was looking up at the stand of trees.

'Gwion, Ifor, Howell,' ordered Radewych, 'loose!'

The three loosed: the soldier who'd turned fell. The others started scrambling for weapons.

Wulfrun glowered at Radewych.

'Concentrate on the edges. Bunch them in together. Take their knees or crotches if you daren't risk the head or the chest's armoured.'

The Welsh loosed.

The soldiers started coming up hill, some with drawn swords, others raising shields and hiding behind them.

'Don't worry about the shielded ones,' Radewych ordered, 'we'll take them out.'

'When they near –'

'I know how to fight!' Wulfrun cursed.

Radewych faced him calmly. He noticed, out of the corner of his eye, another soldier fall.

'We hit their ends, spin round, come at them before they can turn. When they turn,' Radewych grinned. 'They're caught between us.'

'I wasn't planning to charge head-first into the middle of them.'

'Good. Leave one alive to question.'

He glowered at her. She stared back calmly.

Another fell. Half a dozen were nearing, hiding behind shields. Two flagged behind. The rest were down or dead.

Radewych drew her swords.

The Welsh loosed: arrows weighed on shields, but none fell.

'Ullr! For Freya and Iseulde! The Hooded!'

Wulfrun flung himself out of the trees, axes in hands, crashing into the middle of the ragged shield wall deliberately, surging through and sending the soldiers falling back.

Radewych screamed a war cry.

The Welsh started singing, deep and wordless.

One came at him, stupidly only holding his shield. Wulfrun snagged the shield and pulled. As the man stumbled, he brought his second axe down on the man's unprotected head.

'Ullr! The Hooded!'

One of the soldiers flung his shield at him; Wulfrun dodged it and the man charged, sword in hand.

'Where's your parrying weapon?' Wulfrun screamed at him, blocking his sword, using the other to break the man's nose.

He crumpled, blood streaming down his face.

A limb flashed past, trailing streams of blood. A quick glance showed Radewych working coolly, methodically.

'Freya!' He bellowed.

Another soldier fell, spitted by arrows.

He heard a sound: glanced back. A soldier had been sneaking past, heading for the archers, but Alain had moved out of the shadows, dagger in hand, trying to stop him.

'Help Radewych!' he screamed, moving to help Alain, but he was too far away as the soldier pushed the youngster to the ground, drawing back his arm.

**

The tourney ground was taking shape pleasingly. He had selected a large, mostly flat, area, beyond the walls of Nottingham but close enough to be seen from the walls.

Barracks were being built. The land was being levelled so there could be knightly tourneys – which no Anglo-Saxon would ever be permitted to be a part of – in addition to the archery contest, wrestling, and whatever else could be thought up.

One side of the field rose gently; the peasants and Pagans could stand there.

'You would elevate the peasants, my lord?' asked his seneschal.

'I was just considering having them all slain after the event.'

'I am not sure the King –'

St. John waved the worried man's comments away. 'They are His peasants.' He scowled. 'Mine, really. Without them I get no tax money, no grain,' he shook his head. 'And still this Hel-archer, Hurnungaz, has their loyalty.'

'Everyone dreams of freedom, my lord. He is an – inspiring – figure.'

St. John turned. 'You are inspired by a wolf's head?'

The seneschal shook his head hurriedly. 'No, my lord. But those who live in the mud, they dream of him. They dream of freedom, an easier life, wenches –'

'Fah,' the Sheriff snapped. 'They are lazy. They do not work as hard as they should. Perhaps I should increase the taxes to pay for this for them.'

'You could –'

He scowled. 'Come out with it! I have no time for an indecisive man!'

'Perhaps – a mumming play, my lord. With this hooded hero figure being killed at the end. Or a hanging.'

St. John scowled. 'They sing of these Hooded. They are heroes to the minstrels, the poets, the,' he shook his head. 'A mumming play. A peasant, Anglo-Saxon thing.' He grinned. 'But a hanging.'

'It could be more – involving. My lord.'

He arched an eyebrow.

'Give a prisoner the chance for release. They simply need beat one of your soldiers in combat. They never will win, but the peasants will root for them. When they die at the hand of your man –'

The Sheriff grinned. 'I like it! We need to ensure we have some worthy prisoners. Send for Paol.'

**

'You are not going out looking like that!'

Abbot Simon glowered at Lucianna. She was wearing a long, loose, white robe that he always liked seeing her in for the fact it was sheer.

But now Lucianna filled it, her belly beginning to show, her breasts beginning to swell.

'Your Grace,' she murmured. 'I can still carry out my duties.'

'And when – anyone – sees you are pregnant?' he shook his head. 'No. I will not have the scandal. You will remain in this room until your time. You can still service me, never fear.'

'What about – this tourney that your brother is arranging?'

'You think I am going to parade my mistress, a pregnant whore, on my arm?'

'Your Grace!'

'You seduced a woman, Lucianna! Evgania might be safely locked up by the Abbess Winchester, but your sin still shows.'

'It is not my sin that shows, your Grace.'

He back-handed her and she fell, half bouncing off the bed and falling to the floor.

'Remember what happened to your mother,' he hissed. 'I can have you whipped from my grounds at any time.'

'I carry your child, your Grace!'

He knelt beside her, drawing his belt knife and pressing the edge into her cheek.

'Do you know what the Black Bishop will do to me if he discovers this? You are vile in his eyes already. I will be –' he shuddered. 'I do not know what he will do to me. But I suspect I would no longer be the Abbot, and I like my position here.'

She stared up at him, terrified, but still with a spark of defiance in her eyes.

'Would you like to serve the Abbess? I could send you to her. Without dowry.'

She stared, horror-stricken, tears in her eyes.

'Please, your Grace,' she whimpered.

He grinned, returning the knife to his belt. 'Remember, you are my property, Lucianna. I can dispose of you as I please.'

**

'Do I scare you?'

Bwyd stared at Caerne. The Girl god was leaning against a tree, her eyes half closed. He could see the lazy spiral of the yellow in her eyes. She shifted her thighs, stamping her hooves.

But behind the trees – there was perfect darkness.

Starless.

Treeless.

Just – nothing.

He looked around. He wasn't in the grove they'd settled in for the night. There wasn't anyone else around either.

'Where?'

'Am I dreaming?'

She waited, arms crossed over her chest.

'Yes,' he answered, dry mouthed. 'Where am I?'

She shook her head. 'Good,' she answered, pushing away from the tree. 'You are necessary to me. You must commit yourself to me, but it is pleasing to know you are terrified of me.'

'What must I – do?'

She smiled, sweetly. 'You must die.'

**

They stopped on the edge of a tract of marshy ground. Night was falling and the sky was clouded.

'Will we end in the Trent if we carry on this way tomorrow?' Aneirin asked.

Tam wrapped his cloak around himself, settling back against a tree trunk. Here and there, still visible, a mostly-dead tree broke the surface of the swampy ground.

'I am not sure. Much of Sherwood is known to me, but not this part.'

'It is far from where I know,' Brother Blacwin answered.

'Why,' Tam frowned. 'Are you learning – what you hoped to learn?'

The brother smiled. Genilles was on guard duty; Myfanwy already asleep. Yasha was awake, her eyes bright.

'I do not know,' he answered honestly. 'We are taught Pagans are – wild. Undisciplined. Nasty and dirty, they should be – for their own good – converted or eradicated.'

Aneirin chuckled. 'One word, and a wild heathen might slit your throat.'

The brother smiled, shaking his head. 'That is what we are taught. I believe in the Christ of the East. I loved – I love – supporting those in my charge. And yet if what we are taught in any way is –' he shook his head. 'It will take a far more learned man that I to figure it out.'

'Or a learned woman,' snapped Aneirin.

Tam hid his smirk.

Brother Blacwin nodded. 'Of – course. But I mean.' He sighed. 'Perhaps my faith is at fault. Perhaps I am not strong enough.'

Tam snorted. 'You trusted in – something – to ask to stay with us.'

'It was obvious,' the brother smiled, 'there was honour. You fight – for a better world? That is what I try to do, in my way.'

'Except your Black Bishop burns our homeland and would have us hung if he caught us.'

The brother nodded to him. 'Yes.' He sighed again. 'That is what I will have to figure out.'

**

'A man of de Syloc's?'

His squire nodded. 'A man who proved his worth many times over. The King himself wanted Scarsdale to stay on; the man was a favourite amongst his men.'

'And when he came home?'

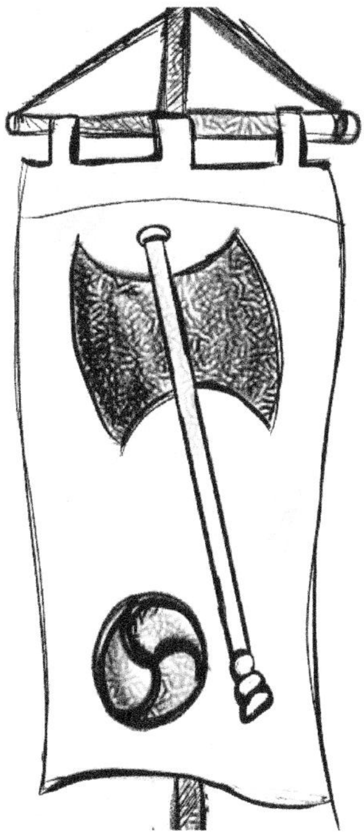

'De Syloc and de Saintcrow killed his family. Destroyed his home. Pillaged his people. Wulfrun,' she shrugged. 'They wanted him hurt but didn't dare kill him in case the King heard.'

Gisborough shook his head. 'So now we've got a highly skilled – and pissed off – member of the King's Own running round with the Hooded.'

'I do not know what led him here. He is Norse; my,' she grimaced, 'my wench-chasing brother is a Pagan, an Anglo-Saxon.'

Gisborough arched an eyebrow. 'And what of the messengers to the villages?'

She shook her head. 'No response yet.' She drew another piece of parchment. 'The Sheriff of Nottingham asks for you and the King's Own to return to Nottingham. He is sketching a plan to entrap the Hooded and teach the peasants a lesson in humility.'

'You are an Anglo-Saxon.'

'Yes, my lord.'

'And how do you feel about that?'

Jenny grimaced. 'I am of Nottingham now, not Loxley. I would be of Gisborough,' she trailed off, catching his gaze.

'A knight ploughing his squire –'

'I am more than just your squire, my lord.'

Gisborough stared at her. 'I know the joys of your cloven inlet –'

'And yet you do not –'

'I don't want you pregnant,' he growled, half rising to his feet.

'I can make it so that I do not.' She glared at him. 'You say you like my mind and my body but this cannot be; I can never marry you.'

Gisborough grimaced. 'You *are* minor Anglo-Saxon nobility.'

'Both the Sheriff and York want Loxley. The Sheriff will not give it up, and even if he did, I cannot rule it. I am a woman.'

'But your child would.'

She stared at him.

'What are you saying?' she asked after a while.

'Once your brother is dead, we will go to York. With her support –'

'Why would she support you?' Jenny frowned.

'She is the Sheriff's wife. It is not a loving relationship. If you worked – for a period – as her maid, or similar. Her recognition would raise you.'

'Would you settle for just Loxley?'

Gisborough grinned. 'It would be a start. Once Robin is dead, my star will be in ascendant. With that to support me, and York's support for you –'

'But why?' she insisted. 'I am just – an outlaw's sister. The Sheriff's former whore.'

Gisborough smiled. 'You are so much more.'

**

Muna scowled. How long will it take them to return to Hurnungaz? I need Hurnungaz –

I – we – need Caerne. We need her – destroyed.

But a man –

You're dead –

Through you, the voice, barely female at times, raged. I am alive. There is a brother of the Christ of the East. We can steal in during the night. Slay him –

It benefits us not. They do not realise they are being tracked.

The voice gibbered with laughter. A Welsh warrior woman. Two young Welsh more interested in each other than any other. The Highland man. A woman from overseas. The brother. We could kill them all in their sleep.

They will lead us back to Hurnungaz. My brother will have taken care of Mar by now.

Mar; the shade, the spirit, grimaced. She will not weaken Hurnungaz or Caerne.

She was – Muna shook her head. The voice was getting stronger. Even since the barrow and the attack by Paol –

I am free! The spirit screamed. They buried me alive and I will kill them all.

No! For Wōden we will drain Hurnungaz; kill Caerne. Then we will see.

**

'Is – wise?'

'Probably not.' Mar grinned. 'But we have no choice.'

They were lurking at the edge of a trackway. A cart pulled by a single horse was coming down it, with one man walking in front and two sitting in the front of the cart.

Mar staggered out from the trees, coming to a halt in the middle of the trackway. She heard a voice from the cart; glanced at it and back in the woods as if there was something to fear following her.

'Hold lass, what's the rush?'

'There's something,' Mar turned to face them, making an act of covering herself. 'I only just got away. I think he was following me.'

One of them snorted. 'This is Sherewode. All manner of things lurk here. You were lucky you weren't killed.'

'Can you help me?'

'What do you need?' the man at the front was drawing close; pale brown hair.

'And how'll you pay us?' the third leered.

The first man glared at the two on the cart. 'We're from the village of Leavingstone. Taking corn to sell. We've not much, miss.'

'Do you have – a spare shift or some cloth? Something – I can sneak back home in. I don't like being – naked in the forest.' She shivered.

One of the men on the cart sniggered. 'Seems we don't often find naked maids.' He exchanged a look with the man beside him.

Mar tensed: knew Hugi was close, watching as well, ready to come out and scare the men off.

'I'm a married man, lass,' the man at the front said, smiling. 'The name's Harald.' He grinned, jerking his thumb at the two men on the cart. 'Ignore them. They're just happy to get a few days to themselves.'

'I'm no –'

Harald grinned. 'If my wife knew I'd been talking to, let alone seen a naked woman, she'd,' he shook his head. 'I love her dearly,' he trailed off expectantly.

'Mar.'

'I love her, Mar, she's a good and bounteous woman.' He kept his eyes on her face, 'If you understand what I mean.'

Mar nodded.

'I keep my own company at night. But if you wanted to join us for a night or two, we can take you south, towards Beaurepaire?'

Mar nodded, grateful. 'That'd be good, thank you.' She glanced back at the woods, hoping Hugi was close enough to hear.

'Here,' Harald said, offering her a piece of woollen cloth and a scarf. 'If you'll cover yourself up, the boys are mostly interested in each other, but I'm sure you don't want to be walking around naked.'

Mar flashed him a quick smile. The one time I want someone to try something. Oh well.

**

'What do you want of me, my lord?'

She looked up at him fearfully.

John shook his head. 'York has given you to me.'

'Yes, my lord.'

She was wearing a simple shift and skirt. Before he could stop her, she had removed them.

'There's no need for that. I'm not here to –'

'Do I not appeal to you, my lord? Is It because of the colour of my skin?'

John shook his head. 'No! I think you're beautiful. But that's not –'

'I am your pleasure-thing, my lord. Few have seen a Moorish girl before. You can touch me. Do whatever you want to me.'

John scowled, exasperated. 'No!'

'Would you prefer a boy, my lord? You can use my bottom.'

John sighed. 'No. Look,' he pointed to the tin bath and the cooling water.

'Ah! You want me to scrub you. If you will get in –'

'No!' he rolled his eyes. 'It was so much easier in Sherewode.'

'What was easier in Sherewode?'

John shook his head again. 'York has given you to me as a gift, on the understanding I take you with me. I am leaving tonight.'

She stared at him. 'Oh!'

'She – knows – you are a spy for Nottingham.'

Angelica bowed her head. 'I understand.'

'What do you understand?'

'You will take me into the forest. No one will see me again.'

'No!' He pointed at the bath again. 'Get in and clean yourself.'

She frowned. 'I am – dirty to you?'

He rolled his eyes. 'Angelica, I am taking you away from York. She wants you freed. I am taking you to some friends.'

'And they will –'

'You will not be a slave, Angelica. You can stay with them, become one of them, or journey on elsewhere. Returning to Nottingham, however,' he shook his head.

'You do not want to – use me?'

'I am not as young as you Angelica. I do not know you. In time,' he shrugged. 'I have had lovers before. There has always been time spent getting to know them before we – made love.'

He blushed. 'Not that I – necessarily –'

'If I – wash as you want, my lord, may I kneel before you afterwards and – thank you.'

'First off, lass, my name is John.'

'Yes, my lord.'

'My name is John.'

'Yes, my lord.'

'John.'

'I –' she broke off. 'I was whipped for using people's names. I was a – commodity. The parts of me that men would want. They wanted to know if a girl with skin my colour,' she glanced at the bath. 'If everything worked the same.'

'I want you to get into the bath, Angelica. I will then scrub your back.'

'My lord!' she gasped, looking up at him. 'It is not right for a lord to scrub a whore's back.'

'Lass, you're no whore. You're a free woman.'

She shook her head. 'I cannot be free. I have nothing. In this country, I am property. I am a whore.'

John sighed. 'Okay. Let's start with you having a bath. If you're not a free woman, then I command you to get into the water.'

**

'Stop, thief!'

Beate sprang off like an arrow loosed from a bow before she realised she hadn't stolen anything. It wasn't Nottingham, thankfully, not that she ever wanted to go back to Nottingham.

The bearded man had given her two coins for using her both ways and she'd managed to keep the coins safe, and survived on her charm, wit and tits.

What the two coins might buy her she didn't know, but it was a small marketplace and she had no need to steal anything –

A hand caught her and lifted her off her feet.

She wriggled and twisted, pulling free –

Another punched her in the stomach and she fell to the muddy ground.

Was hauled up. Struck across the face –

She gasped, crying in pain.

'Thief!'

'Here,' another said, digging fingers into her jaw. 'She's no tongue.'

'Thief,' another echoed.

She was struck again.

'Take her to the cages! She can be tried in the morning.'

**

Hurnungaz stepped back, breathing heavily. Of small consolation, Geoffrey was also breathing fast.

'You fight well Robin. Hurnungaz. Which do you prefer?'

Hurnungaz snorted. 'I was Robin. Now, I am Hurnungaz.'

The warrior nodded. 'Hurnungaz it is. Many an hour we've now fought, and I don't think either has bested the other.'

Hurnungaz inclined his head. Englara and Madoc remained sharp and alert. Raven was scowling. Gwilim and Tegwared were busy searching for branches to use for arrows.

'This is not some trap.'

The man seemed to read his mind. He looked back. The man was mopping his brow.

'You fight well. Oh, there is no troop of soldiers waiting to rush in. Did you ever fight for your lord in the Holy Land?'

Hurnungaz shook his head. 'My place is here, defending my people and Sherewode against the Black Bishop, the Sheriff of Nottingham and others.'

Geoffrey shrugged. 'Perhaps.' He smiled. 'How are we to resolve this? Our skills seem equally matched. Have you been holding back?'

Hurnungaz grinned. 'We shall see, shall we not?' He stepped up onto the bridge once more. 'By the dark breath of earth.'

**

Three arrows struck the soldier and he spun, falling away from Alain.

The remaining soldiers wavered. Radewych swung and took one out, their body crumpling. The three scattered, dropping shields.

Wulfrun nodded at the Welsh.

They nocked and loosed. Nocked and loosed. Nocked and loosed.

The three fleeing soldiers of de Syloc's fell.

'Are you alright lad,' he asked, crossing to Alain and offering his arm.

The youngster took it. Wulfrun couldn't help but notice how small the man's hand was.

'Thank you.'

'We saw the warrior coming,' said Howell, a grimace crossing his face. 'But thank you for trying.'

'You could have got yourself killed,' said Radewych, looking up from where she knelt, cleaning her weapon on the clothing of the dead soldiers. 'So it was a brave thing to do.'

Alain – blushed.

Hid it furiously when he saw him looking.

Wulfrun looked away. 'De Syloc – never had that many soldiers. We – I – need to find where he's staying, how many he has with him.'

'Any of them left alive?' asked Alain, fanning his face.

Wulfrun grinned. 'Let's see, shall we.'

**

'You sent for me?'

St. John raised an eyebrow. 'The correct form of address is, "My lord".'

Paol chuckled, bowing from the waist yet never taking his eyes off him. 'My lord,' he said, the sneer obvious.

'I have decided,' he hesitated.

He is mad. Powerful. But mad. I will need to find something to hold over him. Something – someone – to use against him.

'I have decided there will be a tourney, just outside of Nottingham. I want you to track these Hooded. I want prisoners.'

He took a swig of his ale, ignoring Paol's grin.

'Alive.'

'They are so much more fun when they are dead.'

'But you won't get paid if they're dead. I want them – alive – so they can be hung at the tourney. Entertainment for the masses.'

Paol grinned. 'Can I hurt them?'

St. John nodded. 'Of course. Not their faces; I want them recognisable. I'm sure you can find a few – expendable parts. But I want bodies to hang, recognisable outlaws.'

Paol grinned. 'Robin and his sister.'

The Sheriff shook his head. 'Jenny is assisting Gisborough. She is proving useful.'

Paol chuckled. 'She is a Saxon. Saxons die.'

St. John shrugged. 'It is up to you. The main thing is, that this Hurnungaz and his people are caught. Gisborough –

assisted by Jenny – are hunting them. Gisborough has one hundred of the King's Own to assist him. You?'

'Me?' Paol drawled. 'I need no one getting in the way. Gisborough is a knight. Limited in who he is and what he does. I am not so hindered.'

'Do you need anyone to assist you? Verderers, soldiers?'

Paol curled his lip. 'I hunt best alone.'

**

'So, medic,' the Abbot grinned. 'How certain are you on the figures you gave?'

'Absolutely certain, your Grace. Sir Richard trusts me.'

'And this – boy of his?'

'A foreign child. Dying. The girl, Angel – surely, in itself, an affront to the Christ of the East – is lively and bright. She will make someone a good wife, once she is reined in and tempered.'

'What is her age?'

'She looks to be twelve, perhaps.'

The Abbot nodded greedily. 'This will strip Sir Richard of his money. His adopted daughter can then be offered for sale, her virginity commanding a higher price. See to it the girl remains innocent.'

The medic bowed. 'Yes, your Grace. When will Brother Gascon visit Sir Richard?'

The Abbot waved the question away. 'I want you to return. Suggest more treatments. Bleed every penny from him.'

'You want his property?'

Abbot Simon smiled. 'That is not your concern, medic. You will be well reimbursed. Once Verysdale Hall and grounds are mine.'

The medic inclined his head. 'Yes, your Grace.'

He dismissed him; the man withdrew.

The Abbot grinned. 'Foreign children, as well. Harboured by a traitor in our midst. Children who came to this land on boats.' He took a swig of his wine. 'Things are going to go poorly for Sir Richard, oh yes.'

**

Bwyd gasped, coming to life, choking, gasping for breath. He tried to sit up, banged his head and half-collapsed.

He stared. A blood-soaked girl lay beneath him: he was in some kind of burrow.

'What?'

The girl opened her eyes and blinked eyes of the purest, deepest, green.

'Caerne?'

She smiled viciously. 'Your death has reinvigorated me, Bwyd. You are no longer Sælvatici: you are mine.'

'I am –' he began to protest.

Her hands tore his back and he collapsed, falling onto her. He shuddered, feeling the blood flow.

'Where – am I? What – have you done?'

She smiled. 'He copes better than you thought he would, Wenlock.'

Bwyd turned his head, started. He was sure, in that moment of speaking, that the burrow had simply increased in size.

A dark haired man was stretched out beside him, an almost-grin in his eyes.

'I am Wenlock. I am the last of the Old Ænglish. I have been watching Hurnungaz and his Hooded for a very long time.'

Bwyd blinked. 'How did I get here?'

Wenlock chuckled. 'The Old one – the *previous* Old one – brought Mar from Erin to this land. Like her, I can,' he grinned. 'We are tied to the earth and not tied to a physical location as strongly as those who have come after us.'

He looked back at Caerne. 'What?'

'I killed you. I took you into me. I bore you anew.'

Bwyd blinked. 'What?'

Caerne took his hands and put them on her belly.

He stared, feeling the oceans roar, feeling her heartbeat, aware of the feel of her horns, the constant itchiness of her tail, the heaviness of her hooves, the empty longing, deep inside of her, that nothing could fill –

The longing for – answers. Family. Kin. She was the daughter of a god, the daughter of Cernunnos, born in the slaying of a stag by Robin, born of the Forest, the spirit of Sherewode –

He shook his head. 'How are you – sane?'

She chuckled. 'I am not sane. I am a god. I do not need worshippers but I need family. Sciuridae is dead. He was my kin. You are my reborn son.'

'And Hurnungaz?'

'My – half brother?' she stretched impressively, and the burrow changed again.

There was a huge wolf-kin stretched out on the other side of them.

Bwyd stared, but the creature simply licked its lips.

'In my belly and at my breast, Bwyd, you have learned much. You will never match Hurnungaz' power, but what you do feeds into me as I have fed and given you power.'

'What about – I was – we were watching Gresham Abbey?'

'You will return shortly.' She smiled, caressing his arms. 'I will come for Hurnungaz soon. There is much still to be done. Ullr and Wōden are stirring, their pets are rising.'

'What must I do?'

'You will know.'

**

Tam froze. It was still early; mist shrouded the swampy ground. But the movement had come from elsewhere.

Something heads for us.

He shuffled, as if dreaming, straining to hear.

The crackling sound, of an incautious foot breaking a twig, did not repeat. But still –

There was sudden movement. The twang and whistle of an arrow.

Tam opened his eyes and moved. Aneirin was up and loosing: half a dozen figures were stalking them: seeing movement, they charged.

'Hooded! For the Highlands!' Tam bellowed, getting to his feet and grabbing an axe.

Genilles and Myfanwy were kneeling, loosing into the attackers. Yasha stood up, sword and club in hand. Brother Blacwin sat up, clutching at a small knife.

Another of the attackers fell, but Tam saw a second group behind the first.

'Hooded!' he yelled again.

Three were closing in on their position. He moved with Yasha to stand between the attackers and the brother.

One of the three fell, gasping and clutching for a moment.

'Concentrate on the second wave!'

The mist seemed to be all around them. He struck and parried, hearing Yasha doing the same.

Sparks struck and burned in the strange, dry mist.

He could hear the whistle of arrows, Aneirin and the other two Sælvatici targeting the second group.

But something was still –

'Third group!' called Aneirin.

His opponent was down; so was Yasha's. Four were rushing them, two injured, and behind them another half dozen, though the Welsh were already targeting them.

The air was filled with the sounds of ravens. With monstrous cawing and the stench of burning flesh. With the impression of shadowy wings.

Tam coughed, trying not to choke.

'They buried me alive!' a voice screamed.

The onrushing four half stumbled; Tam dispatched his two easily, as did Yasha.

A body crashed into the ground in front of them, broken-limbed, having been thrown into the air. One of their grey-robed attackers.

The last group of six had one remaining. And he dangled, grasped by the neck by a figure in white.

Tam stared.

It was Muna, and yet –

She seemed to tower, wings scattering the mist. She hurled him to one side: the man crashed into a tree and collapsed.

Muna – sported wings. Her eyes were liquid fire. The dress was sheer and her body was youthful and ripe.

'I'm back,' she snarled, heading for Aneirin.

**

'Well, my lord,' asked Jenny, 'do we stay or do we return to Nottingham?'

Gisborough scowled. 'Are any of the villagers left alive?'

'Very few.' He could see her trying not to smile. 'Berenger grows frustrated. He may message the King.'

He scowled. 'This – sitting here – has not worked.' He stood up. 'It is time we moved. Prepare a route to Nottingham. Pass as many villages as possible. We will let the peasants know what comes of supporting wolf's heads.'

'And me, my lord?'

He frowned. 'What of you?'

'Am I still your squire? Nottingham knows me, thinks me, a whore.'

Gisborough took a step towards her, wrapping an arm around her waist and pulling her close.

'You might have been a whore, but you are my whore now. And squire. I do not know if a whore or a squire can become a lady, but we shall try.' He grinned, holding her tighter, closer, for a kiss. 'Armour me then armour yourself. Make sure your face is covered. The Hooded are out there. I do not want them knowing you are with me.'

She kissed him passionately.

'When we ride,' she grinned, 'think of me. In a proper bed once more,' she promised.

**

'Where – are we?' Hugi asked.

Mar grinned. Harald and the two men from Leavingstone had taken her south for two days as promised.

'Nottingham is that way,' she pointed, 'we need to get under cover. This is a main route.'

He nodded; Mar could see he was tired. Two days of having to follow the cart without being seen; without giving any clue to the three villagers she'd been with that they were being followed.

The two days had also – she grimaced. I am Mar. I am Amar. I was Amarinatha. She shuddered. I was, I am, female. I love women. I would rather be a boy; I would rather have women as a boy.

She sighed. There is no way that can be.

'What's – wrong?'

She looked up at Hugi and patted his arm.

'We will find somewhere to rest. Then I will tell you.'

'Is because – girl?'

She shook her head. I miss the feel of a blade in my hand. She sighed, deeper. *He* is here now, and I am next to naked. Not defenceless, but without a weapon, without Hurnungaz and Wulfrun and the others –

She led the way through a thicket, ignoring the thorns that scratched at her face and arms, her legs. Hugi followed her, brushing them aside, almost oblivious.

They found an oak at the centre, tilted and leaning over, but with an almost burrow-like space at its roots. She lay down, worn out herself, her feet bloodied and bruised, sore and chapped from the heat of the forest.

'Lie down. Curl up. You've kept me safe; let me keep you safe for a while.'

Hugi folded up, all leg bones and bony arms. He curled so his head was in her lap, a monstrous crow head.

She rested her hand on his shoulder. 'Sleep, Hugi. I will keep you safe.'

She closed her eyes, letting her senses extend.

**

Beate grimaced, shifting onto her side. The gaoler had been thorough, having his way with her both ends in return for a mouthful of ale and a lump of hard bread.

So. They hang me in the morning for being a thief.

She sighed softly. And I never even got to spend my coin. She clutched her thin clothing tighter. It was late night, bitterly cold, and dawn was a ways off.

They can't hang me if I die of a chill first.

Such a long way, she thought. And this is as far as I got.

She sighed again.

I wonder is it even true, what my mother said, what those Norse said, before they threw me out.

A daughter of –

**

'I should not be riding, my lord!'

John glanced over his shoulder, trying not to scowl. 'I am no lord, Angelica. I am known as Hereseige John. I am – of the forest. Lady Gloriana of York wanted you – free of York. Free of any debt to the Sheriff of Nottingham.'

He stroked the pony's neck. 'I don't know where my friends are. If they had died – it has been months since I last saw them – then I think I would have heard. So, it's best if you ride, Angelica. I'm used to walking. You're – not.'

'I am a whore,' she muttered, but under her breath.

'My friends – if you want to stay with them, you will be welcome to. They will prove you are no whore, Angelica. You can be who you want to be.'

'I want to be Angelica,' she scowled. 'The Sheriff, he only hit me so York would take me in. You should take me to him.'

John shook his head. 'No, lass. The Sheriff's – not a good man. He'll hurt you.'

She scowled but didn't answer.

Hereseige stroked the horse's mane as they walked. The silence was good. He'd almost had to knock Angelica out to get her out of York's castle.

Will she want to stay?

Will Hurnungaz, Wulfrun, Bwyd and the others still be in the forest? I would have heard – the Hooded are well known. Feared and looked up to. Had the Sheriff caught them – or that Black Bishop – there would have been news, surely.

**

'Why didn't you kill him?' Raven asked.

Hurnungaz grinned. 'I had defeated him. He knew and accepted I won; was the better swordsman.'

Englara shook her head. 'You should have slain him. Such a warrior will turn up again.'

'And now he knows how you fight,' Tegwared added.

Hurnungaz grinned. 'He was most unlike a knight, true. A warrior from the Holy Land, yes. But,' he sighed. 'So far our searches have turned up nothing. The children must be out there. So, I hope, is Mar and Muna. Even Hugi.'

He sighed. 'We will carry on to Edwinstowe. It's only a small hamlet; if there's no word there, we'll circle around the cathedral site and look for the others.' He looked at Raven. 'In answer to your question, yes, I could have killed him. But what would it have gained me?'

Raven frowned.

Hurnungaz nodded slowly. 'True, he's seen some faces and he knows my fighting style now, but I don't think he was holding anything back. Whoever he might be, he's not gained a lot.'

'He knows you are in the forest,' said Englara.

He grinned. 'The forest is a wide, deep, dark, place. Sherewode has its secrets. Even if they flooded the forest with soldiers from all the lords and towns within the forest, there would not be enough to find us. And while they searched the forest, we would be elsewhere.'

'It's too dangerous to go into the towns,' warned Gwilim.

'Says he who's barely left Marcher lands,' said Tegwared.

Madoc chuckled but didn't speak.

'And there's those – King's Own,' added Raven.

Hurnungaz nodded. 'Gisborough sits in a village, waiting for us to fall into a trap. He will realise, soon, that we are not biting.'

**

She was on her back and someone – something – knelt over her.

It's a coin, she wanted to say, but if you can get me away from here it's free.

The person was hooded, their face shadowed.

Fingers touched her. Roamed up and down her, prying, pinching, penetrating.

She stared up resolutely at whoever they were. I will not cry. I will not cry. I will not –

Their hands were on her breasts. A tongue licked the tears from her cheeks.

'You taste,' they hissed.

They sat up, sitting on her belly.

'You don't cry out, you make no attempt to escape.'

Beate glowered at them. Howled, opening her mouth, but only the faintest sound came out.

They shifted again, stretching out over her, gazing into her eyes.

Beate could swear she could almost see yellow in their eyes.

'I have need of you, but I have need of more than you.'

They leant in and she was spreadeagled helpless beneath them, their hands holding her wrists, hooves clamping her ankles – and they thrust their tongue into her mouth, filling her, breathing into her, until it felt as if her whole body was aflame.

**

Wulfrun waited. The moon rose and fell. Stars crossed the sky and disappeared. The sun rose and fell. Days –

'Movement, Wulfrun.'

He opened his eyes. They were waiting on the edge of the forest, hidden from sight, overlooking a small manor house not far from Scarsdale.

The manor house was surrounded by several well-tended fields. No trees grew, no streams or rivers flew, and with its slight rise, the house had a good view over the surrounding territory.

'Was this – where you used to live?' asked Alain, timidly.

He smiled at the youngster. 'Near here. My feudal lord, de Syloc, wanted my wife and my property. He always was a coward.'

A dozen figures stirred from the house, on horseback. Leading them was a tall, black-bearded man.

Wulfrun stared.

'Did you think you could get away with your petty insults?'

De Saintcrow had spoken thus, a typical knight, thinking everything was owed to him. De Syloc was not much better, and now he rode with a dozen men.

'Three of these Welsh,' said Radewych. 'You and I. A dozen mounted warriors. It will be a good fight.'

Wulfrun nodded.

'If we loose, will he flee back in or will he charge?'

Wulfrun shook his head. 'I don't know. He had men at arms, a few cavalry when I was – his man. We've already killed some. I'd say his territory, his power, has increased. A much more influential man. I doubt he will run.' He grimaced, glancing at the Welsh. 'But wait. I want him further from the house. Nearer, before we attack.'

Iseulde. Freya. I am sending de Syloc to you, if he is worthy of the Halls, that is.

**

'Is my brother dying?'

Sir Richard knelt down beside Angel. 'I fear he is. I do not know why.' He sighed. 'That is why that important man was here.'

'I didn't like him.'

He nodded, smiling sadly. 'He is a very important person. A religious man. I hoped, a blessing from him, might make your brother better. But Deederich is slipping away. He might not last long.'

She looked up at him with big eyes, wide, a glimmer of moisture in them.

'I am sorry, Angel. I will continue to do all I can for him. You survived, you are stronger. Do you know why you are healthy and he is not?'

She shook her head.

Deederich lay on a couch on the edge of the garden, close to the stream. Two servants stood near him, fanning him conscientiously. The medic was with him as well, reading a treatise in a soft voice.

I hope for a response to my letters. Three of my friends, I am sure will be able to assist. The other two I am hopeful for. To be in debt to the Abbot –

'Where we – came from. We were orphans. The man who took us in, he took us hunting and feasting. We did everything together. We drank wine. We feasted. Deederich was always a little shyer, but no different.'

'Thank you.' Richard sighed. 'Will you – when the medic is finished – go and talk to your brother? Remind him of those times. Your voice may help him come back.'

She looked up at him. 'Yes. But you need to find Radewych. She would know what to do.'

**

'Lucianna!'

She came – not running, but shuffling as fast as she could. The brown robe she wore was tight around her body.

The Abbot masked his scowl. She *was* a good fuck.

'I have a task for you, girl.'

'Yes, your Grace?'

'I am going to send you, with guards and some of my brothers, to Sir Richard of Verysdale.'

She frowned. 'May I ask why, your Grace?'

'Sir Richard,' he grinned. 'Is in a dangerous position. He is guardian for two foreign children; I do not know how they got here. The boy is dying. The girl will make a good wife to someone.'

'You want me to act as their mother?'

'You are blooming, Lucianna. If you can seduce Sir Richard, so much the better. But make him fall for you either way. I want your child to have his surname, and that does not even require marriage.'

'But your Grace!' tears slid down her cheeks. 'I love you.'

He shook his head. 'Richard is facing financial ruin. I have loaned him money – that was why he came, some time ago. If he cannot repay it, then I may be minded to let him stay on, as a guardian, on the understanding the property goes to your child.'

Lucianna frowned. 'But why your Grace? I am your mistress. Your servant. I cannot serve you and Sir Richard.'

'You will serve Sir Richard. If he wants you to kneel before him and pleasure him, you will.' He shrugged. 'But he is old. When he dies, the property will be held in your child's name. You will return to me then, with your child and this foreign girl and Verysdale Hall.'

'Yes, your Grace.' She bowed her head. 'Did I displease you?'

He frowned. 'No. You are an instrument. I want Verysdale Hall. Your quim or your heart will win it for me.'

'And my child?'

'If they are male, they will become a brother. If female, they will be sent to the Abbess Winchester. But you will return to me, never fear. Older and wiser.' He smiled. 'It is for the best, child. Your mother did not understand. That is why I had to have her whipped from the gates.'

**

'I died!'

Bwyd sat up, looking around.

Godwin chuckled. Llywarch and Tangwystl giggled but said nothing.

'Indeed. You slept long enough,' Merik grinned.

Bwyd nodded to the bear warrior.

'Jerith is on lookout,' said Godwin.

Bwyd nodded. 'And I was asleep just one night?'

'Just one,' Tangwystl grinned. 'What happened in your dream?'

'I died. Was reborn. Caerne was there –'

There was a hiss –

'Jerith warns,' hissed Godwin.

Bwyd got up, gathering his weapons. They were camped close to a trackway leading towards Gresham Abbey; he could hear voices, someone coming down the path.

Was it all a dream? That – wolf creature, that's what Caerne summoned when we attacked the cathedral. And Wenlock, whoever he was –

'I'm not arguing about this, Angelica. The Sheriff's not a good man!'

Bwyd frowned, moving before he even realised he was.

'Hereseige!'

There was a tall man on the path, leading a black girl who sat astride a pony. Bwyd stared. The girl was thin; attractive.

The man turned –

'Bwyd!'

Hereseige crossed to him, grinning broadly. 'It's been a long time, lad.'

'That it has!' He introduced those with him.

Hereseige frowned. 'Where's Mar? Hurnungaz? Wulfrun? Don't say they're all –'

Bwyd shook his head. 'No, they live.' He grinned. 'We're looking for some misplaced children. And Muna and Mar, they've disappeared.'

'Who's the girl?' asked Merik.

'This is – Angelica. She was a slave of the Sheriff. I saved her from York.'

'I was given to you by York,' the girl protested, 'I want to go back to the Sheriff! I do not want to live in this dirty forest!'

Bwyd smiled. 'Would you like to like in a castle?'

She frowned. 'I *know* Nottingham. He wanted me to act as a spy on York. She knew,' she scowled at Hereseige. 'He only hit me to make it look plausible that I would want to run away from him.'

Bwyd smiled patiently. 'If you stay with us a while, Angelica, I can arrange an escort to take you to Clun, in the Marcher lands. You'll be safe there. The Sælvatici will look after you.'

'Who?'

'Think of them as forest guardians. They fight the Normans and anyone who would harm the people of Sherewode.'

**

'Muna?'

The woman in white looked at him. Looked back at Aneirin.

'They buried me alive!' she cawed, the sound of her voice not quite human.

'I am Muna!'

'Is she possessed?' asked Brother Blacwin.

Muna turned to look at the brother. 'You,' she hissed, her eyes glowing and glaring.

He took a half step back but she strode, flapped, sprang, closed the distance between them, seized him by the neck –

'Muna!' Tam roared, hand on the hilt of his sword. 'No!'

She flung the brother away. 'So it's you the power. It's you who'll pay.'

'Pay for what?' asked Aneirin, moving away from him.

'What's the matter?' asked Genilles, also moving away from him, but in the opposite direction.

'Help me,' whispered Muna.

Myfanwy took a half step closer. Muna seized him, lifted him over her head and flung him.

'Muna! Who are you? What's happened? Where's Mar?'

Muna grimaced, her wings wavering in and out of sight.

'She would have raped me if she was a boy!' Muna screamed.

'But she didn't,' Tam spoke softly. 'And – she?'

Yasha had drawn her spear. Genilles carried an axe and a mace.

'You think,' Muna gloated, 'that you can take me?'

'Muna,' Tam asked, gesturing to Aneirin, Genilles and Yasha to lower their weapons. 'What happened?'

'They buried me –'

'Who?' demanded Tam.

The woman in white glowered at him. Flapped her real and not-real wings.

'I am Wōden's!' she screamed in the voice of Muna.

'We are Muna,' said her raspier voice. 'We were buried alive.'

'We need Hurnungaz,' said Aneirin.

'Yes. Bring Hurnungaz. We *need* Hurnungaz,' crooned Muna.

**

'Is this what the King would want?'

Gisborough glanced over at Berenger. 'Nottingham has an idea to draw the Hooded in. To also make it plain that the Anglo-Saxons, the peasants, are nothing compared to the Normans.'

Berenger chuckled.

'You find that funny?'

Berenger shook his head. 'It never ends well, that kind of arrogance. But this touring the villages,' he trailed off.

'Each village we pass, we hang a peasant. Warn them about assisting the Hooded. Offer them money for news. The word will get out. Coming at the Hooded –'

Berenger nodded. 'Nearly a quarter of my men slain, and nothing to show for it. Was sitting in the village your idea or the girl's?' he jerked his thumb backwards; Jenny rode at the back of the column.

If the Hooded trail us, it is the worst place to be. He scowled. But I am smitten by her and that should not be. She is not bride material; I am not looking for a bride.

But she is enticing. And we would have a claim to Loxley, small though it is. I'll not go to the Holy Land again. Not – he shuddered, glancing upwards.

Sherwood was in permanent shadow.

But what would I have to offer to a noble lady? A minor title. A knighthood. If I am the one to kill Hurnungaz, that will be something.

'Mine,' he answered, recalling what Berenger had asked.

'It was too obvious a trap.'

Gisborough glanced over at Berenger. 'If the Sheriff's plan works, you can still return in triumph.'

'Another trap,' the man scowled.

He snorted. 'You've seen their accuracy. We line in a field and charge them, half will be down before we've crossed the field of battle. This is – not warfare, Berenger. This requires cleverness.'

'And your – squire – assists with that?'

'She is the sister to Robin. She has some thoughts.'

Berenger scowled, thin-lipped, but didn't answer.

**

Strigi closed his eyes, leaning on his staff. He could see clearer with his eyes closed. There were shapes in the woodlands, closing in on him, triangulating in on his position. They were flickering shapes of pure darkness in the night, illuminated only by the light of a fractured moon.

The three came on fast, like the wolves of Wōden but in human form. He twisted, striking out with the staff and there was solid impact, one went down, but the other two ploughed into him and he went down, the staff flying from his grasp.

'These lands are Ullr's,' hissed a voice, Norse, and he felt the sting of a blade. Not deep enough to be fatal, but shallow enough to sting and to draw blood.

'Ullr's, Ullr's,' the other crooned, 'we are Ullr's.'

He was struck again, but managed to half turn his back. The blade scored his shoulder, not his neck.

'You fight with your eyes closed? What manner of coward are you?'

Strigi could hear the third rising to his feet. Ullr's. That they should be here, in Sherewode, in Cernunnos' domain – but, ah. Cernunnos was no more.

A branch, his staff, he couldn't tell what, struck his forehead and he staggered back, distracted.

'You are nothing to Ullr. You're not even dangerous.'

'Dangerous?' queried a voice, and Strigi opened his eyes, his night vision flooded with light that sparked green and yellow.

A figure more stag than human held one of them aloft as if they weighed nothing. After a moment they were dropped onto a knee, and there was a terrible sound of breaking. The other two rushed the stag creature even as he found his staff. The creature was inside the blow of one, moving them to block the second, their fingers tearing out the throat of the first. Blood spurted, and the stag creature released the body, blood dripping down their face.

'You're not even armed,' sniffed the third scornfully, raising his sword and charging. 'Ullr!'

'Me,' the creature said with a certain sweetness, stepping forwards, lowering her head.

The oncoming human crashed into her, driving her back. There was a strangled cry; the sword fell from his lifeless grasp. Then the creature lifted her head, the servant of Ullr spitted on her horns. She pushed the corpse off, shaking her head, and advanced on him.

Her horns, her head, was matted with gore, entrails and blood. She licked her lips delicately. Raised the hand that had torn out the throat and began licking her fingers.

'Cernunnos,' he faltered. 'Cernunnos is gone.'

She nodded, audibly swallowing. 'I am not Cernunnos.'

She stalked towards him and he heard hooves in the undergrowth.

'Who are you?'

She smiled a predator's grin. Her hands stroked his furred cheeks, his ears. He shuddered at the feel of blood on his face. It would be worse if it got into his mouth.

'I am Caerne,' she whispered, standing on tiptoe to kiss his dry lips and breathe upon him. 'I am Sherewode.'

**

Paol is here. Paol is here.

Mar shuddered, trembling. He had killed her lovers, killed her instructor, killed her son –

No.

Massacred.

He had massacred and tortured them, living and dead. He had hacked and mutilated them, thinking nothing of slicing them open while they lived.

Two of her lovers had died on top of her. She had kept her eyes shut, their blood drenching her, expecting to die at any moment, to feel the cold steel sting of death.

She had longed for the cold sting of death.

Longed for it.

Every night the three of them had slept in the same shallow grave. Breast to breast, hands between legs, they had shared their bodies, their loves, their lives.

Scáthach had even joined them one night, sharing her body. To have the mighty Scáthach sat on her face while her own lovers pleasured her – and Paol had slaughtered them all.

She sighed, a single tear running down her cheek.

And then – there was Muna. Had she been a true boy, she would have held Muna down. Would have had her way with Muna, delighting in pressing the face of Wōden's crow-girl into the dust as she took her.

Muna was –

Muna was everything she could no longer be.

Do I want to have her – as a woman?

She grimaced at the thought. Didn't trust Muna. Didn't particularly like Muna.

But –

Hurnungaz and Wulfrun were like elder brothers to her.

And the thought of a cock inside her was – abhorrent. The thought of doing anything with a boy was – abhorrent.

But a girl –

The thought of Muna, tied up, helpless –

But Muna had given her to Hugi, expecting, wanting, her brother to rape her.

She felt Hugi tighten his arms around her.

'Shush,' he cawed softly. 'Sleep.'

**

Edwinstowe was a tiny settlement, little more than half a dozen huts clinging to a large clearing. A minor trail led through the middle of the clearing. The forest behind Edwinstowe was dense and thickly packed with oaks. The village survived on small-scale harvesting the wood.

One of the villagers hailed him as they approached.

'Have you heard what that Gisborough is up to?'

Hurnungaz shook his head.

'He's hunting you. Hanging villagers. One in each village. They've upped the reward for you; for all of your people.'

He peered past Hurnungaz, looking at Raven and Englara, Madoc, Gwilim and Tegwared.

'Not that I recognise any of them.'

'You recognise Raven; he's been to the village before.'

The elder looked again. 'I do, that I do.' He sighed. 'I always liked that Muna.'

Hurnungaz chuckled. The old man smiled.

'You've seen or heard nothing of two children? Angenijs and Diederic? They might have seemed strange, not knowing where they were.'

The man shook his head. 'There's nought here but the wood. If people don't want wood, they don't come or stop here. Those who do,' he shook his head again. 'There's talk of a prize, the Sheriff of Nottingham is wanting the greatest archer.'

'Has Gisborough been close by?'

'Five miles north. He's got soldiers with him, lots of soldiers. I hear they're taking liberties.'

Hurnungaz nodded. 'We're regrouping. We'll track them down.'

The man nodded.

**

They tracked them, keeping to the edge of the forest. De Syloc's party were in no hurry: it looked as if their path would eventually take them into the forest.

'That's a main trail they're heading for,' said Radewych, coming up beside him.

'We're at the limit of the archers. We attack from here, and miss, or they draw back, we're forced out into the open. And I don't like that.'

'They get to that track, they can speed up; others could be coming down it.'

'I know,' Wulfrun hissed. 'It's dangerous whichever way we do it. When they're nearer –'

'A single arrow might draw them.'

'This whole thing might be a trap. Their – *his* – guards haven't returned. He might be investigating.'

'Everything *might* be.'

He glanced at the three Welsh. 'Range? Thoughts?'

'It's a distance,' said Gwion.

'A distance we can do,' added Howell.

'And while they're racing, there's plenty of time to loose again.' Ifor grinned. 'I reckon four nocks, at least. Now, we're not as good as your Hurnungaz, but we should be able to make a difference over that distance.'

Wulfrun looked out at de Syloc and his men. Freya. Iseulde.

'Find positions. Loose when ready.'

Three arrows took to the air. Three more before they even landed. The soldiers broke apart, at least one falling from their horse.

Three kept their heads and headed straight for them. The rest, including de Syloc, were milling, checking their horses and comrades.

'Target the main party for the moment. Spur them into movement.'

Another of the main group fell; another three headed for them, though not de Syloc.

'Take out those nearing,' ordered Radewych.

One of the approaching riders fell. Wulfrun drew his axes, moving out into the open. Oh, for Mar, he thought. The lad would make short work of them.

Radewych moved up beside him. The two came on, one injured: the Welsh were now loosing at the three behind them.

He flung his first axe: it struck the lead horse on the head, startling it, and it sidestepped, shuffling into the other. One of the men was thrown. The other struggled to bring his horse under control.

He flung the second axe, but Radewych was already charging. He drew his broadsword.

'Scarsdale! Ullr! For Freya and Iseulde.'

They made short work of the first two. The other three riders were closing, all injured. He couldn't see beyond, couldn't tell if de Syloc was charging or galloping away.

'De Syloc!' he roared, moving to engage.

**

Sir Richard looked up at the knock on the door. 'Come in.'

His servant entered. 'There is a woman here to see you, my lord.'

'A lady, surely.' Richard stood up. The chamber was cold; he didn't want to spare money on heat whilst it was warm outside; none of his friends had responded as yet, but he knew they would.

'A woman, my lord,' the servant bowed and withdrew.

A woman walked in – definitely a woman, not a lady – buxom and overflowing with life. The robe she wore couldn't hide the swell of her belly or her chest.

'What business have you in Verysdale Hall,' he asked, curious.

The woman tried to curtesy, her leg trembling.

He moved to assist her, catching her arm and supporting her to stand.

'The Abbot has sent me to you, my lord.'

'That is generous of him.' Richard smiled. 'But why? You are already – heavy laden with child.'

'I am just a serving maid, my lord. He sent me to assist you – with the children.'

'The children?' he raised an eyebrow.

'I understand one is not well? And the girl – your daughter – who may benefit from an older female companion.'

'What will this,' Richard hesitated, hating himself for thinking it. 'What will this cost me?'

'Nothing, my lord.' She smiled shyly. 'The father is one who cannot marry me. I find myself in disgrace. The Abbot says, by assisting you and the children, my soul may yet be saved.'

Sir Richard nodded slowly. 'That is thoughtful – and kind – of the Abbot. And unexpected. But I cannot pay you as a maid.'

'I do not look for pay, my lord,' she sobbed, her chest heaving. 'The Abbot has thrown me out! I served him faithfully for many years, but falling pregnant he had no use for me. I am disgraced; my mother is long years dead, my father will have nothing to do with me.'

'Oh, you poor child.'

He moved towards her, but almost unbidden, she stepped into his embrace, wrapping her arms around him.

'Oh, thank you, my lord, thank you.'

'I do not even know your name?'

'I am Lucianna. Thank you, my lord.' She stepped back. 'It is very cold in here. Shall I light the fire, my lord?'

He shook his head. 'No fire. Perhaps –'

'Perhaps I can warm you, my lord?' she asked coquettishly.

'I –'

'Oh, I did not mean with my body, my lord. You are far too noble and I am far too common a piece for you to accept the comforts of my body. But if you will not sit outside, accept the warmth and comfort of my body next to yours. I could sit in your lap or sit close beside you, whichever you prefer.'

'I.' Richard stared blankly. She is a poor girl, hard done by, and in her condition also.

'Perhaps we will go outside,' he continued. 'It would not be seemly to be sat in my lap.'

'And I expect I am too heavy, my lord.' She cupped and squeezed her breasts. Rested her hands on her belly. 'My body swells with life and I have no man to comfort me, to look after me, to guarantee the safety and future of my child.'

'Outside.' He nodded. 'Definitely outside.'

**

'So what is the plan, brother.'

St. John scowled at his brother. The Abbot quaffed freely from his wine, several platters of food in front of him.

'And what is with those letters and your former harlot.'

He chuckled. 'Harlot? You mean Jenny of Loxley. She supports Gisborough, now. They are visiting villages. Leaving warnings for anyone stupid enough to support this Hurnungaz or his Hooded.'

The Abbot gave a snort of laughter. 'You think he will fall for this silver arrow nonsense?'

'Any more than Sir Richard will fall for Lucianna being a simple maid. What are you playing at, brother? Verysdale Hall and grounds is not that large. Why cast your mistress aside to obtain it.'

The Abbot scowled. 'She is not my mistress – the way you mean it.'

'So you've not plucked her fruit? Hmm. Shame.'

The Abbot glowered at him.

'Our younger brother tells us his plan worked.'

'Oh?' the Abbot took another mouthful of drink.

'He found Hurnungaz, where Gisborough could not. Challenged him to a duel.'

'So Geoffrey is dead?'

The Sheriff chuckled. 'No. And now Geoffrey knows his style. My command, his knowledge, Gisborough's Kings Own. The trap is hatching, brother, and the silver arrow,' he shook his head. 'Is a distraction, nothing more. If he falls for it, good. If not, he will be caught elsewhere.'

The Abbot scowled. 'Why did you summon me to Nottingham? I have souls to shrive.'

St. John smiled. 'Warwick is not pleased with you. What was done to his daughter –'

'His whorish daughter,' the Abbot scowled.

'Fetch her,' he snapped. 'Ensure she returns to Warwick.'

'Your maid betrayed her! And now gallivants with Gisborough, a common whore and a knight.'

The Sheriff arched an eyebrow. 'Shall I have it suggested to Brother Gascon that the relationship between you and Lucianna needs examination? He is no friend to women anywhere.'

The Abbot glowered, flinging away the empty wine goblet.

'I do not know what game you are playing –'

'One far more complex than you can appreciate.' St. John chuckled. 'Have the – no. Fetch the girl yourself. Escort her to Warwick. I will even loan you soldiers as escort.'

His brother frowned at him. 'Why? What is your plan and where does Warwick's whore and I fit in?'

The Sheriff chuckled. 'Well –'

**

'We go no further. We dare not risk Nottingham.'

Hereseige nodded. 'What is this silver arrow?'

'It's the Sheriff's doing.' Merik grimaced. 'All the villagers are talking of it.'

'Yes,' echoed Godwin. 'A tourney. Free food. Wrestling competitions. Archery. Mummer's plays.'

Bwyd looked at Hereseige. The man raised an eyebrow.

'It's a trap.'

Bwyd nodded. 'But why would the Sheriff bring the Abbot to Nottingham? And is there a prize – the money could be useful.'

'It will bring several lords to Nottingham.' Hereseige grinned. 'They'll have escorts, but nothing we can't take down. And money as well.'

Bwyd nodded. 'We draw back. If the Sheriff knew we were here, he could get soldiers behind us. Circle back; head for the northern trails. Let's see who comes a calling.'

Hereseige grinned. The others headed back into the deep woods, Angelica trailing them reluctantly.

'What of Angelica?' asked Bwyd when they were alone.

Hereseige shrugged. 'She's only known life as a prisoner. First the Sheriff's, then York. She wanted the girl to know freedom.'

'You got to know Gloriana of York?'

Hereseige looked away. 'Sort of.' He frowned. 'She and the Sheriff are married, but each hates the other.'

Bwyd stared. 'They're what?'

**

Wulfrun stared. De Syloc and the remaining man were a distance away, galloping hard for his estate. As he watched, another dozen soldiers appeared on horseback, coming out to protect.

'Bastard!' he screamed. 'I'll get you yet, you treacherous bastard. Teach you to murder Iseulde and Freya.'

Radewych nodded. 'We need to regroup.'

Wulfrun nodded. 'Alain –' he grinned as the lad smiled.

The Welsh bowmen nodded.

'We should never have separated,' said Howell.

'Freya,' he breathed. 'Iseulde. I will return. You will be avenged.'

They headed south.

On the evening of the third day, Wulfrun stopped them early.

'What's up?' asked Alain.

He glanced at the lad and shook his head. 'Something.'

The Forest quietened around them. It definitely wasn't soldiers. No sounds of birds, no insects or creatures in the undergrowth.

But still – something.

Ullr. Aid me.

He turned slowly. There was something – in the trees. Something tall. And white. And mostly hidden – but not.

'Hugi!' he bellowed. 'Is that you?'

The *white* moved.

'No one get scared. Hugi's – one of us.' Wulfrun glanced around. 'He's also different.'

Alain drew back, half hiding behind Radewych. The three Welsh stood close, bows out but no arrows on the string.

'There's nothing to loose at. Hugi's –'

Tall, skeletal white, crow-headed and naked, Hugi appeared in their clearing.

Radewych chuckled. Alain stumbled backwards and fell. The Welsh – stared.

There was someone, he thought, with Hugi. Someone who, when Hugi stepped into the open, stayed where they were.

'Hugi? Who's with you?'

The man shook his head, cawing stridently.

'Stay here.' He crossed to the crow-man. 'Someone's with you. We won't hurt them if they're a friend.'

Hugi half turned his head. Nodded, but didn't speak.

Wulfrun moved past him slowly.

'I mean you no harm. I can see where you are, though I can't see you. I am Wulfrun of Scarsdale. What is your name?'

He moved closer, slowly, trying to appear non-threatening. There was a shape, crouched down, leaning against the tree.

He heard a breath of wind, almost a voice.

'Who?' he asked again.

He moved into the woodlands. The creature – the person, he was sure – stayed where they were.

One step. Another. A third. Dark hair. Small. Pale skin –

They rose smoothly to their feet and Wulfrun stared.

'You hate me.'

Wulfrun frowned. 'Why would I hate you lad. I've missed you. This – doesn't matter,' he pointed up and down.

'But I'm,' they hissed, glowering. 'I'm female.'

Wulfrun shrugged. 'Lad, I don't care what you've got between your legs as long as you've got a blade in your hand.' He grinned. 'I've missed you, lad. I thought you dead.'

They shook their head. 'Muna tried to kill me. She's – possessed.'

'Another spirit,' cawed Hugi, who had joined them. 'In trouble.'

**

The young girl, Angenijs, read from the parchment, but without any interest or understanding. She looked, often, at the bower where her brother lay, wrapped up warm against the mild day.

He lay snug. She had fed him a few drops of water barely an hour early; he had barely been able to take them. Whatever was happening to him, Lucianna knew, he was dying.

But Angenijs lived. Her voice was not passionate or lively, but she was alive. And her lessons would improve. Her learning would improve. Wherever she and her brother had come from – Sir Richard thought they had likely escaped a slaver from another country – she was healthy.

Angenijs sighed, looking again at Diederic.

'Child,' Lucianna said softly, 'come here. Take a rest from your reading.'

The girl looked over. Put her parchment down on the table and set a rock on it to hold it down; came over.

'Up here, Angenijs,' Lucianna opened her arms to her.

The girl scrambled up.

'You're having a baby.'

She nodded. 'I will be. A younger brother or sister for you and Diederic.'

Angenijs glanced at her brother and back.

'Sir Ricard has adopted you and your brother as his own, until more can be found about you.'

'Radewych.'

She nodded. 'I know not the warrior. But Sir Richard will keep you safe. I will keep you safe.' She sighed, gently stroking the girl's cheek. 'If Sir Richard grants me shelter, I could be a mother figure to you and your brother. Would you like that?'

Angenijs looked up at her. 'I never knew my mother.'

She stroked the girl's hair. 'No, and I am not trying to replace her. But every young girl needs an older, female, confidante. And your brother needs someone soft to care for him as well.'

She drew the girl's head down to her breast. 'Rest. I am watching your brother. He is safe and loved.'

Angenijs snuggled in to her, eyes closed. In a few moments she was asleep.

'How is –'

Lucianna flinched. 'My lord, sorry, you startled me.'

The old man smiled. 'I am sorry. How goes Angel's – ah,' he frowned.

Lucianna smiled. 'She was missing her mother, my lord. I may not be a mother, but every child needs the comfort of a mother's breast from time to time.'

Sir Richard nodded, distractedly. He was wrapped in a woollen robe over his clothing despite the mildness.

He is not long for this world.

'Any change to her brother?'

Lucianna shook her head. 'He is fading fast. I fear we will have to bury him soon.'

He sighed deeply.

'What is wrong, my lord?'

He shook his head. 'It is not a problem for a maid to solve.'

Lucianna looked away.

'I – am sorry,' he answered after a moment. 'You are an innocent – mostly innocent – child in all of this.' He sighed again. 'I borrowed money from your master. It is due soon and my friends,' he grimaced. 'Those I thought were my friends –'

'He is not my master anymore, Sir Richard. I am your property, to dispose of as you will.'

Sir Richard frowned. 'I will not dispose of you. But there is no money, and money will soon be due –'

'When my time is past, my lord, I am sure I can think of a few ways to earn some coins.' She smiled at him, deliberately coquettishly.

'No! I will not have you acting as a whore for me, Lucianna.'

'I would be mother to your children, my lord, if you not thought it beneath you to have a poor, penniless, maid as their mother?'

He stared in wonderment. 'This is no battle the like of which I have faced before. Perhaps this is why I left the Holy Land.' He smiled. 'Yes, Lucianna, you may act as mother to my children.'

**

The boat undulated. The sea heaved and shivered. Pale cloud light scattered diamonds of surf amidst the writhing ocean waves. Salt spray stung his eyes. He was far from the shore, far from the land, a tallow-candle hour before the dark. The fish should be biting, should be rising to his bait –

Ycenthwaite sighed.

He clenched his fingers against the cold. His wife would berate him if he came home early, if he returned, afraid of the sea –

He went to stamp his feet and scowled instead. Huffed. Sat back down, stiffly. Wrapped his jerkin tighter around himself.

It's just the night. The cold. The rising waves –

He shuddered.

Memories of the Girl god – he flinched. *That* had been terrifying. To be caught by a mad god girl – he shook his head.

'I must have been mad.'

He grinned, sourly. She hadn't believed him, of course, his wife. Why should she? He'd been babbling like a moon-struck calf about the mad godling, daughter of Cernunnos. He gritted his teeth. It would go full dark soon, and in the dark the fish would rise, and they would eat for another few days.

Another few days. He shuddered.

Hwitebi was safer than the heartlands of Sherewode – well. The Norman hold was not so strong, the law not applied so viciously. But it had its own dangers. Priests of the Christ of the East and old Norse families warred, not caring who got caught between them.

There was a – *moment* – of stillness.

Ycenthwaite raised his head.

His craft bobbed lightly, as if caught by a sprightly current in a sheltered bay. The water was near-reflective. The waves, calmed.

He could see the shore, far-distant. The monastery rose on the hill, visible high out to sea. At times, on calmer nights, the night-singing of the monks could be heard out on the water.

Ycenthwaite could see the ocean growing restive. Something rising, something boiling, something coming from the deep –

He blinked against the cold and the salt spray, shaking his head.

'Dreaming, I am. Mad. Moon-cursed.'

He could hear something, not the monks, whose song was high and plaintive. This – what he could hear – he shivered. It was more feel than hear. Goosebumps rose on him. He shivered. The boat heaved, caught by the rising sea-swell.

Something – *was* – rising.

The sound was muffled. Watery, but deep.

Ycenthwaite shivered.

There were creatures in the deep. Horses of the deep, he'd heard them called, that occasionally took fishermen who wandered too far out to sea. Even more occasionally, their carcasses washed up on shore, looking nothing like horses.

Ycenthwaite shook his head. They were outsiders, foreigners, new to the area, new to Hwitebi, and not let in on the jokes, made fun of because they were not born in the locale. He shrugged. The idea of a horse of the deep – however would it breathe underwater?

The ocean broke and suddenly all was roaring and screaming and tentacles filled the air and there was an impenetrable *black mass* that was not the night and the dark but was alive and sound boomed –

He screamed but there was no sound, drowned as it was by the rising behemoth.

Not a horse of the deep.

A mammoth of the deep.

A demon from the annals of the brothers of the Christ of the East.

Black it was and the ocean was sloughing off it and it was rising and light glittered brightly on its skin and there were tentacles, like ferns waving gently in an unseen breeze –

A gaping maw yawned, darkness upon darkness, and the maw was descending, opening, and the sea roared and crashed and the water was white, like miniature mountains, roaring and crashing and –

**

Berenger grinned. He stood silently, an eye to Gisborough's tent. They had paused – again – in their searching for the Hooded and the Hel-archer.

He could see the knight's squire on her back, legs spread, the knight above her, ploughing her, while her hands scrabbled at his back.

He grimaced, moving away, beckoning one of his men. The man hurried over – he hissed at him to be silent, drawing him further away.

Hastily, Berenger wrote out a note and gave it to his man. 'See that it gets to the King. Our commander entertains his mistress more than he hunts the Hooded!'

The man saluted and hastened off.

He beckoned to another. Wrote a second note and gave it to his man.

'No one but to whom it is addressed, you understand?'

'Yes, my lord.' The man saluted and withdrew.

Berenger smiled. 'Soon,' he whispered.

**

'Your Grace?' the Abbot asked.

Abbess Winchester looked up. 'Are you still fornicating with your mistress, Gresham?'

The Abbot blinked in horror.

'Your – your Grace!' he blustered. 'Why – why say such things? She is a simple peasant maid.'

'A simple peasant maid,' the Abbess drawled. 'Whose mother you fucked into pregnancy and now she herself carries a child.'

'Your Grace, I must protest! Such scandalous rumours are not –'

'You know the girl's cunny. You knew her mother's cunny, before she was a mother.'

The Abbot stared. 'I do not know who has spread these scurrilous lies –'

'You came for Evgania?'

The Abbot gasped, blinking. 'Yes. On Warwick's behalf.'

The Abbess chuckled. 'Brother Gascon has not yet received your gift, Abbot.' She named an amount.

'I cannot afford that!'

'You will, or he will know your deeds. You will be stripped of rank and position, property and titles. You will end your days – soon – in the Tower or in some holding of Brother Gascon himself.'

The Abbot seethed. Forced himself to nod. 'Would he take property? Verysdale shall soon be mine.'

The Abbess waved her hand airily. 'If it is not yours to give lawfully, it cannot be given by you.'

'Your Grace, in a matter of weeks – Sir Richard has no one who will assist him. He owes much.'

'And you ingratiate your pregnant daughter into the house to ensure it comes to you, one way or another.'

'She is not my daughter.' He shook his head vehemently. 'I was never married to her mother. I cannot marry, women are too much trouble and it is not legal. Therefore she cannot be my daughter.'

The Abbess indicated the heavy bag of coin he had brought with him. 'Is that for the daughter of Warwick?'

He nodded. How am I to escape the Black Brother's snares? If I do not pay him, Winchester will betray me. 'It is, your Grace.' He inclined his head to her.

'It has been a long day.' She smiled. 'Nottingham's men rest; they eat and drink. You will spend the night here.'

'Your Grace, that is kind –'

'While you take your rest, I will have Warwick sent to your chambers. Remember she is but a serving girl. Take her in every way imaginable.'

The colour drained from his face. 'Your Grace! I am sent to retrieve her, not molest her.'

Winchester inclined her head at the bag of money. 'Such a princely sum. It buys the girl for the night. In the morning you may take her out with you.'

'Thank you, your Grace. I am not minded –'

'Abbot.' Winchester scowled. 'The Christ of the East commands you defile the girl tonight. Her rapist and rescuer. She will be grateful to you. Ensure her cunny and arse are well-used before the night is finished.'

'But why, your Grace?'

She looked at him pityingly. 'Pathetic worm. I command it. The Christ of the East commands it.' She smiled. 'You are rotten through and through, Gresham. A single girl, and not even innocent?'

**

'So you lead the Sælvatici?' breathed Muna.

'I am Aneirin.'

It was early. The woman was on her way back from the river and water still sparkled on her skin.

'I was older than you when they killed me,' Muna crooned. 'They thought me too old and shrivelled to be worth entertaining. They crushed me beneath stones so I could not move and sealed the barrow up with me inside.'

She traced her hands over the woman's shoulders, her arms. 'A warrior woman. What kind of power do you have?'

'I can summon –'

Muna drove her to her knees effortlessly. 'I am a god!' She caressed Aneirin's face. 'And I am a witch.' She slid her hands up the woman's head. 'I am memory,' she hissed.

Bwyd. An eager, though uncertain, lover. Llewellyn, the true leader, the king of the Sælvatici. Paol –

She grinned, digging deeper.

Helpless, as the hero-lighted man sodomised her. As he filled her mouth, her throat, with his fiery seed. As he filled her quim, burning her from the outside all the way in.

She screamed in pain, in terror –

He delighted in her terror. In her fear.

'Mine,' Muna crooned, 'you're all mine.'

**

'Will you tell me,' Mar asked. 'Of your wife. Your child.'

Wulfrun looked up and grinned. 'Freya was – is – my life. There is no other woman for me, brother.'

Mar smiled.

'They wait for me in the Halls.' He moved, shifting his back against the trunk of a massive oak. 'She was always a better warrior than I was, though the King would never take a woman into his army.' He sighed. 'She wanted to see the Holy Land. I promised her, when Iseulde was older,' he grimaced.

'I am sorry.'

He nodded. 'We were going to go, for Freya, and Iseulde, when we were older.' He sighed, deeper. 'They are both with me still, and coming back from the Holy Land, I had had enough. I wanted no more fighting. I wanted to be a father. To be a farmer. Look after the few families who looked to me. Support them, support my wife and daughter.'

He shook his head. 'One of the men who did it, de Syloc, seems to have risen in power.' He looked up. 'I will speak to Hurnungaz. I want him dead,' he growled.

There was an answering growl from the tree line. The wolf and boar padded out of the darkness.

Mar stretched their hand out and the boar came over, lying down, their head on their thighs.

**

'You think – you can get her to these Sælvatici lands?'

Bwyd looked at him and grinned. 'Aye, Hereseige. Angelica has no place here. A castle, a position, yes. The Forest is not for her.'

'She was the Sheriff's – servant. She might have useful news.'

Bwyd shook his head again. 'No. She's – startled. Once she's safe at Clun, maybe, but if you push her too much, she might run – and if she ran back to the Sheriff.'

Hereseige nodded.

'So what did you do – how came you to York?'

He grinned. 'You wouldn't believe me if I told you it all.'

Bwyd chuckled. 'I died. Not that long ago. Caerne,' the druid shook his head. 'I don't know. But Caerne's powerful.' He sighed. 'She was powerful before we attacked the cathedral site. I think she's even more powerful now.'

Hereseige nodded. Frowned. 'What?'

Bwyd chuckled. 'I'm a Sælvatici. Forest guardian; resister against the Normans and anyone who would control, harm, destroy the Forest or its inhabitants. As is Robin – Hurnungaz.'

'But you died?'

'And reborn in Caerne. And,' he grinned. 'You wouldn't understand it, but I think I met one of the Old ones, an old Ænglish.'

Hereseige frowned. 'What's one of them?'

Bwyd chuckled. 'Before the Normans, it was the Norse. Before the Norse, Saxons. Before the Saxons,' he shrugged. 'They lived in burrows. They were far more in touch with – gods.'

'Is every one of these Sælvatici a druid?'

Bwyd shook his head. 'No. I have studied most of my life to be a druid. To be one with the world, with the Forest.' He grinned. 'We are not like the brothers of the Christ of the East. We fight for what needs to be fought for.'

**

'I am sorry, my lord.' Lucianna rested her hand on his arm for an instant. 'The boy is – gone.'

Sir Richard's face crumpled in on itself.

Deederich lay in the bower. His sister sat on the edge of the bed, crying helplessly.

She held her arm out for Sir Richard: he took it, and she assisted him over the garden to where his adopted son lay.

'He liked the sunlight,' Angel whimpered, looking up at her. 'More than being inside.' She sobbed.

Lucianna held her arm out and the child ran to her, pressing her face against her belly.

She stroked the girl's head. Smiled when, absent-mindedly, Sir Richard put his arm around her waist, breathing heavily.

'I am undone, dear child,' he said softly, stroking Angel's hair. 'My friends will not support me. I cannot repay the Abbot. If I throw myself upon his mercy, will he be generous?'

**

'What do you need from me, Caerne?'

She smiled viciously. 'Everything.'

He sensed – a weight hit him and he fell to his knees, something large on his back. He could hear, scent, its terrible breath.

Teeth bit into his neck. Claws tore at his arms.

'Caerne!'

She smiled, moving closer. Lunged, her teeth closing on his throat.

Tore it out.

**

Hereseige held his hand up for silence. 'I hear something!'

Voices, arguing. One raised and female, strident – and yet there was more to it than that. A voice with power.

Gloriana – Lady York – had a voice born to order, born to command, but it was not the same at all.

The voice he heard – he did not think was Caerne's, but there was something of that aspect about it.

He moved closer, Bwyd and Jerith flanking him.

'No! This will not be!'

Hereseige frowned. It was almost –

'And who's going to stop me? I am the Hand of Wōden! I am the vessel of a god –'

'I will stop you!' Bwyd roared, moving past him.

Hereseige blinked. The normally placid druid moved past him, stave in hand.

He followed Bwyd into the clearing ahead – and saw Tam and Muna; a number of others he didn't recognise, but it was Muna who caught his gaze.

Wings almost fluttered from her back. Her eyes seemed black, lit by internal flames.

'I am Muna!' she roared.

Bwyd strode across the clearing.

'I am the Raven of –'

Bwyd's stave struck her head and she staggered back.

'I am –' she screamed.

Bwyd struck her again.

'Muna!' she cried.

Bwyd struck her in the side. She collapsed onto one knee.

'I see you in there, shade. Spirit.' He shook his head. 'That is not the place for you. You are long dead.'

'She has no one else,' Muna begged, in her own voice.

'You are a creature of malevolence. I will not let you be.'

'I. Want. Hurnungaz!' she screamed.

Bwyd shook his head, unruffled. 'You have two options. Leave –'

'You want me dead!' shrieked Muna, in a voice not her own.

'Leave,' he repeated, 'or live in peace with Muna. With us.'

'Never!'

He dropped the stave and seized her by the throat. 'Is Aneirin your doing?'

Hereseige blinked. 'Who?'

Bwyd nodded to an older woman. She was slumped, eyes downcast, looking worn out and derelict.

'She was so easy!' cackled Muna. 'I am memory!'

Aneirin flinched.

'He was there,' Muna spoke softly, emotions flickering across her face rapidly. 'Paol. He hunts Mar. He hunts the false boy!'

'Look at me, Muna,' Bwyd spoke tenderly.

Muna raised her eyes. 'I will not be tricked –'

'You will not get to Caerne. You will not get to Hurnungaz. You will not get past me. I hold you, Muna and deceased woman who was witch.'

'They buried me alive!' the not-Muna voice screamed.

'They who did that are dead. There is no one to seek vengeance on.'

The woman in white struggled in his grip. 'You are choking me,' she whimpered.

**

Hurnungaz awoke stiffly, his face pressed to a warm, furry, belly.

He pushed himself up, finding he had been lying with his face pressed against Caerne's stag-belly. She smiled tenderly down at him.

He frowned. 'What? You tore my throat out.'

He became aware they were not alone in the burrow. An immense wolf-like creature lay next to them, its head crowned with horns, hooves instead of paws. It dreamed, twitching sporadically.

'You had to die, Hurnungaz. As Bwyd died. But your rebirthing is incomplete; you awoke too early.'

'Where am I? What's – going in?'

She caressed her belly. 'I carried you in my womb, Hurnungaz. The idea of you. You are purely mine now, Hurnungaz. No one has any call or claim upon you.'

'How? Why?'

'Because it must be.' She sighed, shaking her head. 'I drew forth a creature for you.' She stretched her hand out to ruffle the fur of the beast next to him. 'I have tamed it, or it has tamed me, I am not sure. But,' she sighed again.

She stroked his hair. 'We need to be stronger. The cathedral,' she shook her head. 'Powers are shifting. Ullr and Wōden are manipulating their pieces, but they are not the danger.'

'Who is then?'

She shook her head. 'There are many standing against you. The physical, this time, that is where the challenge will come.' She stroked the creature's head. 'The Sheriff of Nottingham. The Abbot of Gresham. The Templars – I do not know. York, perhaps. The Abbess Winchester, she is stirring at the edges. Gisborough,' she shook her head, eyes closed.

'He,' she spoke softly, having been silent for several minutes. 'He is the hammer. He has one with him – and many warriors. Do not let him meet up with the Sheriff's forces. He is gathering an army. The Sheriff has plans of his own.'

She lifted her hand to stroke his cheek. 'Gisborough is far too powerful to unite with the Sheriff. He hunts Sherewode to kill you. To destroy the Hooded. You must seek him out –'

She broke off, frowning.

'What?'

**

Tam stared as Hurnungaz simply appeared, moving past Bwyd and drawing Muna up.

'How?'

'I need –'

The point of a blade pricked Muna's throat and she stilled.

'Muna. You are one of Wōden's Ravens. You are memory. There is a shade inside you, a spirit, the spirit of a woman murdered before her time, by her friends, by the villagers she trusted and relied on.' He shook his head. 'It is they who betrayed you, not us.'

'I have –' she struggled, but the blade remained pressed close against her throat.

'You have life, in and through Muna. You can assist her, make her powerful. Or you and Muna can die. This is no barrow. Your spirit will not be trapped, held, here. It will simply depart. You will – finally – be gone. But in doing so, you will condemn the life of another.'

'You condemn her to death.'

'If one of Wōden's Ravens threatens one of the Hooded, they die.' He smiled grimly. 'This is not Wōden's territory. Caerne will come for him, in time, if he continues to encroach.'

'She has no power –'

Tam saw Hurnungaz smile. Saw Muna's expression change.

'Work with Muna,' he spoke softly, though Tam saw everyone in the clearing could hear. 'Work with her. Make her more powerful. Help her in her cause – so long as it is not tilted against me, Caerne or the Hooded.'

The knife blade appeared. 'Tell me of Mar. Where are they?'

Muna swallowed. Nodded. 'They are, last I knew, with my brother. With Hugi.'

Hurnungaz nodded. 'Tam. Hereseige!' he broke out into a grin. 'It's been a long time.'

'Aye,' the Yorkshireman strode forward, seizing his arm.

Bwyd moved to Aneirin. 'Aneirin? Are you alright?'

'I,' Muna hesitated. 'I provoked some memories in her that were painful. Unpleasant.' She looked around. 'I can – overturn that.'

'Without intervention, will she improve?'

Muna shook her head.

'Then undo the damage done.'

**

Myfanwy led Genilles away by the hand.

'While they are distracted.'

Genilles smiled, as eager as he was.

Aneirin was going to be alright – it had hurt them both to see her broken and limp: Aneirin was the mother of the Sælvatici, had taught them all sword-play, or of myths and legends. Not a few she had helped bring into the world or suckled. Some, including Genilles, he knew, had shared her bed, but only ever once.

They stopped a distance from the camp.

Genilles shifted the jacket from her shoulders and let it fall. She was muddy beneath; streaked green and brown so that her body would not show in the dark night.

'I know you like me – dirty.'

Myfanwy grinned, kicking off his boots and loosing his trews. He grabbed and kneaded her breasts, licking and nibbling at her neck.

She pried him loose; pushed her skirt down.

'Get on the ground, love.'

He obeyed, licking his lips. She crouched, naked and muddy, above him. She eased herself down.

Myfanwy clasped her buttocks, tucking into her delight.

She shivered and moaned above him, trembling, undulating, pushing herself more and more on to him.

**

Raven looked up as a figure crouched down next to them.

'Who are –'

Their eyes whirled a lazy green, flecked with yellow. He stared at their hands, which were unnaturally long. Small horns rose through their hair.

'I am Caerne.'

Raven blinked. 'You're a god.'

She shrugged. 'I'm not human. I'm not the Forest. I'm not my father. God is as good as anything.'

'Why are you here?'

If this was the deity that Hurnungaz and the others worshipped –

'I am here for you.'

'Me?' he stared.

She smiled again. 'You fight for my people. You are barely a child, not quite a man. But your heart beats and your soul rages against the injustice you see.'

He nodded. 'Am I – you said you're here for me?'

She nodded. 'Terrible times are coming. Too many forces. If they are allowed to join up, the consequences –' she shook her head. 'And so I must ready my champions.'

He frowned. 'I'm no champion. I'm just a boy.' He sighed. 'This is not where I wanted to be, not wanted to be doing.' He sighed.

'I cannot change that. But I can prepare you for the upcoming battles.'

'You'll change – me?'

'I'll make you more powerful.'

Raven shook his head. 'No, thank you.'

Caerne stared. 'Why?'

He smiled cautiously. 'Because I won't be me. I'll be beholden to you.' He grimaced. 'I'm sure – Hurnungaz and the others, they talk about you occasionally. But I'm just a peasant boy. I'm nothing special.'

Caerne stared at him.

'You reject my gift?'

He nodded.

'Knowing, without it, you might die?'

He nodded again. 'I loved a boy. He thought it a foul thing. I thought the church would save me. They wanted to condemn me, to make me commit suicide for my supposed sins.' He shook his head. 'It's hard, but I'd rather survive on my own than rely on anyone else for anything.'

Caerne stared, her eyes glittering. 'The Hooded will stand for you, Raven. You are one of us, truly.'

**

'Are you sure about this, my lord?'

Gisborough smiled, his hand on her back. 'When we are alone, I am William.' He grinned. 'We hie to Nottingham. The tourney is due to begin soon. With the Sheriff's man, with the King's Own, we will bring an end to these Hooded. To Hurnungaz. To your brother.'

Jenny grimaced. 'He is my brother no longer.'

He eased the robe from her shoulders; let it fall.

'This will be our last time – for a while. Nottingham may hate you for what you did to Warwick's daughter. The Abbot definitely would. I would keep you safe, keep you secret, for as long as I can.'

He drew her down, divesting himself of his clothes as he did so.

'I want to be there,' she whispered, 'when you slay him. I want to drive a knife into his body.'

William nodded. 'It shall be so.'

**

'What?' Aneirin asked, blinking.

'You are safe.' Tam smiled gently.

'Muna!' she sat up, terrified.

Tam held her, shushing gently. 'Hurnungaz has returned. Muna is – tamed. She undid what she had done to you.'

She burst into tears and Tam was there.

'It was horrible,' she shuddered. 'Paol. What he did. What he threatened – what he will do.'

Tam kissed her gently on the lips. 'There is only the moment, if you want it. Hurnungaz is rebuilding the Hooded. You are safe. The Sælvatici –'

Aneirin pulled him down, kissing him savagely. 'Let me know warmth,' she hissed. 'Let me not be alone for a while.'

**

The tourney field was ready. The main part was set aside for knightly combat, and most of the lords were already in attendance with their entourages.

Another part had been set aside for the archery contest. The Jews had created not one, but two silver arrows for him. One, a false one, as the prize for – whosoever would win. The other, he held safe.

St. John grinned. Brothers of the Christ of the East were on their way to keep him wife – meek. He had passed orders to them that they were entitled to act in his name, to stop her acting in any way which was not appropriate to her position. He did not care if she received blows for it. He had given them directions that they were entitled to put her in a coarse-hair shirt and keep her penitent, keep her humiliated.

His brother – the Abbot – was ensconced in his Abbey. His absence from the tourney was no loss.

He smiled at his companion.

'There are bodies to hang, my lord?'

He nodded. 'Yes, your Grace. Three, so my man instructs me. Two are of these Hooded; one, an associate. All will dance and wriggle later.'

'Good.'

He nodded. Wrestling and other peasant sports close to where the peasants, the Pagans, the unbelievers, would be gathered.

His people. People who owed their very, miserable, existence to him.

His other brother – the mad warrior, the Black Bishop's man – was on his way, with both warriors and several brothers of the Christ of the East.

Oh yes. It was going to be very entertaining.

**

Wings fluttered where there should not – could not – be.

'Why are we here?' asked Muna.

Hurnungaz grinned. It was still night, a night that lay heavy, cold and damp upon the Forest.

Muna wore a short shift. It was thin and did nothing to hide the swell of her breasts, her muscled thighs and tight arse; the black feathers that grew thickly upon her quim.

Her wings stretched and creaked.

'Does the spirit sleep within you?'

Muna smiled, pulling her shoulders back. 'I cannot seduce you. Even if I knelt before you, draining you would give me none of your power.'

'It is not mine. It is Caerne's.'

Muna laughed.

'I am the witch and the hand in one. There's nothing I want so much as –' she chuckled. 'I have another chance of life. A body shared. I want to feel a man once more. But, failing that,' she grinned.

Her wings flapped and disappeared from view.

'I am Wōden's. When my task is done or I am failed, I will return to him, imprisoned once more until he has need of me.'

'Have you no choice?'

She shook her head. 'His spark fills me. Gives me life. I am his Raven-messenger. He can extinguish me in an instant. He –' she hesitated.

Hurnungaz waited.

'He wars with himself. With Ullr. Both want this land – but both are wary of Caerne.' She smiled at him. 'Caerne terrifies them both.'

Hurnungaz grinned. 'She terrifies many. She *is* terror.'

Muna nodded slowly. 'I do not know how this will end,' she began.

Hurnungaz smiled, turning back to face the trackway. 'With death. As it started with death, so shall it end with death.'

**

Aneirin held Tam close as the pleasure burst through her. She gasped and panted, trying to keep quiet but the pleasure – she arched her back, clutching him as he drove himself deep into her one final time.

She shuddered back to the ground, him collapsed atop her.

'When was the last time you had a woman,' she asked, when her shudders had eased a little.

'A while,' he murmured, moving.

'No,' she caught him, held him, 'stay a while.'

'Bwyd said – you only stayed a night with people.'

Aneirin chuckled, stroking his back with her nails. 'I guess this is different then.' She grinned. 'Truth is –'

'Truth is what?' he asked, lifting his head, gazing at her.

'I am an old woman, Tam.' She smiled. 'I know I taught Bwyd sword craft when he was younger. I know I read to him, of tales of our people and legends of Wales and beyond.'

Tam propped himself up on one elbow. His hand caressed and fondled her breast.

'See the nipples, so black,' she whispered gently.

He bent his head. Kissed. Sucked.

She clutched him tighter, holding him in place. 'Would you were more capable than a man. Would that you could fill me again, even as I feel you slide out of me.'

He stopped sucking and kissed.

'Give me a moment.'

She chuckled. 'You may have more than a moment, Tam.' She stroked his back. 'I do not know who has suckled these more, babes in arms or lovers, but I know I enjoy both.'

He lifted his head and kissed her lips. 'You may not be my wife,' he said gently, 'but I do not think she would object.'

Aneirin smiled. 'I would like it if – I have a reputation of only sharing my body once with a person.'

He nodded, sliding out of her fully, pulling himself up and kissing her nose.

'I would like to grow to know you properly, Tam of the Highlands.' She grinned. 'You have sated me.' She giggled softly. 'More than Bwyd. He was good – but you are better.'

He sighed, leaning down, kissing her, sharing a kiss.

'You have a secret,' she said, after the kiss broke.

He nodded. 'You may hate me for it. You may tell Hurnungaz, or Wulfrun or any of the others of it. But – it needs to be told.'

'Oh?' she smiled softly. 'Tell your tale. Rest yourself on my bosom and share the words that haunt you.'

Tam laid his head upon her breast. 'After my children were – raped. Murdered. I came south. Left Alba.'

She stroked his back wordlessly.

'I fell in with an outlaw band. I,' he shook his head. 'I had no cares. No wish to live.' He sighed, deeper.

She had one arm around his shoulders: rested her other hand on his hip.

'The Sheriff caught me. Offered me a deal.'

Aneirin moved her hand to his lap.

'He –' Tam gulped. 'He gave me information. Orders,' he grimaced. 'Told me who to rob. Who to let pass through the heartland of Sherwood unmolested.'

She could feel him growing stiffer beneath her touch.

'With that knowledge, I came to lead the band.' He looked up at her. 'A little more time.' He smiled shyly. 'I want to be inside you when I tell you. Then if you hate me,' his smile faded. 'Smother me on your breast. Tell the others you stopped a traitor. I will not resist you.'

She tightened her grip: he stiffened. She moved her fingers up and down until she felt him gasp.

'Slide down a little and take me: fill me. Then spill your – secrets.'

He slid inside easily.

'I was the Sheriff's man,' he gasped, falling over her, panting.

Aneirin stroked his back. 'And now?'

Tam looked up wearily. 'Robin – Hurnungaz – destroyed my band. Let me live. Since then,' he shook his head. 'Since then I am not a servant of the Sheriff but a true outlaw, wanted all the more for betraying the Sheriff.'

**

'Sir Richard.' The Abbot smiled rapaciously. 'Please, take a seat.'

The old man smiled, sinking into the fur-lined chair the Abbot had prepared for him.

'How is it with your children, hmm?'

The old man hunched in on himself even more. 'Deederich has passed, your Grace. I could not, not even the medic, could save him.'

The Abbot sketched a cross in his direction. 'No more to suffer. That is good for him, though whether his soul will get to Heaven –'

Sir Richard looked up angrily. 'I paid for prayers to be said for his soul. He was an innocent!'

'He was a foreign child,' the Abbot said gently. 'Who knows what he had done before he came to you. And surely someone would have claimed him and his sister, were they rightfully here and worshippers of the Christ of the East.'

The knight stared at him angrily.

'And talking of the girl.' The Abbot smiled rapaciously. 'She is of marriageable age, I believe?'

'Your Grace!'

'I take it that is a yes. I have a number of possible suitors for her, bearing in mind she has no dowry save your property.'

'I cannot,' Sir Richard trembled.

'I believe my former maid now resides at Verysdale, yes?'

Sir Richard nodded. 'Lucianna, yes. She looks after Angel as a mother would. Her time is near.'

'There is the matter of the considerable amount of money you borrowed from me, Sir Richard.'

'I thought to save them,' he almost wept. 'The best of everything. They were strangers. I wanted to comfort and support them.'

The Abbot smiled. 'I doubt the wealth of your property will cover the amount you borrowed. The amount you wasted, with no hope of returning.'

'I – I did the right thing!' he protested.

He nodded. 'And you shall be punished accordingly. Now then,' he smiled. 'What value shall I attach to Angel's virginity?'

**

'Why do you – sleep in the earth?'

Mar looked up at Wulfrun. The boar lay atop them, snoring and belching in sleep. Wulfrun was stretched out next to them, the wolf at his back.

'It keeps us – me – unattached. I am of Scáthach. We are trained warriors. We live for the blade. The tribe. The family. Sleeping in the earth – we die a little every day. We know not when our end may come.'

Wulfrun nodded. 'Would I had known when Iseulde and Freya's time was near. I would have returned sooner; I would never have gone.'

They nodded. 'It would have been better if I had died at Scáthach's. The one who slew my people – my family, my kin, my lovers.' They shook their head.

'They are here?'

They nodded. 'Yes. I can – I can almost sense them. They were near; went after Muna instead. Something came between the pair of them and – whatever shade or spirit Muna picked up.'

Wulfrun nodded. 'I sought vengeance. Sought to bring down de Syloc. His position has risen.' He shook his head. 'He is still a coward. We slew many of his men – he flew back to his house, brought more soldiers out to protect himself.'

Mar grinned. 'Help me end the hero-lighted man I seek. I will help you end this de Syloc.'

Wulfrun grinned, extending his arm. 'Agreed, brother.'

Mar clasped his arm. 'Sealed.' He grinned. 'Scáthach and Scarsdale stand as one.'

**

'Where do we go?' Madoc asked.

Raven grinned. 'South, and then east. We head towards Nottingham. There we will find Hurnungaz and the others.'

He glanced at Englara; she nodded, a faint smile crossing her face.

'Caerne spoke to you?' asked Tegwared.

He nodded. 'She did.'

'And she powers you now like Hurnungaz?' asked Gwilim. 'Will be good –'

'She does not.' Raven smiled. 'I turned her down.'

The three Welsh stared at him.

'You turned her down?' said Madoc.

He nodded.

'Why?' asked Gwilim. 'Are you a fool? In this fight –'

Raven smiled. 'It seemed right. Mar is – he – themselves. Hereseige is a stone mason.'

'And Hurnungaz has the power of Caerne flowing through him!'

He nodded at Tegwared. 'Yes. And I do not. I am,' he shrugged. 'I have already become who I was. I don't need Caerne.'

Gwilim stared at him disbelievingly. 'You won't be saying that when the arrows fall –'

Raven smiled. 'I only ever wanted to be me. Myself. As I am.' He grinned, nodding towards the trackway. 'Shall we be off? There's a distance to cover.'

**

Alain whimpered quietly.

'What ails you, child?'

Alain glanced at Ifor, the speaker, and shook his head.

'Is it the – creature?'

Hugi crouched off to one side of their encampment. Even in the dark night, he glowed. Pale skin, veined in black. Too human, too – male.

He nodded.

'No man's a man in comparison to him.'

Alain nodded. He'd seen Mar with them. Mar – confused him. But if Mar was comfortable with them –

Mar. They'd seen Mar emerge from the shadows, following Hugi's arrival.

Mar. Who some called Mar the assassin.

Mar the *boy*.

But a Mar with shallow tits and a quim. A Mar –

He shook his head. Mar was a girl. A boy.

His own brother –

He scrunched his fingers into his palms. He had been too a'feared – had risked everything –

His brother had died. Been murdered. So had –

But for Caerne they would have died in the cathedral site. But for Tam –

Ifor had shrugged and wandered off. Alain looked again at Hugi.

Without thinking about it they got up and slipped silently across the rough camp.

Hugi's eyes were deep-set. He was awake, watching them –

'Are you – lonely?' Alain breathed, sliding down to crouch next to the crow-headed man.

Black-on-black eyes watched him. Intelligence glittered deep within.

Alain put his hand on Hugi's cock. 'You don't have to be lonely – if you don't want to be.'

He stared at them, his expression unreadable.

'I cannot kiss you,' he spoke softly. 'There isn't much I *can* do,' they trembled slightly, but it wouldn't give them away.

'But I can give you some warmth, on this cold night.'

He caressed the creature's cock, which trembled beneath his touch.

'I cannot kiss your – beak,' he said, softly. There was a heat in his belly. 'You are a creature of – Hel. A nightmare. But Caerne woke me from,' they shook their head. 'And you are lonely. I would ease some of your loneliness, if you would let me.'

He opened his beak. Spoke, though it was the softest voice he had ever heard, a bare fluttering of air.

'Yes.'

**

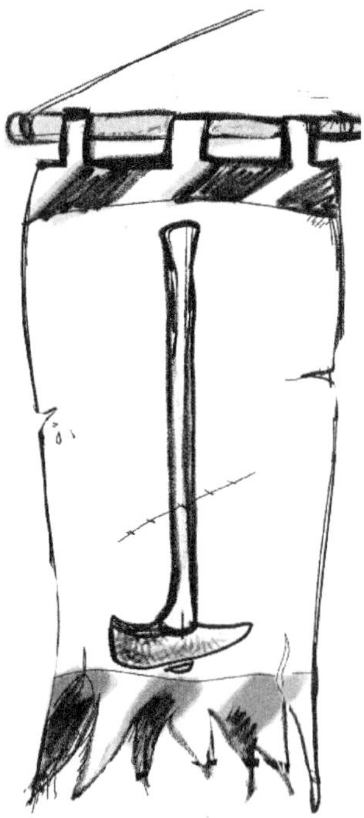

'The men are ready, my lord.'

St. John nodded to his captain of the guards. 'Details.'

'We have verderers in the forest beyond, a half mile beyond, the field. All hand-picked by Paol.' The man grimaced.

The Sheriff took a sip of the wine.

'The three prisoners are – mostly alive. They will hang at midday. They are double-guarded. A full third of the men sent are in disguise, scattered and ready for the peasants.'

He nodded.

'One third patrol the borders of Sherwood itself, beyond the field, an obvious deterrent to force any fleeing deeper into the undergrowth, closer to Paol's men.'

His captain of the guards referred to a scroll, listing all the lords who had sent entrants and soldiers to assist.

'The single biggest gathering of soldiers. If they attend – they will not escape.'

'If?' his captain queried.

The Sheriff waved his comment away. 'My guest?'

The captain paled. 'She spent time with the prisoners yesterday, hearing their last prayers.'

'And?' St. John raised an eyebrow.

'All seemed to – bleed heavily, whilst atoning.'

He nodded. 'Of course they did. The Abbess has a – way – with those who wish to atone. Do not question the ways of the Abbess, captain. Your life may become quite interesting. And short.'

The man nodded.

'Any news of Gisborough?'

The man nodded again, flourishing a scroll. 'Berenger sent word. They are not far; arriving today.'

St. John took the scroll, broke the seal and scanned it.

He grinned. 'Berenger is not happy with Gisborough.' He chuckled to himself. Gisborough seemed to have fallen fully for Jenny's – charms.

It will be interesting, what she can tell me of him.

**

'The Sheriff – wanted me to spy on you.'

Jenny watched William's face as he rounded on her angrily.

'You spied –'

She shook her head. 'No. I have not reported back to him. He will hear what you wish him to hear.'

'Why?'

She shrugged. 'I am – in love with you, my lord. I do not know if – *we* – can be. But you have lifted me out of Nottingham, and for that I would gladly spend my life with you, as wife or servant or whatever role you wish.'

He half-scowled.

'Everything is a game, my lord. Gisborough. The Sheriff – a man of machinations, though he rarely stirs from Nottingham himself. He is,' she thinned her lips. 'He had some secret scheme, something which went awry. An outlaw band, I think.'

'The Hooded?' Gisborough stared at her incredulously.

'No. Before them. And that is all I suppose. He knew who would be attacked before they were. And then the Hooded,' she shrugged.

'So he might have a man amongst the Hooded?'

Jenny shook her head. 'I – don't know. He was angry. If – *if* – the man still lives, he is no longer the Sheriff's.'

'Have you any proof? Would be good to have something to hold against him.'

Jenny shook her head. 'Unless we can find the man, I doubt –'

Gisborough raised his hand. Turned slowly.

**

She burned.

Beate felt the fire burn her body.

Felt her skin aflame, though all was silence and darkness.

Felt her bones crack, splinter and shatter as the heat rose.

Felt her blood boiling.

She screamed, tongueless, her teeth exploding –

Her skin was gone, her body was gone, she was –

**

There was a shadow in the trees above him, far, far above him.

Something stalking him.

The shadow of long, hooked claws, scrabbling at trees, at rocks – but at the same time, from the lack of reaction from Jenny, he knew it wasn't there.

'I think you are in trouble.'

William looked around. Jenny – wasn't there. He was in the Holy Land, the rock scorching beneath his feet and above him –

'The shadows are its hunting grounds.'

He turned back. The woodlands were empty. He'd often felt the memory of the manticoras, but the forest was empty.

Silent.

Too silent.

Claws scrabbled.

**

She was Beate and she was not.

Something filled her mouth.

Her body was on fire but it was different.

It was her, but it wasn't her body.

Her bones had been shattered and reformed and she was not who she had been.

Her heart pumped blood.

'Taste me,' a voice said, and all she could see was a pair of yellow – green eyes.

Lips brushed hers.

Hands gripped her shoulders: her shoulders were higher, the grip was painful –

The feel of fur against her body – warm fur.

Living fur.

A living creature.

Beate grabbed them, pulled them to her, and thrust her tongue into their mouth –

**

The woodlands were silent. They were not far from the King's Own encampment; Berenger would be rousing the men, getting ready – they were riding into Nottingham today, though William had warned her – several times – she was to remain discrete, hidden, so that the Sheriff would not realise she was amongst his men.

The forest was silent.

She detested the forest, but knew something was wrong.

Two figures appeared, a tall, black haired bowman and a woman barely clothed.

'Bastard,' she hissed. 'My brother and one of his trollop women warriors –'

'Let me –'

The air was screaming and the sky was black and she heard the shrieking of crows, the bellow of rutting stags, the terrible howls of wolves –

William staggered back a step.

'What –'

As he collapsed to the ground at her feet, sheathed in arrows, the two figures retreated back into the woodlands.

**

Richard stared. 'Her what?'

'Her virginity,' the Abbot quipped. 'I take it she still *is* innocent? You have not plundered her innocence the way you plundered my wealth with no hope of return.'

'How dare you – I'll –'

He rose out of his seat, intending – he didn't know what.

The Abbot grinned. 'You are an old man, Richard. Shrivelled.' He chuckled. 'Debts you cannot afford to pay back. A young, budding, girl whose innocence you couldn't pluck.' He shook his head. 'A whorish, pregnant, maid, whom you couldn't even conspire to have suck you for warmth.'

He stared. 'You sent – Lucianna – to me.'

'Of course. She is rather appealing.' He grinned. 'I had hoped she would straddle you in your bedchamber and fuck the last of your life out of you – everything would then have fallen easily to me.'

Sir Richard stared. 'She said – you –'

The Abbot chuckled. 'I have known the pleasure of her cunny. And her mouth. Her arse.'

He stared in horror. 'You raped the poor maid –'

'I did no such thing.' The Abbot sat back in his chair, resting his hands on his belly. 'This is a tale long in the telling, and – given that you are unalterably mine now, Sir Richard – I am inclined to tell you it all.'

'I am not –' he protested.

The Abbot raised the scroll. 'Is this not your signature? The small plot of Verysdale Hall, your lands, title, everything you own, against a sum of money leant.'

'Yes, but –'

The Abbot chuckled, rubbing his hands together. 'I am not inclined to tell you quickly – or easily – what has happened. What I have done. You will spend the rest of your days as a brother. A *silent* brother.'

Sir Richard stared in fury.

'You will, of course, sign over everything to me.' He lifted the parchment. 'I could do it through this, but it will be easier.' He chuckled. 'Sign your daughter over to me. Sign your property, your lands, everything over to me.'

'And – Lucianna?'

The Abbot grinned, ringing a bell. 'Two of my brothers will begin your instruction – Richard. No more the sir. No more the lord. You, and your lands, and your daughter – they are all mine.'

**

Wenlock stared.

A large field, a tourney field. On one side, peasants, workers, Anglo-Saxons and kin, cheering on the combatants. On the other, noble lords and ladies, Normans, the ruling class. Predators.

He grimaced.

Knight battled on horseback. An archery contest was underway. Three figures hung from gallows, swaying in the breeze –

There was no scent of Caerne. No trace of the Hooded.

One of them, he didn't recognise. A young Moorish maiden, her belly slit open, her body desecrated before death.

Wenlock looked away, feeling sick.

The other two – the other two he recognised.

They were naked but for hoods covering their heads. Their bodies bore many fresh marks, scars, jagged lines where blood had run.

The Sheriff toasted the crowds, cawing with laughter. A man beside him, a face of steel, red haired – a keen intelligence, eyes darting around, as if seeking –

Wenlock flung himself backwards, crashing backwards into his burrow.

'The hero-lighted man,' he whispered.

**

Raven grinned as Hereseige seemed to appear out of the mist.

'John!'

The man grinned. 'Brother Raven! Bwyd is here with us already, some part of Caerne's doing.'

Raven grinned, nodding to his comrades. 'All's well? Tegwared, Madoc and Gwilim; Englara.'

Hereseige nodded to each of them in turn. 'Hurnungaz is elsewhere. You let Raven lead you?'

'We did not let,' Englara said, surprising him. 'He led. Age is no bar. Radewych, Jerith and Yasha?'

Hereseige half-nodded. 'Radewych is still out with Wulfrun. The others are here. All's well.'

**

Wulfrun scowled. 'I don't like the look of that.'

Twenty men at arms, in heavy chain and bearing halberds, had taken up position on the crossroads. One way ran to Nottingham; another towards Wales, the other south. The tabards they wore were of silver and purple, unknown to him.

'King's Own?' asked Mar.

He shook his head, glancing at Radewych. 'No. I don't recognise their banner, but they're not King's Own.'

'Three bows,' said Howell softly. 'And that's heavy armour. Those weapons will have the reach on us.'

Wulfrun nodded. 'But we can't leave them. If the Sheriff is gathering forces then we need to stop them, scare them, shatter them.'

Radewych shook her head. 'Those are not soft troops. We *can* take them, but there will be a cost.'

Wulfrun nodded. 'The cost may be worse if they join up with crossbowmen or archers. A tight unit.' He grinned, beckoning the others closer.

'Mar, go right. Hugi, left.'

The giant nodded.

'Get behind them. Wait until they scatter.'

The man nodded, almost grinning.

He looked at the three Welshmen. 'Separate. Aim for faces. Under arms. You don't have to kill, just bring them down.'

'What about me?' asked Alain, glancing at Hugi.

He glanced at the youth and shook his head. 'Stay out of sight. If they scatter, if one's distracted,' he half nodded to himself. 'Be careful.'

He looked again to the Welsh. 'Take your time. Place your arrows. Pinging off armour is no good.'

The three nodded, slipping away. Mar had already removed himself. Silently, Hugi slipped away, glancing at Alain as he did so.

**

Berenger reined in, scowling. There was a body, crumpled in the grass –

'Fan out! Dismount, look around, may be a trap.'

He vaulted down, drawing his sword and heading for the body. The grass was trampled, still dew-damp. Footprints, a single pair. And the body –

He scowled. Gisborough lay on his back, sightless, arrows in his chest and belly, legs and face.

'Hooded,' he cursed silently.

'Single track, prints, leading away,' one of his men reported.

'Signs two waited up here.'

'Two?' he frowned. The number of arrows in Gisborough's body, it would have taken considerably more than two to catch him unawares, to slay him instantly.

'Track the single print. They can't be far!'

Half a dozen men followed the trail.

'Half a dozen more,' he bellowed, 'find the nearest village. Get a cart. Whoever's done it, has just murdered a King's Man and an officer!'

**

'So. The penitent Richard.'

The former Sir Richard was on his knees, wearing a coarse, sack-cloth, robe. His hands were shrivelled, veins standing out. Beneath the robe his body was twisted and bruised, lashed daily.

'Verysdale is mine,' the Abbot gloated. 'As is your former daughter.' He grinned. 'She is even prettier than I was led to believe.'

'None would betray her,' Richard tried to scowl.

'Oh, but most of your people were never yours, *Sir* Richard. The medic, the whore, most whom you arranged to assist in,' he shook his head. 'Taking in refugees. Fleeing from wars we care nothing about. Godless heathens.' He shook his head.

'The – medic?'

Abbot Simon chuckled. 'You have been sold out from within and without, *Richard*.'

He smiled, stroking his belly. 'Verysdale is mine. You will end your days in this place.' He signalled to the brother who stood in the corner.

'Fetch a scribe. And arrange for our guest to be reminded about not speaking. Or eating.'

**

'My lord?'

St. John glanced at his guest. 'Oh, your Grace. Do you approve?'

The Abbess looked at the three heads. 'I recognise none of them.'

The Sheriff nodded. 'That one,' he pointed at the head at the end of the row. 'They were never an outlaw. A gift, to my wife. They were obviously given away or sold. Three of Brother Gascon's brothers have gone to ensure she remains – modest.'

The Abbess Winchester frowned. 'Given the sinfulness into which woman is born, perhaps her – faith – would be better overviewed by one equally – cursed.'

The Sheriff stared. 'You would personally attend to her – to ensuring she remains – the best that a woman can be?'

The Abbess bowed her head. 'The Christ of the East tells me I should ensure York remains – pure.'

St. John nodded. 'Good. Let me know any needs – financial or otherwise – and I will arrange for them to be met.'

The Abbess nodded. 'These other two.' She shook her head. 'They were the best your man could get?'

St. John chuckled. 'Oh, no.'

'No?'

He grinned. 'He is,' he shook his head. 'A bloodhound. There were others available. Others, more prominent, he could easily have captured or slain.'

'Then why these two?'

The Sheriff smiled. 'Because he believes in the excise of terror. In time, Hurnungaz, the others, they will realise who is missing. Paol will hunt them down – he found these three easily enough. He will hound them, take one out here and there.'

'A problem would be better eradicated, not toyed with.'

The Sheriff inclined his head. 'Of course, your Grace.' He smiled. 'However, whilst these Hooded run free, they gather other malcontents to them. He will pluck their feathers, one by one. Everything is in place.'

'And that – tourney?'

St. John smiled. 'It achieved its effects. In the knightly trials, in the archery, every winner was a Norman. The Anglo-Saxons were hopelessly outmatched. They are,' he grinned, benignly. 'They are a doomed, dying people. We will assist their passing. The cathedral will rise, these Hooded will have expended their efforts and for nought.'

'And all the lords you summoned here?'

The Sheriff smiled. 'I reminded them of their duty to Brother Gascon and the cathedral. Several left with significant coinage. They are more than receptive. Construction can begin, unmolested, as Paol hunts the Hooded down.'

The Abbess nodded. 'There is another matter. A – private matter.'

The Sheriff glanced around. His soldiers, distant and out of earshot as they were, withdrew.

'Your brother. The most ungodly Abbot of Gresham Abbey.'

He nodded. 'A greedy, grasping man. The lengths he has gone to, to obtain a small property, Verysdale Hall –'

She waved his comment away. 'He has – claimed – Evgania, Warwick's daughter.'

The Sheriff scowled. 'There was a tithe sent for her. Jenny of Loxley –'

'I know the sordid tale of how your former mistress seduced and stole the money, attacking brothers of the Christ of the East as she did so.'

'She is now – ensconced – with William of Gisborough. I believe he never found serving Brother Gascon – to his liking.'

'Have you heard word of the *poor child* being returned to her father?'

He shook his head. 'No. And it is very unlike him to offer money for something, unless the money was not his.'

'Oh, I believe it was his.' She smiled.

'Your Grace, what am I missing?'

She chuckled. 'I believe a search of the Abbey – with Brother Gascon's permission,' she withdrew a scroll and gave it to him. 'I believe it will reveal the girl, Evgania. Your brother has been keeping her – entertained. Or perhaps, she has been entertaining him. I care not which way.'

He nodded. 'I should imagine Brother Gascon –'

'Then there is also the matter of his mistress.'

'Lucianna.'

The Abbess nodded. 'I see you are familiar. Are you aware she is his daughter?'

St. John stared. 'She what?'

'And now she is pregnant by him. Without any duress, she has been ill-treated, I imagine she will provide any supplementary evidence required.'

The Sheriff stared. Such a thing – he shuddered.

'You will take – appropriate action?'

He nodded firmly. 'I will. My brother,' he shook his head grimly. 'I knew he – strayed. But such a thing as you have told me.'

'See to it,' Abbess Winchester hissed, moving closer, 'that your man acts quicker. I want to hear of corpses of known Hooded being found. Nothing can stop, nothing *must* stop the plans of Brother Gascon.'

The Sheriff nodded. 'I will see to it, your Grace.'

**

He heard the twanging of bow strings even as he charged.

Radewych came from another direction, screaming wordlessly, and Hugi from another, silently, a lumbering giant suddenly amongst the silver and purple tabarded soldiers.

Bodies fell. Arrows pinged. Hugi snatched one up and flung.

'Scarsdale! The Hooded! Ullr!' screaming, Wulfrun charged them. He was past the reach of the nearest and axes flashed, axes slashed.

Arrows loosed cautiously; a soldier fell back, one in his throat.

Wulfrun slashed and fought, the bodies thick around him, hearing Radewych scream and slash and fight; hearing Hugi roar and caw, shriek, and the thud of bodies, the ugly, meaty sound of weapons on bodies.

**

Geoffrey grinned. In the morning light the cathedral gleamed. It rose, polished stone, already taller than him and dominating the field. The original cathedral, the one Hurnungaz and his men had attacked, was barely a quarter of the size of the new one.

That, had been mostly wood. Stone corners, stone supports, but wood other than that.

The Bishop had ordered that pulled down. And now something far larger rose, a strong, redoubtable fortress-cathedral.

The stone gleamed, polished and dark, rising like a pennant over the blessed field. Within near-sight of it the field was cleared of trees, the ground mud and rubble, all grass removed, everything not inert removed.

The fissures to Hel had been blessed. Streams had been diverted, blessed, poured into them until they had stopped steaming, until the ground could be filled.

And everything was blessed. Brothers of the Christ of the East crossed the site in pre-arranged patterns, blessing and re-blessing the site and the stone, the dark earth and the rock.

From the entrance of the cathedral, currently a gaping hole but soon to be an immense door, twice, at least, the height of a man, a road led. A road of crushed stone and fire-blackened earth, but a road.

'From this road, from the Cathedral itself,' Brother Gascon had told him. 'We will build anew. This is not a Cathedral, Geoffrey of Hallowcross.'

'No,' he whispered, seeing the shape and scheme of the brother's plans, 'this is a city. The cathedral as its jewel. Born from the inside out.'

The Bishop had nodded, pleased. 'Yes, yes, you see it! Clean, neat, ordered lines. We will crush the peasants, any who stand against us, the way we are crushing the forest.'

'Salt and burn the ground,' Geoffrey whispered, shaking his head.

There were rough guard houses in a wide circle around the site and soldiers from all the nearby lords. The King commanded – he grinned.

Almost daily they were extending the site, pushing the guard houses further out, reiving the trees, the grass, rerouting the streams and rivers to their needs, creating the perfectly formulated city where there had been nothing before.

**

Radewych struck and fought, creating a shallow space around her. Too long had been spent with the Hooded, the children forgotten.

Angenijs.

Diederich.

Hurnungaz' battles were not hers, not her peoples. His searches, their searches, had not found her charges.

And so we are in this strange land, brought here by the Undrentide path, and we cannot return and we cannot find those we must protect.

She blocked and parried, slashed and struck fluidly, never letting anyone get close. She was aware of Hugi, battering away at the halberds that struck at him.

Of Wulfrun, holding his own.

The three archers now together, targeting one soldier at a time, trying to find a weakness in their armour.

Alain remained out of sight.

Mar remained – out of sight. The fighting was too intense, too bloody – despite their three pronged assault, not one of the soldiers had broken and run.

It would be a hard, grim, fight.

Radewych smiled.

**

Jenny sank to her knees, exhausted, torn open, empty.

William was dead. William – slain by her brother.

She grimaced, baring her teeth, heaving and shuddering, tired, too tired to continue on.

She'd heard Berenger's men for a while, tracking her, but they had turned back. The King's Own were meant for tourney fields and straight warfare, not desperate battles in blighted forests.

She knelt, trying not to cry.

'What ails you, child?'

Jenny looked up. A woman stood close by, a horse further back, cropping the grass.

The woman –

Hair of green and black and white fell in a cascading roil and swathed her. The grass, the trees, the clearing, seemed pale and vapid in comparison to her. Barring the hair the woman was naked, but the hair itself seemed to move as if alive and not scattered by slight breezes.

'Who – are you?'

The woman chuckled. 'I am Godgifu. Once I was Mercian. Now,' she grinned, reaching out and stroking Jenny's hair. 'Tell me your troubles.'

Jenny sighed. 'My man – Gisborough. I was a,' she grimaced. 'My brother betrayed, disowned, abandoned me. Sold me to the Sheriff of Nottingham. He whored me out.'

The woman – Godgifu – nodded, though a dangerous look flashed across her face.

'I am eager for my brother's blood. His death,' she hissed.

Godgifu chuckled. 'I can arrange that.'

Jenny snorted. 'He is Hurnungaz, of the Hooded. He has the power of some stag-bitch behind him, Caerne.'

Godgifu chuckled. 'I can drown him deep in the mires of this forest. I can bury him in the Trent or any tributary. Who he is, who he has supporting him, is nothing to me.'

Jenny shook her head. 'My brother is a bastard. He has gods on his side, supporters, the forest itself. The Sheriff, Gisborough,' she gulped, 'others, even the King's Own, they hunt him, but he eludes them all.'

'What do you want for him? A quick death, slow death, torture?'

Jenny blinked. 'Who – are you?'

Godgifu chuckled. 'My husband sought to limit me. Define me. Fence me in.' She grinned. 'His body lies in a deep lake now, never to be found. Water snakes and lizards strip his skin, chew upon his bones.'

Jenny shivered. Nodded. 'I want Robin – Hurnungaz – dead. I want him to know I brought about his end. I want him to watch all his – whores – being tortured, dying first. I want him helpless as everyone is broken around him. Then I want him to die. Slowly. Painfully.'

Godgifu smiled. 'It can be done. This forest is old but is intersected by rivers, meres, lakes, even pools and puddles. Come – seal the deal with a kiss.'

Jenny got to her feet and crossed to Godgifu. Her hair wrapped itself around her; she could feel the hair sliding inside her clothing, caressing her skin.

'Just one kiss,' Godgifu smiled.

Jenny leaned in.

**

Richard heaved himself up. The cell was cold. All was lost –

Not all was lost. He had been foolish – alas, poor Henry, he thought, his mind flitting back.

No. Not all is lost. Angel lives. Under Lucianna's care, as poor and haphazard as it may be, I hope. And here, he grimaced.

Here I rot. A forgotten warrior. A fool.

He turned away. The cold had settled into his bones. It will not be long. I may never see Angel again.

He sighed. I tried to do right by her and her brother.

I tried.

**

Hugi seized another by his weapon, lifting him. The man slipped; fell. He crushed his neck easily, thrusting the weapon backwards into the meleeing press of bodies.

A weapon kissed his side. He screamed in fury and rage, cawing wordlessly, and from all around hawks and crows, ravens and blackbirds took to the air, screaming their fury.

The soldiers hesitated in their attack.

**

Evgania lifted her head. She was alone in the cell, which was nothing but a cold floor for a bed and a thin blanket for warmth. The merest sliver of light showed it to be near-dawn, but it also kept the cell cold.

She shivered. She'd had nothing to eat since the Abbot had taken her from the Abbess bar a thin gruel.

The Abbess had made her a serving maid, a kitchen maid, kept her flogged regularly and the property of any man who cared to use her.

Many men had used her, but their attempts had been – as of nothing. Pathetic, half-hearted, not the vigorous nature to which she was inclined.

Not that she was inclined to assist any who sought to use her without consent, without payment.

Lucianna – now there had been a one worth spending more time with. Soft and plump, barely used though poorly by the Abbot, unaware of the ways –

She grinned, despite the cold. It had been something, to slake herself on the plump mistress of the Abbot. To show her the ways one woman could please another.

And then Jenny had betrayed her. Little more than a kitchen-born drab, a minor Anglo-Saxon bitch the Sheriff should probably have disposed of long ago.

That had led to the Abbess and thence to the Abbot.

She shivered again.

The Abbot was scarcely capable, so Lucianna had whispered in the aftermath of warm embraces. He liked to think himself the powerful man, a man of the cloth and the church, but truthfully a small man with a small penis and no idea how to enjoy female company.

At least. She stretched, grimacing. The Abbess' predilection with having her whipped had left her body scoured, but now the wounds were healing, though slowly.

**

Mar watched as several soldiers burst from the main group, charging the three archers where they hesitated – unwisely – in a group on the edge of the trackway.

They moved without hesitation: the archers would be cut down before they even had a chance to defend themselves.

A knife caught one in the neck, but not deep enough: the man staggered, knocking it out, glancing in puzzlement at his blood-stained fingers.

Mar flung themselves onto his shoulders, driving two knives in deep. The man collapsed.

Four soldiers pounded towards the archers. One of the archers, Gwion, was fumbling putting an arrow on the string. The other two had abandoned their bows and drawn what weapons they had, knives and axes, swords and clubs.

Mar plucked the fallen knife from the ground, chasing the four.

**

'I am York!' Gloriana screamed.

The black robed brother of the Christ of the East struck her across the face.

'You are a whore in god's sight!' he raged. 'Property of Nottingham. Your place is grovelling at his feet!'

The three brothers closed in on her. One caught at her arm; another grabbed the thick jacket she wore. The third thrust his hand against her belly.

'Your belly swells with life! Whoresome harlot, you should be abed in Nottingham, compliant to his needs!'

The one at her back caught her jacket and tugged, attempting to pull it down. One slapped her again and her head rocked back: she saw stars.

'On your knees, harlot! Profess your duty to and love for the Christ of the East!'

'I never denied –'

One of them struck her across the face, sending her spinning, crashing, to the floor.

'Harlot!' screamed one of them.

Gloriana clambered back to her knees. Her belly was tight, not long filled –

'A better position for you, bitch,' one of the brothers crooned, his hands on her back sliding down to her hips.

'I am Nottingham's,' she hissed in fury. 'How dare you touch me!'

'You are but a shelter for Nottingham's line,' one at her head crooned, 'the line is important but the shelter is not.'

She was pushed onto all fours.

Hands were on her shoulders, on her back. Hands tore at her skirts.

'I am –' she tried again.

One of the brothers sank to his knees in front of her. 'You are nothing. A receptacle. The king may be a relation of yours, but we follow the King of Kings.'

Gloriana slumped to the ground. In her own chamber it would be then. Fearghal was outside, she knew, but would not – could not – act against the brothers of the Christ of the East.

Her skirts were lifted. Her underthings torn down.

She moved her hands to her thighs, arranging herself better, no doubt, in their eyes, for the inevitable.

'That's a good whore,' crooned the one behind her. 'This shall be your daily service. Are we nought but poor men, beguiled by a woman.'

'We will atone,' the second added, a laugh in his voice.

'Daily,' the third sniggered.

Gloriana closed her hands on the blades strapped to her thighs, hidden by the weight of her skirts.

'Now then –' fingers touched her.

She drew and launched, taking down the one in front of her. Her knives flashed and cut and he burbled, blood dribbling from his mouth.

She turned and grabbed the man who'd touched her: thrust her knife deep into his throat, holding his gaze as the life died.

The third brother stumbled backwards, staring in horror.

'What have you done, foul woman?'

Gloriana grabbed his ankle and tugged. He fell and she yanked him closer. Drove her knife deep into his crotch.

'My lady?' asked Fearghal, respectfully, from outside her chamber.

She sliced the brother's throat. Did the same for the other two and sat back, shuddering.

'It is done.'

Her captain entered softly, closing the door behind him.

She drew her skirts around her. 'How many saw the brothers arrive?'

He shook his head. 'Too many. Word will reach Nottingham, the Black Bishop, that they are here.'

She nodded. 'Arrange for three of your men to wear their robes. Make them loud. Public. Have them lead a procession somewhere – away from here. After that burn the robes.'

Fearghal nodded.

'What they attempted –'

He nodded. 'My faith weakens, my lady. I am sorry I could not – did not –'

Gloriana waved his comments away. 'There would be no trial, no apology from the Black Bishop. He festers in the heart of Sherwood. Sherewode,' she grinned.

Fearghal frowned. 'Sherewode?'

She nodded. 'I heard a man call it that once.'

'A man of the people, an Anglo-Saxon, no doubt.'

'This is my territory. My dominion. I want any brothers of the Christ of the East in my land watched. If they are local, they may well be loyal. We do not want to hurt them. But any rabid, any fervent, maniacal followers of Brother Gascon, keep them under observation.'

He nodded. 'Shall I extend the guard?'

Gloriana nodded. 'Yes. But keep them at length until we know they can be trusted.'

'The Sheriff's – child – may well spell –'

She nodded coldly. 'I will write to the King. He has – had – no intentions of passing my property on. I will need wise counsel,' she grimaced.

Why did I send him away?

None can know.

None can guess.

'I will need wise counsel. Strong hearts. Nottingham, the King, the Black Bishop, they all play games. I have a need for more than mere soldiery, as loyal as they are.'

Fearghal nodded. Coughed. 'It would also be wise, my lady, in your condition –'

'It is not for several months, the wise woman tells me. There is time for – envoys.'

'Envoys?'

She nodded. 'Allies, possibly, against the Black Bishop. And the Sheriff.' She grinned. 'Choose one, or go yourself, but the first to be sent must be to the Abbot of Gresham Abbey. The Sheriff's brother; a man at odds with both Nottingham and the Church.'

'A dangerous position to take.'

She nodded again. 'That's why the best man must be chosen for the matter.'

Fearghal nodded. 'It will be done, my lady. I do not like the thought of leaving you a while for this, but I will be swift, careful and – cautious.'

**

Lucianna stroked Angenijs' hair gently. 'Would you like to go from this place?'

The angelic child looked up at her. 'It grows cold here. Without Diederich. Without Sir Richard.' She shivered.

Lucianna folded an edge of her wrap around the child.

'It is not safe to travel these parts, even with the blessing of the Abbot.' She grimaced. 'But I think there may be worse to be had here.' She sighed. 'This is not my home. Do you think this not your home?'

Angenijs looked at her again and shook her head. 'My – our –' tears welled in her eyes. 'Is far beyond the sea. We came in no boat. There was a path, blackness and light, a,' she shook her head. 'It was an adventure. I – we – never thought that,' she trailed off.

Lucianna nodded. 'I am not minded to go back to the Abbot.' She sighed. 'I loved him. I did,' she shook her head. 'I do not know where may be safe.'

Nottingham, perhaps. There was never any love between brothers.

**

Wulfrun breathed heavily, aware of the blood on him, of cuts and bruises, fresh scars. He wiped his brow, grinning as Mar approached, and Alain slipped out of the bushes.

'We were hard pressed, lad.'

Mar nodded, cleaning his blades.

Radewych staggered to her feet, spitting. 'They are done at least. I fear –'

Howell limped over, face downcast, soaked in blood. 'They are ended. Gwion and Ifor are no more. Whoever the soldiers were, that was hard-fought.'

Wulfrun nodded, grasping and holding the trembling warrior for a moment.

'They fought for freedom. They are safe now.'

The Welshman nodded. 'Brother will look to brother. Kin will look out for kith. Divided we stand. United we rise.'

Wulfrun nodded. 'Kin, aye. What is the Sælvatici tradition? Burn or bury?'

'Burn. A warrior's send-off.'

Wulfrun nodded. 'Radewych. Alain. Mar. Howell. Where's Hugi?'

Alain turned and pointed.

Hugi leant against a tree, breathing heavily. His body was criss-crossed with cuts and blood, but he seemed alive.

'Will you look to him?'

Alain blushed a little. Nodded.

'Thank you. The rest, we've a pyre to build, then seek Hurnungaz once more. We must unite; stand together.'

**

'I am the champion of Sherewode!' Broga chuckled, holding aloft the silver arrow.

It gleamed – dully.

'I am the best archer,' he crooned, turning it this way and that, happy to let the donkey trace its journey back to his master.

When the Sheriff had held it aloft, it had sparkled.

'This accursed forest!' He turned it around. 'I can buy freedom from my master. I must declare myself poor Norman to enter in his name. This will free me. I will be a free man, resident of Sherewode. They will seek to have me join them. I will lead –'

Something made him look up. The trail he followed was narrow in places, circuitous, lesser used. And all the safer for it. But on it –

A creature stalked towards him on its hind legs. Female – a deer – horned – a woman.

'Are you a by-blow of Hode?' he challenged.

The creature hissed, opening a mouth too full with teeth. 'Sister-daughter of father mine,' it screeched, licking its lips.

'I won this – I won this –'

It seized it from his grip, twisted and bent it. 'Plaything of your master. Of the Sheriff.'

'I –' he stared at it. At its mad, yellow-green eyes. At the way its gaze ran up and down him; at the way it licked its lips.

'Who – who are you?'

It chuckled. 'I am Caerne. Stag-daughter of the Forest. To whom do you owe your allegiance?'

Broga whimpered. 'To you?'

**

Jerith placed his weapons carefully upon the tree. They were no closer to finding the children. Their pentamerous was broken, nothing – worked.

He peeled off his armour and clothing. They were far from home. Too far, but there was no way back and no way of knowing where Angenijs and Diederich were. Where those who looked to them for safety and security were.

He placed his boots carefully on the bank. The river was not deep but it had been too long – too long, and his body stunk and ached from many nights sleeping in armour, on lumpy ground. From too many nights not sleeping wrapped in the embrace of the pentamerous.

He slipped into the water carefully, wincing at its coldness, at its sharpness. It was just too wide to cross with a running start; not deep, but deep enough.

He waded out to the middle, sinking down, letting the cold close around him. It shuddered and stung and bit at scratches and scars, reminding him he was alive.

We just need find the children. Find a fifth we can all live with; can love.

He didn't feel the hand close around his ankle.

But the hand that grasped *him*, that tugged him down into the suddenly surprisingly deep –

He gasped, water flooding him.

Hands, tendrils, entwined him, dragging him down and holding him deep in the water.

**

Hurnungaz returned to their makeshift camp, Muna trailing him silently.

A low fire burned. Hereseige and Bwyd squatted before it, attending to the hares upon it. The brother of the Christ of the East – Blacwin – sat opposite them, warming his hands.

'Who's on watch?'

Bwyd looked up and grinned. 'Tam and Aneirin to the north.'

'Godwin, Merik and Llywarch elsewhere.'

He nodded. 'No call was heard? Muna and I simply strolled into the camp.'

Yasha and Englara sat side by side, sharpening and cleaning weapons.

He heard movement –

'I saw you.'

Madoc appeared behind him. 'Gwilim and I tracked the pair of you.' He grinned. 'You're good, both of you. We heard no sound from Tam or Aneirin; Gwilim has gone to check.'

Hurnungaz nodded.

'The others?' he frowned, looking round.

'Tangwystl and Tegwared sleep,' Bwyd said.

'Raven?'

'I'm here.'

Raven sat up. He'd been lying under a mound of leaves and soil.

'Angelica,' Hereseige said quietly. 'I don't know where she is.'

'Likely ran,' said Bwyd softly.

'And Genilles and Myfanwy. They only had eyes for each other. They may have slipped away,' Madoc shrugged.

'Jerith is bathing,' offered Englara.

Hurnungaz stilled himself.

Caerne.

He felt the stillness surround him. Felt her presence.

**

'Why?' cawed Hugi softly.

Alain had taken Hugi deeper into the forest. The pyre was being built behind them, but Hugi always seemed – stronger, better, when there were fewer people around.

'Why what?' Alain asked.

Alain tore their tunic, licked it, and pressed it against one of the scars that still wept: it wept a grim, red-black blood.

'Why?' Hugi gestured towards his man – *crow*hood.

Alain shivered. 'My – sister – was murdered. By her lover. I killed him.' He trembled.

'You – *killed* – him?'

Alain stared at Hugi. The creature, the crow-headed man, was so gentle. So not the giant, the Hel-crow, that many thought him.

'You know?' they said softly.

Hugi nodded.

'What do you know?' he challenged.

Hugi laid his hand over their heart.

He trembled. 'No one knows,' he hissed.

'Not tell.'

He reached up and stroked the handsome face. 'I am so far beyond – what I ever thought.'

Alain glanced back. They were far enough in; Wulfrun knew where they were, but he also guessed it'd be a while before they were ready to move on.

He looked back at – Hugi. 'Are you strong enough?'

Hugi nodded, caressing his arm gently. 'Yes. Cannot do much.'

Alain removed his jacket. Am I seriously considering this? Removed his shirt.

Again.

The feel of Hugi – against his lips. Too big to take into his mouth. A secret only Hugi knew.

Removed his undershirt and the tight binding.

Hugi's hand was on his chest. He gently removed it and stood up.

Took off his boots. Pushed his trews down and stepped out of them. Removed his underthings.

Alain sat in Hugi's lap. Cradled his cock to her belly, rubbing him gently. Leant forwards, so that her breasts just touched it.

His hands were on her shoulders. He held her gently as she worked him.

**

'So, brother.' St. John smiled coldly at his brother. 'What is this I hear of you taking Evgania from the Abbess?'

Abbot Simon grimaced. 'It was your whore who stole the money intended for her – good treatment.'

'And she's in one of your cells at the moment, being fucked nightly?'

'I am a –' the Abbot began.

'You're a degenerate power seeker.'

His brother glared at him. 'And you're not?'

He shrugged. 'I am Nottingham!' He grinned at his brother's shocked face. 'I am responsible to the King! You – what is this I hear of you fucking your own daughter?'

The Abbot quailed. 'It's lies. Lies. She's not my daughter.'

He raised an eyebrow.

'I was never married to her mother; her mother was a servant maid; I had her whipped from my lands. Her daughter was sent to me, I do not know who fathered her child –'

'How do you think the mad bishop will take this?'

The Abbot scowled. 'You can guess how well the mad bastard will take this. Came in here he did,' half rising, 'branded me. Pissed in the fire.'

The Sheriff chuckled.

'And who's tipped you, eh? You never cared. Your own plans and schemes, nefarious plots to undermine the King and steal money for yourself.'

The Sheriff raised an eyebrow. 'A lord who does not gather excess wealth to himself is no use to the King. I do not steal from Him. I do not take from anyone; I take what is my right.'

'My man Jackin – he knew things. He heard things.'

'And where is he now?'

'Slain. The Hooded slew him.' The Abbot chuckled. 'And the King's Men? Your lackey Gisborough not offer you enough confidence to actually track them down?'

He shrugged. 'I don't know where he is. I think the power has rather gone to his head. Hanging villagers,' he shook his head. 'What of Sir Richard of Verysdale?'

The Abbot grinned. 'His property is mine. Legally. I have merely to claim it – and the girl, Angel, or whatever she is called, and one of Sir Richard's maids.'

'And where is Sir Richard?'

The Abbot shrugged. 'At prayers, at this hour, I believe.'

'Prayers?'

Simon gloated. 'He has become one of my Order. Surrendered his property and all to me. I merely need to travel there and assert my rights.'

'Warwick will not be impressed, I warrant, that you hold his daughter.'

'And you failed to provide dowry for her; you allowed dowry to be stolen by your own whore.'

He chuckled. 'The whore is Gisborough's now. She reckons she can find where this thrice-damned Hel-archer is, that was once her brother.'

'So you have both Sir Richard and Warwick's daughter on your premises. All for – Verysdale? It is a pleasant property, but small, no great value.'

The Abbot chuckled. 'The Black Bishop,' he shook his head. 'Despite what he thinks; what the voices he believes whisper to him tell him,' he trailed off.

'Not your religious superior, I know. He carries a writ from the King, giving him power – in the King's name – to do as he will in Sherwood.'

'To stamp out the peasants –'

St. John shook his head. 'The King's own people. They reap the fields. They provide the coin that extend the King's empire.'

The Abbot waved his hand negligently. 'There are always more of them. They are expendable.'

The Sheriff shook his head, standing up. 'You are a fool, brother.'

The Abbot raised an eyebrow.

'Did you think the Bishop had been doing nothing since the Hooded attacked his site?'

'What care I –' Simon blustered.

'Oh, you'll care very much.' He chuckled. 'The site is much bigger, our brother tells me. Built of stone, so it cannot so easily be destroyed. The King's writ has gone across the land. Soldiers are being sent to the Bishop. The King –' he grimaced, shaking his head.

The King takes my titles, my land, my monies, and expects me to shore up the mad bishop.

He shook his head. 'We will talk on this more, later, brother.'

**

'Be yourself!' he whispered, cawed, coughing.

His body was trembling. 'Hugi?'

He stared at her, his hands gripping her tight now.

'You will be stronger as yourself!' he hissed.

He convulsed and warm stickiness plastered her throat, shoulders and chest.

'What do you mean?'

He shook his head, drawing her back into his embrace, his cock tight against her.

'See things,' he hissed, wheezing. 'In passion. Images. Future things.'

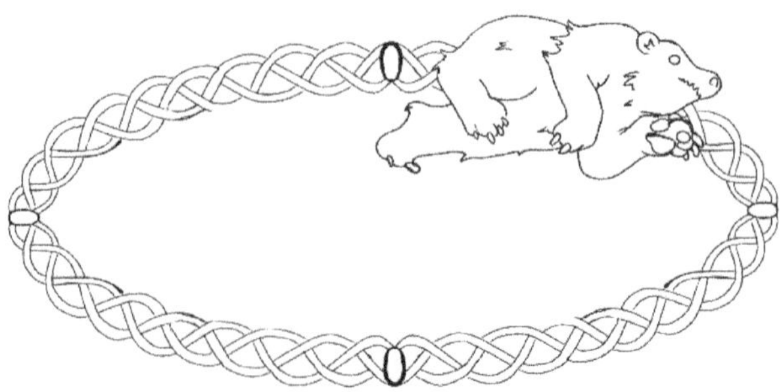

She caressed him gently. 'What does it mean?'

'Means,' he shook his head. 'Not know. Just flashes. Thoughts.'

He took a handful of grass and began cleaning at the clear liquid that trickled down her body.

She stopped his hand when it was on her breast.

'I must be mad,' she smiled shyly at him. 'Here I sit, a maid, a girl in disguise, with the desire of a crow-man all over me. And yet you're the kindest, gentlest, man I've ever known.'

Hugi smiled gently.

'Will save you.'

'You saw that?'

Hugi nodded, his fingers surprisingly gentle as he cupped and caressed her breasts.

'Must go soon,' he smiled shyly.

'We will,' Alain gulped. 'Do this again?'

'Get dressed,' he cawed softly. 'Moving soon.'

**

Hurnungaz looked up at the piercing whistle.

'That was Tam's signal.'

The Hooded scattered. He drew his bow, placed an arrow on the string and waited.

A man appeared, looking haunted, stumbling along, yet his clothes were not tattered and torn.

'Who are you?'

The man looked up in surprise, looked around. He shook his head. 'Caerne sent me,' he muttered, 'Caerne sent me.'

Hurnungaz eased down. 'Who are you?'

The man looked up again, seeming to gather some of his wits. 'I am called Broga. I,' he looked around as some of the Hooded seemed to simply appear out of the surrounding woodlands.

'Brother Bwyd, eh, I've heard of you.' He grinned at the druid. 'And, bless me, the giant Hereseige.'

'I'm no giant,' Hereseige grinned, 'only compared to some men.'

A few of them grinned.

'Caerne sent me,' Broga repeated, shaking his head. 'I was – *was*,' he stressed, 'Warwick's man, but no more.'

'Oh?'

'Under his patronage – the patronage of one of his liege lords, really,' he glanced round. 'I entered the tourney the intention was always to show the villagers that the Normans were the – best.'

'You're Anglo-Saxon.'

He nodded. 'Told to act Norman. Be a poor one, if anyone asked.' He stood taller. 'I won the silver arrow competition, I did.'

'Where's the arrow?' asked Hereseige.

The man shook his head. 'When the Sheriff held it aloft, it gleamed. It glittered. On my way home I held it aloft.' He shook his head. 'It gleamed but dully. And then,' he swallowed, 'then that – Caerne – appeared. Told me the route to take.' He shook his head wondrously. 'My feet knew the route though I scarce did.'

'So why are you here?' Bwyd asked.

'The whole thing was a trap?' Brother Blacwin said softly.

Hurnungaz nodded. 'Of course. Obvious, blunt and unsubtle. The Forest flooded with troops. More undercover in the crowds, no doubt.'

'I don't know,' Broga admitted.

'Was there any mention of,' Englara surprised everyone by speaking, 'Angenijs or Diederich?'

The man frowned at the names. Shook his head.

'Caerne,' muttered Hurnungaz.

'There was,' he paled.

'What did you see?' asked Godwin.

'They hung three people,' Broga admitted. 'The Sheriff told me their names.'

Hurnungaz stared. 'Tell me.'

Broga gulped. 'Angelica, a Moorish – maiden. Two Marcher rebels, the Sheriff called them.'

'Who!' demanded Bwyd, his accent coming through.

Broga blanched. 'Myfanwy and Genilles. Both had been tortured before they were killed. A Sheriff's man caught them.'

**

Mar lifted his head. *They* were hunting. Not him, specifically – he glanced around.

'Wulfrun!'

The Norse came at a run.

'What?'

He shook his head. 'We must leave the pyre and go. Gather Alain and Hugi. Something,' he grimaced. 'Something evil hunts this day. Our strength is in numbers.'

Wulfrun whistled.

Out of the undergrowth appeared the wolf and boar. Both raced to them, panting and stamping, looking around suspiciously.

'I know where to go, where to aim, in what direction,' he glanced back at where Hugi and Alain were, half-hidden in the undergrowth.

'We must go. Now!'

**

Berenger led the column slowly into Nottingham. His men were restless, angry. Gisborough had been – until his distraction by the Sheriff's former whore – a good man.

The idea of staying in the village hadn't been great – inspired, no doubt, by that woman. But that he should simply be slain and left by unknown – likely the Hel-archer of these Hooded.

And more than that. They'd had no good engagement. The only good encounter had involved those foreigners, and Gisborough had been injured in that, men had been slain – and all had escaped them.

We will do better, he grimaced. Nottingham will do as our base for the moment. I will send a missive to the King. Obtain His directions.

**

Hereseige stared gloomily at the cooking fire. The wood burned smokeless, but what bother if it smoked.

He sighed.

'You did what you could for her, brother.'

He glanced at Bwyd grumpily. 'I didn't even notice she was gone!' He scowled. 'She tried my patience sorely. I wanted to give her freedom, to get her away from the Sheriff, away from,' he trailed off.

'York, you said.'

He nodded. York was –

'Was that a dream as well, I wonder?'

'Was what a dream?'

He glanced at Bwyd. Looked around. 'Nothing.'

'You've not been the same since you came back. Was a troubled journey to York?'

He sighed, looking at the druid again and shaking his head. 'Not really.'

'And Quellavera and Sir Roger got onto a ship all alright?'

He nodded. 'Aye, some while ago.'

'Then what – ails you. And since you've been back, and before Angelica – was gone.'

Hereseige grimaced. Rose. Arleigh. Gloriana. And Angelica, though she was not even – he shook his head. Best put thoughts of Gloriana out of my head. None can know. None must know.

He grinned. The Sheriff's child may inherit York. Just imagine that. From stone mason to father of the man who commands both York and Nottingham.

**

'Jerith is gone too long.'

Yasha looked at Englara and nodded grimly. 'None seem to have noticed. This company,' she grimaced slightly.

Englara nodded. 'Would Radewych were here. And Kugene. I miss –'

Yasha stilled her with a glance. 'I know where Jerith intended to bathe.' She sighed. 'Would I had gone with him.'

'Take me there.'

**

Wulfrun ran like a bear. Great strides, bouncing off things, moving forwards sideways, unhampered by the profusion of axes he carried.

Radewych ran like a deer, light-footed, swift and nimble.

Mar ran like the wind, silently.

Howell ran like a boar, low to the ground, slow but unstoppable.

He carried Alain on his shoulder. They were not fast; it was quicker and she was almost no weight.

He knew Mar was right. He couldn't – quite – sense what had been close. But it was something –

Coming out of the underground chamber, when Mar had been injured. A terrible power, something which had chased Muna, something – she had not spoken of it – which had caused another spirit to inhabit her.

A dangerous, damaged, soul.

**

Fearghal reined in. The Abbey of Gresham was in sight. The lands were rich and opulent. A river ran through the grounds; brothers tended the farm lands, the herb garden, the other places.

Everything seemed quiet and still.

Will he be use to us or not, he wondered. The sooner I am back – but if there is any who may be of use, against Nottingham, against Brother Gascon.

Narrowing his gaze, he eased his horse on.

**

Lucianna stole away at first light. Angenijs was awake and ready. She reasoned night was the worst time, and the afternoon and evening not much better.

I hope we find fair company, support, before then. I know roughly the way to Nottingham, she caressed her belly.

It is not time yet. We will be taken pity upon. The daughter of a nobleman, her pregnant maid. We pose no threat.

She stole away from Verysdale without a backward glance. Angenijs knew it was a serious thing, a dangerous thing they attempted, but she was bright and alert.

'Sir Richard did what he could for you and your brother,' she said softly.

'He liked it there,' Angenijs said wistfully.

She nodded. 'With Sir Richard – gone, and with the Abbot of Gresham Abbey – interested.' She shook her head. It was nothing for Angenijs to hear.

'We shall find company soon. Company we can share with as we journey to a safer place.'

**

Wenlock stared.

The cathedral was being rebuilt and all in stone – in stone and taller, already, than it had been before the attack, and several times larger.

A path, a makeshift road ran from the huge front door. There were demarcations for large buildings; beyond the cathedral, little else had been started work upon but the road, and rough barracks, observation posts that encircled the site.

In one area, several hundred soldiers were being trained. They seemed competent already, in their gleaming silver and purple tabards. There were cohorts bearing halberds. A single cohort of crossbowmen. Several of long spears. All appeared equally armoured and heavy.

How can the Hooded stand against those numbers?

**

St. John noted the presence of the King's Own on his streets before he reached his castle. He stripped off his gloves, flinging them to a squire, and stalked through to his hall.

'Gisborough? Where were you!'

Berenger appeared, looking dressed for war.

'War-clad, in my hall? The axe on your back –' he gestured and several of his soldiers appeared, loaded crossbows pointing at the captain of the King's Own.

'Gisborough is dead, my lord. Apologies for appearing so armed, I am no threat to you.'

'Gisborough? Dead?'

Berenger nodded. 'Yes, my lord. A slight mystery. On investigation, we found the prints of two. But a dozen or more arrows feathered his body. There had been someone with him – this Jenny. Lighter than him and light of foot. We tracked her but she disappeared, crossing a river.'

St. John shook his head. 'Jenny is mine. I sold her to Gisborough, but she was mine. She had no part of this.'

Berenger shrugged. 'I have sent a missive to the King. We are about a quarter down in number. With Gisborough dead, my lord, I am requesting quarters here until I receive instruction.'

He nodded absently. 'Yes, yes. That is not a problem.'

The man bowed and withdrew wordlessly.

**

Angenijs froze. 'Wait –'

'We must hurry on,' Lucianna protested.

Angenijs glanced up at her and shook her head. 'It is not safe.'

'Yes, it's not safe, we must hurry –'

A growl filled the air. Lucianna quivered in fear, clenching her thighs together. They were on a main trackway: what looked like a crossroads was a little way ahead, hopefully with signs. But before them –

Mist seemed to form out of the very air. The growl was repeated, coming from it.

'What?' she whispered.

A shape appeared in the mist. A large, bulky, shape, moving through the mist towards them.

'Do not run,' she hissed, tightening her grip on Angenijs' hand. 'If you run –'

The creature padded out of the mist. A wolf – or wolf-like – but larger, with a stag's horns. And it walked sedately, on stag-like legs, not on a wolf's paws.

But still it half-snarled, and its immense jaw and sharp teeth were those of a wolf.

The mist swirled. Flickered with flashes of green and yellow.

'Oh, Christ of the East, save us,' Lucianna whispered, sketching a cross in the air.

The large wolf moved off to one side, eyes fixed on her, lips peeled back, growling deep in its throat.

From within the mist a figure appeared. Slight, human, colourless but for the light of their eyes. The mist faded away – a horn-headed woman strode towards them.

I must have imagined the colour. She is – she is –

The woman walked on hooves. Her hands were immeasurably long, and wrong. The wolf turned back, circling the woman; she rested a hand on it and the growl turned to a croon.

'Who – who are you?' Lucianna asked.

The woman smiled. 'I am Caerne. I am here to bring Angenijs to her people.'

**

Hurnungaz threw his head back. The Forest *shifted* –

He could sense Wulfrun, Radewych, Mar, Hugi, the others – they were running.

Something was hunting in the forest. Something – unholy. He caught an edge of their power and shivered.

Caerne was out – he caught a fleeting image of a child and a pregnant woman –

Something else was roaming –

**

Ranulph lifted his head, staring, his hand automatically reaching for the crossbow at his belt. The dark forest was silent. Still. Not a bird sang, nor insect chattered. No creature crashed through the woods, hunting or hunted.

All was still.

All was silent.

Then the trees were splintering and the air was roaring with a foul stench and Ranulph found himself falling backwards and sound returned to the dark forest – the sound of terror, of fear, of everything fleeing, by wing, hoof and burrow.

He raised his head.

A howl raped the air. He blinked, bleeding, blood dripping from his nose, aware he'd soiled himself. The ground shook and shivered. The dark forest smelled of Hel, and a creature from it stalked him.

It was an immense hound – but not. It seemed to have a black mane, and moved with the grace of a cat, but from its body grew fronds, which appeared to be testing the air, turning this way and that, independent of the creature.

Pure malevolence eyed in gold and green stared at him. The creature breathed and smoke and mist and flashes of fire filled the clearing.

Trying to move away, trying to escape the horror, his roving hand found the crossbow at his belt.

He considered for an instant and abandoned; sketched a cross, symbol of the Christ of the East, in front of himself.

The creature *howled* and trees exploded, caught fire, shredded.

Ranulph screamed.

The gold in its eyes burned brighter.

Ranulph could smell the brimstone and incense like the priests of the Christ of the East used. Beneath the burning smell was the stench of something rotten.

It grinned, baring its teeth – and pounced.

**

'What – what do you want?'

The Abbot slumped in his chair, a hopeless look in his eyes. It had been easy to get in to see the Abbot. His steward was gone; there were no lay brothers it appeared, only brothers, most of whom were otherwise engaged in their faith.

'I have come – to extend the hand of friendship.'

The Abbot's eyes widened. 'Who did you say you represented?'

'I am Fearghal. Captain of York's guards.'

The Abbot stared. 'What does Nottingham's wife want?'

Fearghal raised an eyebrow. 'Long before the King ordered her marriage to your brother, she was her own man. Own woman.'

The Abbot grimaced. 'She dresses as a man. She gives herself airs and graces she has no right to. She disports herself as a man –'

'Is your position so secure, Abbot, that you can strike away the hand of friendship?'

He glowered. 'From the trollop the Sheriff married to beget his line with, yes.' He drew himself up and out of his chair, unsteady. 'This – ' he blinked. 'This is over. Get gone!'

Fearghal shook his head. 'The Sheriff has always looked down on you. I'd wager the Black Bishop has no liking for you. Your position is precarious –'

The Abbot seized his tumbler and flung it. 'Be gone! I will call for – Lucianna! Lucianna, damn it, where are you, girl? Lucianna!' He sank back into his chair. 'Just like her mother. I will have to have her whipped.'

**

'Cover!' Hurnungaz bellowed.

The Hooded scattered – in an instant the clearing appeared empty and he could feel the onrushing –

'Scarsdale! Ullr!' a voice roared and Hurnungaz grinned.

Five figures were pounding towards the clearing as if Hel itself was on their trail. Wulfrun, side by side, with Radewych –

'The Hooded!' he bellowed, 'up and to arms. Allies approach!'

The Forest flourished the Hooded and Hurnungaz stared.

Wulfrun and Radewych. Mar. Alain. Howell. He frowned –

Wulfrun almost ploughed into him and he seized the Norseman, steadying him.

'Wulfrun! You're safe!'

The Norseman grinned, panting hard. 'Mar! Mar – what do you sense?'

The assassin came up, their eyes wild. 'They are still there. We are safe. They –' he looked around. 'They have someone.'

Wulfrun looked around. 'Alain! Where is Hugi?'

The young man shook his head, dishevelled, dirty, on the verge of tears.

'He put me down. He said, he said,' the man collapsed, sobbing.

Mar went to him –

'Hugi?' asked Muna, moving up besides Hurnungaz.

'Something –'

She shut her eyes. Screamed. Ravens took flight and crows took flight and blackbirds took flight and the air was filled with black feathers and raucous cawing and shrieking and Muna was shrieking, her wings shredding the air, screaming in fury and helplessness.

**

Radewych glanced from Englara to Yasha.

'Jerith is gone?'

They nodded.

'Drowned.' Yasha answered. 'He had been held down. Clothes, armour, weapons on the bank. Went into a river to bathe. Something –' her look became dangerous. 'Englara had to stop me going after it. This land,' she grimaced.

Radewych sighed. Nodded. 'We have faced no worse in our own land. But Angenijs and Diederic are without us and no more –'

She broke off as the druid, Bwyd, approached them.

'I know where you must be,' he looked at each of them in turn. 'They are safe – the two of them. Head for Verysdale Hall.'

'How do you know?' demanded Yasha. 'If you've known before –'

'Caerne told me,' he answered in a voice cold and dead.

Radewych nodded. 'Where must we go?'

Bwyd nodded. 'I will give you directions.'

Hurnungaz appeared beside him.

'Take the north road,' they spoke as one. 'After twenty miles –'

Radewych shuddered. The words were burning themselves into her memory. The two voices speaking as one;

the two voices speaking with the voice of a mad stag god in them.

They finished speaking.

Radewych glanced at her remaining compatriots. 'Jerith has been slain. Some – underwater being. But Angenijs and Diederic – we must find them. We owe them our fealty.'

Hurnungaz nodded. 'Of course. Pay attention to the main paths – there are things loose in Sherewode that should not be.'

Radewych nodded. 'We will heed them. Thank you, Hurnungaz.' She grinned. 'Divided we stand.'

Hurnungaz grinned, offering her his arm. 'United we rise. Until we fight side by side again.'

She nodded. 'North, sisters.'

**

Wenlock woke, frowning.

The village of Briggstowe, located in a deep bowl on a steep hillside, slumbered in the early morning. The hillside was stark and sheer, bereft of crops, too stony for farming.

At the base of the hill an impenetrable copse gave way to darker Sherewode. Mist rose from the trees and the swamps and the inhabitants.

A shallow stream bisected Briggstowe. Too shallow to fish in, the water drawn down by their invocations to clouds and storms, forgotten gods and old goddesses.

Wenlock frowned. He could smell the brimstone.

The copse heaved and writhed.

The Hooded were too far away. *Something* hunted the Old Forest. Something born of human – and something definitely not born but drawn, summoned, unleashed –

A roar echoed across the hillside.

The village awoke and there were screaming babies, yipping foxes, terrified villagers –

Villagers stumbled out and the stream burned green fire –

It stood, illuminated on the skyline. A monstrous black dog, but so much more. Tentacles grew from its back, waving and sniffing the air independently.

It roared again and fire flickered around its mouth.

Its tongue was forked, split, lashed the air.

It gouged the ground with its claws.

Villagers broke and ran.

The creature ran down the hillside, gouging chunks out of it, leaving burning claw-prints in its wake. It leapt –

Wenlock blinked, gasping, looking around. He was still in his burrow, though the air was thick with the scent of brimstone and Hel.

'The Hooded. Hurnungaz. I must warn them –'

**

'Your Grace,' the Abbess Winchester sank to her knees before Brother Gascon. She was in the Cathedral; stone walls were rising all around, though the entrance was still an immense hole, waiting a door.

'Forgive as well,' she hurried on, 'my appearance and my speaking thusly.'

'We believe you are loyal, sister.' His voice was cold, low, almost a whisper. 'Your sin is being female, but that can be atoned for.'

She bowed her head.

'What news do you have for me?'

'The Abbot of Gresham Abbey,' she whispered.

'Hmm. I have heard his mistress is pregnant.'

The Abbess nodded. 'His mistress is also his daughter.'

She could hear the stone masons working, cutting and shaping the rock in readiness to be added to the walls. The distant sound of hymns, of brothers at prayer.

'His – daughter?'

She nodded.

'Hallowcross!' the Bishop bellowed, surprising her with the volume of his bellow.

Through the open doorway a warrior came at a run, heavily armoured and armed.

'Hallowcross,' Brother Gascon scowled. 'The Abbess appears before us. She must atone for the fact of her sex.'

'Your Grace,' Winchester rose to her feet, discarding her robe and letting it fall. 'I have already started my atonement.'

The horse-hair shift itched and rubbed, enflaming her sinful body.

'Fifty lashes, Hallowcross. Punish the wicked woman.'

'Your Grace,' Winchester dared to speak again, 'the horse-hair aroused my female body. Fifty lashes are not sufficient. Your Grace. I wish to atone.'

She bowed her head again.

The Bishop's man, younger brother to the Sheriff and the sinful Abbot, stepped forwards. Tore the horse-hair from her.

'Fifty lashes, Hallowcross. We must whip the evilness out of her. Concentrate on her feminine aspects. Let them bear the brunt of her chastisement.'

Winchester smiled as a whip lashed across her waist. Her breasts. Her thighs. Her belly.

She closed her eyes, praying gently. Whips scourged her back, her buttocks, her breasts, the unholy entrance to her body.

She prayed more and more fervently, enjoying the pain, the feel of flowing blood.

'Christ of the East!' her eyes rolled back in her head.

The pain, the blood loss, stirred her to greater and greater devotions.

**

'Brother Blacwin,' Alain asked quietly, 'I would have you hear my penance, if you will.'

The brother smiled gently. 'Of course, young man. Let us walk a ways from camp, enough not to be overheard.'

Alain nodded, leading the way. I do not need to do this – I do. I – I think I –

'This will do,' Brother Blacwin said from behind them. 'These are perilous woods. Best not to go too far.'

Alain turned back, nodding. The Brother was settling himself against the base of a tree.

'What is on your mind, Alain? You have always seemed an honest, faithful, member of the flock.'

'But,' Alain hesitated. 'I'm with the Hooded.'

Brother Blacwin shook his head. 'Their aims are different to mine, but they,' he crossed himself. 'They are not completely unholy men. They seek to do good, though in their own way.'

'That is not,' Alain tried again and hesitated.

'Something weighs on your mind?'

Alain nodded. 'There is. It – it is a terrible burden.'

'Then lay your burden aside. Confess your sin and seek atonement.'

Alain untucked his undershirt; drew it and the overshirt up; pulled the binding loose and down. 'I – it is easier to show. Brother.'

'Sister,' Brother Blacwin smiled. 'You may cover yourself up.'

Alain re-tied the binding; let her shirts fall. 'My name – my name is really Alais. Alain was my brother.'

'What happened, to force you onto this path?'

'My brother was the scribe. Our father had me learn my letters as well. He thought I would suffer none for knowing what my brother knew.'

She sighed again. 'There was a suitor. An accident. My brother died; the suitor died.'

She bowed her head. 'I lied,' she continued softly. 'Became my brother. Became a scribe. Found I liked it. Ended up working for the Black Bishop,' she shuddered.

'And what do you want me to do, judge you for your actions? Force your secret into the open? Punish you for making a desperate choice?'

She lifted her head and looked at the brother. 'Raven,' she hesitated. Shook her head.

'I am not the brother that Raven went to. Yes, you have sinned child, but you have made the life your own. Everyone believes you Alain; no one believes you a girl.'

'Hugi,' she looked up, blushing.

'The crow-man?'

She nodded. 'I – he told me,' she looked away.

Sat in his lap, pressed against him –

She shook her head. 'He said I had to be myself. Be a girl.'

Brother Blacwin nodded. 'Do you want to be? Your secret is safe with me if not.'

Alain frowned. 'Why? I heard enough of the Black Bishop's preachings –'

The brother smiled gently. 'If he interrogated me now – I mean questioned.'

Alain smiled.

'I suspect I would be struck off. At his mercy. I – I do not take everything blindly. Anymore. We were taught,' he shook his head.

It had been painful and awkward, pretending to be a boy. Having to find privacy for ablutions. Always being bound up.

And as a boy – she shook her head. I wasn't much of a boy. As a girl – perhaps Muna can help. She has lost a brother.

'Faith,' Brother Blacwin murmured, 'is all very well until the evidence challenges it. Heresy, I know,' he smiled at her.

'Faith,' she murmured.

**

'You saw?'

Hurnungaz blinked. He was in a burrow; there was a short, dark haired man stretched out beside him, his face sharp and triangular, wizened.

'I've seen you before?'

'I am Wenlock. You saw?'

He shook his head. 'I saw – a trail of fire. Something descending. It was so fast.'

'Briggstowe. There is a creature loose.'

'How? Where from?'

Caerne was walking towards him – except she wasn't, he knew. Some trickery of Wenlock's, one of the Old Ænglish.

Her eyes were green, the merest of yellow streaks in them. She was staring at something, entranced, at him –

'Cernunnos?'

Hurnungaz could sense but not see the figure; they were taller and broader than Caerne but that was all.

'Caerne!'

'Father,' she whispered.

'He's dead!'

'Father,' Caerne whimpered, stepping closer. 'I loosed something. I didn't know what I did. I tore a hole between this world –'

Hurnungaz could hear the whisper of words but not make them out. Something dark, a cloak, perhaps, wrapped around her –

He could still see the woods, but it was fading –

'Caerne is gone.' Wenlock shuddered. 'You must return to your people.' He shook his head. 'I do not know what that was, but it was not Cernunnos.'

Hurnungaz nodded. 'We can go after her.'

Wenlock shook his head. 'There is a Hel-beast loose in Sherewode. It is tracking your people, it has been summoned for this purpose.'

'That creature?'

Wenlock nodded. 'The one called Paol is also loose. Working for the Sheriff, he hunts Mar but will kill any he finds. He has already plucked two of your Welsh and given them to the Sheriff; the Moor girl as well.'

Hurnungaz shuddered. 'We will stop both. Then we'll go after Caerne.'

Wenlock nodded. 'Return.'

**

Radewych stared. A heavily pregnant woman held Angenijs by the hand. They were on the edge of a property, secluded deep within the forest and she could hear a stream nearby.

'Radewych!' screamed Angenijs, pulling free and running to her.

Radewych sank to her knees. 'Angenijs! You are safe!'

The girl flung herself on Radewych: she hugged her tightly.

'How came you here? Where is Diederic? Who has kept you safe, this woman?'

'There was a man, Sir Richard, he was nice.' Her smile fell. 'Yasha! Englara!' she looked around. 'Where are Kugene and Jerith?'

Radewych shook her head. 'Our male companions are dead, slain.'

Her heart ached. It had not been right since they had come to this land. The pentamerous was broken – Kugene and Jerith were gone, there would never be any others like them. She loved Yasha and Englara, but it was not the same without the men. To be in the middle of four lovers –

She shook her head. Angenijs was crying silently.

'They gave their lives to find you, Angenijs. Where –' she looked around. 'You know this property?'

'It is called Verysdale Hall,' the woman said. 'It is Sir Richard's property, though the Abbot of Gresham Abbey may own it now. I lived here a short while; Angenijs longer. Sir Richard took in Angenijs and her brother,' she trailed off.

'Better the hall than the forest,' said Englara. 'We can prepare a defence, if needed.'

'Is Diederic – no longer with us?'

Angenijs nodded. 'He couldn't adapt.' She shook her head. 'Sir Richard was a kind man. Lucianna looked after me the best she could. There was this woman, with horns. A wolf,' she shook her head.

'What is your will?' Radewych asked. 'We serve you, the three of us. Will you seek to return home or make a home here? We are at your service.'

The other two knelt down, flanking her.

'We are at your service, Angenijs,' they echoed.

Angenijs smiled. 'I choose –'

**

Bwyd looked around the archers. 'We go to the site of the cathedral – or as near as we can, safely. The mad bishop was absent when we attacked it; the ground was riven. I want to know what is going on there.'

The men and women nodded.

'Just the seven of us?' asked Tangwystl.

He nodded. 'It's not a full assault. We need to know what is going on there. If we can take out a patrol or two at the same time,' he grinned.

And Caerne, he frowned. He could feel her power flowing through him, but not Caerne herself.

'It's that way,' he pointed. 'Tegwared, Howell, bring up the rear. Llywarch, with me, we'll lead.'

**

Wulfrun grinned at Mar and Raven.

'Do you know where we are?'

Raven shivered. 'I do.' He shook his head. 'I don't want to be here.'

'This is your option,' he grinned at the youngster. 'If you don't want to, we'll return. But if you do,' he chuckled at Mar, 'then we could walk through the village, you with two men at your side.'

Raven shook his head. 'I don't want to. My family,' he shook his head. 'You're my family, Mar, Wulfrun. Them,' he gestured to the village, 'they're nothing to me. I don't want to see them. I don't want to be – in front of them. Who I am,' he looked at the pair of them. 'Thank you, but no. They are nothing to me.'

Wulfrun nodded. 'Then we don't.' He grinned. 'Freya and Iseulde, I will be avenged on you, in time.'

Mar nodded, his hand on his back for an instant. 'We will support you in this, Wulfrun.'

Raven nodded. 'Thank you, Wulfrun. Mar. You've cared more for me than my family ever did.'

**

Tam parted Aneirin's robe. She looked up at him playfully.

'Old I am, and wrinkled and sagging –'

'Do you think I care about that? You're a powerful woman, Aneirin.'

'Powerful,' she chuckled. 'Greying thatch. Fat belly. Puckered breasts. Calloused hands.'

'Beautiful,' he stopped her with a kiss. 'Powerful and beautiful.'

'You're just saying that,' but there was a light in her eyes.

He stopped her with a kiss again. Kissed her cheeks, her forehead. Kissed her chin, her neck, her throat.

'I am as old as time,' she whispered.

'And time does beautiful things.'

He kissed his way down to her navel. She giggled when his tongue pierced it.

'I'm not sure what you'll achieve –'

He moved up, taking her breast in his hands, kissing, licking, nibbling.

'What would you have me do?'

'Less talking. More worshipping.'

Tam grinned, moving from one to the other.

'I am ready, whenever,' she whispered.

'I am not,' he raised his head and grinned. 'There's more to be tasted.'

He kissed his way down. Teased his way through the tangle of grey and white fur.

She moaned softly. 'You do not have to.'

He caressed her thighs. 'You are a goddess, Aneirin. To be worshipped. Delighted in. Eaten.'

He returned to her lap.

**

'What manner of woman are you?' Brother Blacwin asked.

Muna sniggered. Wings, near-visible, near-invisible, flapped behind her, creaking, whispering.

Alain stared, biting her lip. Muna wore next to nothing, thin and tight, sheer. She was undeniably, openly, female and yet so – seeming powerless.

'I am woman and witch and Wōden's right hand, brother,' she cawed. 'I am three in one, your holy trinity.'

Brother Blacwin sketched a cross in the air between them.

'Do you think your symbols hold any power?'

'To me, they do.' He smiled. 'As your power works for you.'

Being a god's right hand would do it. I am but, he sighed. A false boy, sister to the true Alain. I am Alais. I want to be open, but –

Muna whirled. 'Child,' she cawed. 'Scribe.'

'Alain is a scribe –' the brother began.

Muna tilted her head. 'My brother loved you.' She narrowed her gaze. 'He gave a little of his power to you.'

Alain shook his head. 'No, he didn't. I mean, he liked me, yes, but there was no – transference.'

Muna chuckled. 'I see the lie in your eyes, girl. You brought him a vision. Release, pleasure, did that. He has returned to Wōden.'

'Will he – come – be reborn, I mean?'

Muna laughed at her. 'I do not know. Wōden's task is not finished. He may. I am just,' she sighed, wrinkling her nose. 'I am Wōden's spirit, not the keeper of his secrets. I cannot act against Hurnungaz, against Caerne. Wōden wanted,' she shook her head. 'If I speak too much I may be shorn.'

'Will you keep my secret – that I am a girl?'

Muna cawed. 'You want it to remain a secret?'

'Alain,' Brother Blacwin said gently, 'is a young woman. A talented scribe. But she finds herself in Sherewode, in a notorious outlaw band, with no discernible, forgive me, Alain, skills as a warrior.'

Alain nodded. 'Raven has some small skill with a knife. A hunger for –' she shrugged. 'I like straight lines and columns and numbers and everything was secret – everything was like that until Caerne came to me.'

'I could – give you something,' Muna leered. 'You carry a piece of my brother. Dedicate yourself to Wōden and I will spill a little power into you.'

'What must I do?'

'Child?' Brother Blacwin frowned. 'Are you sure of this? You are a believer in the Christ of the East.'

Alain nodded slowly. 'I have neither skill nor courage. I wish to be myself – but I am afraid.'

**

'Hold,' Bwyd held his hands out. 'Let them come nearer.'

They were close to the edge of the cathedral site. A column of soldiers, about a dozen, led by two black robed brothers of the Christ of the East made their way down the trackway.

He nocked an arrow on the string. Caerne, guide my aim.

'Loose,' he whispered.

The brothers and the front rank of the soldiery fell, spitted. The others squawked and grabbed for weapons – another three fell.

'Sælvatici!' Bwyd roared, the cry taken up by the archers all around him.

Another two fell; the remaining three turned and ran, falling as arrows took them.

**

Hereseige grinned. 'There's a penalty to pay, crossing through our kingdom.'

'Your kingdom!' the knight shrieked, glancing at his two men at arms. 'I'll pay no price to godless heathens –'

'I'm not godless!' Merik scowled. 'I worship the bear goddess.'

The knight stared.

'Broga,' Hereseige grinned. 'Stick an arrow in one of his men at arms.'

'We had no need to stop!'

The arrow bounced off the man's leather armour.

The knight chuckled. 'We are victorious! You cannot defeat those who –'

Hereseige stepped forwards and swung his hammer. The knight crumpled, sliding off his horse.

One of the men at arms fumbled for a crossbow, the other his sword.

Godwin, Merik and Broga loosed. The crossbowman stumbled backwards, the bow dropped, an arrow through his hand. The other stumbled backwards, arrows in his leathers.

Hereseige stepped forwards and swung the hammer once more.

One of the soldiers turned and ran. Hereseige flung his hammer and brought the man down.

The other turned to flee: Broga brought him down.

'Check the other's dead. Check for coin, anything.'

**

Berenger grinned sourly. He was leading the King's Own back to the cathedral site. There had been no word from the King. Nottingham knew to forward any missive, but in truth –

He grinned. The cathedral was a ways away still, but it was good to be out of Nottingham. The man was planning something; the town was noisy, dirty, dishevelled, scarce worthy of the appellation city.

Here we will make a difference, he thought. Rebuild this country, that Athelstan built, in a better image. Strip out all the Saxons. All the Pagans. Build in a better image: the Christ of the East.

His horse neighed and he looked up. Something moved in the forest ahead.

'Ware outlaws,' he cried.

The road was narrow, too narrow for more than four abreast. Three moved up beside him: he could hear the column rearranging itself, bunching in tighter.

'Orders?'

'We –'

The forest spewed a huge black creature, already galloping towards them, some kind of monstrous black dog. There seemed to be a haze around it; undergrowth caught on its back.

'Charge!' he bellowed, drawing his sword. 'Meet it head on and ride over it!'

**

Mar looked at them both. Wulfrun had built a low fire; they were returning to Hurnungaz, but sheltered the night in a deep hollow on a thickly wooded hillside.

'I was a woman,' he said. 'I bore a child. I had a son.' He shook his head. 'There is a man called Paol. Blessed – cursed – with the hero-light. He slew the warrior woman Scáthach. My lovers. My son. He left me for dead, thinking me dead.'

Wulfrun sat silent, as did Raven.

'I wanted vengeance. The Old one, one of the old Ænglish, gave me passage over here. Caerne came to me first. Told me to seek him out. I was here before him.'

The fire warmed, but not his heart.

'He hunts me now. It was he who caught Hugi. Others.'

'I will not let you face him alone.'

'I alone can kill him,' Mar answered softly.

'We have Caerne. Ullr. Muna, Hurnungaz –'

Mar shook his head. 'The child I bore was Paol's. He has my scent in his nostrils. It is no one's fight –'

'It is all of our fight,' Raven glared at him. 'You all took me in. We all stand by you, Mar. Brother.'

'Brother,' Wulfrun echoed.

Mar gritted their teeth. I will not cry. I will not.

**

'Are you ready?'

Alain jerked awake. Muna was bending over her, naked, her eyes black, her wings beating heavily.

'Yes,' she whispered, sitting up. 'What must I do?'

'Strip. And come with me.'

Alain removed her tunic. Undertunic. Her thin boots and trews.

'Naked.'

Muna ripped the binding from her chest, making her gasp.

'You will never wear that again.'

She pushed her underthings down.

Muna took her hand. 'Follow me. We have a long path to follow.'

Muna set off. Branches struck her in the face. Thorns and plants tore at her skin; roots and creatures underfoot threatened to bring her down, until she was having to scurry to keep pace with Muna, who marched on relentless, uncaring.

**

'Did I not warn you, Aneirin?'

She turned, too late, too slow, encumbered by Tam's sleeping body atop hers –

A blinding flash of pain. And then unconsciousness.

**

Bwyd grinned. Half a dozen mounted warriors cantered down the path. They were as close to the cathedral as they could get, but the stone-built building was visible even at a distance.

The ground was solid, no longer riven by whatever his mistress had summoned. The air itself felt dead, destroyed.

He glanced at his archers. Llywarch, Tangwystl and Madoc to one side; Gwilim, Tegwared and Howell the other. Seven of us. Enough.

'Loose!'

Arrows bounced or struck and the soldiers didn't fall.

'Caerne!' he bellowed, loosing again.

Another wave struck the charging soldiers and one fell, another stumbled, and then the horsemen were upon them.

**

'There,' Muna pointed.

There was a clearing in the midst of the forest. Moonlight bathed it, but Alain could feel – something.

'Stand in the open there. Call to Wōden. If he hears you, if he can use you, his messengers will come.'

Alain – Alais – stumbled out into the clearing. She was weary. Cut and bleeding, half blinded by sweat and trickles of blood.

'Wōden! Hear me,' she asked, moving around the clearing, looking up, waiting, wanting.

There was a fluttering in the trees: she turned to look, but it subsided.

'Wōden! I beseech you! Come to me.'

There was a rustling in the branches again, but it fell to nothing.

'Wōden! I dedicate my life to you if you will hear me! Give me strength. Give me courage!'

Laughter echoed around the clearing.

'What will you give me?' said a voice in her head.

She turned. The clearing was empty: no one was there.

'Myself. As Alain I was nothing. I want to be – more. Hugi said –'

The trees exploded with cawing and shrieking and the sky was hidden by ravens, crows, choughs, others too numerous to see. They scratched and tore at her and she whirled, holding her arms up to protect her face.

'Wōden! I am yours if you can use me!'

**

Hereseige pointed. Three men on horseback ambled down the trackway. They carried swords but looked more like merchants, traders, than soldiers.

'You three wait in the trees. I'll accost them.'

They all nodded, readying themselves.

Hereseige walked into the open. 'Hold! There's a price to pay for being in Sherewode!'

The man at the front raised an eyebrow. 'We are but simple brothers.' He grinned. 'From the preceptory in the north. You know, perhaps, Grimgyth?'

Hereseige nodded, relaxing. 'Aye, that I do. Godwin?'

Godwin appeared, an arrow on the string.

'That's not Grimgyth.'

'Correct,' the man smiled. 'Grimgyth said to use his name should we be stopped.' He looked up and around. 'I reckon you hold no more than half a dozen in keeping. The three of us could end that, but,' he smiled. 'Grimgyth, Dægmund, they said you were honourable men.'

Hereseige nodded, reluctantly. It was good – to be back. To be in the forest once more. As enjoyable as –

Angelica. If I had refused York, left her there –

The Sheriff would likely have taken her. She would be being used, forced to betray – he shook his head.

'Aye, the way is clear for you.'

'Thank you,' the man smiled. 'I have news you may not have heard. Rumours. Tales. Something – Hel-bound, smelling of brimstone, a creature that is unnatural, of fire and claws, something stalks the forest lands. It comes and goes. Villages have been destroyed – Briggstowe. Soldiers slaughtered. Buildings razed. Take care.'

Hereseige nodded his thanks.

'Godwin. Merik. Broga,' he sighed. 'Let's return to Hurnungaz. News he needs hear.'

**

Tam raised his head muzzily. He was lying on the ground, alone. He sat up slowly, looking round. His clothes were in a heap where he'd dropped them.

Of Aneirin, there was no sign.

He sat up and started pulling his clothes on. 'I guess Bwyd was right. She didn't want much more than a night or two.'

**

A metal collar choked her throat. There was blinding, bleeding, pain in her wrists, her ankles.

'They will not like it,' chuckled a voice.

She tried to speak. Her mouth was full of pain. Probing with her tongue, there were teeth missing, raw, sharp pain –

'I had such fun, breaking the storyteller's teeth. The warrior's teeth.'

She tried to focus, to concentrate, but various different levels of pain were circling her consciousness.

'I have nailed you to a tree. Nails through your wrists. Nails through your ankles. I do not know if your deluded god worships this specific tree, but I thought you a worthy offering to them.'

The voice chuckled, nearby.

She could feel their – his – breath on her skin.

'The Christ of the East will certainly not like the parallels.'

Pain bit into her belly, sharp and intrusive.

'You are dying, Aneirin. I am killing you deliciously slowly.'

A hand seized her breast cruelly tight.

'You will never know pleasure again.'

There was sudden, intrusive stabbing pain and she screamed.

'I am almost tempted to leave you like this. To prolong your suffering. But I do not personally hate you. I did so enjoy fucking you. Your cunt was welcoming, your mouth obedient.'

She felt the cold kiss of the knife again and passed out for a moment.

'I have been shadowing you for so very long. You fucked the druid. You turned the man of the Highlands into a lover. How will they feel when they find you –'

She could hear, feel, the tearing, ripping, of her body and she screamed –

Fingers caught her tongue.

**

'What did they say?'

Hereseige grimaced. 'Something Hel-ish loosed. A creature; fire and claws.'

Hurnungaz nodded. The thing Wenlock had shown him – and Caerne –

He looked up as Bwyd appeared, the Welsh behind him.

'What news from the cathedral?'

The druid sighed, shaking his head. 'Tegwared and Gwilim did not make it. We took out two patrols. The,' he scowled.

'The cathedral rises,' said Llywarch.

'We could not get near it,' added Tangwystl.

'Two patrols slain,' Bwyd added bitterly. 'He's more soldiers there than before. The ground is dead. Healed but,' he shook his head. 'Cursed. Nothing grows but stone buildings. Whatever they're building there –'

'Even were all the Sælvatici here, there would not be enough to attack,' said Madoc.

'Nor should we try,' said Howell. 'It is – insurmountable.'

'Nothing is,' Hurnungaz half-smiled.

Brother Blacwin smiled. 'With faith, mountains can be toppled.'

Hurnungaz frowned. 'Have you seen Alain and Muna?'

The brother nodded. 'Alain,' he hesitated. 'Alain went with Muna. They were talking about Wōden.'

Wulfrun sniggered. 'What next?'

'We're ready,' said Raven, glancing at Mar.

'There's Templars loose in the forest,' Godwin added. 'Not the two we've met, but they knew them.'

Hurnungaz nodded as Tam appeared, looking dishevelled.

'No Aneirin?'

Tam glanced at Bwyd. 'When I woke up, I was alone.'

Bwyd looked away. 'She always leaves,' he muttered.

Broga and Merik shared a look.

**

Wenlock stared.

Sherewode was besieged. Hel-creatures stalked it, hunting the Hooded –

'Hurnungaz!'

**

Hurnungaz raised his head. He'd heard his name, recognised the voice –

'To arms!' he cried. 'We are under attack!'

**

Bwyd stared.

Aneirin had been nailed to a tree. There was a metal chain around her neck, a slaver's chain. Her torso was raw, bloodied, having been shredded with knives and whips. Nails had been driven through her wrists and palms, her ankles. There was a bloody, raw, ruination, her belly, between her legs, a heaped mound of entrails and blood and viscera on the ground.

'He was gentle with her,' Mar said softly.

'Gentle!' screamed Tam. 'He –'

'Gentle!' Mar roared. 'Paol butchered, gutted, everyone I knew while they lived! This is his handiwork! He ripped some of them open and they still lived! Now he is here in Sherewode, we are all –'

Wulfrun pulled Mar round. Punched him in the face.

'Aneirin?' Bwyd said softly. 'You were the best of us. You were there so long, for so many of us.'

Mar was on his knees, screaming wordlessly at Wulfrun, who gripped their arms tightly.

The Welsh, the Sælvatici, nodded grimly. They've seen this Paol's work before. As have you.

He looked up at her. She was beautiful, even ruined. Had brought up so many generations of the Sælvatici. Had been Llewellyn's confidante and right hand for so long. He moved closer, frowning.

Her jaw was soaked in drying blood, her mouth open. He stared, swallowing grimly. Her tongue had been cut off.

'Where's this bastard?' hissed Madoc.

'You don't want to –' he began.

The growl made him shiver. Sent icy fingers down his spine. Bwyd turned –

**

Wenlock stared.

The creature was immense, sheer black, almost reflective. Fire glowed in its eyes. Its claws ripped the ground beneath it every time –

Hurnungaz loosed, arrows flowing from his bow. Llywarch and Tangwystl stood beside him, loosing into the creature.

Hurnungaz roared – there was an answering roar and into the clearing thundered a bear. It launched straight at the Hel-hound –

And was flung away.

A wolf, Wulfrun's familiar, and a boar, Mar's familiar, thundered out of the darkness, attacking the creature.

Wulfrun and Bwyd attacked; Hereseige and Merik plunged into the battle. Madoc and Howell leapt into the fray, short swords and knives stabbing.

The creature roared, shaking itself, and bodies went flying.

Bodies flew.

Bodies flew, and some did not rise again.

The creature inhaled.

'Do not –' screamed Bwyd.

Mar leapt on the creature's back, knives flashing.

Fire flamed from its mouth: for a moment Godwin was caught – and then he was falling, shredding, collapsing, bone and sinew, cloth and steel, smoking.

Hurnungaz loosed.

Merik was ripped apart.

The creature rippled: Mar was thrown clear into the trees.

Wulfrun, Hereseige and Bwyd charged as one. Tam, Raven, Madoc and Howell charged.

For an instant the creature's body was hidden.

Hurnungaz, Broga, Llywarch and Tangwystl paused in their loosing.

The creature rippled again and the Hooded were thrown clear.

It snarled, growled, head turning this way and that, flames flickering from its mouth.

Wenlock saw Brother Blacwin offer something to Raven. There was a heated discussion.

Wulfrun's wolf howled, bowling out of the undergrowth, and this time a pack came with it. They leapt upon the creature, snapping and biting, tearing at the fronds on its back, its tail, anywhere but its face or paws.

The creature caught Wulfrun's wolf in its mouth. Crunched.

Wulfrun howled in despair and charged, Raven and Tam beside him first. Hereseige and Bwyd a moment later.

The creature lashed out – Wulfrun flew backwards, hitting a tree solidly, sliding down and lying still.

Wenlock stared as he saw Hurnungaz drop his bow. There were bodies everywhere – burnt trees, crumpled Hooded.

The creature was injured – blood flowed, and from some cuts little tongues of fire raged.

'Hurnungaz, no,' he whispered.

'It's me you want,' Hurnungaz drew his sword. 'Come on then.'

The creature loped towards him – and Hurnungaz charged.

Wenlock closed his eyes.

**

'Caerne!' Hurnungaz bellowed, 'aid me!'

'Caerne!' Bwyd was beside him, axe and club in hand, charging the Hel-beast.

From the corner of his eye, he saw Raven charging in as well –

'No! Caerne! Aid us.'

**

Hereseige charged. Tam, Llywarch, Tangwystl and Broga beside him, all bows abandoned.

'Hereseige!' he bellowed. 'The Hooded!'

'The Sælvatici!' voices echoed.

He struck out with his hammer and there were bodies, Hooded, all around him, and the air was filled with fire and fronds – tentacles – that curled and licked and stung and bit –

'The Christ of the East!' he saw Brother Blacwin charging in, something in his hands –

'Caerne!' screamed Hurnungaz, drawing a bloodied sword back.

The creature inhaled.

'Freya!' bellowed Wulfrun, back on his feet, running but staggering, axes in hand. 'In Iseulde's name!'

'Scáthach!' screamed a voice of pure fury.

Hereseige stumbled – Mar, their face soaked in blood, somersaulted onto the creature's back, their knives extensions of their arms and the knives plunged and stabbed and slashed and –

The creature rippled once more; half staggered back, but blood was flowing faster now.

'Wōden!' screamed voices and two more appeared, naked and black-feathered, a crescendo of crows and Corvidae following them and the air was thick and heady with fire and brimstone and the howl of wolves –

**

Wenlock stared as the Wulfenstæg erupted from the woodlands, leaping onto the Hel-beast's back, ripping and tearing with sharp teeth.

The creature howled, fire spitting skywards.

The Hooded charged once more.

**

Brother Athelwright knocked on the door. 'Your Grace? Your Grace, are you within? You are wanted.'

There was no sound from within. To enter the Abbot's private chambers without permission carried penance, but the Abbot was needed and no brother had seen him for a day or two at least; there had been a stream of visitors, but none in the last day.

'Abbot Simon? Your Grace? May I enter?'

The silence stretched out. He pressed his ear to the door. There wasn't even the sound of the fire crackling, and the Abbot liked warmth.

'Your Grace?'

He turned the handle slowly, waiting for the Abbot to shout at him. There was no sound; he wrinkled his nose, smelling something off.

'Your Grace?'

He pushed the door open fully.

The Abbot sprawled in his chair, his robes drenched in blood. The fire was long dead in the grate. The room was cold and the Abbot's eyes open, staring Heavenwards.

'Your Grace,' he whispered, crossing himself.

Continuances

The tale weaves its way from 'Hurnungaz' and reaches a conclusion in 'Hurnungaz Dissever me Never'.

There are a number of short stories set before, during or after 'Hurnungaz', or during the timeline of 'Hurnungaz the Dark Breath of Earth'. Think of them as annexes to this, or continuances.

'Mælmoth the Wanderer' takes place just after the events of 'Hurnungaz' and was inspired by a piece of art from Nimue Brown.

'Gelert's Hound' is set in between 'Mælmoth the Wanderer' and this book, announcing the arrival of Paol, as well as our first proper look at the Sælvatici, including Llewellyn and Aneirin.

'Barrow witch' is the tale of what happens when Paol arrives in Sherewode; he detects Muna and begins hunting her, but the storm he precipitates has unforeseen consequences.

There are a number of other tales, still to be written, set within the timeline of this book or elsewhere and these will be annotated in 'Hurnungaz Dissever me Never'.

Afterword & Thanks

To Mark Hayes and Nimue Brown for 'getting it'.

To John Chadwick for the fantastic cover art on this, and the cover art and internal art on 'Lore of the Sælvatici', as well as 'Hurnungaz' and 'Barrow witch'.

To Tamsyn Swingler for giving me the opportunity to perform 'Rise of the Sælvatici' all those years ago (twice!) at Montol, and for artwork and inspiration.

To Laura Jane Round, my co-conspirator in so many things.

To CD Phillip for the wonderful imagery breaking up the text, and for the 'Gelert's Hound' image.

To Tom Brown for starting a Christmas tradition with 'The Littlest Krampus'.

To 'The Sælvatici' fb group for sharing and suggesting things.

To Daniel Martin for editorial suggestions and proof reading, for pruning and honing.

To the Black Meadow legends, as annotated by Chris Lambert, in written and sonic iterations. If ever the mist falls and you're outside – particularly in the North Yorkshire Moors or in fields of brambles – then it is simply too late. I was driving in the West Country and as the album came on, the mist came down.

The Stone Tapes' 'Avebury' and 'The Kingdom of Mercia' were an early influence, particularly when thinking about musical or spoken word interpretations of the Hooded tales. Find them at thestonetapes.bandcamp.com.

To William Westwater for the theme tune to 'Lore of the Sælvatici'. You can find the song on Dark Sinfonia's album 'Incantations'.

Whilst it had no direct inspiration or impact upon this, the album 'Evelyn Evelyn' should be sought out. Like the Black Meadow legends, there is a lot that can be done simply, and it is these that I have tried to emulate, with the material given me.

About John Chadwick

John Chadwick is a writer, illustrator, animation filmmaker, spoken word performer and co-host of The Innsmouth Book Club podcast. A former university senior lecturer and writer/illustrator in residence at The Yorkshire Sculpture Park, his work has been exhibited, published and performed through several medium since his film Spiritual Love was nominated for Young Narrative Filmmaker of the Year at the 1996 British Short Film Festival.

About Steven C. Davis

Steven C. Davis describes themselves as a word witch. They have created the 'Sælvatici' [Robin Hood myth cycle in a folk-horror / dark Pagan style] and the 'Less than Human' [an examination of society through the medium of genetically-based shape shifters] worlds and regularly create and release multi-media content for both. Their play, 'Mother Hode', set in the Sælvatici world and a forerunner to Hurnungaz, toured the UK in 2023 to resounding success.

They are the Creative Director of Tenebrous Texts and one half of 'Poetic Malevolence' a gothic-influenced performance poetry duo, with Laura Jane Round. They are also a storyteller, a performance poet, a publisher, a playwright, a presenter, an artist, a master of ceremonies, one of an alternative artistic collective known as 'the fringe dwellers' and are occasionally considered driven.

They are *near*-infinitely patient, demisexual, and feel malevolent joy frequently. They are considered creatively feral and should be approached with caution, unless you identify similarly. They like the taste of words: bring them a gift of some new ones, or some very, ***very***, old ones, and they may feel gratitude towards you. It should be noted, they are often passionate and pissed-off in equal nature.

About CD Phillip

CDPhillipwrites was an art kid who grew into an art adult (which is much the same except with more back pain.) Xie can be found on Instagram where xer art and writing is on occasion displayed.

About Wulfenstæg

Wulfenstæg is a frequent attender at historical conventions and Pagan fayres. He has little time for the nonsense of modern times so do not expect a presence on the dreaded "social media".

He is at his happiest when he's whittling wood or watching a fire spitting sparks into the night sky. Walking in a forest and letting its senses absorb his personality. Watching a river flow, the water churning and bubbling, going about its business without human intervention.

He is grateful to Steven, and Tenebrous Texts, for handling the commercial aspects of this project, which has inspired him greatly.

GASP's Trading Card #7

Gurdybird

Bio: Based in Cornwall, Gurdybird plays a Hurdy-Gurdy over her backing tracks which she performs, programmes, and records herself, creating original compositions and unusual renditions of traditional folk tunes and shanties, performing with her music videos projected where possible for a multimedia storytelling effect. She also roams acoustically at events, performs plugged and also dabbles in remixing.

Link: gurdybird.bandcamp.com.

Raising Steam: Appears on 'Raising Steam II', and the 'Raising Steam 2022' and 'Raising Steam 2023' festival samplers. Raisingsteam.bandcamp.com.

Printed in Great Britain
by Amazon

50226776R00208